STRIXHAVEN
OMENS OF CHAOS

Also by Seanan McGuire
and available from Titan Books

War of the Spark: Ravnica
War of the Spark: Forsaken

MAGIC™

STRIXHAVEN

OMENS OF CHAOS

SEANAN McGUIRE

TITAN BOOKS

Strixhaven: Omens of Chaos
Print edition ISBN: 9781835418123
E-book edition ISBN: 9781835418185

Published by Titan Books
A division of Titan Publishing Group Ltd
144 Southwark Street, London SE1 0UP
www.titanbooks.com

First edition: April 2026
10 9 8 7 6 5 4 3 2

This is a work of fiction. All of the characters, organizations, and events
portrayed in this novel are either products of the author's imagination
or are used fictitiously. Any resemblance to actual persons, living
or dead (except for satirical purposes), is entirely coincidental.

A CIP catalogue record for this title is available from the British Library.

EU RP (for authorities only)
eucomply OÜ, Pärnu mnt. 139b-14, 11317 Tallinn, Estonia
hello@eucompliancepartner.com, +3375690241

Printed and bound by CPI Group (UK) Ltd, Croydon CR0 4YY.

For Kyra, the best study hall buddy a girl could have,
and for Ruby, who was always bound for Strixhaven.

The Multiverse: an endless collection of planes, each with its own worlds, magic, and laws of nature, connected by the roiling brilliance of the Blind Eternities, the space between tangible creation, filled with energies that will vaporize anyone directly exposed to them. The exception: Planeswalkers, individuals protected from the force of the Blind Eternities by the powerful spark burning within them.

But recently, the impossible has shaken the Multiverse. The Phyrexians, a powerful society of biomechanical monsters motivated by their belief in their own superiority and a ceaseless need for expansion, breached the walls of the Blind Eternities and invaded planes without number, leaving death and destruction in their wake. They were stopped, at great cost, and in the aftermath, the very fabric of the Multiverse has been transformed.

Many Planeswalkers have lost their sparks and innate connections to the Blind Eternities, leaving them unable to travel as they once did. As if to compensate for this, fissures have formed through the Blind Eternities, connecting previously separated planes. These fissures, called omenpaths, are on the cusp of changing everything.

The Multiverse may never be the same.

FALLING STARS

Kasmina isn't sure she's had a single other dream since the Phyrexian Invasion shattered the Multiverse as she knew it—since everything changed. She's never been much of a dreamer, preferring to keep her flights of fancy to her waking hours, where the shifting stars and unfamiliar skies of the planes she walked between always satisfied her need for escape. What need for dreams when you *live* in them?

But now, every night when she sleeps, she finds herself back under the endlessly spiraling expanse of the Blind Eternities, buffeted by winds blowing from nowhere, everything around her painted in colors her eyes no longer understand. The Blind Eternities never look the same twice, for all that the dream they hang from is unvarying: change is the nature of the Blind Eternities, and here, in dreams, she sees them only as clearly as a non-Planeswalker ever can.

In her dream, she carries a candle, thin and ocean blue and guttering in the wind. She cups her hand around it as she searches for safety, for shelter, for someplace she can protect the flame, but there is nothing to hide her and nowhere she can go. She is lost. She is alone.

As the dream progresses, the Blind Eternities sicken and shudder, fissures forming like cracks in the substance of creation itself, splitting the colors and swirling shapes asunder—cracks that, when she looks more closely, become the roots of Phyrexia's mighty Invasion Tree, their terrible Realmbreaker. They grow denser and denser, tangling more and more tightly around one another until the Blind Eternities are all but consumed and only the horrors of the invasion remain.

And she runs.

Night after night, knowing it won't save her, she runs, fleeing across formless ground under a root-scarred sky, unable to reach deep enough into herself to finish the transit she must have been attempting when she was trapped here, unable to escape the fast-approaching disaster.

And then the roots close over the last of the Blind Eternities, blocking their light, leaving only the candle in her hands. Until her flight hooks her toe under a root and sends her sprawling, and her candle hits the ground, and the flame is lost.

She wakes gasping and clutching her chest, her heart as hollow as an eggshell, the flame that once burned there as dead as her candle, extinguished in the dark.

It's been months since she's had a decent night's sleep. She's beginning to think she'll never sleep properly again. She doesn't deserve to rest.

She failed. She was entrusted with the legacy of all the Planeswalkers who came before her and with the preservation of the Multiverse, and she failed both her tasks and didn't even see her failure coming. She deserves the emptiness in her chest and the sleepless nights in her room.

But the Multiverse deserves a chance to survive.

Breathing hard, her mind still swimming with a haze of shattered images, she rises from her bed. She doesn't bother turning on the light; two of her owls are here, and borrowing their eyes is as easy as opening her own. She walks to her desk, reaching for pen and paper.

The administration listened when she recommended the Kenrith twins. It's time for something larger now, something more important. And they'll listen. Even if she has to change their minds herself, they'll listen.

The work doesn't end this way.

The work is just beginning.

ONE

BROKERS AND BARGAINS

"Blue! Watch yourself!"

The shout comes a bare breath before the sound of crumbling masonry. Eula Blue, unwilling cleanup worker and self-trained shield mage, throws her hands over her head, a dome of pale, misty light forming around them as the rest of her team presses in beside her. This has happened often enough that they've learned the safest place to be during a collapse is as close to Eula as possible.

The bricks raining down from above hit her shield and bounce harmlessly off, clattering to the pavement. The impacts stop. Eula holds the shield, watching the sky until she's sure the collapse has finished, then releases it and lowers her hands at the same time, sending the last of the dust and grit to join the rest.

Her foreman is already striding toward her. He's a big, barrel-chested ogre, a Riveteer by birth and allegiance, and he was openly dubious about allowing her to join the cleanup crews after the Invasion. "What good is some soft-handed little wannabe Obscura going to do?" he'd asked, and the other recruits had laughed, and any chance Eula would have been willing to try looking for another job had died. It was cleanup or nothing.

Not that she likes the work. If she's being honest with herself, she hates it. It's all hot, muggy Caldaia air and physical effort, and tears in her clothes that she can't afford to have properly mended. But the work needs to be done, and her family needs the money, and so here she is.

The foreman waits until he's only a few feet away, the rest of her crew already back to work collecting broken glass and shards of Phyrexian exoskeletons from the street around them. Elias is picking up the bricks that fell on them. They'll leave this stretch of New Capenna better off than they found it if it kills them—and based on what just happened, it still might.

"Blue," says the foreman brusquely. "You think about my offer?"

"Yes, sir."

"Make a choice yet?"

Eula composes her face. She needs this job, at least until she can save enough to hire a private tutor. There's always work to be done in New Capenna, but if you don't belong to one of the five Families, there are things much worse than cleaning up the streets. She was lucky to get this position, and she managed it only because the foreman's sister was a friend of her brother's when they were her age; that tenuous connection got her onto the crew when the foreman would have preferred another Riveteer.

Of course, the Riveteers don't tend to produce shield

mages, and her talents have saved her coworkers often enough to attract attention that she wasn't necessarily looking for.

"I'm still discussing it with my parents," she says, as neutrally as she can.

Not neutrally enough. The foreman frowns. "This is a big opportunity, you know. Could open a lot of doors for you."

"I'm aware, sir."

"They may not be the doors you were hoping for, but with Park Heights gone, I don't know the Obscura will be opening their doors anytime soon. You could make a name for yourself among the work crews if you wanted to get serious about this."

"I know, sir. Thank you, sir."

The foreman looks at her carefully, but she controls her face, refusing to let her true feelings show. She did her primary schooling in Park Heights, at the best elevator school her parents could buy her way into. She should be halfway through her first year of university right now, learning how to bend the law to her own ends, courted by the Brokers and the Obscura alike. Instead, she's here, cleaning up the wreckage of the campus she's been dreaming of for most of her life. This isn't what she wanted. This isn't the way it's supposed to be.

This isn't right.

The whistle blows, signaling shift change. With this many workers in need of a paycheck, there's no overtime available, for anyone. Eula trades neutrality for a bright smile, tipping her cap at the foreman before she says, "I'll see you tomorrow, sir," and she's off and running.

He pushes his own cap back as he watches her go, and he doesn't try to call her back. She's done her hours, she'll draw her pay, and if she doesn't want to go the extra mile, that's no skin off his nose. It's her family that needs the money, not his.

There's always another pair of hands in New Capenna.

Eula puts his offer out of her mind as she runs. She can't delay him forever, but she can have tonight, and the days since the school fell have taught her that time is the dearest coin there is. Once it's spent, it's gone, and even the Obscura can't snatch it back for you.

She knows she's the best shield mage on the work crews, which is easy enough when she's the only shield mage on the work crews. Most of the shield mages in the city belong to the Brokers, and they're too important to waste their time on petty make-work and physical labor. That's the future her father wants for her, whereas she wants to join the Obscura in their dazzling dens of blackmail and illusion. She's not your standard Obscura, but a shield mage is welcome anywhere. That's why the Riveteers are willing to offer her a formal apprenticeship with their Family. They need her, and she needs them, and it could be so easy. All she has to do is say yes. They'll give her more hours, more responsibilities, and the shining golden chains of admission to their Family at the end of it all. If she becomes a Riveteer, she can grant her family the stability they lost when Park Heights fell.

She can save them. She can give them security, authority, respectability, all the things Phyrexia took away. And all she has to give up is her own future.

Not that her future has ever been her own. The Brokers have never offered her father membership, but he's always been their man, and he's all but promised her to them if she masters her magic well enough. Her mother's side of the family used to work for the Cabaretti. Most of them died with their masters when Park Heights fell. And here's Eula, dreaming of the Obscura and knowing she'll never have their attention the way she wants it. The way she needs it.

She moves fleetly through the Caldaia, the lowest level of New Capenna, where the Riveteers hold sway and the products of their endless industry are never far away. Before the Invasion, Eula had only ever come this low on dares and bets; she'd been a true child of the Mezzio, eyes fixed firmly on Park Heights, and she'd been sure nothing was going to stop her upward climb. There was no force in New Capenna that could contain Eula Blue.

Well, that had turned out to be true. There *was* no force in New Capenna. But there were forces outside it that didn't care about her dreams or aspirations, and Phyrexia had brought her hopes for an education crashing down to earth, tangled in the wreckage of the school where she'd been intending to craft her future. Now here she is, one more child of the Caldaia gutters, caught between a lifetime of hard labor and preserving her slim chance at an escape in exchange for locking her entire family into that same fate.

She's nineteen. This shouldn't be on her shoulders. So Eula runs, temporarily free, racing toward an uncertain future.

Before Park Heights fell and took both her family's fortunes and their neighborhood tumbling down with it, Eula knew exactly how her life was going to go. Now everything is uncertain, and she hates it, almost as much as she hates the tiny apartment she shares with her parents and younger siblings, who are young enough that they still view their new lives in the Caldaia as a long vacation from the expectations of the upper city, rather than a sudden and brutal limitation on their futures. Her older brother has his own place in a Riveteer neighborhood, more permanent, more secure, but the apartment she shares with the rest of her family is safe and quiet enough that Eula can sleep at night, and she wants to be grateful for that. She just doesn't know how.

Resting her backside against a silvered stairway rail, she half slides, half rides it to the bottom of the granite stairs and trots down the last short block between her and home, slowing as she nears the door. She hates her job. She hates coming home almost as much. She's never wanted to be an unhappy person, but she is now, because she hates it here.

Eula Blue is trapped.

She unlocks the door—no open doors this deep in the Caldaia—and lets herself into the crammed front room, packed with secondhand furniture and children's toys. The air smells, as always, like boiled vegetables and whatever Mom's roasting for dinner. She can't think about food yet—she never can before she gets a shower—and all it does is turn her stomach.

"Eula?" Her father's voice comes from the narrow doorway connecting the front room and kitchen. "Is that you?"

"Yes, Dad, it's me." Who else would it be? Unless someone's lost a key, everyone else who lives here should be home by now.

"Can you come in here?"

He sounds uncharacteristically serious. Eula frowns as she moves toward his voice, wiping her grimy hands on her jacket. Maybe something happened to Alton? He doesn't have the physical presence or strength of most of the Riveteers he works with, and she worries about him every time he goes out on a job site—

No. No point in borrowing trouble. Eula takes a deep breath, lifts her chin, and steps into the kitchen.

The whole family is there, save for Alton, which just makes the fear she's trying so hard to suppress spike harder. The kids have bowls of cut fruit distracting them, and her parents sit at either end of the small breakfast table, her mother looking worn-out and worried, her father holding a letter in his hands. Eula's eyes go to it immediately. The paper is thick and looks expensive, with the texture that comes only from money. She doesn't recognize the seal at the top, but that looks expensive, too, like someone invested in making sure it would be identifiable at a distance.

"What's that?" she asks, and her voice is too loud for the space, and she can't pull it back.

"Eula," says her father, lowering the letter. "This came for you."

Anger flares atop fascination. It's not enough that she's been forced into a small room with two younger siblings, lost her neighborhood and her privacy and her future, but now they're opening her *mail*? She forces it back. They mean well, she knows they mean well, they're just not used to living on top of one another like this. Hopefully they never will be.

"Why did you open it?" she asks, as politely as she can.

"It was delivered by that new courier service, the one that brings messages through the omenpaths," he says. "We couldn't imagine what someone off-plane might have wanted with you, so we felt it was necessary to see for ourselves."

Depending on when the mail arrived, they would have needed to wait for only a few hours for her to get home. They didn't need to open something addressed to her. She wants to hold on to the anger over the invasion of her privacy, but in the end, curiosity is stronger, and the omenpaths are new enough to be sources of endless curiosity.

"You knew my shift was almost over. You could have waited until I got home."

"I'm sorry we didn't." It's a rare admission from her father, that he was wrong about something, and so she settles, irritation soothed by novelty.

"We just didn't know you knew anyone off-plane," adds her mother uncomfortably.

When the Invasion tore through the membrane dividing Capenna from the rest of the Multiverse, it left scars. Tunnels of a sort, bored through the fabric of reality itself, connecting the worlds in ways they had never been connected before.

Eula had already known Capenna is a plane—one of many—scattered across a near-infinite Multiverse. Wrapping your mind around the true nature of reality is one of the first challenges of a magical education, and people who couldn't manage it didn't tend to last long in her classes. But despite all of this, the omenpaths had been a shock. They made the Multiverse seem small and accessible in a way it's never been before, trading some of its grandeur for the hope that maybe someday, even people like her will be able to reach out and touch another world.

She's considered buying a ticket through one of the omenpaths and going off to seek her fortune in a place that might be able to put her talents to better use than a work crew, but she's never been willing to take the leap and commit to trying. She certainly hasn't gone looking for an off-plane pen pal.

And now her mother is looking at her like she's been hiding

something, and she doesn't know what to do about it. This isn't something she can cast a shield against. The silence in the kitchen grows cold and heavy until she turns her attention back to her father.

"What is it?" she blurts, desperate for anything to break the silence.

"It's an invitation," he replies.

"To what?"

"To a school," says her mother. "A place called Strixhaven, on a plane called Arcavios. They teach wizards there."

Eula's heart leaps in her chest, choking her with hope and *wanting*, wanting so pure it's like sunlight in her veins, like sipping Halo at a year's turning party and knowing the whole world is at your fingertips. She forces it down, not quite letting herself embrace it, and asks, "Oh?"

"Yes," says her father. "I don't know how they heard about you . . ." He pauses meaningfully, giving her the opportunity to confess to sending in an application, to inviting their attention. She doesn't say anything. She didn't do it, and protesting her innocence will only make her look guilty. ". . . but they did, and they'd like to offer you a place in their incoming class. Tuition and supplies fully covered, although we can't afford to pay the extra fee for a private room. They included a ticket through the omenpath network to Arcavios, in case you want to accept the place."

"I do," she says without thinking, taking a half step forward, already reaching for the letter. Her father twitches it away.

"I don't know that we want to let you go to school off-plane," he says. "How will you learn to be a proper Capennan law mage if you're learning another world's laws?"

"If I'm a fully trained shield mage, you know the Brokers will teach me the law," she says. "They still have the people for that, even if we've lost the wizard's college. I can do it."

"So you still want to be a Broker?" There's a hard edge in his voice, one she understands better than she wants to.

Eula swallows. "Yes, sir," she lies. It's all he's ever wanted for her; she can learn to want it for herself the way he needs her to, even if she knows she would be happier among the Obscura. Even if she wants to sit at Raffine's feet and listen to everything the ancient seer has to teach her. She can put her own desires aside. For the sake of the family.

But her father isn't thinking about the Obscura at all, or Eula's oft-derided ambitions. "You haven't decided you'd rather be a Riveteer workhand for the rest of your life?" he asks.

Eula recoils. "No, sir! I'm only working cleanup for the money to help this family, not because I want to. They'll get by just fine without me, and if I go to this school, I . . . I'll get to learn. That's all I've ever wanted."

Fear strikes then, sharp and biting: maybe he's asking all these questions because they can't get by without the money she's been bringing in. Maybe he's not going to let her go.

"This school, it's not something we have any information about. It's not something I've ever heard of before. And things being what they are, it's entirely possible the *Brokers* don't have any information about it, either."

"Yes, sir," she says, automatically.

Her father nods, frowning to himself. "So any information *you* could gather would be something new. Something valuable."

"Sir?"

"You'll go to this school, if they're so eager to pay your way. You'll learn everything they have to teach you, and everything they don't *intend* to teach you, and you'll bring it all back here, to New Capenna. To your family. To the Family."

It's the same word. The way he stresses it the second time he says it turns it into something else entirely. Eula swallows.

She wants to belong to a Family, even if she doesn't agree with her father about which would be the best fit for her. Joining one of the five Families and having access to their resources and protection is what every citizen of New Capenna dreams of. It's what she's been working toward since the first time she managed to summon a weak shield, barely strong enough to stop a soap bubble.

It's what she thought she lost when Park Heights fell, and now that it's possible again, all she can think is, *I'm going to school. I'm going to go through an omenpath to a different world, and I'm going to go to a real school, where they'll teach me all the magic I want to know. I'm going to school.*

She feels like she's walking on air as she follows her mother out of the kitchen and through the small apartment to her room.

"You leave tomorrow," her mother says, voice clearer now that they're alone. She always sounds more sure of herself when her husband isn't in the room. "We have to pack."

"Yes, Mama," says Eula, and she smiles as her mother gets the carpetbag from the closet. They begin packing her scant belongings, and the work crew has never been further away. She's leaving. She's on her way into the future.

She's going to *school.*

TWO

OMENS AND EMBERS

Sleep doesn't come easy. Eula tosses and turns until she realizes she's keeping her younger siblings awake and slips from the bed, pulling on her housecoat and creeping out of the room. They mumble sleepy protests at her desertion but don't fight too hard; they have class in the morning, and they need to be awake enough to pay attention and answer their teachers' questions.

Guilio is five and Noemi is six, both born when Eula was moving into the upper classes at her Park Heights school. Her parents had been anticipating her beginning to pull an apprentice's salary by now, moving out and leaving them with the resources to feed two more mouths. Well, that's what anticipation gets you: five people in a tiny apartment and not enough of anything to go around.

There are schools in the Caldaia, of course, but they're meant to make laborers, not scholars; instead of penmanship and history, the little ones are learning the foundational skills for the lives it now looks like they're going to lead.

Eula can change all that. She just has to get to this Strixhaven place, and she'll be able to turn the family fortunes around. Her upper-city friends who didn't lose their neighborhoods in the Invasion will start speaking to her again, will welcome her back into the circles she used to move through so effortlessly, and she'll be home. She'll forget about the Obscura and become a Broker like her father wants her to be, or she'll finally convince him to let her follow her own path into proper Obscura black, and either way she'll fix everything, and it'll be like the Phyrexians never came.

She holds that thought as firmly as she can as she stretches out on the couch, using it to keep other, less pleasant thoughts at bay. She finally slips off to sleep a few hours before dawn, only to wake what feels like minutes later to the sound of the city stirring around her. Morning seems to come earlier in the Caldaia, where it happens without the aid of the sun. They've calibrated their lives so that they don't need the sunlight here, although everyone's happy when it makes its way down through the city to shine on the alleys and the window gardens, warming and brightening the world.

Eula yawns, stretches, and opens her eyes to find Guilio inches from her face. Her inhale becomes a startled squeak, and she falls off the couch to the uproarious laughter of her younger siblings, who have apparently never seen anything this funny in their lives. They're still laughing when their mother comes and herds the pair to the kitchen for breakfast.

She stops in the kitchen doorway to look back at Eula, her expression grave. "Your carriage leaves in two hours," she says. "I've laid out your good dress in the bathroom. Go get ready, and remember, this is an opportunity not just for you, but for your family and all of New Capenna."

"Yes, Mama," says Eula, too groggy to argue. She wipes her eyes with the back of her hand and staggers toward the bathroom where, true to her word, her mother has laid her best blue dress across the sink.

The sight of it makes her flesh crawl, and she wishes, suddenly and fiercely, that she'd managed to wake and escape the apartment before anyone else was up. She wonders if her mother remembers the last time Eula had a reason to wear that dress—to do anything to make herself look even remotely in fashion, rather than blending in to the work crews. Wonders if her mother remembers how many funerals there were in the weeks following the Invasion.

Eula remembers. They went on for so long that it felt like the funerals were never going to end, like the people of Capenna were going to run out of the living before they finished burying the dead. First they'd buried the people who died fighting Phyrexia, and then they'd buried the people who died when Phyrexia lost, and finally they'd buried the people who died almost incidentally, the ones crushed when the city fell, the ones who never had a chance.

The last time Eula wore her good blue dress, it was for her friend Inez's funeral, and she'd sworn afterward that she was never going to wear it again, out of respect for the friend she'd buried. But here it is, and she doesn't have anything else to wear, and so she slips it on, does the buttons, fastens the belt, and looks at herself in the mirror. Her hair is too long to be fashionable; it hits her shoulders, rather than holding an obedient wave, but it's still white-blond and striking enough to be worth looking at twice. The dress has clearly been worn before, the cuffs frayed and the hemline funeral-long, rather than society-short. She doesn't have any stockings, and her shoes are scuffed.

She takes a deep breath, pushing memory and preconceptions aside, and forces herself to look critically at every aspect of what she sees. She's an attractive girl. Hard labor in the Caldaia hasn't changed that, and if there had been a risk it would, her father wouldn't have let her join the work crews, no matter *how* much they needed the money. The family needs her to catch the eye of a Family, and that means being properly groomed and mannered, as well as magically talented and clever enough to know her own limitations. If anything, the lack of direct sunlight has been good for her complexion, which no longer risks tanning or freckling. She might as well have been designed to look her best in Brokers' colors, white and blue and gold, and one day she'll wear them if she has to, even as she'll mourn the Obscura black she dreamed of. One day she'll put tattered dresses far behind her, whatever colors she wears, and she'll be the toast of the town.

Just not today. Today, she leaves.

She opens the bathroom door to find her whole family waiting, even Alton. Her mother is in the middle of them all, beaming, offering Eula's carpetbag like it holds the treasures of the city itself. Her father is more stern; he looks her up and down, then thrusts a slice of toast into her hand.

"You need to eat. You won't shame New Capenna by letting yourself get faint with hunger on a simple journey."

"Yes, sir," she says automatically.

Noemi frowns, looking between the two of them. She appears to be trying to puzzle through what's happening, and as her eyes settle on the carpetbag in her mother's hand, she reaches a conclusion and wraps her arms around Eula's legs, beginning to wail. The sound is too shrill for this hour of the morning. Eula winces, then bends to stroke her sister's hair with her free hand, attempting to soothe her.

"It's all right, pigeon," she says. "I'm just going to school, like I said I was before we had to move. I'll be back before you know it. Promise."

Noemi looks up at her, blue eyes filled with tears. "Really promise?" she asks.

"Really promise," says Eula. She straightens, taking the carpetbag from her mother, still watching her younger siblings. "Be good for Mama and Pop, okay, you two?"

"Okay, Eu," says Noemi.

"'kay," says Guilio, less interested in whatever weird thing she's doing now than he is in the delay to his breakfast.

Eula offers them all a wavering smile, quickly embraces Alton and her mother, nods to her father, and heads for the door, pausing only to get her coat from the rack. She doesn't look back.

Outside, the air is dark and cool and oddly still, for all that the sounds of the waking city are everywhere. The cleanup crew will be starting their first shift soon, and Eula feels a pang of guilt. Has anyone told her foreman she's not going to be there?

Probably not, but there's no point in dwelling. Alton got her that job, and Alton came to say goodbye; he'll tell the Riveteers where she's gone. They'll replace her soon enough. She knows better than to think she's somehow indispensable, and that means she can go.

She's already going. She's walking, although she didn't realize she'd started, heading for the omenpath processing station indicated on her ticket. Two omenpaths appeared and anchored down here in the Caldaia, and she's never used either one. Tickets are expensive, even though no one can quite explain why that should be; the Riveteers seized both omenpaths as soon as they stabilized, and they started selling tickets shortly thereafter, claiming the funds were essential to rebuilding the city. The Obscura control the omenpaths in the upper city, and they charge, too, although she hasn't heard anything about those funds going toward rebuilding anything.

It's not Eula's job to argue with the Families—it doesn't matter why they charge to use something they had no hand in creating. What matters is the ticket in her hand. What matters is her education.

What matters is getting out of here.

Her feet carry her all the way to Lower Bassomer Station, brick and tile and tarnished filigree, the occasional rush of hot air from a passing train rich with the promise of ascent to the Mezzio and beyond, to lost, lamented Park Heights. Eula pauses to blow a kiss at the station, like a promise that she'll be coming back, and walks onward, circling the building.

People begin to appear around her, some with luggage of their own, their eyes lit with the fanatic fire of someone on their way to a bright, much-desired future, some wiping tears away as they wave their loved ones on. A few, wearing unfashionable clothing that marks them as out of synch with the society around them, huddle near the walls with bowls of coins by their feet. She makes eye contact with a girl roughly her own age in tattered leather trousers etched with strange diamonds and a loose linen shirt. Cheeks burning, Eula looks quickly away.

Not quickly enough: the girl is already moving toward her.

"Please," says the stranger. "No one told me they charged just to walk through the gate on this side. Home is only a few feet away, but no one wants to help. Please. I need to get back to Thunder Junction."

Eula tries to harden her heart, but the yearning in the stranger's voice is impossible to ignore. She's never heard of Thunder Junction. It must be very warm there. Turning her body slightly toward the stranger, so as to obscure what she's doing, she dips a hand into the pocket of her dress and pulls out the coins she'd taken to buy herself something to eat on the journey. She's sure this new school won't let their students starve.

The stranger beams as Eula drops the coins into her bowl, then counts them with practiced efficiency. "I think I have enough to buy a walk-through ticket now," she says after a moment, and springs to her feet, grabbing a leather pack Eula hadn't even noticed. "May the Thunder treat you kindly in your travels, adventurer. Perhaps we'll meet again."

She takes off at a run, heading for the barrier that spans a narrow, otherwise unremarkable alleyway. Eula watches her go until she loses sight of her, then starts walking again, heading for the same alley.

A booth stands to each side of the barricade that blocks it: one accompanied by a snaking line of people handing cash to a bored elf in exchange for slips of paper with their destinations printed on them, the other with no line at all, manned by a stern-looking magpie aven, his feathers perfectly preened despite the early hour. The sound of the queue hits as Eula approaches, a constant clamor of rubber stamps, jingling coins, and complaining children. It's like a neighborhood fair.

There's even a man roaming the line, selling twists of waxed paper with roasted nuts and candied fruits inside.

The gleam of the omenpath's entrance is visible from the mouth of the alley, blue-white and somehow alien in its geometry, like something that shouldn't be. Carriages are lined up around the entrance, and people mill among them, studying their tickets and clutching their bags as they face the great unknown. Some people walk into the omenpath under their own power, like the girl from Thunder Junction, while others climb into carriages and are driven through. Motor vehicles aren't allowed in the omenpaths. She's not sure exactly why, just knows that they're not permitted, and no one really wants to argue about it.

Eula approaches the second booth, aware of her shabby dress and scuffed shoes and the stares from the people waiting in line, the ones who can't imagine she has the money for a ticket. The aven ticket-taker fixes her with a stern eye, holding out one feathered hand in expectation.

"You'll need a ticket to go any farther," he says, and while his voice is brusque, it's not unkind. "Are you here to use the omenpath?"

This is it, then: this is the moment where she finds out whether this has all been some sort of unspeakably cruel trick. Eula pulls the ticket from her coat pocket and hands it to the ticket-taker. "I'm traveling for university?" she says, and it comes out as a question, even though she didn't mean for it to be.

The ticket-taker, thankfully, only nods. He looks critically at her ticket, then at her. "Do you have any fruits, vegetables, or protected intellectual property? Family grimoires are included on the list of prohibited items."

"No," says Eula.

"Any pets? Recent parasite infestations? There's no telling what we have here that could get out of control somewhere else."

"No, sir," says Eula, getting flustered.

The aven nods again, then stamps her ticket and hands it back. "Lucky girl, traveling by private coach," he says. "Although maybe not so lucky, with as long as this is going to take. On you go, then, head on through. You're right on time for the switchover from Thunder Junction to Shandalar. Wouldn't want to drop you in the wrong neighborhood."

That explains why the strange girl was able to cut the line, if the omenpath is about to change destinations. Eula's heard they tend to do that; this one goes to four different planes, depending on the time of day and the phase of the moon.

The ticket-taker waves her grandiosely past the barricade. Eula goes, more than a little overwhelmed by how quickly this is all unfolding.

The coaches wait in dark, silent ranks, surrounded by the chatter of the people who've come to ride them. Most of the fleet is very old, recalled from retirement when the omenpaths appeared. They're pulled by a motley assortment of harnessed pegasi, massive mastiffs with drooping jowls, and even a few enormous crocodiles.

Eula eyes them warily as she approaches the man checking tickets on this side of the barricade. He takes hers, frowns, and then frowns again as he looks at her face.

"Eula?"

She pauses, blinking. "I'm sorry, I don't . . ."

"Enzo," he says, handing her ticket back, suddenly smiling. "I was in the year behind you at school, on the enhancement track. No talent for shielding, but I could help my classmates take a hit without going down."

"I'm sorry," says Eula. "I don't remember you."

"Never expected you to. A pretty girl like you never looked back." His smile dims back into professionalism. "This says you're heading for Arcavios. That's a multi-leg trip, and you're only paid one way."

"Yes," says Eula. "I know."

"Coming home will be a pretty penny."

"I know that, too." She didn't, but she'd guessed even before she met the stranded stranger. Things like this never come cheap.

"Then, if you're sure."

Eula nods. They don't speak again as he leads her to a carriage pulled by a chestnut pegasus whose wings have been carefully strapped against her sides. It doesn't seem to be causing the mare any discomfort; her head is up and her ears are forward as she watches the pair approach.

Enzo opens the carriage door and offers Eula a hand, boosting her inside. "Your driver will be along shortly," he says as she settles into the plush bench, setting her carpetbag on the floor at her feet. The aven who stamped her ticket said she was traveling by private coach, and so she doesn't worry about scooting over to make room, just closes her eyes and enjoys the clean leather and brass polish scent of the carriage's interior.

"Have a nice trip," says Enzo, closing the door. It's rude, but Eula doesn't reply; she's already half asleep and drifting.

She'll kick herself later for missing her first trip through an omenpath. But right now she's safe and comfortable and *alone* for the first time in what feels like months.

No one could have seen the Invasion coming. Not even the Families had been able to look that far into the future, or across that many planes of existence. But it meant they hadn't been prepared when the branches of that horrible tree started tearing down the very walls of reality, or when the monsters came pouring through the cracks the tree had made.

People died.

It's easy for Eula to fixate on the loss of Park Heights and her carefully planned future, but she knows those didn't matter as much as the lives that were lost. So many lives, and the survivors will be rebuilding for years to come. And it's so easy to lose track of that when crammed into an apartment a third the size of the one that had already felt like it was veering toward too small, doing work she doesn't enjoy and getting pulled deeper and deeper into a life that doesn't feel like hers.

Being in the carriage is like having all those weights removed at once. She's so light she feels like she could fly. And so, comfortable and conflicted, she sleeps through the carriage starting to move, through the change in the air and the rattle of the wheels across an uneven surface.

The carriage hits a rock hard enough to make the whole thing bounce, and Eula jerks awake, looking around with wide, bleary eyes. Sunlight streams through the carriage windows. Bright, clean sunlight, unfiltered by layers of city. Cautiously, she twitches one of the curtains aside and looks out.

They're driving along a coastline, brilliant blue sea stretching out to touch the horizon. The sky is an equally flawless blue, and Eula gasps as a vast scaled creature that looks something like a dragon, only smaller—and she can't imagine anything *but* a dragon that would make this thing seem small—soars overhead, vanishing over the top of the carriage window. They're still moving, bumping their way along on what must be some of the most broken pavement she's ever encountered.

Still cautious, she cracks the window open and is rewarded by a gust of fresh, clean air that manages to smell salty and sweet at the same time. She can't take her eyes off that impossible ocean, that endless expanse of blue.

This isn't Capenna. There's no way this is Capenna. She's on another plane. The carriage passed through the omenpath while she was dozing, and she's so far from home that she's on a different *world*. The thought is dizzying, and she leans back into the cushions again, grappling with it.

She's still grappling as they rattle to a stop, and there are voices outside the carriage, accents unfamiliar. Then the carriage door is opened, and she blinks in the sudden brightness, waiting for her eyes to adjust before she tries to get out.

A good thing, that: the opening is filled an instant later by a man loading cases into the carriage, three of them, old-fashioned steamer trunks with solid brass latches patinaed by the salty air. They take up most of the space in the other half of the carriage, and the man doesn't acknowledge Eula at all, not even with a grunt.

When he withdraws, she finally leans forward, intending to ask why someone's bags are being loaded into her *private* carriage, and pauses at the sight of a girl about her age, hugging an older man.

The girl is shorter than Eula herself, slim without being skinny, and if she jumped into the sea, she would disappear, because her skin is a shade of blue almost identical to the water, marked with thin white lines like the foam that tops the little waves. It's perfect camouflage for someone aquatic, and Eula is impressed, even as she can't help picturing how the girl would look in a Brokers' uniform, perfectly suited to their aesthetic.

In place of hair, the girl has layers of long pink and purple fins that hang midway down her back. Her traveling clothes consist of a green tunic and brown pants slit to the knee, leaving the fins on her calves room to extend.

The man is clearly a relative, with skin the same shade of blue and similar features. He's powerfully built and wears the skull of some great beast as a hat. Eula thinks it might have come from one of the things that flew over the carriage earlier. She can't imagine what it would take to bring one of those down.

He releases the girl, and she turns toward the carriage, a look of grim determination on her face. Eula almost gasps. Another of those strange flying creatures is sitting on the girl's shoulder, this one roughly the size of a crow. Its wings are folded close along its back, and it clings to the fabric of the girl's tunic with small, sharp claws, canny blue eyes taking in everything about its surroundings.

The man nudges the girl toward the carriage, and she nods, her expression growing even grimmer. Her first step appears to take an impossible effort. Her second is only a little easier, and by the fourth, she's climbing into the carriage, cramming herself into the narrow slice of space left across from Eula. The little creature climbs down from her shoulder to curl in her lap, where she begins stroking it with nervous motions of one hand.

"Hello," says Eula cautiously. If the new girl doesn't want to talk, this is going to be a very awkward journey.

To her relief, the girl gives her a sidelong glance and replies, "Hello."

Someone shuts the carriage door. They begin moving again.

"I'm Eula. I didn't know we were going to be taking any other passengers this trip. I'm on my way to a school called Strixhaven, to learn to be a better wizard. Who are you?"

"I . . . um." The blue girl hesitates, and for a moment, Eula is struck by the perfect ridiculousness of her thinking of the newcomer as "the blue girl." Her *name* is Blue. If anyone here is going to be "the blue girl," it should be her!

"I'm Alandra," says the girl finally, and she's named: she can't be a stranger any longer. She rests a hand on the little creature's back and says, "This is Orestes. He's coming with me to help when I get too anxious about all the new people and new things I'm going to be seeing. Father says nerves are a sign of wisdom—the sea has trouble sneaking up on you when you're always on edge—but they're not going to be so useful in a classroom, where I'm not supposed to be on watch for bigger predators all the time."

"What is he?" asks Eula, with sincere interest. "We don't have anything like him where I come from."

"Orestes is a drake," says Alandra. "He'll be much too big to sit in my lap when he's grown up, so he does it as much as he can now. But he says he'll always be my companion, for when I need to be calm in new places."

". . . Huh," says Eula. "Are you also going to Strixhaven?"

Alandra nods, stroking the tiny drake again. The fins

atop her head bristle, reacting to her nerves. That must be unsettling, to be betrayed by one's *hair*.

"Is this your home? This plane? I've never been off my own plane before. It's truly beautiful here."

"The deep down is better," says Alandra. "That's where Father and I live, with the rest of our family. He talks to the drakes, and so do I, so we come to the surface the most often, to be with them. He's the ruler of this whole ocean."

The ocean looks bigger than New Capenna, and unimaginably deep. Eula can't even start to wrap her head around what it would take to control something so vast. Five Families are barely enough to keep the city in check.

"Wow," she says. "That must be a lot of work."

"It is," says Alandra. "He had to learn to control his magic before he could conquer the sea, but he had to teach himself. None of the human wizards he met were willing to train him. He wants me to go to the school so I can learn all the things he never had the chance to."

"Human wizards—are you not humans?"

"No," says Alandra, sounding faintly affronted. "We're merfolk. What are you?"

"Human," says Eula. "We don't have merfolk where I'm from."

"No drakes, no merfolk—this place you come from must be very boring."

"Oh, no, it's not boring at all. It's called New Capenna, and it's a city that's almost as big as your ocean, on a plane called Capenna. Where are we now?"

"This is the Mistral Isle, in the Kapsho Seas. Father was *very* surprised when the strange portal opened on our island.

He tried to go through it, but the first time he did, he wound up in a terrible hot place where even the grasses were made of spines and spikes, and the sun was like a hammer from above. He tried again, but he found a barrier on the other side, and unfamiliar people who said he'd have to 'pay' if he wanted to come home after coming out on their end. He came back here, and we didn't think anything more of the hole in the world until the invitation for me to go to Strixhaven came." Alandra pauses. "Our plane is called Shandalar, if that's what you were asking."

"It was, but the name doesn't mean anything to me."

There's a sudden lurch, and Eula scrambles to look out the window, convinced she's going to see them plummeting toward the water. Instead, she sees the island dropping away as they rise into the air.

Shoving the window open and sticking her head out, she realizes the driver has removed the band from around their pegasus's wings, and four medium-sized drakes have grabbed the rails atop the carriage and are hoisting them into the sky.

Eula withdraws, her stomach churning uncomfortably. "Alandra, I don't mean to worry you, but I think we're being abducted."

"Oh, no," says Alandra, smiling for the first time. "Right now, the omenpath leads back to where you came from, and we don't want to go there, so Father got the drakes to agree to take us to the next pathway. That's why my cases are inside the carriage with us, instead of up on the luggage rack."

"That makes sense," says Eula faintly, and she waits to see what will happen next.

THREE

THE LONG ROAD TO SCHOOL

The drakes set them down on a much smoother road, screeching like unnaturally large falcons before they wheel and fly back toward Mistral Isle, presumably to tell Alandra's father that she's been safely delivered to solid ground.

Eula isn't sorry to see them go, although she's grateful for the safe passage, and happier than she ever thought she could be *not* to be in the air. Slowly, she peels her aching fingers off the bar on the door, shaking her hands until the tingling begins to die down.

Alandra watches her with concern. "Eula? Is something wrong?"

Not to be left out, Orestes chirps an inquisitive note.

Eula swallows, hard. "Did the Invasion happen here on Shandalar?" she asks. "Did Phyrexia come out of the sky and try to take your world?"

"They did," says Alandra, sinking back into her seat. "From the sky, and from the deepest depths, they came. The world fought back. Many drakes and merfolk died to protect our waters, but we won. We drove them to the edges of the world, and they died there."

"Where I'm from . . . we won, too, but we paid a terrible price. My home was built near the top of our city, but still under another layer of city. That layer fell. And when it did, it smashed through our whole neighborhood, and we fell with it, so far . . ."

So far, from the Mezzio all the way to the distant ground. If Eula hadn't been home, her whole family would have died; if the shield she'd thrown up against the impact hadn't been able to hold, she'd be dead, too, another casualty of the Invasion, another untended grave . . .

A hand touches her shoulder. She snaps out of her brief fugue as she recoils, then steadies herself, finding Alandra watching her with concern.

"Sorry," she says, awkwardly. "I guess I just . . . don't like heights much anymore."

"I adore them," says Alandra. "To fly with a drake is the greatest gift they have to offer. One day, when Orestes is grown, I'll fly with him. I'm sorry you fell."

"I'm sorry your world got invaded the same as mine did."

Alandra shrugs. "War is a constant in the sea. It's like the tide. Peace flows out, and violence flows in, and all we can do is try to build our channels where the waters will protect them. What I learn at Strixhaven will help me build better channels against the wars to come."

"What sort of magic are you hoping to study?"

Alandra shrugs again. "I can already speak to the drakes, as Father does, but I can't compel them the way he does. We had a great storm sculptor on my mother's side of the family, several generations ago, and I'd love to follow in her wake. I think I could have a gift for it. You?"

"I'm a shield mage?" Eula holds out one hand, calling a quick disc of light to form a dome around her fingers. "I can use my magic to stop people from hitting me, or to hit harder, or to protect the people I'm with from falling objects. I'm not super strong yet, but I could be, with the right training. I'm hoping Strixhaven can help me with that."

"Wow," says Alandra. She sounds genuinely impressed. "We don't have that kind of magic here."

"Well, I've never heard of sculpting a storm. Maybe we can learn from each other as well as from our classes."

Alandra smiles, and Eula relaxes a bit. She's made a friend already. Maybe this is going to be easier than she thought.

She glances at the window as she releases her shield. "Any idea where we are now?"

"Father said the drakes would take us to a place called Thune, where we could get to the portal. I'm guessing we're there, or near there."

"Huh."

The name doesn't mean anything to her, but the land outside is very different from Alandra's oceanic home. The carriage is passing through a vast scrubland, level and growing green with verdant grasses. Mountains break the line of the landscape in the distance, but where they are, everything is flat.

The carriage slows, stopping, and the driver hops down, boots crunching against the ground. He opens the door and starts pulling Alandra's bags out, hoisting them onto the luggage rack atop the carriage. Between the second and the third he pauses, explaining, "Next stop's our last before the school. You'll need the room."

"Why do this here, instead of on the other side of the passage?" asks Alandra.

"The carriage network guarantees a measure of safety on the roads here in Shandalar. We don't have the same guarantee on the other side of the omenpath. Fiora's a lot like *her* plane," he adds, his attention going to Eula. "They charge to use their omenpaths, and they've been fighting over who owns which passage. We've timed this so we've got a pretty straight shot to Arcavios after our pickup, but we don't want to spend any more time in Fiora than we have to."

"Is charging for the omenpaths not normal?" asks Eula.

"Only a few planes we've seen that do it," says the driver. "Yours and those toffs in Ravnica are the only ones in the primary carriage network who've been charging, and not all the guilds put a price to passage. About half the destinations we can reach from Ravnica don't have a fee associated. Fiora isn't in the primary network. You have to pay extra if you want us to connect through there, much less stop."

"Why don't we want to spend much time in Fiora?" asks Alandra, stroking Orestes with one hand as if to calm them both. The tiny drake butts his head against her fingers, chirping for her to scratch just so behind his gills.

"Fiora is a perfectly lovely place and plane, as long as you don't have to deal with the people," says the driver. "Since we're making a pickup in one of their main cities, Paliano, avoiding the people isn't as much of an option as we'd like."

"Why do we not want to deal with the people?" Eula is starting to feel worse and worse about this trip. Alandra had the right idea—she could use a tiny drake to soothe herself.

The driver inhales, thinks for a moment, and then exhales slowly. "Begging your pardon, ma'am, but the carriage network is based on Ravnica—that's where we get our muster and assignments—and it's not entirely accurate to say that most people don't pay. People pay if they want to use our services. Drivers don't come free, and draft animals need to be fed. It's just that most planes don't have an organized system of tolls for passage or tariffs for goods, so your ticket is only for the ride from where you start to where you finish off, not for using the omenpath in the first place, or for any of the things you might be carrying with you."

"All right . . . ?" says Eula.

"One of the first things we learn when we take this job is that we're not here to judge other people's societies or traditions. Your plane is your plane, and just because it doesn't do things the way someone else's plane does, that doesn't make it wrong. We're Ravnican."

"Like the toffs," says Eula, amused.

The driver gives her a wry look. "There's common folks and toffs everywhere you go. One side sets the rules, the other follows them."

"Fair enough," agrees Eula, thinking of the Families.

"As I was saying, we're Ravnican. That doesn't make us better or worse than anyone else, and we're not supposed to pass our prejudices on to passengers."

"That doesn't answer my question."

"I think it does," says Alandra. "He's saying that avoiding the people on Fiora is a matter of cultural judgment, and he feels bad about trying to explain it to you."

The driver looks relieved as he nods and says, "That's the size of it. Fiora is a . . . special place. They backstab each other as a way of saying hello. Marriages look more like hostage negotiations. Their monarchy is less based on succession than it is on assassination. One of my aunts married into the Orzhov Syndicate back home, and she says her guildmates are less likely to slit your throat for your pocket change than the friendliest person on Fiora would be. We get in, we pick up your classmate, and we get out, hopefully without a fight."

Eula has absolutely no idea what any of that meant, but she can tell from his tone that he's trying to make a point. She frowns. "I don't like any of this."

"Nor should you. I saw your ticket. It didn't say anything about the route we were supposed to take. *I* wouldn't have started by collecting the two of you, if it'd been up to me, but someone up the line decided this was the fastest way to get you to school, so that's the route we were assigned, and it's more than my job's worth to argue with my employers." He grabs Alandra's last case and hoists it onto the roof. "The two of you stay alert, and we'll get this done as quickly as we can."

He doesn't move to take Eula's carpetbag, and she doesn't offer it. Instead, he closes the carriage door. There's a series of rattles and clangs as he secures the bags to the top. Then they start moving again, veering off the straight, level path they've been following and striking out across the plains with bone-rattling speed. Orestes squeaks indignantly, climbing onto Alandra's shoulder. Eula and Alandra clutch the bars on the ceiling, trying to brace themselves against the jostling.

"What are we doing?" asks Eula.

"I think the omenpath isn't on the road," says Alandra.

They're heading straight for the nearest mountain. Eula pulls herself over to the window and slides it down, sticking her head out to watch with wide, round eyes as they charge directly toward the high stone wall.

There's a glimmer there. Not much, just a bright line of glittering blue-white light, like the inside of a geode. Eula tries to focus on the dancing brightness, forgetting the rest of their surroundings. It's so beautiful, like a song turned into something solid and concrete. Seeing it makes her want to reach out and touch it, and only the need to hold the bar in order to keep from being bounced out of the carriage stops her from trying. *What could it hurt?* she thinks. *Isn't it strange to go to a new place—a whole new world—and not try to touch any part of it?*

Then the pegasus at the front of the carriage reaches the geode, and although the sparkling seam is narrow—barely wide enough to slide a hand into—the entire galloping equine is pulled inside, seeming to flatten and distort before it vanishes into the glitter. Eula pulls herself back with a gasp and watches through the still-open window as the world is replaced by a scintillating wall of prismatic light and mirrored surfaces, a hundred points of geodesic shine bouncing her own reflection back at her.

It's still so beautiful. She never realized the omenpaths would be beautiful. Alandra appears to be realizing the same thing, because she leans forward, eyes locked on the light, and watches raptly as it rushes by.

The tunnel of geodesic brilliance lasts for only a handful of seconds, and then they're breaking back into the sunlight—sunlight that seems dim by comparison, although the sky is clear above them and the sun itself is no smaller or darker than the one they just left behind. And they *did* leave that sun behind: this sun is a different shade of molten brilliance, more copper than gold. It still lights the world, but it does so in an obscure, gentler way, like everything is filtered through a veil of honey.

With the window down, the air of this new world fills the carriage, dusty and clean and bathed in the scents of a hundred kinds of unfamiliar flower and tree. The mountains are gone, but they're still in the plains, these ones vast and lush and stretching in all directions like they're determined to go on forever. The grass is tall and green, studded with yellow and purple flowers. They smell like sunshine and safety, like receiving an admissions letter to the university in Park Heights, like acceptance. She wants to gather them, to fill her hands and breathe in deeply. She reaches for the handle, intending to open the door—

Alandra leans closer to her, one hand cupping Orestes's back. "Close the window, please," she urges, voice low. "I don't like the perfume."

Eula blinks, snapping out of her fugue, and closes the window. The smell of the flowers dissipates quickly, and the plains, while still beautiful, no longer look like the most alluring thing she's ever seen. "I'm sorry," she says, half laughing out of nervousness. "I don't know what just came over me."

"It's all right," says Alandra. "Father warned me that different planes might affect us in strange ways. No harm was done."

"No harm," agrees Eula, faintly. Alandra's father is a powerful wizard. Eula's father is a bookkeeper, and while he'd argue that numbers are their own form of magic, none of the lessons he had to give her are going to be half so useful as the ones Alandra's father gave to *her*. A small thread of bitterness works its way through the day's delights, reminding her how far behind she is already.

The carriage is traveling along something smooth and level now, a road of some sort, or a particularly well-worn foot trail. Eula leans back in her seat, watching this new world roll by. There's so much Multiverse out there. She wants to see it *all,* and she knows she'll never have the chance. There aren't the hours in a lifetime to see *everything* the omenpaths have to offer, and there's so much more beyond even that.

Then the driver pulls them into a turn, and the most impossible sight of all comes into view.

It's a city, like New Capenna, and like New Capenna, it appears to have been built in layers. Not sensible, self-supporting tiers, where each is slightly larger than the one above it, maintaining stability while reducing the living space of each successive tier just enough to make it more exclusive and desirable as a place to live, oh no. This is a city as a single massive tier, vast and dense and imposing, placed on a vast pedestal and lifted above the world. There is another city built around the pillars that hold the first so firmly in the air, covering the ground like soap bubbles coat the bottom of an empty tub; and like soap bubbles, the second city manages to seem faintly grimy, as if all that is good and worthwhile and desirable has been lifted into the sky, leaving the dust and dregs behind.

They're approaching the outskirts of that lower city. The carriage slows but doesn't stop. Watching through the window, Eula gets her first look at the inhabitants of Fiora. For the most part they appear to be as human as she is, although there are elves and other, unfamiliar humanoids among the crowd, moving easily with the others. All watch the carriage with assessing eyes as it rolls by, and Eula fights the urge to shrink away from the glass. It feels like they're traveling into a predator's den, something huge and hungry and unknowable, and she wants to be anywhere in the Multiverse other than here.

The people are dressed in odd fashions, puffed sleeves and thick velvet tabards over thinner shirts; she thinks it would be difficult to stab someone wearing one of those tabards, and maybe that's the entire point. Their faces are like the faces she would expect to see at home, except for a seemingly universal wariness. Every one of them is watching the carriage like it could be either a treasure or a trap, and they haven't made up their minds yet.

She turns her attention back to Alandra, who has moved Orestes to her lap and is stroking the tiny drake with quick, anxious motions of her hand. "Are you all right?"

"I don't think I like it here," says Alandra. "I'd like to go now, if we could."

The carriage rattles to a stop, and there's a scuff on the pavement as their driver hops down from the seat. A moment later, the door swings open and a boy steps inside, clutching a duffel bag and crouching to avoid hitting his head.

Their driver appears behind him, expression anxious. "I trust you can introduce yourselves," he says. "We need to move if we're to reach Talon before dark."

He slams the door then, and the carriage dips as he hoists luggage onto the roof rack, then drops himself back onto the bench. A snap of the reins and they're off, racing toward some unfamiliar destination—Talon, wherever that is—with the boy still half stooped in the middle of the carriage.

He stumbles as the wheels hit a dip in the road, and Eula scoots herself and her bag to the side, motioning for him to take the other half of her bench. He eyes her warily as he does exactly that, clearly questioning her motivations, and she smiles at him, as wide and open as she can manage.

"I'm Eula," she says. "This is Alandra and Orestes." The merfolk girl waves at the sound of her name and indicates her drake at the sound of his. She doesn't speak, apparently trusting Eula to handle this part. That's fine. You don't make inroads with the snobs in Park Heights without learning how to handle yourself. "You are?"

The boy continues to watch her warily. Unlike Alandra, he's skinny rather than slender, thin enough for her to see the bones of his wrists under his lace cuffs. Eula suspects half his bulk comes from the heavy velvet tabard he wears, in fashion with the other people she's seen on this plane so far. His hair is rough-cut, messy, and black as spilled ink; his eyes are almost as dark, deep brown irises around black-hole pupils. Meeting his eyes is like falling into a deep chasm in the earth, and Eula looks away before she can fall too far.

She thinks he might be attractive. It's hard to say, with his eyes swallowing everything he looks at.

"Segante," he says, finally, and there's an air of newness to his name, like he's admitting it to the world for the first time. Maybe people in Fiora don't like to give their names? If everyone here is waiting for someone else to betray them, they may not want to hand out ways to target themselves.

"It's nice to meet you," says Eula. "Are you going to Strixhaven, too?"

"I am," he allows, and that seems to be the end of it: they pass the next several minutes in silence, the carriage gathering speed as their driver rushes to get them away from the low, dangerous-looking city.

The land outside the windows passes faster than ever, their driver pushing the pegasus pulling their carriage to its limits. Eula finds herself thinking fondly of the drakes—at least if they were being hoisted in the air, they wouldn't be hitting what feels like every bump and divot in Fiora, jarring them until she feels it in her teeth.

The driver shouts something, and they're skidding to a halt, the carriage sliding into a sideways position. The speed of the switch sends them all tumbling together, with Alandra winding up on top of the pile and Eula on the bottom, instinctively throwing up a shield to keep Segante's elbow from landing in her kidney.

For a moment, everything is silent, save for their labored breathing and Orestes's frantic peeping; the little drake has fallen between Eula's carpetbag and the wall and is unable to see his charge. Alandra sits up and reaches over to pluck him loose, gathering him against her chest. He stops peeping but watches between her fingers, wary of danger.

Eula and Segante are slower to recover, tangled together and tossed aside as they are, flattened hard against the carriage wall. There's another shout from the driver, and the carriage rocks.

That stirs Segante into motion. He rushes to peer through the window, then spins and shushes the others. They weren't making any noise. That doesn't appear to matter, as he holds two fingers to his lips and glares at them both, expression fierce and shoulders tight.

Someone outside yells. Eula moves. She pushes Segante out of the way, moving to look out the window herself. A barricade has been set up across the road, and four men are there, swords in hand, menacing the driver. He's still seated at the front of the carriage, and their pegasus doesn't appear to have been hurt, but there's no going forward.

"He needs to just pay them and we can get on with it," murmurs Segante, so close to Eula's ear that she jerks away, turning to stare at him. He shrugs. "They're highwaymen. You pay them and they let you by. If you protest too much, they decide you have something worth protecting, and they get curious. That's when people get hurt."

Their driver doesn't appear to have been informed about the customs of Fioran highwaymen. He's continuing to protest, and as Eula watches, two of the men advance on him, swords aimed low. The other two turn toward the carriage door. Segante grabs her, pulling her away from the window.

"Blue girl," he snaps. "Can you not be blue?"

"Excuse me?" asks Alandra.

"We don't have anyone who looks like you around here. They're likely to decide you're someone important—daughter of a noble household or dignitary from another city-state—and try to take you for ransom. Even if they don't, that little pet of yours is going to be nigh irresistible. Lots of fine ladies in the high city who'd pay well for something as unique as that."

Alandra's eyes darken, literally, sunny yellow trending toward orange, like sunlight filtered through heavy cloud cover. She clutches Orestes more tightly to her chest.

Eula glances back out the window. The men are moving slowly, unhurried and unconcerned, but they're almost to the door.

Can't open a door you can't touch. She raises her hands, holding the dimensions of the carriage in her mind, and throws a shield away from herself, covering the side of the carriage in a shimmering film of white shot through with inky black. The window goes hazy, distorted by the shining dome of the shield.

Segante blinks, then moves to peer through the thickened window. "They've stopped," he reports. "They're looking confused. Can you make this thing cover the whole carriage?"

"No," says Eula, voice strained and tightly clipped off. "I can't hold this forever, either."

"No stamina, huh?"

"I don't see *you* helping," she snaps.

"I'm not the one who provoked the brigands. All the driver had to do was pay them," he says. "Highwaymen are a normal part of travel. You can't just go around killing them because you don't like them doing their jobs."

Alandra screams.

It's less like the shriek of a frightened teenage girl and more like the wail of a seagull: loud, wild, and undulating up and down the scale of what sound can be, impossibly shrill, going on and on and on, long past the point where she should have run out of air. Eula stares at her in disbelief. The sound goes on, getting bigger and bigger in the close confines of the carriage. She claps her hands over her ears, fighting to maintain her concentration and hold the shield. The highwaymen have reached it now: she can feel them banging their fists against it, testing its limitations. Holding it intact while Alandra screams is getting harder by the second.

"What is she *doing?*" demands Segante. "Blue girl! What are you doing?"

Alandra continues screaming.

A peal of thunder announces the arrival of a sudden storm. A crack of lightning splits the sky, and torrents of rain crash down across the plains. It sounds like a wave the size of a city park slamming into the ground around them. Around them, but not—Eula sneaks another glance out the hazy window— not directly on top of them. The rain appears to be falling everywhere except for where the carriage sits, leaving it dry and undisturbed.

The hammering on the door gets stronger, hands beating at Eula's shield until it feels like they're hammering against her body. She moans and drops to her knees. Segante steps around her.

"Let it go," he says, his voice surprisingly soft.

She gives him a startled glance. He looks back at her, expression gentle, and nods.

Eula releases the shield. It collapses from the outside in, unraveling like a lace doily, until the final strands dissolve and the magic snaps back on her, leaving her gasping and unsteady. She braces her hands against the carriage floor as she struggles to catch her breath, and so she misses what happens next, as Segante opens the door and steps out into the rain-drenched afternoon.

He closes the door behind himself as he says something, his tone quiet and reasonable, but his words are taken by the storm. A minute or so later, the carriage door opens again, and

Segante climbs back inside, dripping wet and perfectly calm.

"They're gone," he says, simply enough. "Alandra, if you could shut down the monsoon long enough for our driver to get us out of here, I'm sure he'd appreciate it."

Alandra stops screaming and blinks at him, the orange bleeding out of her eyes and leaving them bright yellow once again. "What did you do?" she asks as she holds Orestes close against her chest.

"Nothing," he says.

He retakes his seat. The carriage rolls on, gathering speed as their driver resumes his journey toward the omenpath, and as there's no window in the back of the carriage, none of them look back.

None of them see the bodies.

FOUR

SHADOWS AND SNARLS

The journey to the next omenpath takes long enough that Eula nods off again, head lolling as she sleeps through miles and miles of Fiora countryside, soothed by the rattle of carriage wheels and the occasional peep from Orestes. Her dozing mind translates them into the vibration of subway tracks and the cries of pigeons, the sound of ordinary life in the Mezzio, back when the world made sense.

They hit a bump, and she snaps awake, sitting upright and blinking, bewildered, at the small, dim confines of the carriage. It had seemed so big when it was just her, but now, with Alandra and Segante crammed in beside her, it feels even smaller than her room back in the apartment she's been sharing with her family.

The thought carries a pang of guilt—and hunger. They've been traveling for hours, and there's been no offer of food. Her stomach rumbles, and she presses a hand against it, sitting upright.

"She lives," says Segante dryly.

"Be nice," says Alandra.

He looks at her with interest. "Where's the value in that?"

Alandra sputters but doesn't answer.

"Are we going to stop soon?" asks Eula. "I could use a drink of water, and something to eat." They hit another bump in the road; she grimaces. "And a bathroom."

"We're almost to Talon," says Segante. "But with the delay from the highwaymen, we're barely going to reach the omenpath before the sun goes down and it closes until morning. I'd rather go hungry for a bit and reach Arcavios than stop for supper and end up stuck. Aside from the limited potential sleeping arrangements, you do *not* want to be on the main roads after dark. That's when things get dangerous."

"As opposed to before?" asks Eula.

"Highwaymen who travel by day can be paid off with gold or jewels," says Segante. "The sort who travel at night require dearer payment, and I, for one, like my skin where it is."

Eula pales. "I changed my mind. I'm not hungry."

"I thought you might."

They continue on for a few more minutes in silence before curiosity gets the better of her, and she asks, "What did you do back there?"

"I understand that in some places, friendship is considered a valuable and desirable thing to have—more, even, than leverage or debts," he says. "Is it like that where you come from?"

"Yes."

"Me, too," says Alandra.

"I don't want to be a constant outsider at school, held at arm's length and unable to interact with my peers," he says.

"So?"

"So it would be better if I didn't tell you what I did to make those highwaymen leave us alone. We're unhurt, we're continuing onward to our destination, and the rest is chaff to be swept away." He makes a careless gesture with one hand.

Eula wants to argue, wants to tell him it doesn't work like that. She can't. She's tired and overwhelmed and she's starting to wonder whether there's a school at the end of this interminable journey. How could any school, however glorious, be worth all this?

The carriage rattles as it slows, and their driver knocks on the wall three times before he yells, "Hold fast! Omenpath ahead!"

Either this one is unguarded or their driver is getting more aggressive about busting through barricades. Whatever the case, the carriage speeds up and doesn't slow down again as it races toward a thick copse of trees to the side of the road. There's no glimmer this time, nothing to indicate that they're running *toward* something, not just charging headlong into a collision. She clutches the security bar so tightly it imprints into her palms, and she fights to keep her breathing smooth and regular as they slam into the trees—

—which distort and unfold around them like endless chains of folded paper, delicate and cut with unbelievable care. She gasps, looking back as best as the shape of the window allows, and sees those unfolded paper chains streaming out behind them, whipping in the wind of their passing.

The carriage gives a mighty jolt, and they break out of the waving cascade of paper possibilities into a bright afternoon. The sun is higher here than it was on Fiora, and the shadows it casts are odd, fuzzy at the edges and almost seemingly doubled. Eula opens the window and leans out, shielding her eyes with her hand.

There are two suns. They burn in slightly different shades of plasma, one marginally larger than the other, but that matters less than the fact that there are *two* suns burning overhead. Eula drops back into her seat.

"New plane," she says.

"This should be Arcavios, then," says Segante.

The carriage rolls on, slower now, like the driver no longer sees any need to hurry. They're getting where they're going, and he'll set the speed he likes to get there. Eula, Alandra, and Segante reposition themselves inside the carriage, peering out the window, commenting on the scenery outside.

Arcavios—if this *is* Arcavios—appears to be a lush and healthy plane, not overbuilt like Capenna, more landlocked than Alandra's slice of Shandalar. There are mountains in the distance and trees growing near the road, which feels like a proper road, smooth and even and easy for the pegasus to run down.

They round a curve. Eula's mouth drops open. No, this isn't anyplace she's ever been before, or ever even imagined. She barely notices the carriage starting to slow.

In the distance, a shining arch floats above the grassy plain. Its structure appears to be made of floating stones, suspended in a precisely angled line, the gaps between them forming the rays of a stylized star. Alandra pushes over to look with her, and the pair of them stare at this impossible formation, rapt.

Only Segante doesn't seem interested. He remains in his seat, twisting a piece of frayed black ribbon between his fingers to form a complicated pattern of loops and snarls, all of which collapse when he tugs upon the end.

The carriage comes to a stop, and Eula and Alandra pull back into their seats, waiting to see what happens next.

What happens is their driver opens the door, clearly worn and weary but uninjured. He smiles encouragingly at the trio. "Thanks for the save back there," he says. "I knew the highwaymen could get pushy on Fiora, but supposedly, they're to let the omenpath runs through without bothering us—we paid a tithe to the Black Rose, and that's meant to buy us passage. I'm sure the Firemind will be having a few words with her once I get home and tell him what happened."

If that's supposed to mean something to Eula, it doesn't. Still, Eula's pretty sure she wouldn't want someone called "the Firemind" mad at her. She musters a wan smile. "Is this our destination?" she asks.

"Close to," he says. "We just have some folks who need to speak with you before I help you with your bags."

He steps aside, leaving them room to pass. Eula is the first out, hauling her carpetbag and looking attentively around the whole time, almost overcome by the magnitude of the moment. She passed through Shandalar and Fiora, but she didn't *touch* them. She's stepping onto the soil of a whole new *plane,* a world so far from home that she doesn't have a way to measure the distance.

Her shoe, designed for the streets and stairs of New Capenna, has very little tread; she steps down from the carriage and promptly slips as the gravel slides underfoot. She begins to overbalance and is stopped by Segante grabbing her arm, preventing her from going sprawling.

She mumbles a thanks. He doesn't respond, just looks at

her impassively until she gets her balance back and then lets her go, moving to help Alandra down.

Orestes moves to Alandra's shoulder as soon as they're outside the carriage, peeping at the sky in what Eula can only describe as a proprietary tone, like he's informing anything that can hear and understand him of his ownership of Alandra. Alandra strokes his wings with one hand as she moves to stand near the others.

A pair of people are waiting in the road, wearing green-and-gold leather armor that seems to have been stylized to invoke the idea of some strange, great serpent. One, short and blue-skinned and sturdily built, consults a clipboard as the three of them blink at this unexpected greeting committee.

"You're the off-plane students?" asks the person with the clipboard.

"Er," says Alandra.

"Yes," says Eula, calling on all the lessons her mother taught her about being a proper society lady. This is an inspection of some sort. If someone has the money for bribes, it should be over quickly.

"Please cooperate with all Pathwarden instructions, and we'll have you on your way in short order," says his companion, a tall, dark-skinned elf with long pink hair.

"What's a Pathwarden?" asks Alandra.

"Think of us as the guards at the gate," suggests the elf. "We're here to check your paperwork and make sure you're not carrying anything that could be dangerous to Arcavios. We're still fairly new, so we don't have permanent checkpoints at all the known omenpath manifestation points, but we will."

Eula blinks. "What are you talking about?"

"Do you have any fruit or fresh vegetables? Any plant cuttings or seeds?" asks the one with the clipboard.

"No," says Eula.

"No," says Alandra.

"Yes," says Segante.

The figure with the clipboard looks up sharply. Segante smiles.

"I brought packets of dreamwaste flower seeds with me," he says. "I have a cultural exemption for them."

Eula looks at him, stunned. Alandra does the same. Of the three of them, he was apparently the only one to receive sufficient time to prepare.

The figure with the clipboard frowns and goes back to the list. "Any live animals?"

Eula manages not to scoff. Alandra's drake is perfectly visible. What's the point of asking a question when you already know the answer?

"This is Orestes," says Alandra, taking the little drake down from her shoulder. "He's my friend."

"That isn't a species native to this plane," says the elf.

Alandra clutches Orestes and takes a step back. "He keeps me calm. He's my *friend*."

Overhead, clouds begin to gather and darken.

Eula clears her throat. "The drake is a piece of medical equipment," she says, thinking of people back home who use miniature topiary dinosaurs and artfully groomed poodles for the same purpose. She's seen them carry their companions into places where animals were distinctly not allowed because those companions ceased to be animals when they went to work. It's semantics, but semantics can be a powerful thing.

Indeed, the Pathwardens murmur and nod, and the one with the clipboard makes several quick check marks, then turns to the carriage driver. "Passenger manifest?" he asks.

The driver hands over a folder while the elf withdraws a brass branch from inside her uniform. White enamel bells dangle from it in an elegant arc. She shakes it, then cocks her head, listening to the chimes. As they fade, she looks to the figure with the clipboard, then nods.

"No diseases, poisons, or communicable curses," she says.

"Excellent," says the figure with the clipboard, flipping though the folder with one hand. He tucks it under one arm and smiles at the group. "Welcome to Strixhaven," he says. "I hope you'll have a wonderful education."

"Or at least a survivable one," says the elf.

The Pathwardens turn and begin climbing into a small, aerodynamic-looking cart, drawn by a clockwork construct of gears and silver pistons. "The school will be sending someone to collect you and your bags as soon as we tell them that you're clean," says the figure with the clipboard. "This is where we part ways."

"Wait," says Eula. "We didn't get your names."

"Abtin," says the one with the clipboard, settling into the cart.

"Veil," says the elf. "We'll see you at school."

The automaton whirrs to life and trots away, drawing the cart with it, and the three of them are once more alone with their driver, who begins unloading their bags from the top of the carriage.

"That was strange," says Eula.

"Yes," agrees Segante. "But painless, as far as such things go."

"I guess," says Alandra, and Orestes chirps as firmly as if he's trying to get the last word in.

They're at a wide spot in the road: while the road itself is smooth-worn ground, running in a tan line back the way they came and onward until it vanishes around the hills, this spot is surrounded by a small circle of green grass and wildflowers. It looks cultivated and wild at the same time, which is a nice trick. There's a picnic table off to one side, made of some weathered, antiquated wood.

Eula looks around and frowns. "I guess they don't get a lot of unscheduled traffic from Fiora," she says.

"Not at this hour," says their driver. He gestures back toward the omenpath. "The gate has closed and won't reopen until morning on Fiora." He finishes taking their bags down from the carriage roof, flashing the group a smile as he sets the luggage on the ground. "You three all right?" he asks.

"We don't have any food or water," says Eula, in case he hasn't noticed.

He nods. "Someone from the school should be right along to collect you," he says. "I promise."

Eula's not sure how much weight his promises carry when he's trying to leave them alone in the middle of nowhere, but she doesn't have a good argument, so she moves to the picnic table with the others. Now that they're not moving, her stomach is beginning to complain in earnest.

"I wish I'd thought to pack a lunch," she says. Or eaten a more substantial breakfast than a piece of toast. At least she's not hungry because of her own actions: the money she gave the girl from Thunder Junction wouldn't have done her any good without a place to buy food *from*.

"I have a lunch, but it's probably poisoned, and I don't really feel like trying to figure out the antidotes while I'm choking to death," says Segante glumly. Catching Eula's startled expression, he says, "It doesn't contain fruit or fresh vegetables. I answered the questions I was asked."

"I don't know what to say to any of that," says Alandra. She opens one of her smaller bags and pulls out a packet wrapped in wax paper, unfolding it to reveal strips of dried fish and some small, hard-looking rolls. She picks up one of the rolls, offering it to Eula.

"We call this 'bread,'" she says. "We trade for it with the humans who travel through our waters. They bring us bread; we give them oysters and fish that live too deep for them to catch."

"We have bread on Capenna," says Eula. "You eat fish?"

"Why wouldn't I? It's not like I *am* a fish," says Alandra. She looks to Segante. "Would you like some?"

"Is it poisoned?"

"I'm planning to eat it, so no," says Alandra. "Look." She breaks off a bit and offers it to Orestes, who swallows it without chewing.

The carriage starts moving, heading onward without them, and Eula feels a pang of sudden fear. This is it, then: no going home from here.

She nibbles at the hard, dry roll Alandra gave her and tries to focus on the future. She's going to become a great wizard. She's going to master her natural talents and learn a hundred less ordinary applications of what she can do, and when she goes back to Capenna, all the Families will fall over themselves to offer her and her family the protection they deserve.

All she has to do is what she's always wanted: she just has to go to school.

The bread is faintly sour but familiar enough for all of that. The fish, when she takes a piece, is a revelation. It's rich and sweet, heavy on the tongue without the unpleasant "fishiness" she's experienced in the past. She eats slowly and politely, not gulping, and watches Segante and Alandra do the same.

Orestes is less patient. He leaps off Alandra's shoulder and snatches flying insects out of the air, filling his stomach at his own pace. His swoops and dives are funny things to see; Eula giggles as she watches him, amused by his hunger.

It's been about an hour when another vehicle comes rolling up the road. This one is less plush than the carriage that brought them here, more like the sort of wagon used for hauling provisions and supplies. It's drawn by a pair of tall deerlike creatures with vast, branching antlers covered in small flowers and flowing white tails like the pegasus that brought their carriage here. The driver is a humanoid figure in a long red-and-white robe. Eula assumes they must be some sort of aven, although she's never seen an aven who looks like this, with brown and white feathers and a face like a smooth dish, beak nestled deep into the facial feathers so that it almost disappears.

Eula glances to Alandra and Segante, both of whom look as confused as she does.

"He has a head like an owl," murmurs Segante, voice pitched low to keep it from carrying.

The driver laughs. "Whispering doesn't do much good when you've got hearing like mine," he says. "You must be our trans-planar students, no? I'm what's called an owlin, but more precisely, my name is Bricen, and I'm your escort to campus. If you have any questions about the school, I'm your man."

"That's very kind of you," says Eula carefully. "You'll forgive us for being cautious, but we're new to this place—and this plane. You're intending to take us to Strixhaven, yes?"

"Yes, to Strixhaven," he says reassuringly. "We're expecting you, and the deans will be glad to see you've made the trip safely." He flicks the reins, bringing the wagon to a stop, and climbs down to start hoisting their bags into the back. "If you're concerned about the school itself, I've been attending for the last three years, and I love it there. I'm sure you will, too."

"It's a school for mages, yes?" asks Alandra.

"All sorts," says Bricen. "Strixhaven is divided into five colleges, each specializing in a different style of magic. You won't be expected—or allowed—to declare yourself straightaway. You take your first year of classes as a generalist, and when that's done, you can choose a college. I belong to Lorehold. We study the duality of order and chaos as they've manifested in the past so we can better bring history to life, and we're always glad to have a new researcher join us. Although, I promised not to go recruiting you for my college before you could even go through orientation, so that's enough of that." He looks around, then frowns, an expression that's more about the tension in his eyes and the slight lift in the feathers of his head than it is his mostly obscured beak. "There were supposed to be four of you."

"Does Orestes count?" asks Alandra, holding out one arm for her drake to make a graceful landing upon. He looks at Bricen and chirps.

"No, I'm afraid it doesn't," he says. "You're the storm caller from Shandalar—I used to study with a student from our local merfolk population, and we did a report on variations across the Multiverse, all theoretical, of course, and I recognize your fin structure—and I'm assuming the young lady in the blue dress is our shield mage—"

"And I'm from Fiora," says Segante, before he can be helpfully labeled.

"Er, yes," says Bricen. "We're supposed to have a Dominarian psychometrist here. Have you seen her?"

"We had a pretty straightforward trip," says Eula. "Capenna to Shandalar to Fiora to here. No stops anywhere called Dominaria."

"Oh well," says Bricen. "I guess the carriage line couldn't find an easy way to combine the trips. I suppose we wait."

"We haven't had much to eat today . . ." says Alandra.

"Oh, I have provisions," says Bricen, suddenly cheerful again. "And I have a pack of cards. Who wants to learn owl's dilemma?"

FIVE

THE OWL'S DILEMMA

Segante's cheating. Eula's sure of it.

She just doesn't know *how* he's cheating, and that makes it worse, somehow. She grew up playing cards with kids from the Families, the ones you allowed to win or else: she could be fine with a little cheating if she just understood how it was being done. But it's a beautiful day, and Bricen has a basket of sandwiches and unfamiliar fruits that taste something like apples and something like walnuts and everything like a satiation she didn't know she needed. He brought water, too, and that alone may have been enough to make him Alandra's favorite person. The mermaid waited for everyone else to drink their fill before dumping the entire canteen out over her head, soaking herself to the scales.

Alandra hasn't been playing cards with the rest of them. She says it's because they don't play cards underwater, and she'll be happy to teach them some rock-rolling games when they get tired of playing with little pieces of paper, but Eula suspects it's because she knows Segante's cheating. Eula glares at him over her current hand, the little ink-and-paint birds on the cards watching her with unseeing eyes, and waits for him to slip.

Before he can, another carriage rattles down the road, this one drawn by a reptilian creature with a crest of feathers atop its head, extending down the slope of its neck to its shoulders. The driver pulls the carriage to a halt, nodding to Bricen.

"Here to collect the new students?" the driver asks.

"I am. Do you have someone for me?"

"I do, and you're quite welcome to her." The driver hops down. From the outside, Eula sees the clever system of straps and buckles holding the bags on top of the carriage; it's a small matter to secure them, and an even smaller one to take them down.

Their newcomer apparently has two bags, neither in a style Eula knows, both outfitted with brass finishings and solid-looking locks. The driver hands them to Bricen, who adds them to the pile on his wagon.

The driver sighs then and turns to open the door. A girl steps out, roughly Eula's age, her skin as deep a brown as Segante's eyes, her black hair done up in a pattern of elaborate braids, each capped with a golden bead. Her clothing is elegant: a blue dress, a red wrap around her waist, and a small half jacket studded with more gold beads, these smaller and more delicately shaped than the ones in her hair. She carries a beaded bag slung over one shoulder and across her body.

She nods to the driver, who hurries to climb back onto the driver's seat and take off down the road. Eula blinks.

"She's the friendly sort, isn't she?" she asks, intending it to be a light comment to break the ice.

The girl turns her attention on Eula, frowning slightly. "She collected me as she was bid, she carried me here, and she has delivered me, I presume, to the next stage in my journey. Was she expected to show fellowship beyond that?"

"Er, no," says Eula. "It's just that our driver was . . . Hi. I'm Eula, Eula Blue, from Capenna. It's a pleasure to meet you."

"Is it?" asks the girl. "I thought more time was needed to determine such things. My name is Kequia Akosa, daughter of Niambi Akosa, Speaker of Femeref upon the plane of Dominaria. I am here to be delivered to a school for magecraft and spellwork, where I can learn to better command my natural abilities."

"We're all on the way to Strixhaven," says Segante brusquely. "You're not special."

Kequia blinks, then lifts one elegant eyebrow. "Or we all are. Your name is?"

"Segante, from Fiora. Are you going to talk like that all the time? Because I might start throwing things if you are."

"Alandra, from Shandalar," says Alandra. She doesn't introduce Orestes. "I don't throw things."

"And I'm Bricen," says their driver, lazily waving one wing as he collects the cards. "I'm your guide for today, and from the way you're talking, I'm betting you got one of the old student handbooks handed off to you."

"My grandfather brought it home as a curiosity before the opening of the omenpaths," says Kequia. "It included comportment and decorum standards for all students, and a code of etiquette as complicated as a weaver's masterpiece."

"Yeah, we keep one of those at the Lorehold dorms, for when we need to remind ourselves that the current code of student conduct isn't as antiquated as it seems," says Bricen, tucking the cards into his pocket. "Contrary to what you may have read, we allow contractions on campus. Nicknames, too, and if you wind up falling in with Silverquill, they'll trade you credit at the school store for teaching them new swear words."

"Oh, thank the sun," says Kequia, shaking her head so hard the beads in her hair chime melodically against one another. "I got about a dozen lectures on upholding the family name and following the rules whether or not I thought they were good ones before my mother let me leave for the omenpath. It's why I was running so late."

"Family honor a big one with your folks?" asks Bricen sympathetically.

"You have *no* idea." Kequia flashes the other three a shy, sideways smile. "You're my new classmates? Is this your first time off-plane, too?"

"It is," says Eula, and moves to take a seat on the wagon. "How did your granddad get one of their student manuals if you're not from here?"

"He used to be a Planeswalker," says Kequia. "For most of my life he was just my silly grandfather who made bad jokes at the dinner table and helped me come up with ways to prank my mother without getting into *too* much trouble. Then, a few years ago, he disappeared. My mother told me the truth: that he was much older than he seemed and had lost something important to him, but it had been given back, and now he had to handle his unfinished business. After the Phyrexian Invasion, he came home to visit while he decides what to do next. When I received my invitation to the school, he dug the student handbook out of his old things and begged

Mother to let me attend, said it would be the best place for me to blossom."

"I guess the Invasion happened everywhere," says Alandra unhappily, watching the pair of them. "I just wish we knew how it all started. People *died*, and there's no one to punish for what they've done. It's not right."

Kequia grimaces, turning her face away, and doesn't comment.

Eula blinks. After the starch-stiff politeness of her arrival, Kequia's bluntness is going to take some adjusting to—as is her inexplicable discomfort. She gestures to Alandra, patting the seat next to her, and the merfolk girl hurries to climb onto the wagon and sit, choosing proximity to the familiar. "So none of this is new to you?"

"*All* of this is new to me," says Kequia, settling on the seat opposite Eula and Alandra. "Do they have stories for children where you come from? Nighttime tales?"

Eula nods. "They do."

"Moon whispers, we call them," says Alandra. "The moons whisper to the seas and change the tides, and parents whisper to their children to change their dreams."

"Nice," says Kequia. "Well, for me, the planes were always nighttime tales. After his spark returned, my grandfather would go traveling, and when he came home, he would bring trinkets and toys, and fabulous stories to go with them. Marvelous tales that touched my daily life as much as your moon whispers may have touched yours. I never expected them to be something I could reach out and lay hands upon, much less things I saw with my own eyes."

"In some ways, this is even stranger for you," says Eula.

"We're seeing things we never dreamed of, but you're walking into your bedtime stories."

"I've had a headache since the first omenpath opened within walking distance of my home," says Kequia. "It hasn't helped that people keep going to see what's on the other side and coming back wanting me to touch their souvenirs and tell them all their hidden stories."

"Bricen said you were a psychometrist," says Segante, sitting next to her. "What are they going to teach you at wizard school, how not to invade people's privacy? The last psychometrist on Fiora was an infamous thief. They're not allowed anymore, by order of the Queen."

"How do you order a whole kind of magic to not exist?" asks Alandra, puzzled.

Eula has some ideas about how you could do that, and they all end on the edge of a knife. She swallows and doesn't comment.

"I'm not that kind of psychometrist," snaps Kequia. "I don't do people, just objects. I'm here to learn more fine control."

"Oh, you want to become a bigger invasion of privacy," says Segante.

"Bricen was telling us about his college, Lorehold," says Eula quickly, before this can turn into a real argument. "If you have a student handbook, you must know about the other colleges. Can you tell us about them?"

"Of course," says Kequia, eyes still on Segante. She seems to be trying to stare him down. Eula's not sure that's possible. "Lorehold are historians and researchers, although every college does their own kind of research, at the end of the day. Witherbloom works with life and death; they're biologists and naturalists, by and large. Silverquill is all about a fast pen and a clever tongue. They'll debate you until you're dead and then convince their Lorehold buddies to call back your spirit so they can keep the argument going. Prismari are the art students; they like to express themselves and feel their feelings. Sometimes those feelings create beautiful sculptures and paintings, and sometimes they explode. And then there's Quandrix, where you go to pull on the strings of the universe and see what unravels. Oh, they must be having the most *wonderful* time with these omenpaths. They're like a Quandrix experiment that's broken laboratory containment and gone feral."

"Huh," says Eula.

"You sound disappointed."

"I am, a bit. I guess I just hoped there'd be a college that sounded more like, well, me." She shrugs. "I wanted to come here to fit in."

"We're not from this plane," says Kequia. "We're never going to fit in."

As if to punctuate this, Orestes warbles, and Kequia laughs. The wagon starts to move, heading back the way it came. Eula stops trying to carry on a conversation in favor of craning her neck, trying for a first glimpse of the campus. Orestes takes to the air, flying along above them, keeping pace with the wagon as it heads down a long, slow slope.

Eula almost gasps when she spots the towers on the horizon, tall and hazy with distance. Bricen looks back. "See something?" he asks.

She points, speechless in excitement, and he follows her finger, laughing when he sees what she's spotted.

"That's the campus, all right," he says. "We should be there soon enough, and then you can learn to take the place for granted the same way the rest of us do. I grew up knowing I was going to attend Strixhaven someday, and probably go into Lorehold. My parents met at school, and they both said Lorehold was the best place they could ever have spent their school years. I like digging, I like people, and I figured this was a shot at a job where I could do both."

"I'm sorry if this is a rude thing to ask," says Eula carefully, "but where's the magic in that?"

"I talk to spirits, and they tell me where to dig; sometimes I talk to stones, and they tell me how to get to what I'm looking for without damaging anything. I can negotiate with the sunlight to blaze a little less brightly and not damage newly excavated finds." Bricen flicks the reins again, keeping them moving. "Not everyone at school is going to be there because they want to be better wizards. Some of them come because you won't find a better grounding in diplomacy or land management than you'll get at Strixhaven. Or because they're really good at Mage Tower and want to play for a while before they go home and take over the family business. It's not rude to ask someone where the magic is in their position, but you can't act like someone's life choices are inferior if they say there isn't any. Does that make sense?"

"I'm just grateful to be here," says Eula. "The only wizard's school in my city collapsed during the Invasion, and right now there's no way to get an education beyond the basics unless your family's well connected or rich or something."

"Isn't yours?" asks Alandra, sounding honestly curious.

"Not really," says Eula. "Why would you think that?"

Alandra gestures at their companions and then herself before shrugging. "It just seemed to fit the pattern."

"My father's a bookkeeper for a minor branch of the Brokers—that's the Family he's hoping I'll join once I finish my education and go home. My mother used to be a dance teacher for another Family, the Cabaretti. She stays home with my little brother and sister right now, and before they were born, she stayed home with my older brother and me. My brother went to work for the Riveteers as soon as he finished primary schooling. He's a mimeomancer, and the college didn't have any instructors who were qualified to teach him even before it collapsed, so he decided to go straight into the workforce. None of them are very well connected, and if we were rich, I wouldn't be sitting here in a dress with tattered hems, now, would I?"

"You might," says Kequia. "If you wanted to stay beneath notice."

"Well, I don't, and I'm not," says Eula. "I'm here to learn. I can't imagine traveling all the way here if I didn't want to learn everything there is."

"You're not our first off-plane students, but the last two were the Kenrith twins, from Eldraine, and they came before the omenpaths opened," says Bricen. "They went home a while ago. I hope they're doing well. Will was always friendly when I bumped into him in the library. Harried but friendly. Rowan was . . . is it rude to call a spark mage a live wire? Because she was one, rude or not. She played Mage Tower like she'd been made for it." His voice trails off as he contemplates the fates of his former classmates.

"I don't understand how that relates," says Eula.

"Oh, just that for most of us, Strixhaven isn't some great

journey," he says. The school dips out of sight for a moment as they go down a short hill, and when they come back up again, the whole thing is finally revealed, towers and walls surrounding a central campus of sturdy buildings and artful gardens. Above it all rises another of those gravity-defying arches, this one gleaming with starlight sparks of circulating power. It's breathtaking in its beauty, impossible to either define or deny, and like nothing Eula has ever seen before.

Even with its strangeness, the school skyline is a comfort to Eula's city-adapted eyes; she hasn't realized how much of a strain it was to see only the natural world everywhere she looked until just now, when she can focus on the unnatural and intentional once more. Bricen is still talking, not seeming to notice how silent his passengers have become: "It's the school our parents went to that we attend because it's expected of us and right there, not a place we dream of and struggle to reach."

"We didn't dream of Strixhaven," says Segante sourly. "We didn't know it existed before we got our admissions paperwork."

"Dreams don't always have a long history behind them," says Bricen. He sounds easygoing as always, just happy to be there.

The ground levels out below them, and they're on the final stretch of road between them and the campus. Eula wants to jump out and run the rest of the way to school, bursting with nerves and anxious energy. Alandra whistles a low note, and Orestes swoops down to land on her wrist, rubbing his head against her arm and chirping before he throws himself back into the air. Segante eyes the school and scowls, while Kequia rides in serene quiet. This is it; this is where everything changes into something new.

This is where their new lives begin.

The school gates swing open as the wagon approaches, revealing a courtyard filled with people of all shapes and sizes. Eula's eyes go so wide it hurts as she looks around, trying to absorb everything at once. There are humans here, and elves, and aven, and blue-skinned people like Abtin, and a dozen other types of people, wearing loose school robes over their clothing and chattering among themselves. It's not the chaos that unsettles her, makes her want to shrink back against Alandra; it's the unfamiliarity of it all. The noise is similar to what she'd find at the subway during shift change, but the people are all so *strange*.

Bricen drives through the crowd until he reaches a low marble fountain. He's moving slowly enough that he doesn't hit anyone, and people move out of his way with only a few curious glances, allowing him to pull the deer-creatures to a stop with no collisions. As soon as he releases their reins, the animals lower their heads and begin to drink from the fountain.

Bricen gets down, moving around to the back of the wagon. "This is where we part ways," he says, echoing the Pathwarden from before in what must be a quirk of the local idiom. Eula makes a silent note that this is how they say goodbye here. "Your resident advisor will be along shortly to collect you and your bags and get you to your dorm. It's been set up special for your needs. It was great to meet you. Come on, out of the wagon now."

None of them move.

"Now's not the time to come over all shy! Welcome to Strixhaven!"

Eula is the first to recover her bearings. Carefully, she unfolds herself from the seat and steps down, turning back to offer Alandra a hand. The blue girl grabs her wrist and holds on tight, moving closer. It's less restraint than it is a quest for security, and Eula allows it, watching the students who still move all around them. There are other merfolk in the crowd, a paler shade of blue than Alandra, with differently shaped fins and patches of peach- and chestnut-colored scales that mimic the tones of human skin, but seeing them doesn't seem to settle Alandra any, as she doesn't step away from Eula.

Kequia hops down, dragging her bag with her, and looks around with bright, curious eyes. Segante is the last off the wagon, managing to make the act of stepping to the pavement look remarkably like skulking. He doesn't need a shadowy alley to loom in; he creates his own shadowy alley wherever he goes.

The thought is a funny one, and it brings a smile to Eula's face even as Bricen is turning to face them. "I need to get this wagon returned to the school stores before I'm late for class," he says. "Your student advisor will be along any second now. I'm sorry I can't stay for the handoff, but Professor Osgir doesn't tolerate lateness well. He says history has waited long enough to be uncovered and deserves our full attention now that we're finally getting around to it. If you need me for anything, anyone in the Lorehold dorms will be able to pass a message along, all right?"

"Thank you," says Eula, and the others echo her, save for Segante, who is glaring fiercely at anyone who seems to take too much of an interest in their little group. At least his nigh-omnipresent anger is turned outward at the world around them and not inward at his companions. Eula can see where he might become a valued friend, if he can just learn the entire world isn't out to hurt him.

Bricen climbs back into the driver's seat and vanishes into the crowd with surprising speed, leaving the four students and their bags standing alone in a sea of strangers. Orestes lands on Alandra's shoulder, crooning and rubbing his head against the underside of her chin until she takes a deep breath and lays a hand across him.

"Thank you, friend," she says. "I'm well."

The other students are becoming less of a jumbled mass as she watches, and Eula sees several accompanied by companions that seem to fulfill the same purpose Orestes does for Alandra: an elf walks with a spiky purple creature on her shoulder, something like the mixture of a salamander and a caterpillar, while another owllike aven holds the harness of a tall white fox with black spots along its muzzle and sides. The fox seems to be guiding the student, who follows its lead across the courtyard. Other companions are less concrete and take the form of living swirls of ink, or dancing patterns of elemental imagery.

Eula nudges Alandra with her elbow and gestures toward the elf with her chin. "You're not the only one who brought a friend with you," she says.

Alandra relaxes further. "Thank the tides," she says. At Eula's curious look, she shrugs, the corners of her mouth turning sheepishly downward. "We're going to stand out no matter what we do. I didn't want to make it worse."

"How much time did you have to worry about coming here?" asks Eula, trying to take in the entire crowd without being too obvious about her rubbernecking. For all the wild diversity of the crowd, there are species missing: she doesn't see a single raccoonfolk or cephalid.

"Father informed me I'd been offered attendance a week ago, and we've done what we could to learn about the place," says Alandra. "Mostly that took the form of asking anyone who came through the omenpaths if they'd heard of Strixhaven and listening closely to their answers. So I suppose I had a little time to worry, but not enough to really upset myself."

"I didn't get any time at all. I have no idea what I'm supposed to be watching out for."

"I'll help," says Kequia, stepping up on Eula's other side. "I have the handbook, even if it's outdated, and all Grandfather's stories. Although I doubt we're going to be sitting down for tea with Planeswalkers, or phasing entire continents into time distortions, so they won't all be that useful to us."

Eula gives her an uneasy look. "No, I don't think we want to do either of those things."

A figure is making their way through the crowd toward them, tall as a rhox, with broad shoulders and a muscular build any ogre would be proud of. Like a rhox, her head is less humanoid and more . . . something else—horned and bovine, if larger than any cow Eula's ever seen. Chains and charms dangle from her horns, ornately wrought in black iron and polished silver. She's clearly arrowing straight for their little cluster, causing Segante to stiffen and move his hand to his hip, like he's reaching for a weapon Eula can't see, while Kequia hugs her handbook a little tighter and takes a half step behind Alandra. Eula narrows her eyes, watching the stranger approach.

The newcomer has a massive steamer trunk balanced on one shoulder, easily large enough to stuff any of the other four inside with room to spare. Orestes flattens himself on Alandra's shoulder as she approaches, mantling his wings and growling low in the back of his throat, the sound rumbling and dangerous.

"Hello," says the figure, once she's close enough to speak without shouting. Her voice is feminine, soft and rich and gently pitched, like she understands how intimidating her size can be. "I was told the rest of my kine would be found here, waiting for our advisor. Are you the trans-planar student body?"

Eula's heart sinks as she realizes the others are looking to her; even Segante appears to assume that she's going to speak for them. It's nice to be seen as an authority. It's intimidating, too. "Is it that obvious?" she asks.

"To me, perhaps," says the newcomer. "I have been waiting for you. My name is Jamira, and it's a great pleasure to meet you."

"Eula Blue, of Capenna," says Eula. Introducing herself by plane seems odd, but she's sure she'll get used to it eventually.

"Alandra, Shandalar," says Alandra, following her lead.

As the others follow suit, even Segante, Eula's nerves calm somewhat. Then Segante adds, "Why did you get here early?" in a blunt, almost interrogative tone, and she winces.

"My father brought me here as soon as he could find a navigable omenpath," says Jamira, voice still warm and calm. "It took some time, as our plane did not weather the Invasion well."

"Where are you from?" asks Eula.

"Aranzhur."

Kequia gasps. Eula looks sharply at her. The smaller girl shakes her head. "I'm sorry. That was . . . I'm sorry."

"You've heard of my home, then?" asks Jamira.

"My grandfather was a Planeswalker. After the Invasion, when it became clear how many had been repaid for their service to the Multiverse via the snuffing of their sparks, he became hungry for news of the places he no longer felt obligated to protect. He sought news from all who passed, and gathered great lists of the lost." She looks at Jamira with a naked sympathy that makes Eula uncomfortable. "He said Aranzhur was destroyed by the legions of Phyrexia. That the whole world fell."

"Some of us survived," says Jamira, uncomfortably. "My family was fortunate: we were as trapped on our plane as anyone else, but we had my father with us, and he, too, was a Planeswalker before the worlds changed. He fought for us like he could repay every moment his spark stole from his family, and my sister and I fought alongside him. When the machines fell, our home was a great shell of frozen iron and burning ash, and none of us had been transformed from what we were. But there is no home for us on Aranzhur, not any longer."

Eula swallows, thinking of the fall of Park Heights, the rebuilding of her city, how endless the work seems—but no one has ever called Capenna "lost." She can always go home again.

Jamira shrugs. "I don't know how the letter offering me a place here found us. We've been traveling plane to plane since the loss of Aranzhur, seeking a safe place to settle. But my father agreed it would be foolish to refuse such an opportunity, and he and my sister escorted me. They've moved along to the next place Father thought might offer them shelter, a world called Innistrad."

Kequia makes a small, choked-off noise, and Eula guesses this "Innistrad" isn't renowned for its hospitality.

"It's lovely to meet you," says Eula. She still doesn't know what the large, friendly woman is, but it seems rude to ask people about their species, especially when they're going to be together for a while. Information will be volunteered, she's sure. Information always is, if you're patient and pay attention.

And indeed, the answer to her unasked question comes only a heartbeat later as Jamira looks at her with a smile and asks, "Do they have minotaur where you come from?"

"Is that what you are?" asks Eula. Jamira nods, and Eula shakes her head. "This has been a day filled with new things, and you're just the latest in the line. Are all minotaur so . . . tall?"

Jamira laughs. "Yes, we tend to be pretty tall. Are all humans from Capenna so short?"

"No, I just got lucky that way," says Eula. Jamira laughs again, and this is nice: this is something they can live with, five people and one drake and a whole campus full of new things.

The teeming population of the quad is breaking off into smaller groups, the noise level dropping steadily with the migration. Eula looks around. Some of the groups have banners with strange sigils on them, flags she doesn't recognize, echoed in the scarves and jackets worn by the people who gather beneath them. Her eye is drawn to a cluster of elegant, beautifully composed students in black and white whose banner is blazoned with what looks like a pen nib set in front of a black crescent moon. They remind her of the Obscura-in-training who used to loiter around the university before it fell, utterly in control of themselves and their reality, prepared to fight the world if that's what they had to do.

Other groups are more ragtag and gather under white pennants displaying the school crest. She sees the pen and moon reflected there as well, one of the top sections of the crest's shield. Her heart lurches in her chest, excitement and frightened anticipation building. Orestes chirps, and she looks over to see the drake nuzzling Alandra, whose scales have gone a paler shade of blue, her own excitement trending more toward anxiety.

"Hey," says Eula. "It's okay. No one's freaking out. I'm sure this is supposed to happen."

"It is," says Kequia. "As Bricen said, the student advisors are coming to collect their groups. The banners with the emblems on them represent the five colleges that make up the university. We'll be able to pledge to them in our second year and start pursuing a more focused course of study. This year, we're supposed to try new things and look for something that makes us happy, so we can choose the right college."

"Pledge?" asks Segante warily. "As in allegiance? I'm not sure my Queen would appreciate that."

"It's only allegiance to the extent that we'll give you access to the college dining hall and let you sign up for some more specialized classes. It would be a mean joke if Witherbloom started letting undeclared students into Professor Vess's Botanical Necromancy seminar. You need a good grounding before you can come out of that one without zombie ragweed in your lungs." The voice is new, cheerful and fast-talking, with an accent similar to Bricen's, if not identical.

Eula turns. The others turn with her, looking at the woman

who has come up behind them while they were distracted. She's green-skinned, with leafy hair that makes her resemble one of the topiary dinosaurs that sometimes wandered the more upscale parts of Park Heights. She's studying the five of them with unshielded curiosity, and she has another of those salamander-caterpillars riding in the crook of one arm, about half the size of Orestes, dangling placidly and chewing on a leaf from her tunic. The banner she holds aloft in her other hand is blazoned with the university crest, but a smaller symbol is stitched on the edge of the black-and-green scarf she wears, showing what looks like a stylized beaker surrounded by curved sunburst lines.

"You're my off-plane students, right?" she asks. "Oh, please tell me I didn't just scare the sanity out of a bunch of locals, I'm only supposed to terrify the incomers who've been assigned to me."

"Um," says Eula.

To her surprise, it's Segante who steps forward, bowing to the stranger. "If we're unique as a grouping, then yes, you've found us. If we're not, I'm sure you've still found the best of the lot, and you should count yourself lucky for it."

"You know Silverquill won't take you until second year, right?" asks the stranger.

Segante blinks at her.

"That's the college of eloquence and debate," says Kequia. "Diplomacy."

"Ah. They won't have me at all, then," says Segante. "I know how to flatter because I didn't want to die, and my aunt would view the absence of flattery as a request for a quick execution. Learning diplomacy wouldn't suit me at all."

"Well, that's disturbing," says the stranger. "My name is Dina, and I'm a Witherbloom student, meaning I'm with the college of essence studies. If that doesn't mean anything to you yet, that's fine, you have plenty of time. I'm also your resident advisor during orientation, and I'm here to take you to your dorm. Since you can't pledge a specific college yet, you'll be in with the rest of the uncommitted: because you each represent a plane that hasn't previously been part of our student body, you'll be in your own block of rooms. We figure you'll be experiencing ongoing and dramatic culture shock for the first term, and we'd rather you didn't spread it around. Any questions?"

"My father has made a generous donation to the school to guarantee me a solitary room in your 'student housing,'" says Segante. "I trust this is included in your paperwork?"

"Yes, and it actually makes my life easier, since I was told I'd be meeting a group of all female students," says Dina. "Not needing to explain to your *actual* advisor why I went and stuck you in with the girls keeps me from being forced into an argument I'd really rather avoid."

"How many advisors do we have?" asks Eula.

Dina glances to her. "For the duration of orientation, you have two: me, who's been where you're standing recently enough to have a scrap of sympathy for your questions and confusion, and your primary advisor, who'll be with you for the duration of your time at Strixhaven. Once you choose your colleges, you'll also receive a collegiate advisor, who can help guide you through your more advanced studies. If any of you choose to come to Witherbloom, for example, that might be me. Might not. And if you go Quandrix, your primary advisor could also be your collegiate advisor. It's only confusing right now because it's new. After you've been here for a while, this is all going to be as straightforward as crop rotation."

Only Kequia laughs at that, while the rest of them stare at her in bewilderment. Dina gives Kequia a crooked grin. "At least one of you has a sense of humor," she says. "All right, let's get you to your dorm. Can you get your own things?"

Alandra's cheeks flush a deep cobalt as she begins to shake her head but stops when Jamira nudges her with one massive elbow. "I can help you," she says.

Alandra blinks, then nods, relaxing a bit.

Segante has only one bag, as does Eula: between them, they hoist one of Alandra's, while Alandra helps Kequia with her second bag, and Jamira takes Alandra's third. In a matter of moments, all five of them are looking attentively at Dina, waiting for the green-skinned woman to lead them to their dorm.

Their time at Strixhaven has truly begun, and soon they'll all be able to find out what that means. Eula glances at the bright eyes of her fellow students and believes they're as eager for those answers as she is.

A new adventure is getting under way.

SIX

ORIENTATION

The "dorm" Dina leads them to is a tall brick building with a flowering vine clinging to the outside, covered in trumpet-shaped purple flowers that fill the air with a sweet, unfamiliar perfume. More of those odd salamander-caterpillars hang from the vines, chewing on leaves or occasionally sticking their entire heads inside particularly large flowers, drinking the nectar they find there. The one on Dina's arm squirms, and she laughs, placing it gently on the nearest unoccupied branch.

Catching Eula's bewildered expression, she shrugs. "The pests like to eat the climbing snarlflowers, and since the snarlflowers will damage the masonry if they're not kept under control, it benefits everyone if we help it happen."

"Your college—" says Segante.

"Witherbloom," affirms Dina.

"You manage the botanical health of the campus?"

"Among other things," she says. "Growth, death, decay,

and rebirth—they're all essence in the end. Our pests help us channel the opposing forces in constructive ways, and we can get extra credit for keeping things like the snarlflowers under control. There's a lot to learn about campus management. Some of our graduates stay on as groundskeepers every year. It's a very well-regarded position and essential to the university as a whole. You'll get to tour the whole university tomorrow, and the Witherbloom campus next week."

"Does every college have their own campus?" asks Alandra.

Dina nods, waving them inside. "Yes, and you'll have the chance to tour them all. No one's going to force you anywhere. Some introductory courses are mandatory for all students, and you five will be taking a required class on Arcavios history, covering the creation of the plane, the foundation of the school, and the lives of our Founder Dragons."

"Dragons?" asks Alandra, while Orestes chirps in echo of her audible dismay.

"Yes. The five founders who created our respective colleges. They're still around—dragons live a long, long time—but they don't show up often on or around campus, and you're unlikely to meet them. It's still essential that you know about them, and your reactions to the class will help us set the curriculum for future off-plane students. You'll meet your primary advisor in your Arcavios history class. She developed it and will be your instructor."

"What's her name?" asks Jamira.

"Kasmina," says Dina.

Kequia frowns but says nothing.

Dina leads them down a long hall set with narrow doors on both sides, stopping when she reaches a wide oval room at the hall's end. Eula thinks it may correspond with one of the building's rounded corners, which bulged from the outside as if they were being encouraged to develop into towers one day, organic and anatomical and utterly at odds with the sleek lines and cultured curves of New Capenna. This room is the first place she's been that felt at all like home, built with no angles to it at all, only the smooth curve of perfect engineering.

There are four doors, as well as the hall they just came along, and another hall stretching out from the right-hand wall, presumably connecting to the next corner along the line.

"Eula, you'll be with Alandra in room 6A," says Dina, gesturing toward a door. "Jamira, you're in 6B with Kequia, and Segante, based on your paperwork, you'll be in 6C. 6D is being left unfinished until our next round of trans-planar students, and it's important you not try to rearrange your assignments, as your rooms have been tailored to your specific social and physiological needs."

"Is our room flooded?" asks Eula. "Because I don't have gills, and that won't end well."

"Not entirely," says Dina. "Administration got basic physiology reports for each of your planes before they determined whether we could extend offers of admission. Jamira's home biome, for example, is environmentally similar to Kequia's, although Jamira is suited to more extreme temperatures. She doesn't require them constantly, but it would be bad for her to stay in a mild climate all the time. At the same time, maintaining a room at a temperature that would be ideal for Jamira could harm Alandra."

Eula nods. A lot of thought has clearly gone into making sure they can survive here, and survival is essential if they're going to thrive. Tend the base of the shield before you build the body, or you'll wind up with something fragile and unstable that collapses under the slightest pressure.

"It's like a logic puzzle," she says.

Dina laughs before beaming at her. "Exactly like a logic puzzle. Get it wrong, everything falls apart. Get it right, it seems so *simple*."

Segante, meanwhile, is moving toward the door Dina indicated as his. When he opens it, a gust of warm, floral air escapes, smelling like sunlight and safety. Segante brightens, a look of genuine delight spreading across his dour face as he looks inside, then closes the door quickly. "How did you already get the dreamwaste flowers to grow here? I thought I'd have to plant them all myself."

"They have a space in one of the Witherbloom greenhouses, and I'll make sure you have access once you're through orientation. Getting the seeds was easy—and that's part of why it was possible for you to get a cultural exception to bring your own seeds," says Dina. "The flowers were already approved. One of the stable omenpaths not far off campus connects to Fiora about half the time—I assume that's the one you used. When we heard we'd have a student coming through the omenpath, we added Fiora to our planar research. All five colleges worked to be sure your rooms would be suitable."

"Do you do this for all incoming students?" asks Eula.

"No, because we don't normally need to," says Dina. "We know most of the student body can survive and stay physically and emotionally healthy in the environment of Strixhaven. Whether that's true of the five of you has yet to be determined. You'll be in these rooms until you declare for a college, and once you do, you'll relocate to the appropriate dorm, where we'll have new rooms readied for you."

"Thank you," says Eula, as politely as she can manage when her head is spinning. She opens the door indicated for herself and Alandra, revealing a small, square room. She didn't actually see inside Segante's room and can't say whether his private room is nicer or more thoroughly equipped than theirs. She can't imagine it would matter. She just stands at the open door of their room, staring at the walls and breathing in the salt-scented air.

One half of the room is filled with water, a wall of shimmering light keeping the liquid from spilling out into the side with the door. The water side gets the window, which is fine, as it turns the sunlight coming from outside diffuse and rippling, like the light that makes it down to the Caldaia.

Unlike the sharp angles of the campus, which had already been starting to make Eula's head spin, the walls in here have been softened with curves and filigree swoops, the baseboards and even the small closet door turned into elegant lines that echo home back to her in ways she could never have articulated needing. There are no bookshelves on the water side but two on the air side. There is also a bed on the air side of the room and a piece of shaped coral in the water.

She's been staring for a while when Dina steps up behind her. "This was a challenge," she says. "The sculptors from Prismari were more than happy to rise to it, and the wall containing the water Alandra needs should hold up to any spellwork you need to do as part of your classes. It's fully permeable. Getting it that way took a while." She pushes past Eula to approach the dividing line between environments, reaching out to tap it with a finger.

A ripple spreads out from the point of contact. Dina waits for it to fade before touching the water again, this time pushing her hand through the barrier. She flexes her fingers, showing that her hand is still her own, then pulls it back. It emerges completely dry, and she beams at Eula, looking smug. "The first iterations of the spell took 'keep the water inside' to mean it should pull the water out of the person who was passing through the barrier, and we had to get a few Quandrix students on tweaking that to be something less potentially fatal. But now you should both be able to be comfortable here."

The water doesn't go all the way to the ceiling on Alandra's side of the room, and there's a small shelf above the window that looks suitable for Orestes to sleep on. Eula nods, still speechless, and steps fully inside.

Dina retreats to the door, beckoning Alandra forward, then gestures to Jamira and Kequia's door.

Eula hefts her case onto her bed, distracted by the care taken in creating her new environment, and so misses the moment when the last two students see their room. Hearing Jamira's snort of delight, she sticks her head back into the central chamber, and the reason the minotaur and the mermaid couldn't share a room is made immediately clear: even as Eula's room is half air and half water, Jamira and Kequia's room is half air and half some sort of blackened stone shot through with veins of red. The air on that side of the room is shimmering like the water, heat rolling off of it in waves.

"Prismari again?" guesses Eula, quietly grateful that she'll be rooming with a flood and not a furnace.

Dina nods.

"Wasn't all this expensive?"

"Not really, since most of it is student work—we got credit for helping to set up individualized rooms for the five of you, and the spells have been stabilized enough to hold for at least the semester. As you start to approach the point where you'll need to choose a college, we may ask you to help with the maintenance. Honestly, the hardest part of getting everything set up was making sure all five colleges could contribute: you're the first openly off-plane students we've had, and no one wanted to feel like another college was getting an advantage in wooing you to enroll with them."

"Our driver mentioned a pair of twins? He said they were from off-plane . . ."

Dina grimaces. "We know that now. At the time, we just thought they were from some little village none of us had ever heard of, magical prodigies so powerful that their parents sent them away to Strixhaven for their education instead of doing whatever the people there had been doing for generations. It wasn't until after the Invasion that Professor Vess told us they'd been Planeswalkers. Maybe they still are. I don't know. Either way, I hope they come back." Her grimace fades, followed by wistfulness. "They were my friends. And wherever they are now, I hope they still have each other."

"Excuse me," says Kequia. "That's the second time you've mentioned Professor Vess. Do you mean Liliana Vess, the necromancer?"

"I do," says Dina, sounding delighted. "She's one of our best teachers. Viciously dedicated to the ethics of necromancy, and if you have the chance to attend one of her debate sessions with Professor Yedora, you absolutely should. Professor Vess believes the will of the living comes before the desires of the dead, while Professor Yedora says a burial is like a planting, and it's rude to uproot a growing ghost."

"When will we receive our class schedules?" asks Kequia politely, her expression giving nothing away.

"They'll be delivered to your rooms this evening. Look on the desks when you hear the bell for start of dinner service in the dining halls," says Dina. "Bathrooms are down the hall, marked with the school crest to distinguish them from the other dorm rooms. And the nearest dining hall is straight out the front door and directly across the quad. You all have a basic meal plan as part of your tuition—sorry, Segante, but the people who paid for your room didn't splurge on feeding you, so you'll be eating with everyone else. The colleges have their own dining halls, but I don't recommend seeking them out until you have a basic idea of how the local cuisine sits in your stomachs. Sometimes they can get a little . . . extravagant with their flavor profiles when they think they're cooking for people who know what they're getting into."

"All right," says Alandra, somewhat nervously. Orestes chirps, and she rubs the little drake under the chin, clutching him close.

This catches Dina's attention. She pauses, then smiles sympathetically. "And this is all a lot. Welcome to Strixhaven, we're glad you're here, I'll be back in the morning to make sure you can find your classes. If you need anything else, just stop anyone carrying one of these banners"—she waves the pennant she's still holding—"and they'll be glad to help you."

"Thank you," says Jamira, and the others echo the sentiment with varying degrees of sincerity as Dina turns and walks back the way they came, leaving the five of them alone. Orestes chirps again, and Alandra sags.

"I don't mean to be unfriendly, but does anyone mind if I . . .?" She gestures to the door to the room she's going to share with Eula and looks relieved when the others shake their heads.

"Go ahead," says Eula. "You've been dry long enough."

That's all the permission Alandra requires. She rushes into the room, dragging the bag she carried here with her, and drops it just before she leaps through the shimmering wall into the flooded half of the room. Orestes rides with her, although he launches himself from her shoulder as soon as they're submerged, swimming to the surface and floating there like some sort of scaled seabird.

Alandra does a somersault in the water before pulling herself into a hollow in the coral construct, vanishing. Eula turns to the others.

"Everybody's room to their liking?"

"As though it matters?" asks Jamira. "We're locked in place by spellcraft and courtesy, and the laws of hospitality say we'll remain as we are."

"I'm sure Dina would be happy to help us change things around if we really wanted to," says Eula.

"I will be well content with the environment crafted for me," says Jamira. "I was a blacksmith on Aranzhur before the Invasion. I had my own forge. I bent fire under my hands. The room designed for me is similar to my childhood home, and if Kequia will allow me to store my papers on her side of the room, I see no reason to request adjustments."

"They gave Eula and I both extra desks, just so that would be possible," says Kequia. "I've heard horror stories from cousins who went to Tolarian Academies about sharing rooms with people who insisted on making messes in communal spaces. At least we're not going to have that issue."

"I won't have any issues at all," says Segante, somewhat smugly. "My room is my own."

"You've seen ours. Can we see yours?" asks Eula. "I don't really know anything about Fiora."

"Believe me, you're better off that way," says Segante. "My door remains closed."

"Is anyone else hungry?" asks Kequia quickly, picking up on the beginnings of an argument forming.

Eula looks over her shoulder. Alandra is still inside the coral construct in her pool. "I'm going to need to find a method of communicating with her while she's in the water," she says with a small sigh. "I don't want to leave her here while the rest of us run off to the dining hall."

"What is a 'dining hall'?" asks Jamira. "I didn't want to ask while Dina was here. The rest of you seemed to know, and I would prefer not to highlight any gaps in my own education before I absolutely must. On Aranzhur, minotaur were often viewed as less intelligent than some of the other humanoid species, and I refuse to feed into negative stereotypes of my own people if it can possibly be avoided."

"A dining hall is like a feasting hall, but instead of a banquet hosted by a specific person or community group, there's communally prepared food and drinks available for sale," says Kequia.

"I don't have any money," says Segante. "Not for this plane."

"The meal plan Dina mentioned will see to our basic needs," says Kequia. "The student handbook explains the meal plan tiers. I'm sure you'll get a book of your own as part of orientation. Hopefully one that's slightly more up-to-date."

"Are you telling us that because you don't want to look like a know-it-all, or because you don't want one of us to steal your precious book in the night?" asks Segante.

"Hey," says Eula. "We're not going to find much commonality in the rest of the student body if they're all from here. We're the only people not from Arcavios."

"Us and Professor Vess," says Kequia.

"All right, us and—what?" Eula turns to blink at her. "What do you mean, 'us and Professor Vess'?"

"She's from Dominaria, same as I am," says Kequia. She sounds uncomfortable. "Grandfather mentioned her, but even if he hadn't, she's a little, well, infamous. Some of the things she's done—I'm amazed she's still alive. I guess she came here to start over."

"She's a Planeswalker?"

Kequia nods.

"All right," says Eula, suppressing the urge to ask Kequia whether all the Planeswalkers know each other. Maybe they used to travel in flocks or something. She's gone her whole life without needing to deal directly with a Planeswalker, and now she's barely a full step removed from two of them. "Us and a random Planeswalker who likes to raise the dead. We need to get along, or this is going to be hard on all of us. Even harder than it's going to be already, I mean. We're going to have our differences, even beyond planar origins. So can we at least try to play nice?"

"Of course," says Jamira. "The forge feeds on what it's given and doesn't pine for better fuel."

Segante makes a scoffing noise and turns to drag his trunk into his room.

"I'm going to go see if I can rouse Alandra," says Eula, and flees back into her own room before things can start feeling any stranger.

This is supposed to be the beginning of her new life, the point where she finally gets to learn how to become the mage she was always meant to be. She looks around the room with its echoes of New Capenna on the wall and sighs. This isn't home. Neither is the Caldaia. Home is lost, fallen under the weight of Park Heights, and it's better for her to adjust to this place, which isn't haunted by the screams of the people who died in the Invasion, than it is to cling to impossible dreams of what's gone forever.

She opens her bag, pulling out pen and paper, and writes a quick note inviting Alandra to dinner. This done, she walks to the shimmering wall that contains the water and taps her fingers around it, feeling for the edges of the spell. They're solid, rooted deep into the walls of the building and, from there, into the snarlflowers climbing up the outside. More of those essence studies Dina was referring to, using living things as anchors for ongoing workings. It's clever, and Eula wants to take the time to understand it. She doesn't. For now she just checks those anchors to be sure she's not about to pop the bubble, then forms her thumb and forefinger into a circle, pressed against the wall.

Holding the note in her other hand, she moves it in a careful, intricate pattern, explaining what she wants to her magic. A shield begins forming inside the water, twisted to form a bubble, with the opening lined up to the circle she's made. Once the shield is formed and empty of water, she pushes the note through the circle, which she then twists off, sealing the piece of paper in the dryness.

Stepping back, she gives the bubble a mental push, sending it bobbing toward the coral structure. A blue hand emerges from the hole at the center, followed by the rest of Alandra, who holds the bubble curiously in front of her face before swimming to the surface. As soon as the shield is out of the water, Eula releases it, dropping the note into Alandra's hand.

Alandra unrolls it and reads quickly, then swims to the side and sticks her head out through the wall. "I would love to come eat with the rest of you, if you can wait just a moment," she says. "Thank you for thinking of me! How did you do that trick with the bubble? I can't make solid bubbles unless the air's moving a *lot* more than that, and then they tend to pop in people's faces and make a big splash."

"I told you, I'm going to be a shield mage when I finish my schooling," says Eula.

"Seems to me you already are one, and you're just going to get better," says Alandra. She passes the note out through the wall, dropping it in front of Eula. "I'll be right there!"

She withdraws into the water and dives back into the coral, although Eula can't imagine what she's going to retrieve— all her belongings are in the dry part of the room. Still, she's coming to dinner, and for right now that's enough. It seems oddly important to keep the group together, at least until they have a little more of a sense of what's going on here.

Alandra emerges from the coral, kicking herself free and swimming back to the wall. She slides out into the main room entirely dry, a newly healthy sheen to her scales. She whistles, and Orestes perks up, spreading his wings and following her through the spell wall.

"Where are we going?" asks Alandra.

"Dining hall," says Eula.

"Great."

They emerge to find Kequia and Segante waiting, although Jamira is nowhere to be seen. Segante has taken the time to change his vest and brush his hair, making him the best groomed of the lot of them. Eula looks down at her mended dress and feels suddenly grubby, wishing she had time to clean up before they eat. She's sure they'd let her, but since going out was her idea, it seems better not to ask.

Jamira emerges from her room, smelling of char and tying a leather apron around her waist. "Thank you for waiting," she says with exquisite politeness.

"No problem," says Eula. "Well, we're all here. Let's head out."

Together, they leave the common area outside their rooms and retrace the path they walked with Dina, emerging from the dorm into the evening air. The trumpet-shaped flowers are in full bloom now and covered in the creatures Dina called "pests," which rip and crunch at the vines, the soft sound of their chewing filling the air. It's odd but soothing, in its own way.

The paths around them are less busy than the quad where they arrived, although students still wander by in all directions, most moving in small groups, some wearing what Eula now recognizes as the colors of the colleges, others dressed as plainly and eclectically as the five of them. No one gives them a second look. It's refreshing, really.

Back home in New Capenna, everyone knows Eula and her family fell from the Mezzio, and while surviving the Invasion is officially a good thing, she's heard whispers from some of the work crews, people saying it's strange that a gifted shield mage should have been able to protect only her own family, leaving her neighbors to die. Even the people who don't blame her for surviving tend to see her as a bit of a snob, thinking herself too good for them. She'd never stopped looking upward, never stopped planning her escape. Her clothes were always too fine for the lower city, even as they had been too shabby and secondhand for the Heights.

Here, though, she's just another student among the throng. She's neither in nor out of fashion, but entirely parallel to it, a representative of a whole different social ecosystem.

It's the same for most of the others. Even Jamira, who would have been a strange sight in New Capenna, doesn't attract notice. There must be minotaur on this plane, because no one gives her a second glance. Alandra isn't quite so lucky. She doesn't look the same as the other merfolk Eula's seen, and Orestes attracts attention every time he takes off to circle overhead, wings catching and controlling the wind.

Eula is beginning to worry about finding the dining hall when a large boxy building comes into view ahead of them, made of the same brick as the dorm, but with benches and low stone tables scattered around outside, many of them occupied by groups of students. Here, the college colors are more obvious, as is the fact that people seem to sit with others who share their affiliations. They pass a table where a group of elves and humans in red and white are eating some sort of baked cheese dish that smells amazing and looks like it's been dropped from a great height. One of them points at Alandra and says, in a voice that probably wasn't meant to be overheard, "Witherbloom, for sure. All the amphibians go there."

The rest of the group snickers. Alandra looks uncomfortable and walks faster, forcing her friends to hurry to keep up.

Only Segante doesn't hurry. He stops, looking at the group of students with a cold, all but unreadable expression, eyes hard. Bit by bit, their snickering tapers off, until the one who actually made the comment scowls and asks, "What?"

"Nothing," says Segante. "I simply wanted to take note of which college encourages such incomprehensible rudeness toward new members of the student body. Did no one teach you to refrain from offending strangers until you know how useful they may or may not be? Lorehold is not for me, if it fosters bullies."

The students he's addressing flush and mutter, none of them quite meeting his eyes. Eula backtracks to set a hand on his arm, murmuring, "Jamira found a table inside. Come on, let's get dinner."

He doesn't say anything, simply makes an imperious noise and keeps watching the offending group. But he moves with Eula when she starts walking toward the cafeteria again, letting himself be led.

It's not until they're inside that Eula sighs, shaking her head. "That was brave and stupid, so points for style, none for subtlety, I guess. Is that what they teach on Fiora?"

"No." He gives her a level, unblinking look. "I would be shunned on Fiora for being so direct. We teach the art of the knife between ribs, the poisoned plate, and the slit throat. I didn't think Alandra would appreciate any of those things, and I'm reasonably sure murder is grounds for expulsion among these fine, soft people we find ourselves surrounded by. But I meant what I said: Lorehold is not for me. I have little interest in history, and even less in calling back the dead to answer for their lives. Let those students think they cost their college an enrollment, especially if they're meant to be courting us. It's little enough punishment for their rudeness."

"If you say so," says Eula, and leads him to where the others are waiting. Jamira has spread her heavy leather duster across a table near the front of the dining hall, protecting it from other claimants while the five of them go and line up for their food.

The dining hall is as large inside as it seemed from the outside, the air heavy with the smell of unfamiliar foods, bright with the sound of student chatter. Long counters take up one end of the room, and people move along them with trays, accepting plates and bowls from the servers on the other side. Eula lines up with the others, taking a tray from the stack at the end of the line, and waits.

It's a simple system, and very similar to the one she's seen in the Riveteers' mess hall: approach each station and either take their offerings or politely refuse them in favor of moving to the next. She's somewhat relieved to realize she recognizes the basics of all the dishes on offer, if not the dishes themselves. Breads and root vegetables, pasta and cheese, some sort of heavy stew and a salad made of incongruously black-and-white lettuce.

The meal plan they've been given covers servings of any dishes on offer, as well as a drink and a slice of questionable pink cake from the dessert counter. Eula gets a cup of hot coffee, beige with cream and sweet with too much sugar, and makes her way back to the table. She tries to be surreptitious as she looks at everyone else's trays. You can tell a lot about where people come from by the sort of things they choose to eat.

Segante has a bit of everything, while Jamira has several bread rolls and a slab of some unidentifiable meat. Kequia has three slices of cake and a plate of fried root vegetables with some sort of dipping sauce, and Alandra has a massive monochrome salad with little pink shrimp scattered through it like confetti after a parade.

Really, Eula's own sandwich, coffee, and cake feels almost boring compared to everyone else's dinner, but it's what she wanted, and she's glad to have it. They're halfway through their meal when Jamira puts her fork down and looks to Alandra.

"What that boy said hurt you," she says. "I would like to know why."

"Er," says Alandra, while Orestes chirps.

Jamira doesn't say anything, only waits with attentive politeness for an answer.

Finally, Alandra says, "An amphibian is something that can live in air or water, which I do, but amphibians transform from one thing to another as part of learning to breathe air. They're soft and squishy and usually pretty fragile. I can live in air or water, but that's because I have gills, and I'm not squishy or fragile. Calling a merfolk like me an amphibian is a pretty major insult."

"We don't have merfolk in Capenna," says Eula. "We have cephalids. And if you called the cephalid who taught my penmanship classes an amphibian, she'd staple you to the wall to think about why that was a tactically poor idea."

"There *are* amphibious people on Shandalar," says Alandra. "They're called amphin, and I don't look anything like them."

"He was trying to be cruel. I don't think he was looking too closely," says Jamira.

"Do you think he knew he was being insulting?" asks Alandra.

"They have merfolk here, I've seen them," says Kequia. "I would be surprised if he didn't know."

"But I didn't *do* anything to him!"

"Some people just need to be mean in order to feel good about themselves," says Kequia.

Alandra stabs her salad with her fork. "I don't think Lorehold is for me, either. But it was never going to be. What about you, Eula?"

"I don't think so," says Eula. "I'm going to find the college that helps me to become the best possible shield mage, and I'm going to join the Obscura after I graduate, and I'm going to lift my family back to the heights of the city." Saying it so bluntly makes her feel brave. Let her father dream of the Brokers. She'll go where her heart says she belongs.

"That didn't make any sense at all, but it sounds very admirable," says Segante, and Eula laughs, and the momentary tension is broken.

They have so much to learn. Not only about this new place but also about each other and all the new places they come from.

They clean up their dishes and trays when their meal is finished, putting things into the bins set out for that purpose, and exit the way they came in. The little cluster of judgmental Lorehold students is gone, and their absence somehow reignites the discussion of which colleges might be worth pursuing.

Jamira confesses, in her deep, oddly gentle voice, that she's interested in the theories of magic, especially as they relate to the omenpaths and planeswalking. "It was magic that stole my father for much of my childhood," she admits, "and that same magic saved my family from being prisoned on a dead world after the Invasion razed everything I'd ever known. I want to understand it. I'm sure there will be many paths to understanding that magic, but right now it appears I would find the most support among the Quandrix, if they are as described."

"I think Lorehold would be *wonderful*," says Kequia. "Not the students we saw at the dining hall, of course, but Bricen, and the historians, and all the people who want to understand the lessons of history well enough that we won't have to go back and learn them a second time. That's what history is, really. It's an instruction manual for not making the same mistakes over and over again. I don't like making mistakes more than once."

"And you won't be mean to me if you go to Lorehold?" asks Alandra.

"Of course not! I try not to be mean to anyone if I can help it."

"Oh. Good." Alandra shrugs. "I don't know. Maybe Prismari? Storm sculpting is an art, and it sounds like they could help me with that. And also, a really good storm is sort of like an explosion you've stopped in the middle of exploding, so if their stuff blows up all the time, they might not mind so much."

"Witherbloom," says Segante, and nothing more. Eula looks at his serenely set expression and is unsurprised, if a little concerned, that his studies might take him in the wrong directions.

That leaves the others looking at her. She shrugs, putting

on her best expression of unconcern. "The Obscura are all that really matters, where I'm concerned. I'm going to be one of theirs, and it's going to be perfect, and no one back home's going to know what any of these silly colleges are. But I'll still be the first Strixhaven graduate in the Family, and they like people who can talk fast and think faster. It's Silverquill for me. I'm sure of it."

"I wonder if we were the five they recruited because they could tell we wouldn't all clump together and go to the same college," says Segante. "It shows sensible planning, if that's the case. No one gets an advantage over anyone else. No one gets angry because they feel they were left out. If they want to be able to scale up bringing in more trans-planar students, this is how you do an introductory program. Cater to our individual needs while also selecting students who will spread across the campus, giving the appearance of fairness."

"That's calculating," says Eula.

"That's Fioran," says Segante.

"And that's your answer for everything."

"It's the truth."

They continue on through the early evening dark to their dorm, where the snarlflowers have begun to glow, illuminating the walls and the pests that still munch on their vines. As they approach the building, an owl takes off from the roof and flies silently into the night, white wings spread like unmarked banners as it soars.

Inside the dorm, the halls are empty. If there are other students in the building, they're dealing with their own affairs and allow the five newcomers to pass quickly back to the central chamber leading to their rooms.

Someone has been here while they were busy eating. Someone has scrawled INVADERS GO HOME across the wall of the antechamber in messy, drippy lettering. The five of them stop dead in the doorway, staring at the message. Alandra makes a thin squeaking sound and steps halfway behind Eula, hiding from the letters like they might bite her.

Kequia moves cautiously forward, eyeing the words more closely. Then, with a quick, jerky motion, she reaches out and touches the edge of one letter, pulling her hand sharply back again.

"It's some sort of sap," she reports. "Whoever smeared it here didn't touch it directly, so I can't tell anything about them, except for a thick core of bitterness and insularity. I don't . . . Why would anybody already hate us?"

"Some people are prepared to hate anything they don't understand," says Segante. "We need to remove this."

"We can call Dina," says Alandra.

"No," says Segante. "How do we know she'd be on our side in this? We handle this ourselves."

The atmosphere in the antechamber is different with the reminder on the wall that they don't belong here: the air of new beginnings and hope that filled it before is gone. Jamira escorts Alandra and Kequia into Alandra's room, the three of them leaving Eula and Segante to clean up the offending message.

"I've dealt with graffiti on the cleanup crews at home," says Eula. "Magic isn't always the most efficient way to handle it, but it works." She presses a shield thinner than a sheet of paper and slides it up the wall, under the words, separating the sap from the paint. "Is there anything you can . . . ?"

Segante touches her shield, and a film of oily green spreads across the surface, making her fingers sting and burn. The letters rot away, and she drops the shield, allowing the decay to dissipate as she shakes her hands, trying to chase the feeling of rot away.

Segante gives her a frosty look, then turns and walks to his room, slamming the door behind himself.

Eula exhales and goes to her own room, where Alandra is already in the water, concealed in her coral cove. Jamira and Kequia look at her, concerned.

"We cleaned it up," she says. "You can go to your room now."

Still concerned, they get up and go. Eula crosses to her desk, where her class schedule is waiting next to Alandra's, each in a carefully labeled envelope sealed with a wax impression of the school crest, a many-petaled symbol that could be a star or could be a snarlflower pressed flat under a sheet of glass. If there's one thing Strixhaven seems to love, it's branding.

Whoever left the graffiti must not have been able to get into their locked rooms. That means it wasn't a member of the faculty. That makes Eula feel a little better as she removes and unfolds her schedule, checking it carefully.

They'll be starting the next day with a tour of the university, focused on the main campus and led by Dina, followed by History of Arcavios with Professor Kasmina. After that, they'll be scattered, sent off to classes more tailored to their skills and interests. Eula is pleased to see that her schedule includes an introduction to shield magic, as well as an advanced geometry class that looks similar to one she'd been looking forward to before Park Heights University fell. There's a surprising amount of math in proper shielding.

She makes a bottle shield for Alandra and pushes her schedule through the bubble wall. Orestes swims over to collect it; he pokes his head through the wall, and Eula scratches the back of his neck before he pulls back into the water and drags the shield-bottle into the coral cove for his mistress. This accomplished, Eula turns to unpacking and is almost done when the midnight bell rings, signaling the campus to silence.

Eula sits on the edge of her bed, breathing out, trying to give her jangled nerves a chance to settle. This has all happened so quickly. One day, she was home in New Capenna, facing a life rewritten by the Invasion, unsure of how she'd ever be able to achieve the things she'd dreamed of. And now she's the first person from her home plane to be invited to attend this impossibly distant school, where she can learn everything she's ever needed to know.

This is a chance beyond all price, and she's not going to squander it, even if she doesn't understand the social rules surrounding her, even if people have already decided she's an intruder. Eula gets up, collecting her toiletries kit, and heads to the bathroom to brush her teeth before she sleeps. Tomorrow is a new day, and she's going to make the most of it.

SEVEN

CHOICES AND COLLEGES

Alandra's watery habitat filters the sun through the window but doesn't block it entirely, and the bell to signal the start of breakfast service wakes Eula in a room filled with diffuse, dancing light. She slept better than she'd expected to, pulled under by exhaustion and exhilaration to spend her night running through tangled streets woven of purest dream, never quite getting her feet under herself, never quite falling down. She sits up, rested and breathless at the same time, and looks around the meticulously familiar unfamiliar dorm room with widened eyes.

Orestes is curled on his shelf with his head resting on his tail and one wing folded over his eyes. Of Alandra there is no sign. Eula slides out of bed and moves to the closet, flicking through her scant clothes as she tries to decide what to wear on the most important day of her life. Before last night at the dining hall, she would have assumed students at an elite magical university would be . . . not better, necessarily, but kinder than the ones she knew from home. Now she knows better. People are people no matter where they come from, and people are always capable of being cruel.

In the end, she selects her second-best dress, knee-length and cream-colored, but without any secondary colors to imply a college affiliation she doesn't have the right to claim—yet. They'll learn more about the colleges during their tour of campus, but she's already pretty sure where she's going.

She emerges from the room to find Jamira already in their little foyer, horns polished to a mirrored gleam and wrapped in iron and copper chains, leather duster replaced by a long blue vest that hangs almost to her knees, open at the front to leave her white top and brown shorts exposed. Eula nods to her and keeps walking.

It's not a surprise when Jamira follows. None of them are feeling secure enough to spend much time alone just yet.

"Where are you going? I read the clock tower as saying we had time for breakfast before orientation."

"Need to brush my teeth and get dressed, figured I'd do that in the bathroom."

"Ah. I have already done these things."

"Cool, so I'll see you—"

"But I will accompany you. How did you rest?"

Eula briefly considers pointing out that she can find the bathroom on her own but dismisses the idea. A little company can be a welcome thing. "Quite well. You?"

"Better, I think, than I would have without the environmental spell. As Dina said, I can function in lower temperatures—this is fine—but I relax more fully in the heat. Aranzhur had a substantial amount of geothermal activity, due to a multiplicity of volcanoes. Father said that was likely why we were targeted by the Machine Legion with such ferocity, and why our attempts to defend went so poorly. They infected the flowing rock of our magma channels and came from beneath before most even realized we were under attack. By extracting the liquid metals from the lava flows, they equipped themselves with more and better weapons than our forges could contribute."

"I'm sorry," says Eula, somewhat numbly. She lost her home, but her city was saved. Jamira saved her home but lost her world. The two aren't even comparable, don't feel like consequences of the same war.

"All survivors are, in one manner or another. Did you fight?"

"No." Eula's memories of the Invasion are of flight and shielding, of riding the place she had always known as home to the bottom of the world on a shield like a child's toboggan, constantly sure that she was about to die. She saw people die. She saw people transformed. They were lost either way. Sometimes she feels like she was lost at the same time.

"My sister and I did, by our father's side," says Jamira. "It was . . . terrible. Heat and pain and the smell of burning, screams like hot blades plunged into freezing water, bodies everywhere. The Phyrexians took them apart for parts, whether or not they had already been completed. Nothing was left intact, until even what was broken fell to pieces."

Eula shudders. The joining of the planes isn't entirely a positive thing, college educations aside. This new reality has its price, and it hasn't been paid evenly. She'll do well to remember that, and not to assume that what looks undamaged is.

This campus must have sustained its own wounds during the Invasion. She may never know where all the scars are, but there's no way Strixhaven—or Arcavios—weathered the storm unscathed.

The rest of the walk to the bathroom is made in silence, and Jamira remains outside while Eula slips in to brush her teeth and get dressed, smoothing the wrinkles out of her bodice with the heels of her hands before wetting them and running them through her hair. A look in the mirror confirms that she's presentable enough not to bring shame upon her family. Her hair complements her dress, and her shoes, while scuffed, are in fine enough repair to be worn in public. She gives her reflection a nod, then exits the bathroom to rejoin Jamira.

Jamira looks at Eula's outfit and frowns, her anatomy making the expression difficult to read. "Is this a particularly complicated uniform where you're from?" she asks.

"What? No. No, New Capenna just has rules about what you wear when, and what's appropriate for which situations, and I don't want to break them, even if they're not followed the same way here." Eula shrugs. "Call it a comfort thing? Everyone needs their security blankets."

"I have my jewelry, Alandra has her drake, Kequia has her student handbook, and you have a skirt that will show any stain it encounters. I see."

Eula is tempted to ask what Jamira thinks Segante has but manages not to, only following the minotaur back to their foyer.

Kequia and Segante have emerged by this point, both yawning and rumpled but—and this is far more important at the moment—dressed. Eula frowns at the closed door to her own room.

"Any of you good enough at holding your breath to pop in and let Alandra know she's about to oversleep?" she asks.

"I could try, I suppose," says Segante uneasily, following Eula's gaze to the door just as it opens and Alandra emerges, Orestes on her shoulder and a fresh green dress wrapped around her body, tied with a belt of braided twine and shells.

"I'm sorry," she says. "Am I late?"

"Not yet," says Jamira. "Are you prepared for the day?"

"I have my schedule, and as long as our tour of campus includes someone who can walk us to our classes, I shouldn't have any issues," says Alandra blithely. "I'll only need to be shown once. After that, Orestes will know the way."

"We'll stop by the bathroom on the way out for anyone who needs it," says Eula, just as the next bell rings, signaling the midway point of breakfast service.

Crossing the quad to the dining hall feels almost familiar after last night, something comfortable and understood. Students stream dense and quick in both directions, some clutching pastries as they head for class, others with the dim eyes of the unfed, still waking up. Eula can't help tensing whenever a group comes too close, trying to guess who left that message on their wall the night before, prepared for any interaction to become an attack. And for all of that, few give Eula and the others so much as a glance: they're new here but nothing strange when set against the rest of the campus population. That's reassuring, in its way. Anonymity is a rare gift. They reach the dining hall to find it no more than half full, echoing with the constant buzz of too many people talking at once to leave any of their words truly distinct. The serving stations are open as they were before, offering pastries and baked egg dishes and flat discs of fried dough that aren't quite like any pancake Eula has ever seen. They seem to baffle Jamira and Segante, both of whom spend as much time investigating their breakfasts as eating them, and Eula has to remind herself several times that laughter isn't polite.

They're still picking at their meals when Dina appears, accompanied by a tall, tan boy with black hair dressed in black and white and looking deeply beleaguered by the entire situation. Eula stands quickly, smoothing her skirt with her hands, and flashes him a friendly smile, which he answers with a blank expression and a glance to Dina.

Ah. Not feeling friendly, then. Eula turns her attention to Dina.

"You're the prompt sort, aren't you?" asks Dina, laughing under her breath. "Not a criticism, although you're not the one I was expecting to play teacher's pet. Everybody fed and rested? No nightmares or issues with your environment spells?"

This is where they either tell Dina what happened the night before or keep their secrets to themselves. Eula knows which she would prefer, but her breath still catches as she waits to see what the others will do. They didn't discuss this ahead of time.

"The temperature is perfect," says Jamira.

Kequia nods. "I wouldn't have expected it to be, but she's right. I slept fine."

"My room is ideal," says Segante.

"Good," says Dina. "Great, even. Now that you're getting settled in, it's time for me to drag you all over the university and give you a vague idea of where things are. There's no way we can cover everything in a morning, so if you get lost at any point, just find a campus guide, and they'll be able to point you to where you need to go."

"A campus guide?" asks Segante.

"You still have those?" asks Kequia, with audible excitement. She produces her student handbook, flipping it open to an early page. "Campus guides are constructs built with an encyclopedic knowledge of campus. They help students navigate the university."

"We lost a bunch of them in the Invasion, but we've been rebuilding the fleet," says Dina. "They're not as uniform as they used to be, so your illustrations probably won't match, but they're still around."

Kequia looks like she wants to clap her hands in excitement. Instead, she hugs her book and waits for the others to fall in around her, all five of them watching Dina for her next instruction.

"Clear your dishes and we'll start," she says.

Eula's cheeks flush red, and she hurries to clear her dishes, leaving the table where they ate as clean as they found it.

Dina smiles when the five of them reassemble. "Excellent. Now, this is Killian"—she indicates the boy who's with her—"one of my fellow upperclassmen. Can anyone guess his college?"

"Black and white are Silverquill," says Kequia promptly.

"Precisely," says Dina. "Killian is our debate master, and he can argue day into night if you give him the opportunity."

"Flatterer," says Killian.

"Takes one to know one," says Eula, earning herself

a raised eyebrow and what seems to be the flicker of an approving expression from Killian.

Dina laughs. "And on that note . . . come along, you five. We only have an hour allocated for today's tour, and it's a big campus." She begins walking, and the rest of them follow her out of the dining hall and back to the outside, where Eula sees other advisors leading clusters of students like ducklings through their own iterations of the tour. It's a pleasant feeling, knowing she's a part of something that's happening all around her. She's fitting in already.

"Technically it's six big campuses, but you'll be getting your detailed tours of the colleges after orientation," says Killian. It's clear the two spend a lot of time together, just from the easy way they interact. "Central campus, where we are now, is used for shared classes and first-year students. The Mage Tower grounds are here as well, so if any of you are the sporty type, you'll be spending a lot of time here even after you move on to a college."

"Mage Tower?" asks Jamira. "I don't know this game."

"Oh, you'll love it," says Kequia. "I'm really looking forward to watching a game. If you sit with me, I can explain the rules."

"I prefer to learn the rules to a game from the field," says Jamira. She looks at Killian. "Can undecided students play this game?"

"If you can run, catch, and throw, you can play," he says.

She nods ponderously. "I can do these things."

"There's more to campus life than sports," says Dina, wresting the conversation back onto her planned itinerary. "The Biblioplex is under repair, but it remains the largest magical library in existence. According to the stories, every spell that has ever been crafted by any mage, anywhere, is copied and stored in the private stacks at the Biblioplex. You won't have access to everything, of course, but the things you *will* have access to should be more than sufficient to guide you through any course of independent study you want to pursue."

"*Every* spell?" asks Eula, feeling dazed. Even the shallow end of a pool like that will net her the sort of secrets that her father not-so-subtly asked her to seek out and bring home; he'll be able to buy his way as high up in the Brokers as he desires, and once he's a Family man in his own right, it won't matter that she's heading for the Obscura as fast as her legs can carry her.

"Every spell, and histories of planes across the Multiverse," says Killian. "Honestly, I don't know why we were so surprised when the Invasion happened. We had so many of the pieces already."

"How is that even possible?" Kequia is staring at Killian and Dina with eyes so wide they look like they're on the verge of turning perfectly round.

"I don't know," says Dina, half laughing. "Ask a librarian. Or become a library page and maybe they'll tell you so you can shelve things more efficiently."

They continue walking, Dina pointing out landmarks like the administration building and the various buildings dedicated to general subjects. The Mage Tower field is more like a stadium, round and self-contained, with excited students chattering out front as they prepare for their shot at whatever the game entails. Most of them are wearing athletic clothing. Eula decides it's probably not her sort of thing. She can run when she needs to, and some of these buildings look like they'd be fun to climb, but sports for the sake of sports have never been her preference.

"You'll learn the basics of Mage Tower in your physical fitness class," says Killian. "It's a popular sport here on campus, and you may find you enjoy it. Or you may find you enjoy having arms that only bend in the usual places, and choose less aggressive pastimes."

"I suppose we know who isn't a player," murmurs Segante, and Eula smothers her laugh.

They continue on, finally reaching the first of the tour's proper landmarks. The Archway Commons looms so large as they approach that Eula can't entirely understand how it hasn't dominated every moment of their tour so far. A massive parabolic arch rises from the ground to a point that seems designed to frame the plane's two suns, circled by floating slabs of stone like those same suns' rays. The students who've been passing them on the paths, chattering and vibrant, quiet as they approach the Commons.

Then Eula sees why.

The arch is the crowning element of a lush park, benches and quiet picnicking spots scattered among patches of glorious green. Tall stone pillars line the walkways through the park, their tapered points floating a few inches above the ground, still clearly new and unweathered. Atop each of them is a statue, and a name. Many of the statues are of older people, some with hands outstretched as if caught in the act of shaping some incredible work of magic. Eula blinks, then glances to Dina and Killian. Somehow, it's not a surprise to see that both of them look to be on the verge of tears, their expressions drawn and miserable.

"I'm so sorry," says Eula quietly. She doesn't need to ask what she's offering her condolences for. They've mentioned the Invasion enough, and this space is clearly new: this is where Strixhaven has chosen to show its scars, the still-bleeding wound that Phyrexia left behind.

"Everyone lost something in the Invasion," says Killian, his words a wall for her sympathies to break against. He puts a hand on Dina's arm, and she shoots him a grateful look. "We're not special. We're just recovering."

"Which includes giving you a tour," says Dina, managing to sound almost cheerful. "Reaching the individual college campuses would take half an hour each way and eat your whole day. But we planned for that. This way."

She waves for them to follow as she turns away from the arch and its silent statuary, leading them out of the park and to a broad patch of cobblestone where a strange conveyance is waiting. It looks like a closed carriage with an owl's head and flat silver "wings." There is no exterior driver's chair: instead, their driver is seated inside the contraption, behind the stylized head, his face visible through the owl's "eye."

It's Bricen, a pair of goggles covering his own eyes, which is an odd sort of relief, as Eula thinks she'd start laughing and never stop if the owl had four eyes of its very own. The thing is comic-looking enough.

"Welcome!" he calls. "Nice to see you all again!"

Dina gestures for them to climb into the vehicle, and they do, with varying degrees of unease. That unease only grows as Bricen pushes a button and the thing begins to move, rolling rapidly forward.

"Safety belts, please," says Killian, and the whole thing

lifts into the air, causing Eula to yelp and grab for Segante's arm, Alandra to laugh in delight, and Kequia to lean closer to the window.

"What *is* this?" asks Segante, voice like ice.

"A Quandrix invention," says Dina. "We call it a Skycoach, and it can get us to the rest of the locations on our tour without taking up your entire day. Don't worry about falling. My friend Zimone assures me the math is solid."

Segante quiets uncomfortably, and Eula relaxes her grasp on his arm as the university rolls by beneath them.

Perhaps fittingly, their first stop is the Quandrix campus. The Skycoach lands with surprising delicacy, and the seven of them file out, leaving Bricen in the driver's seat as Killian leads them to a tall metal gate worked into a continually dwindling geometric pattern, one that refuses to be followed by the naked eye. It almost seems to shift when not looked at directly, as do the walkways beyond, which gradually rise up via a series of ramps until they wend gently into the orbit of a complicated hall whose geometry is as impossible to follow as the gate's.

"Torus Hall," says Dina, gesturing grandly. "This is where the Quandrix mages study their craft. This is the college of mathematical magic, of numbers and nuance, and you may wind up here if what you want more than anything is to understand the equations at the center of everything there is."

Jamira looks impressed. Eula notes, silently, that Quandrix is absolutely not for her.

They return to the Skycoach, and the tour resumes.

Their next stop is a towering cliff face that seems impossible in comparison to the rest of the campus. It doesn't fit the landscape. Eula looks around in disbelief, trying to find the trick that allows this optical illusion to exist. She doesn't find it. Students in red and white stroll down the central avenue sliced into the cliff, walking between statues of figures she doesn't recognize but who must have done something impressive to be immortalized in stone.

"Effigy Row," says Dina, indicating the walkway. "The entry to the Lorehold campus. This is the college of history and archeology, which are often but not always the same thing. This is where you go when you want to understand the bones of the problem, rather than the meat of it."

"Fascinating," says Kequia, hugging her handbook a little tighter.

Again, they resume, stopping next at a winding, beautifully paved pathway that twines between sculptures of frozen flame and slowly morphing water, pieces of elemental majesty frozen in place as works of art. A loxodon with some sort of stringed instrument is sitting in front of a topiary made of breathing ice, playing a stirring ballad for a group of dewy-eyed admirers. She doesn't seem to notice them but continues to play and sing in a sweet, carrying voice that's only slightly too far away to be comprehensible.

"The Opus Walk is a testament to Prismari creativity and the heart of their campus, although the soul is in the Furygale," says Dina. "This is the college of performance and passion, stormsingers and pyromancers. You'll never be cold here. You'll never be warm, either. They thrive in the pause between ignition and explosion."

Alandra beams, and Eula knows her mind is made up, if it wasn't already.

After their next flight, they disembark and approach a building that makes Eula's heart ache with missing Bassomer Station. It looks like a train station reinterpreted to become dazzling and as eye-catching as a sphinx's aviary. The windows are colored glass, and she knows the light inside must be jeweled and transformative, gloriously enriching anything it happens to touch. Some of the students wave or nod to Killian as the group slows to a stop, and Dina nudges him rather than stepping forward to speak. He sighs and moves to address the rest of them.

"This is Grandloft Hall, the largest and most essential part of the Silverquill campus," he says. "Silverquill is the college of eloquence. Amusingly enough, that clarity of purpose means we don't need to dress up what we do in pretty words. We *are* pretty words. Wit and style are our greatest achievements, and we don't accept those who refuse to put in the work."

Eula feels suddenly shabby, like he's assessing and judging every snag in the fabric of her skirt, every scuff on her shoes. She'll do better. She'll do whatever she has to, and she'll be good enough for this beautiful building, for these beautiful people. She'll wear the black and white here, and add the blue of the Obscura when she goes home, and she'll be the best shield mage either of these two planes has ever seen.

Segante joins her in her rapt contemplation, and for a moment, she can see the two of them on this campus together, learning their magic side by side. Only for a moment, though: Silverquill wouldn't suit all of him and might put him in danger when he goes home. He'll be happier in Witherbloom, and so she lets the image go.

Dina frowns a little at the look on Eula's face, glancing to

Killian before she says, "All right, and as they say, we've saved the best for last. Follow me."

Onward the tour wends, the Skycoach letting them off near a dirt path leading into what Eula first assumes is a drainage ditch. Dina gestures toward the green, indicating the treetops that loom above the tall grass, and says with some pride, "Witherbloom campus. The great bayou Sedgemoor."

"Your campus is a *swamp*?" asks Segante. He sounds impressed.

"Our campus is *in* the swamp, but we need the essence Sedgemoor produces to do our work as effectively as possible," says Dina. "Witherbloom is the college of essence studies, which doesn't seem to mean anything if you're unfamiliar with the concept, but means everything once you know what it's referring to. We study the interaction of life and death, and that requires us to understand the living and the dead intimately. We produce healers and necromancers, naturalists and people who never met a natural order they wouldn't be overjoyed to warp to their own ends."

"Hmm," says Segante.

"And with that, your introductory tour of Strixhaven and its colleges is concluded," says Killian. "If any of you want a closer look at one of the colleges, or at a specific facility, let Dina know. She's your student advisor, and she'll get you situated. But don't let her know right now. She's busy."

He takes Dina's arm. With a tight smile for the group, he begins to turn away, tugging Dina with him.

"Killian, this isn't very advisory," she chides, but doesn't pull away or particularly resist. Finally, laughing, she says, "All right, pop quiz—can you find your way from here back to the central campus? You should be able to, if you were paying attention to what was below us as we flew. It's about a thirty-minute walk—you can make it to your first class on time if you start now."

"It won't be a problem," says Jamira. "Please, go about your business."

Granted permission, Killian pulls Dina away faster, and the five of them stand on the edge of a vast, largely unseen bayou, watching the pair go.

EIGHT

THE COMPANY OF OWLS

"All right," says Eula. "That was . . . educational. My feet already hurt, and we haven't even started classes yet. Much less finished walking back to our dorm."

In the distance, a bell rings to signal the turning of the hour. Eula groans.

"I think Dina was way too optimistic about our walking speed. We're going to be late. Do you think we get a pass if we're late because our advisor ditched us to hang out with her boyfriend?"

"I'm certain our new instructors will be forgiving," says Alandra.

"I'm not," says Kequia. "According to the handbook, punctuality is prized and a base expectation of all Strixhaven students. We should hurry."

"I can find the central campus, but I don't know how to find a specific building from there," says Jamira.

Kequia's eyes light up. "Oh, don't worry about that. We can use a guide!"

She starts walking briskly back toward the distant curve of the memorial arch, eyes on the walkways around her, clearly searching for something. Eula hurries to catch up. "What do these campus guides look like?" she asks.

"If they've been redesigned post-Invasion, I don't exactly know," admits Kequia. "But the ones in the book were about half as tall as Jamira, and presumably they're still designed to help students navigate the university. Watch for them around the edges of any crowd."

They join her in scanning for a guide as they walk. Other students begin to appear before they've gone very far, moving in little groups and clusters. Alandra whispers something to Orestes before tossing him into the air, and he flies above them in wide circles, clearly looking for a construct in the tangled crowds below. In the end, it's Segante who catches a gleam of metal and waves them in the direction of the guide Kequia described, which is rounded and lovely, not merely functional, with a gold-plated exoskeleton whose filigree etching incorporates all five college logos alongside the crest of the school.

Kequia beams.

"They didn't *completely* redesign them," she says, in the tone of someone who's seeing dreams brought to life before her eyes.

"Schedule, please," the guide says, in a flat, somehow still friendly voice.

Jamira holds out her schedule, and the guide looks at it with its large blue eye, symbols etched in white racing across the eye's surface for a moment before something inside its chest pings, sharp as a barrister's bell, and the guide says in an oddly content tone, "If you all have the same class schedule, you will want the Building of General Historical Studies. Please follow me. If you would like, I can provide some interesting architectural facts about the building as we walk."

"That will be quite all right," says Eula. "We just need to get to our class."

"Understood. Facts will be available at a later date, if so desired. Right this way."

The guide begins trundling away, and the group follows, passing other guides leading clusters of students without college symbols on their clothing. That makes sense; Eula supposes that by the time someone joins a college, they probably know where most things on campus are and how to get to them without someone to hold their hands.

That's fine. Familiarity will come later, and for right now, what matters is punctuality, which is an essential part of politeness. One thing every Park Heights child learns early and often: politeness is better than following almost all the other rules. No one assumes the good, tractable, obedient ones are the troublemakers, and Eula is nothing if not very, very good when people are watching her.

The Building of General Historical Studies is smaller than she expects, red brick and silver spires swooping toward the sky, with a large, round stained-glass window above the main door depicting five dragons forming a snarled, complex knot with their wings and bodies. The guide pings again as they reach the front steps.

"We have reached your destination," it says. "Have I been satisfactory?"

"Extremely so," says Kequia.

"Thank you," says the guide. "Your classroom is behind the fourth door on the left-hand side of the hall. Please enjoy today's education."

Duties apparently fulfilled, it turns and trundles away, leaving them to blink after it. Segante is the first to speak.

"We don't have anything like that in Fiora. We melted them all down for scrap when we found out they were spying on us."

"I was thinking how easily we could use them for spies in New Capenna," admits Eula.

Segante snorts, amused, and the group heads inside, climbing the shallow brick steps to the tall double doors.

Inside, the hall is dim and empty, smelling oddly of some sort of floral cleaning solvent. There are no other visible students. Eula looks around, trying to take the opportunity to understand the flow of motion on the central campus better, but there's nothing to indicate where their peers might be hiding. The walls between the doors are clean, smooth plaster, occasionally marred by a poster for a student organization or advertising a sporting event.

Kequia, eager to get to class, leads the rest of them to the fourth door on the left, opening it and slipping through. Eula and the others follow, not wanting to be left behind, and the door slams shut behind them, echoingly loud and impossibly quiet at the same time.

That's not the only impossible thing. The "classroom" on the other side of the door is more like a forest clearing, green grass growing tall enough to brush against their ankles, trees towering in every direction. Owls fill those trees like feathery fruit, their eyes a dozen shades of amber and orange, watching the group's every move, and high above everything else, the sky that has replaced the ceiling is a bruised nighttime purple, spangled with stars.

There are six desks of varying size scattered around the clearing. The largest is labeled as Professor Kasmina's and is sturdy oak, weighted down with books and blotter. The other five are more like the standard student desks Eula remembers from her last school.

One of them is larger than the others by half and is clearly intended for Jamira; another, the smallest of the five, is just as plainly meant for Alandra, marked as such by the perch that sits beside it for Orestes. The other three could be interchangeable, although Eula's sure they're not; everything else has been too precisely planned. She moves among the three, studying them, and on the third, she finds what looks like a doodle of Lower Bassomer Station, done in simple graphite yet still identifiably distinct.

She settles there, then nods toward the next desk in the line, hoping either Kequia or Segante will understand what she's asking them to do without forcing her to say it. They move together to study the desks and, after a moment, seat themselves accordingly.

The sky lightens by several degrees, sliding apparently toward dawn.

"Nicely done," says an unfamiliar voice from the dark between the trees. "You found your seats more quickly than I would have expected, given your tardiness and the lack of instruction. Are you quite all sure you're in the right place?"

"We're the new trans-planar students, and we're here for our mandatory History of Arcavios with Professor Kasmina," says Eula, fighting hard to keep it from turning into a question. She fails the fight on her second statement: "She's supposed to be our advisor?"

"Until you choose a college and limit yourselves to a primary track of study, that's correct," says the voice, before its owner emerges from the shadows. Eula assumes the newcomer must be Professor Kasmina and watches closely as the woman crosses the clearing to lean against the teacher's desk.

She's tall, with the strong, sinewy build of a Cabaretti dancer, wearing a white cloak trimmed in blue over a layered white tunic cut along the edges to mimic the natural fall of feathers. Her leggings and accents are all in blue, making her look oddly formal for the setting she's been placed against. Her hair is long and honey blond, and her eyes are an even brighter blue than her clothing. She holds up one hand and whistles two soft notes, smiling as a white-winged owl glides down from the nearest branch to perch upon her wrist.

"I'll remain the academic advisor of anyone who chooses to go to Quandrix at the end of the year; I'm one of their junior professors, and so I get the enviable honor of guiding their newest students. And if I've done my job correctly, you'll all be able to pass the admission requirements of whichever college you choose to pledge to. As to why I'm your academic advisor before you pledge to Quandrix, it's largely because I was the one to encourage this program. Arcavios is a beautiful, thriving, deeply wounded plane, and we need time to recover from the Phyrexian Invasion. That means we need students to replace the ones we lost, and looking for them across the Multiverse allows us to find them without increasing our on-plane recruitment efforts to a degree that would discomfort the locals. They've had generations to decide whether or not they want to send their children here. The deaths we suffered during the Invasion haven't changed a lot of minds in our favor. While the Machine Legion marched on the entire plane, the campus was a singularly desirable target."

"Why?" asks Kequia, apparently treating this little introductory speech as the start of the class.

Eula doesn't object. This lines up well with her own curiosity, and if she can get her answers without drawing too much attention to herself, she's happy enough to do so. She can make herself impressive later, after she has the lay of the land.

"Ah. That is an answer you'll receive over the course of this class. As I've implied and you've surely guessed, I am Professor Kasmina, your advisor and instructor. I'm a member of the Quandrix College of Numeromancy and will be joined by guest speakers from the other colleges over the course of the semester to guarantee you receive a rounded and unbiased impression of campus life."

Eula frowns at that and puts up her hand, waiting until their professor shoots her an amused look and a nod before lowering it and asking, "Is there a reason everyone we've talked to seems so determined to make sure they're not granting anyone any advantage when it comes to wooing us? Where I come from, you're supposed to present yourself in the best possible light, always, and if your rivals can't match your display, that's on them, not on you."

"Eula Blue, Capenna, yes?" asks Professor Kasmina.

Eula nods.

"I would love to be able to teach a class on the history of Capenna to follow this one, but sadly, I doubt we'd have the demand. Your culture isn't considered one of the more status-oriented, not when compared to a plane like Fiora or Theros, but it should be."

Eula blinks, feeling faintly stung, although she isn't certain why. Professor Kasmina doesn't appear to notice, continuing without missing a beat: "Capenna's systems of manners and personal advancement are ritualized and often obscure when viewed from the outside. Here on Arcavios, we're just as interested in taking the upper hand, but less so in succeeding by stealing the advantage from people who don't know yet that there's a contest in progress."

"How can anyone not know when they're in a contest?" asks Segante sharply. "We're all competing, all the time."

"Ah, yes, Master d'Amati. You'll forgive me if I don't use your first name—I don't believe it's present in your admissions paperwork. You've cut your hair since I reviewed your eligibility for enrollment."

Segante's cheeks redden, but he lifts his chin and looks at her with calm challenge. "I prefer the surname Guarneri. It was my mother's and is less likely to find me hauled before the Queen for interrogation as to my intentions. You may call me Segante, for now."

"All right," says Professor Kasmina. "I'll make a note regarding both names. You were saying, about competition?"

"We don't play silly games with level playing fields and false fairness on Fiora," says Segante doggedly. "We compete, the loser is removed from the board, the winner solidifies their position."

"Your perception of Fiora, while not inaccurate, is colored by your upbringing. Despite what the nobility may think,

Fiora is more than knives in the dark and poisoned posies," says Professor Kasmina.

"I stand by my point," says Segante coolly.

"In that case, there's a passive competition between colleges for every student who steps foot on this campus, and if the colleges competed the way you say people do on Fiora, we'd have to close down due to the death toll. Here, we fight fairly and in the open, and in the interests of our students as much as in the interests of the individual colleges. Over the course of our time together, the five of you will be learning the history of the plane as a whole and of Strixhaven as an institution in specific. Our curriculum is flexible: we want you to be comfortable here, as our first openly trans-planar students, and able to function as a fully integrated part of the student body."

Eula and Alandra exchange a quick, uneasy look, and Orestes chirps, picking up on his mistress's discomfort. Once it becomes clear that Alandra isn't going to, Eula puts her hand up.

"Yes?"

"Some of us are members of species that don't seem to be found on this plane," says Eula, with diplomatic care. "How are we supposed to integrate when that's the case?"

"The inclusion of sentient species not found on Arcavios was discussed when we were selecting our inaugural class," says Professor Kasmina. "It's part of why we knew we would have to be open about your origins. Previous trans-planar visitors have been human, or otherwise able to pass for locals. But it was important to us that we not exclude anyone on the basis of species. You were the best candidates we had, and as such, we had to take what steps we could to bring you here."

"How did we become candidates, ma'am?" asks Kequia. "I had my name down for Tolaria West. I was going to study psychometry there."

"Do you know—no." Professor Kasmina catches herself and shakes her head, a small smile creasing her lips. "That would be an insulting question to ask any of you, but most insulting to Jamira in particular. I'll try this instead: Were you aware that the study of the Planeswalker spark has consumed scholars and mystics for centuries, all of them attempting to better understand that fundamental connection to the Blind Eternities, which form the space between planes? The Blind Eternities are the connective tissue that binds our Multiverse together, and until very recently, they were the only known means of traveling from one plane to another. This wasn't always the case. The nature of Planeswalker sparks has changed before, most recently during the Mending, an event that occurred roughly sixty years ago, and which diminished all known Planeswalkers in power, seemingly on a permanent basis."

"I've heard about the Mending," says Kequia. "My grandfather says it was necessary to repair damage caused by careless mages, and that before it happened, there were other ways to move between planes—machines and artifacts and even some massively powerful spells, which may have contributed to the problem in the first place. Before the Mending, Planeswalkers were immortal."

"Yes," says Professor Kasmina. "And after the Mending, the plane we refer to as Avishkar experienced what they refer to as the Great Aether Boom, when massive quantities of raw aether were discovered and refined on the plane, allowing them to progress their science and technology with amazing speed. Aether is to the Blind Eternities as mana is to the planes where we spend our lives. The Planeswalkers were reduced, and suddenly there was aether for the taking, if not evenly distributed through the Multiverse. Some of the scholars who had been working to better understand Planeswalker sparks—those not now trapped on whatever plane they had been visiting when the change occurred—shifted their focus to this new manifestation of aether. Or most of them did, anyway."

She pauses, waiting for questions. There are none. All five watch her in rapt silence, waiting for the conclusion to her tale.

"Some scholars redirected their attention from the Blind Eternities to the Planeswalkers themselves, and to a group that had been identified by former Tolarian scholar Teferi Akosa as potential Planeswalkers. The spark ignites when it will, and for some, it never becomes more than a possibility—an ember. During the Mending, at least one possible spark was extinguished to complete the healing of the Blind Eternities, and that individual has never again shown the potential to become a Planeswalker." She pauses, giving Kequia a pointed look. "Teferi had matters requiring his attention in the Mending's wake, but others picked up his scholarship and began tracking the potential Planeswalkers who retained their embers. While there was little chance that all of them would one day ignite, they were all mages of incredible potential, people who could, one day, hold the power to shape worlds in the palms of their hands."

Segante scowls. "Are you telling us our names were on this list? That we were offered admission because you thought we might be Planeswalkers someday? A poor investment on your part. There are no Planeswalkers anymore. They all died or were undone in the Invasion."

"Not all of them," protests Eula. "The Archangel Elspeth still moves between the worlds. And I thought they didn't die, they just lost the spark our professor's been talking about. Blowing out a candle didn't kill them." She glances to Professor Kasmina for confirmation.

Professor Kasmina nods. "Many sparks were extinguished in the aftermath of the Invasion. I can't say whether it was most, as no one has ever conducted a full count of the Planeswalkers of the Multiverse, but it seems likely to have been the majority, given what we know and what Planeswalkers we've been able to contact since the change. The omenpaths connect the worlds, much as the old inter-planar technology used to, but without the potential for immediate misuse. Planeswalkers can still travel, but so can everyone else. It seems to be the dawning of an era of equity."

"That isn't an answer," says Segante sharply.

"Yes, your names were on the list of embers," says Professor Kasmina. "All of you had the potential to spark—and may still, under the right conditions. We don't know. The changes are too recent. But that was why you were selected, from all the candidates in the Multiverse, as our first class of transfer admissions. We hope you'll thrive here, and, by thriving, prove Strixhaven is the best magical university in existence, capable of meeting the needs of students from across the planes. With the omenpaths now open and seemingly stable, it's going to be important for us to establish ourselves quickly, or we'll never be able to maintain our reputation."

She waves a hand, and books appear on their desks, sturdy

volumes bound in gray linen, with the name of the class blazoned on the front. "Which brings us, at last, to the topic of our class. The history of Arcavios is a complex one, as all planes are—cultures and civilizations trend toward complexity, given time, although they all end in simplicity. But before the plane as we now know it existed, there was another world here, a plane that never developed intelligent life and thus never had a proper name, although various names have been used for it throughout the literature. The Archaics—whom you will learn of in more detail as this course continues—refer to this half-formed plane as 'Karudis.' They've never explained their reasons, and as such, I'll be referring to it throughout this course as 'Apex,' to give it a designation with meaning that you can all easily spell in your notes."

Another wave of Professor Kasmina's hand and the sky above her clears all the way into airy morning, stars replaced first by sourceless brightness, then by an orb rotating alone in the emptiness. Seas and continents form, marking the outline with landmarks viewed from such a vast distance that they have no refinement. A sun forms, and the orb rotates around it, too quickly to be marking actual years, the seas and landmasses shifting as it circles.

"'Apex' is a trifle pat, perhaps, but sometimes one must go with the easy answer for the sake of learning, if not scholarship, which is not always the same thing," says Professor Kasmina. She waves her hand again. A second orb begins forming on the opposite side of the sun, the two worlds rotating together. "Time passed, and where other planes might begin to develop life and stability, Apex began to develop a sibling, a twin, anchored to the same point in the Multiverse, occupying the same impossible space. Where Apex was a world of physical reality that might one day have been able to support complex intelligent life, the new plane was a world of luminous mana, bright and burning and inherently destructive. The two planes might have been able to coexist like this forever, had not the newcomer—Zenith—continued to grow and spread to encompass celestial bodies of its own."

A second sun appears in the sky, close enough to the first that the orbits of the two planes begin to become erratic, weaving in and out of harmony with each other.

"The Archaics have a name for the newcomer as well. They call Zenith 'Ezroi,' and they claim the two planes were natural enemies, opposite in every way, destined to fight to the death, until they defied that destiny and fell in love. While some planes have shown manifest worldsouls that seem to represent them as if they were thinking individuals in their own right, I prefer not to think of planes as capable of making their own decisions. We would be little more than the mites on an owl's wings if that were so."

Jamira puts up her hand. Professor Kasmina snaps her fingers, and the scene above them freezes in place.

"Yes?" she asks, with a hint of frustration.

"Forgive me, but what *is* a plane?" says Jamira. "Is it a world, a planet? The sky of Aranzhur was forever full of stars. I assume they shine there still, even after the Invasion consumed our world. Father told us every star was a sun like our own, and every sun was orbited by planets of its own making. Was our sky full of planes?"

"An excellent question for your Planar Theory course," says Professor Kasmina. "The short answer is that every plane is a reality, and every reality contains a universe. Worlds without number, stars and constellations, all the pieces of a cosmos, replicated again and again into bubbles held within the Blind Eternities. A plane may be as small as a continent, as on Theros, or as large as several worlds held in frozen cascade, as on Kaldheim. We name the planes after the worlds that have intelligent life and access to the wider Multiverse."

"But by that logic, couldn't Aranzhur and Arcavios exist on the same plane, just behind different doors?"

"Again, that's an excellent question for your Planar Theory course," says Professor Kasmina. "We're here to learn the history of Arcavios, not of the entire Multiverse. May I resume my lesson?"

"Yes, Professor," says Jamira, half sullenly.

Professor Kasmina snaps her fingers again. The orbs resume their rotation, pulling farther apart and then coming dangerously close as their suns shift in the space around them, which is not yet recognizably a sky.

"Apex and Zenith danced around each other for a time and then, inexorably, began to fall into the reality wells at the heart of their opposite number. Part of what defines a plane is the behavior of the mana that powers and sustains it—the magic of Innistrad is not the magic of Zendikar, however similar it might seem at first taste. The plane sets its own rules. And the rules of Apex and Zenith, while similar enough to exist in the same space, were inevitably antithetical to each other. Their mana did not merge, but snarled, forming pools of contrasting power, patterns of permanent antagonism."

Above them, the orb designated as Zenith crashes into Apex, the two of them grinding more and more interminably together. Continents shatter. Mountains are formed as slivers of stone are driven beneath the continental plates, lifting what land remains high into the air. Seas are formed, destroyed, and spilled into emptiness, to evaporate and fade away. Professor Kasmina snaps her fingers again, and what remains of each plane lights up with a web of scintillating light. Only a glance is required to see that the two webs are out of alignment with each other, dancing with rainbow flashes that clash and conflict, never smoothing out into anything that resembles peace.

The gleaming orbs continue to grind together, their brilliant webs gradually beginning to overlap. The colors still don't align. Every time a line brushes against another, they stick together and pull tight, drawing the rest of the web more and more taut over the surface of the conjoined planes. Bit by bit, the two orbs are smoothing into one, larger than either was on its own, with the continental maps of the two originals mashed together and canted oddly to the side. The tangled lines become a single web, until the only signs of what must have been a massive cataclysm are the two suns in the sky, and the strange snarls of magic that dot the globe.

They mark the points where the two webs first came together and adhered, creating an artificial and impossible unity. There are dozens of them, dozens of dozens, but five stand out with a bright and burning light, difficult to look at directly even in this abstract re-creation of something that happened long before the birth of recorded time.

The other snarls dim and ebb, fading into the background of the web without disappearing. They will remain, it seems, for as long as the plane endures. But the five points keep getting brighter and brighter until, one by one, they burst.

The orb is cast at such a scale that it should be impossible to see anything emerge from the rupturing snarls, but five tiny dragons tumble out of them, spreading moist, bicolored wings, and roar dominion to the sky.

"The exact moment Arcavios was born is as difficult to chart as it is with any plane. When you're measuring time in millennia, even the strongest of chronomancers have difficulty seeing where the path begins. But it seems likely that Arcavios as we know and understand it was born in this moment, when the Snarls of opposing magic formed by the union of Apex and Zenith birthed the five dragons who would go on to found Strixhaven and its colleges. Their intervention tamed a world, shaped its civilizations, and brought us, gradually and gloriously, to the place we stand today. The Dawning Age birthed the Snarls, star arches, and Archaics, and it endured until the other humanoid intelligences of the world began to rise to prominence and take their place in the great story of the plane." Professor Kasmina brings her hands together, and the orb shatters into prismatic glitter, drifting down to cover them all. "And that is the end of our introductory lesson."

The bell rings outside the classroom, tolling low and mellow, less an alarm and more a reminder of the time.

"I'll see you all tomorrow morning," says Professor Kasmina. "And Jamira, I'll see you next period, for my Theory of Omenpaths course."

"How do you know so much about the study of Planeswalker sparks?" asks Kequia.

"Why, because it's been my life's work," says Professor Kasmina. "And I will continue it, even now that my own spark has been extinguished. Everything changes. What's been mended once can break again, and this scholarship may yet prove essential. Hurry now, or you'll all be late to your next class."

They file silently out of the room and head for the exit. Once outside, Eula knows, they'll find individual campus guides and go their separate ways. But for right now, they remain together, united and out of place.

She can't say she entirely likes it, but she's not sure what she'll do when it's over. Find a new group to belong to, she supposes. That's always been a skill of hers.

For now, they walk on.

ONTO THE FIELD

The school week passes in a blur of classes and tours, deadlines without end, and a pop quiz on methods of mana filtering that leaves Jamira as wrung out as she is after smelting the impurities out of iron ore. A quiz is a mental exercise, but she feels like she's been physically dragged across several miles of rough terrain by the time she returns to her dorm after the final class of the week, collapsing into the comforting embers of her bed. When Kequia comes in some hours later, she finds Jamira fast asleep, horns still wrapped in her daily jewelry.

Carefully, she untangles the chains from Jamira's horns, straightening them with careful fingers before returning them to Jamira's jewelry box. Every link sings a song of war and sorrow to her psychometry, of lost Aranzhur and her eternal, deep-banked fires. She sees glimpses of people she presumes to be Jamira's family: her sister, her father, and her memory-faded mother, gone but never forgotten. The grief of it all is neither surprising nor unique: everyone's wounds are still healing after the Invasion. That may explain the feeling of almost frantic playfulness that sometimes sweeps across the campus. *See,* shouts joy in these bruised times, *see, we're still here! We're still alive! We won.*

We won.

Kequia goes to sleep on her own side of the room, Jamira's sorrow echoing through her fingers, and dreams of home.

Classes at Strixhaven don't restrict themselves to a narrow period of time like they might at other schools. At Strixhaven, the bell for the start of breakfast service rings shortly after the suns begin their daily trek across the sky, and classes begin not long after, not ending until well after the midnight bell has rung. All seven days of the week have their own lesson plans, although most students have a schedule that gives them two days off sometime during their personal week.

Jamira and the others have been scheduled so that their breaks correspond, five days on and two days off, during which they're free to do whatever pleases them on and around campus, unless there's some sort of holiday. The next morning is their first without classes since their arrival, and it dawns to find Jamira staring at the ceiling, still exhausted, the room's hot air baking her skin to a comfortable degree. Kequia is gone, crept out at the breakfast bell, and Jamira doesn't expect to see her until nightfall. That's well and good. She likes the little human more than she'd expected to like any of the other students when she decided to come here, but that doesn't make them *friends,* not really.

She likes all of them more than she expected to, and that's a problem, because it's going to make her time away from her family more difficult than it needs to be. Well. She never expected this to be easy.

Jamira stretches her arms over her head as she rolls onto her side, transferring her momentum into the act of standing up. Even in a room designed for her use, her horns almost brush the ceiling. Everything on Arcavios is built so *small*. Despite the loxodon and ogres native to the plane, too much of the campus has been designed for use by human-sized students. It's a subtle sort of prejudice that serves to remind Jamira constantly that this is not her home, this is not where she belongs, this is not Aranzhur.

Aranzhur is gone. Nothing she does is ever going to bring it back. Her father, who was still a Planeswalker when the battle began, couldn't save her world, so how could she recover it from the wreckage? Phyrexia was defeated, but the damage they did lives on, and they shattered the magma channels, drained the reservoirs, darkened the skies with oil and ash—the plane still exists as a physical place, but it will be decades, if not centuries, before it can support life again. Her daughters will call some other world home, will fit themselves into imperfect spaces and learn to endure the soft indignity of ceilings that are too low and beds that are too small.

The thought is infuriating. No one else is here, and so she snorts and shakes her head, making no effort to repress the instinctual behaviors she knows make humans uncomfortable. They're remarkably open-minded, these humans of Arcavios and elsewhere, but they still believe every intelligent species is essentially human at its core, just human wearing a fancy costume of some sort. Show them a dust-bathing viashino or a minotaur with a salt stick and they react with confusion and, at times, concern. Kequia is good about not commenting when Jamira is openly inhuman, but she knows the other woman notices. It would be impossible for her not to.

Jamira's vest is waiting at the foot of the bed, clean after a night in the superheated confines of her luggage. She picks it up and shrugs it on, lacing the front with quick, practiced gestures. She knows Eula judges her for always wearing the same things. She also knows Eula is not as clever as she thinks she is and can't read the messages spelled out by the jewelry Jamira adorns her horns with every morning. She wears the chains and jewels appropriate for an unmarried woman, yes, but also the charms that declare her a master blacksmith in her own right; the trinkets that make her hoped-for college alignment clear; the arrangement of bells that says she's not currently open to courtship, but if she were, she would prefer the company of women to the company of men. Another minotaur from Aranzhur would be able to look at her horns and know everything they needed to know about her.

Not that she's likely to ever see another minotaur from Aranzhur again, outside of her father and sister, who have hopefully found a place for the family to settle by now. She should really take this free time as an opportunity to learn more about Innistrad, if that's where her father hopes to find them a new home. The thought is off-putting. She doesn't want a new home. She wants Aranzhur. She wraps her horns in the day's jewelry, not remembering that she went to bed still adorned or asking herself how her chains were untangled, and huffs lightly, feeling utterly alone in the Multiverse.

Prepared to face the day, Jamira leaves the room, stomach rumbling as she continues onward, out of the dorms. There is no graffiti today, has been none since their first day. Maybe it was just some prankster with poor impulse control; maybe that will be the last of it.

She doesn't think so.

A flicker of motion catches her eye as she steps outside. She turns, focusing on a tree to the right of their dorm, tall and rough-trunked, with leaves like open hands. The snarlflowers twine along its trunk, claiming it as they claim so much else, and for a moment she thinks the motion must have been a hungry pest looking to fill its belly at a higher vantage point.

Then her eyes adjust, and what she'd taken for a pattern in the tree bark resolves into an owl with brown feathers patterned in black stripes, visible mostly due to the orange slash of its beak and the round yellow circles of its eyes. Jamira scowls at it.

There seem to be owls everywhere on this campus. She sees them on the rooftops, she sees them in the trees, and she sees reminders of them in the feathers Alandra's lizard drops all over everything after snatching unwary songbirds from the air. The owls watch them, and she's quite sure she knows who the owls are watching them *for*.

Jamira turns away from the tree and the owl, growling stomach forgotten in the face of her growing anger. Instead she stalks toward the building where they have their History of Arcavios course, where she might be able to find out why this is happening.

She doesn't know what she's going to do when she gets there. She wasn't planning on a confrontation this morning, didn't wake up thinking now was the time to ask their advisor why she insists on spying on them—why they aren't afforded any privacy, or the respect given to most of their peers. They're not *children*. Back home in Aranzhur, she was considered old enough to own her forge and start her own household. She didn't, purely because her sister needed her, and they both needed to believe their father was coming back.

And then he had, and Phyrexia had followed, using paths pioneered by Planeswalkers to destroy the world. The thought is sudden and bracing and reminds Jamira that her anger is nothing new. She's been mad for a very long time.

There are no classes in the general history building today, but the door is still unlocked, and she stalks along the empty hall on quiet feet, not quite storming, definitely not advertising her approach. Professor Kasmina said she was available every day between breakfast and lunch for any questions they might have. Well, Jamira has questions. She only hopes that "every day" includes the weekend.

When she reaches the classroom, she tries the door. It, too, is unlocked, and so she steps inside, not bothering to knock.

Professor Kasmina, who is seated at her desk, looks up without a glimmer of surprise. She lifts an eyebrow. "Jamira," she says. "To what do I owe the honor?"

"Why are your owls following me around campus?"

"It's not just you. You're not special. They're following all five of you. I didn't think you'd be the first to notice; I thought Segante would be paranoid enough to realize most of the student body isn't being stalked by predatory raptors. He's not as careful as he makes himself out to be, and half his stories of Fiora are so exaggerated by his paranoia as to be useless. I suppose being related to the Black Rose of Paliano left him with a skewed opinion of the world. But yes, Jamira, my owls have been following you."

"Why?"

"I need to know how you're all settling in, what's working and what's not, what might upset or harm you. Whether any of the other students are giving you any grief." Kasmina sounds utterly calm, unruffled by this confrontation. "I need to *understand* you."

"Because we're your 'embers.'" Jamira can't keep the bitterness from her tone.

For the first time, Kasmina looks surprised and almost interested. She shifts in her seat, turning to fully focus on Jamira. "Yes."

"Do you think we could still—" Bile floods Jamira's mouth, and she swallows it back before she continues. "Could still be Planeswalkers someday?"

"You had the potential before the worlds changed. You may yet. I don't have enough information to know yet."

"But Planeswalker sparks can be extinguished."

Kasmina's face twists, bitterness washing the surprise away. "They can. I don't know how it was done. People have used rituals and terrible magics to steal sparks before, but I never studied those paths."

"If my ember catches fire, can you fix it?"

"Fix what, Jamira?"

"I don't *want* to be a Planeswalker. My father was a Planeswalker, and it ruined us. He wasn't even home when my mother died. My sister and I had to tell him he was a widower when he finally returned to us. The Blind Eternities have taken *everything* from my family. I will not serve them."

Kasmina looks at her with something that may be pity or may be disappointment. The two are such close kin at times. "You want me to extinguish your spark, should it ignite."

"Yes."

"That's not possible."

"Why not? It happened to yours, didn't it?"

Kasmina goes very still, as still as one of her owls. Then she blinks, again like one of her owls. Finally she says, "That wasn't very kind, Jamira."

"Kindness and the truth aren't always the same thing."

"I suppose not. If—*if*—your spark ignites, I will do what I can to help you control it. But it might be better if . . . no."

"If what?"

"No, it was a foolish thought. I'll help you."

"I want to know what you would call 'foolish,'" says Jamira.

Kasmina sighs. "I belonged to an organization that had been studying Planeswalker sparks for centuries. There have been instances of sparks being transferred or stolen. There have even been recorded times when someone's ember was harvested from them and used for a work of great magic."

Jamira stands straighter. "You mean I might not need to spark at all?"

"Yes, but—it would be very dangerous, Jamira. You might not survive the removal. Think of your sister. Would you choose to leave her alone?"

"She finally has our father," says Jamira. "She would not miss me."

"If I were to agree to do this, I would need your help."

"Anything," says Jamira.

"Anything?" Kasmina taps her chin with one finger. "Well,

anything might be enough. You can't tell your peers about this. The ritual won't allow me to help them all."

Jamira snorts. "Eula would be delighted to spark. She'd think it made her special. Alandra would just hope it brought her closer to the storms."

"You're disdainful of the others."

"Not all of them. Kequia is brilliant. If anyone could make good use of a Planeswalker's spark, it would be her."

Kasmina makes a noncommittal sound. "I'll need to gather some information about you and your home plane, and about the way your embers are reacting to the mana here on Arcavios. You'll come to see me every week, and I may have tasks for you."

"Anything," says Jamira again. "I can't tell you how much this means to me. To be free of this fear . . ."

Kasmina looks at her, seeing the tension in her eyes. Jamira has been afraid of the Blind Eternities since long before she was afraid of the Phyrexians, or anything else. "Indeed," she says. "My first task is this: find something you enjoy here on campus. A club or a student organization, join the newspaper for all I care, just something that will explain your absences in a way that satisfies the others. You need to look like you belong here. Can you do that for me?"

Jamira looks unsure but nods. "I can try," she says.

"Excellent. Come see me tomorrow. I'll have your next task ready for you then." She turns back to her desk, Jamira apparently dismissed.

Jamira waits for a few moments to see whether she can ride out the silence, then turns and walks away, recognizing the dismissal. She looks back only once. Kasmina is focused on her papers and doesn't seem to notice her.

Jamira slips away.

She walks down the hall in contemplative silence, stomach churning. She didn't realize how afraid she was of her own ignition until she was offered a way to be free of it. The relief is so profound that it feels like sickness.

Stepping outside into the bright sun is dizzying. She pauses, blinking back the stinging brilliance of the light, and barely hears the shout from off to one side. She turns her head to see a silver-and-diamond serpent made of interconnected geometric shapes flying toward her as if flung by an unseen hand, and she reacts without thinking, putting her arms up and plucking the wayward beast out of the air. It wraps around her wrist, turning its triangular head to look at her as its diamond tongue tastes the air, and she stares at it in rapt fascination. It's beautiful. It's like a poem written in mathematical perfection, and the sunlight dazzles on its scales, rendered less burning by contact with the spectacular, impossible reptile.

A group of students is running toward her, some in the uniforms of Quandrix mage-scholars, others in the undecided colors of her fellow first-years. They're clamoring as they come, clearly in the middle of some intensive act of sporting.

The first to approach is a tall elf in Quandrix colors. "Jamira, right?" he asks. "Can I get our fractal back? That was an incredible catch."

"Why were you throwing the fractal?" asks Jamira. The snake is warm around her wrist. She doesn't want to let it go.

"Mage Tower practice," says another student, a round-featured owlin without a visible college affiliation.

Jamira frowns. "That's the game where you steal and protect mascots, yes?"

"Yes," says the elf. "Based on that catch alone, you should try out. If you want to join us for a while, we can teach you the rules while we set up a scrimmage."

"Join you . . ." says Jamira. The coincidence of Professor Kasmina ordering her to find something she enjoys right before she stumbles into a group of student athletes seems enormous, but these are Quandrix players; they'll have been running mathematical probability fields to keep their game moving forward. If those fields have found her, well, who is she to argue?

"I think I would like that," she says, and extends the hand that holds the fractal toward the elf.

"Excellent," he says, and smiles, and the game and the day both go on.

NINE

LAUNDRY DAY

The weekend passes in a whirl of homework and exploring the campus, catching up on sleep and trying everything offered in the dining hall. By the time the new week rolls around, it's like they've been at Strixhaven forever, like their homes and pasts are distant dreams. Oh, the fading novelty doesn't make things easier—there are still unexplained glares in the dining halls and on the green, still owls watching them from the walls.

There is no further graffiti in the antechamber, but someone sets fire to several sacks of pest dung on the outside doorstep, creating a smell that lingers for most of the weekend. Someone else throws a rock at Kequia while she's walking back to the dorm, and Jamira asks her not to go anywhere alone. From the way Segante has been eyeing Eula, he's close to making the same request. Alandra hasn't reported any direct harassment, but her scales seem duller and her steps are slower; the atmosphere of the campus is wearing on her. She only really perks up in her room, where she can relax into the water's embrace and let the pressure go.

Eula worries, but there's not much she can do, and Alandra is a big girl: she'll ask for help when she needs it. She busies herself with her own distractions, finding the gathering places favored by the Silverquill students she hopes to join, finishing her essays, and answering cutting murmurs with sharp-eyed looks that promise trouble for anyone who tries to push their luck.

And so, hour by hour, the weekend comes to an end, and classes resume, the first day of the week marching ever on. They know where they're going now, paths becoming familiar, classrooms becoming less intimidating. Thrown rocks or no, it's less disorienting to go off alone, and so the end of classes finds Eula walking back to the building on her own.

She follows the path to the dorm, watching an owl come in for a landing on the roof. It's hard not to take the owls as a sign that Professor Kasmina is spying on them for some reason, and if their biggest advocate at this school doesn't trust them, do they really have a future here? Add that to the looks she's been getting from some of the other students and, well . . .

She's not used to being a social outsider. It was difficult in the Caldaia, but here, it's like standing on the other side of a window while the biggest and most beautiful ball in existence happens only a few feet away. She wants to be in that room. She wants them to trust and welcome her.

She sighs and opens the dormitory door. She has homework to do, and her father is going to expect her to start sending him information soon, beyond the simple campus map she slipped into the weekend mail. She can't just stand around moping because the other students don't invite her to their parties yet. They will, once they realize what they're missing. They'll all rue the day they turned their backs on Eula Blue.

She's starting to question Dina's claim of other students living in this building: she's never seen any of them, and she doesn't see them now. The halls are empty, silent save for the echo of her own feet. She welcomes the privacy, even as she can't imagine why Dina would lie about this.

But then, Dina may have been lying about a lot of things. For all her claims about first-year students being uncommitted and able to go in any scholastic direction they like, it's painfully evident the five of them are being encouraged toward specific colleges. That those colleges mostly agree with the ones they would have chosen on their own is a pleasant coincidence. That, or the project that flagged them as potential students was even more invasive than Eula likes to consider, and so she does her best to put it from her thoughts entirely, focusing on her studies.

In addition to sharing Arcavios History with all four of her dormmates, she shares a Theory of Magical Poetry class with Alandra and a Practical Shield Magic class with Jamira. She and Kequia sit near each other in Introduction to Diplomacy, where Kequia asks armor-piercing questions about local customs and manners, identifying flaws in the logic of their fellow students with remarkable poise. Segante has a biology course rather than poetry, and a flower-arranging course that doesn't seem to fit into any specific college but pleases him well enough.

His flower-arranging course is in the late afternoon, when they have the widest array of blossoms available, and so it's something of a surprise when Segante knocks on her dorm-room door about an hour after she locks herself inside to copy a set of translation spells from the student handbook to send back to her father. She startles at the sound, dripping ink onto her scroll, and shoots the door a sour look, ready to aim a few sharp-edged words at whoever has dared to interrupt her.

"It's Segante," calls a familiar voice. "Can you come out? I need to talk to you about something."

He sounds cagey and uncomfortable, two emotions she's grown used to from her Fioran classmate. Eula rises from her desk and pauses to wave a hand over the watery wall of Alandra's side of the room, turning the surface briefly mirrored. Her hair remains perfectly presentable for receiving company. Alandra is off on her own undisclosed errands, and so Eula doesn't need to check whether her roommate is decent before moving to open the door.

Segante's hair is in disarray, falling to almost cover one eye, and he looks at Eula with an odd sort of pleading in his expression. "I need your help," he says. "I remember what you said about having no local currency. I can compensate you for your assistance."

"You have local currency?"

"Of course. I brought a bag of gems and gold coins from home. They convert easily enough, especially if I take them to the Quandrix professors. To them, a small garnet is an off-plane artifact and worth more than its weight in any precious substance you'd care to name."

"You know we're friends, right, Segante?" asks Eula, trying to shake off the image of someone casually picking up a bag of gems and gold. The relatively high social status of her dormmates is something she does her best to disregard, for the sake of her own peace of mind. "Friends don't have to pay for favors."

"Perhaps not where you come from, but on Fiora, a friend uncompensated is a friend whose tongue may be for sale," said Segante. "I need your help, and I need your silence, so allow me to pay you, if you please."

"All right. What are you paying me for?"

"Your clothing, while mended and sometimes clearly secondhand, is always impeccably clean. I've seen you wear that white skirt of yours more than once, and it would stain if you even thought too hard about sitting on the grass."

"This is true," admits Eula.

"I was not . . . encouraged to learn the art of laundry as a child," says Segante, discomfort growing. "My clothing needs to be cleaned and returned to wearable condition, and of the five of us, you seemed the most likely to have the skills to do so."

"I'd feign offense at you assuming that I know how to wash velvet because I'm a girl, but all Jamira's clothing is designed to be cleaned with fire, I think Alandra grows her clothes from kelp, and Kequia . . . well, I'm pretty sure she does her own laundry, but she'd ruin velvet as soon as look at it. Sure. I'll help."

This doesn't lift Segante's expression. If anything, it turns more dour. "How much do I need to pay you not to mention a word of what you see to anyone else?"

"It's laundry, Segante. How many secrets can laundry have? And don't give me that 'This is how we do things on Fiora' routine again. There have to be *some* chores that aren't veiled in secrecy, or there's no way anyone does the dusting."

Segante sighs heavily. "I still need your guarantee."

"All right, fine. I won't go mentioning your unmentionables, all right? Now, what needs washed?"

"Virtually everything," says Segante, and backs away from the door, letting her exit. He leads the way across the foyer to his room, and Eula brightens. Segante hasn't allowed any of them inside his private quarters since they arrived, and while she knows it can't be *that* exciting—it's a dorm room like any other, no matter how many modifications it may have required—it's still exciting to get a glimpse of something that's been kept secret for this long.

The room is small and square, like the one she shares with Alandra, although the absence of a submerged grotto makes it seem larger, big enough for a desk, a wardrobe, and a generously sized bed, as well as a rounded table inlaid with stone patterning. The walls and angles have been softened in a manner she recognizes, although with strong, geometric lines of brick rather than the swooping, organized filigree of her room's plaster and trim; the rug is plush and slate blue, like a mirrored lake. Vases of carefully arranged flowers sit on almost every flat surface, and a pile of clothing occupies the end of the bed.

Eula stops, frowning. "Do you not have a laundry hamper?"

"A . . . what?"

"Have you ever done your own laundry?"

"At home in my father's house, we had people for that. I would leave my clothes discarded on the floor, and they'd come back washed and pressed and ready to be worn again. I thought at first that the school would have some service to do the same, but as the days passed, I realized my mistake."

Eula feels a surge of pity. She doesn't normally like it when boys pretend not to understand tasks like laundry. Laundry isn't gendered, and pretending not to know how it works is just a way to get out of doing their fair share. Her father was the one who taught her how to use bleach without destroying her clothes. But Segante seems to have come from a household where servants took care of all those things. It's not about being a boy. It's about being some sort of noble.

"There was a hamper in the closet of my room," she says. "Can you check yours and see if there's one here, too? It'll be easy if I don't have to carry everything by hand, and I doubt you want your undergarments scattered along the hall."

The laundry room is located at the front of the building, past the main entrance, down a side hall that doesn't connect directly to any dorm rooms. It helps keep the noise down, Eula supposes. The machines are similar to the ones they use in Capenna, marvels of technology that agitate and rinse the clothes without the tedium of doing it all by hand. Laundry seems to be fairly universal from plane to plane. Alandra, whom she really does suspect of hand-growing her clothing every morning, had never seen a washing machine before she went with Eula to the laundry, and she says that on Shandalar, clothing is washed by beating it against wet rocks and rinsing it in streams. Kequia knew what a washing machine was, and even how to operate one, but not how to separate her colors. Really, it's a wonder these people aren't just wandering around naked.

Segante finds a hamper in the closet and helps Eula gather his clothing from the bed and floor, piling it into a tangled heap inside the basket. He carries the hamper as she leads him to the laundry, which he eyes as if it might be some sort of venomous snake preparing to strike at him.

"First, we have to sort the colors and pull out any fabrics that need extra care," says Eula, digging into the hamper. She doesn't notice the way Segante flinches, or how firmly he turns his eyes away. She has a task to accomplish, and while she's happy to both help a friend and make a little money, she doesn't get that much free time. She needs to get back to her transcription so she can start on her homework. The last thing she wants to do is fall behind when she's representing all of New Capenna, and when all of her hopes and dreams for the future are riding on her performance.

She's always done well under pressure, and so she keeps digging, fishing out velvet vests and jewel-toned sashes to go into their respective piles. Most of Segante's shirts are white or off-white, and those go into their own pile, along with a surprising assortment of thick cotton wrappings and undervests, tailored to button so tightly that it's a miracle he can catch his breath at all.

She pauses with one of those vests in her hands, rubbing her thumb across the small, flat button at the top and frowning. She's seen something like this before. Where has she seen something like this?

Finally, in a calm voice, she says, "When I was in my fifth year at school, one of my classmates wanted more than anything to be a newsboy. I don't know why anyone would want that—it's dangerous work, carrying the news between neighborhoods, always yelling and making a spectacle of yourself, just so you can bring home a few extra coins at the end of the day. Most of what you'll make goes to the families who own the printing presses, and if you carry the wrong paper into the wrong territory, you can get yourself into an awful lot of trouble."

"Is that so?" asks Segante, his voice mild as anything.

"Do you have newspapers on Fiora?"

"I've never heard the term before, so I'm assuming not."

"Broadsheets, maybe? Declarations from the local government, news about what's been happening where and when and to whom, postings about job fairs . . ."

"Ah. No. We have printing presses, but the Queen would never tolerate such a potentially uncontrollable means of making her will known. City criers suit her much better, and they know that to deviate from her decrees is to risk a slit throat or a stolen tongue."

Eula lifts her head and blinks at him. "Newsboys get rolled for their bank sometimes, but nobody dies. Usually. Um. I don't think this story translates well to Fiora."

"Yet you started telling it. Please, continue."

"Oh. So this classmate of mine really wanted to be a newsboy. Thought it was about the best job anyone could hope for without joining a Family, and that takes years on years of work and skill and effort. But there was one big problem."

"What's that?"

"It's in the name of the job, isn't it? News*boy*. And everyone who looked at my classmate thought he was a girl. So he got a cousin of his who worked as a seamstress to make him these real clever vests that kept everything compressed the way he needed it to be, but not compressed enough to hurt him, and he went and he got to be a newsboy, just like he'd always wanted." Eula tries to focus on the laundry, not wanting to see

Segante's face as she lays out what she thinks she knows. "He survived the Invasion, as far as I know. Most of the newsboys did. They're nimble, and they know the city more than just about anyone."

"And this boy, this classmate of yours, you don't think less of him?"

"Should I?" Eula shrugs. "Nobody gets to choose how they're born, but we choose how we live, and who we grow into being. He knew who he was, he chose it, and he's been shaping himself the right way ever since. He told me once he'd only need the vests until he was done growing. After that, there's spells and surgeries and such that can help him sort himself out."

"A good alchemist—or essence-witch, if you're using the local term—can make potions that help even before a deeper correction can be made," says Segante, formal as always. "A flask in the morning, another at night, and a properly fitted compression vest, and everything is as it should be."

"But a man who doesn't want his secrets spread around might not want people discussing his laundry," says Eula. She looks at Segante, meeting his eyes and not looking away as she says, "A pity there's nothing interesting about it."

That would have been laying it on a bit thick with almost anyone else, but with Segante and his tendency to assume that every hand holds a knife ready to be buried in his back, it's better to be direct. When she doesn't blink or waver in her steady gaze, he relaxes slightly, some subtle tension leaving his neck and jaw.

"Thank you," he says. "You'll have your money tomorrow."

"Don't worry about it," she says. They're alone in the

laundry room, and so she risks another question: "Are you still considering enrolling in Witherbloom when the year's finished?"

"If they'll have me," he says, somewhat stiffly.

"I never pictured you as the type who'd want to go to school in a swamp."

"Nor did I take you for the sort to seek a stage," he says with a quick, rare smile. "We're all filled with surprises, are we not?"

"I suppose. I just didn't expect you to waste that silvered tongue of yours on flowers." She's pushing the bounds of safe teasing, and for a moment she's afraid she's gone too far.

Then his smile becomes a true grin. "Flowers speak their own language, and I'm reasonably fluent," he says.

Eula frowns, perplexed. "I wish I understood you better. I like you, but you confuse me."

He shrugs. "Confusion is also its own language. My father says I'm a liability. I have the potential to be a great healer, or an even better killer. If I pick healer, I'm weak. I'll never sit on a throne or wear a crown either way, but I'll still be used by people with the strength it takes to do those things. If I pick killer, I'm a threat. My aunt will never let me live. So he sent me to school on another plane of existence, where I can't bring shame or draw a target on our family."

Eula's frown deepens. "That sounds *awful*."

Segante looks at her, expressionless, so close that she can smell the faint perfume of dreamwaste flowers from his skin, stronger than the soapy smell of the laundry. "I thought we weren't here to make cultural judgments."

"We're not. It's just . . . it sounds so *lonely*."

"I have less cause to miss my family than any of the rest of us do. Perhaps I'm the least lonely of our motley lot."

"But—" she begins. He's already walking away, leaving her alone with his laundry and her unanswered questions.

Unanswered for now, anyway. This is a school. Why are they here, if not to learn everything they need to know?

TEN

STUDY HALL

Adjusting to the rhythm of life at Strixhaven is surprisingly easy after the first few weeks have passed and the issue of Segante's laundry has been dealt with. All of them have their weak spots, some as mundane as laundry, others as fantastic as Kequia's genuine inability to take out the trash. Her psychometry makes a simple chore into a form of torture. So they help each other, and they make each other better.

And there are benefits to supporting one another. Helping Segante leaves Eula with money in her pocket, which has been a nice change; money means she can afford snacks between meals, and to begin upgrading her wardrobe at the student store. Not that it's easy to find things without college affiliations already displayed on breast or sleeve, but still, being able to supplement what she brought from home has been an incredible improvement to her quality of life.

After spending a month watching Eula get increasingly unhappy about her hair, Alandra returns to the dorms after a sculpture class with a taciturn Prismari upperclassman who brings his own scissors and exclaims with delight over the lack of any need for bleach before sitting Eula down and reshaping her shaggy locks into something she's not ashamed to be seen with in public. He refuses payment but slips her a piece of paper with his dorm number on it and tells her to come see him in a month for a touch-up.

Eula watches him go, euphoric and trying to keep her attention off the mirror, then whirls to gape at Alandra.

"Do you *have* haircuts on Shandalar?" she asks.

The mermaid shrugs, sitting on the edge of her desk and resting most of her weight on her hands. Her scales have continued to dull; they barely glitter in the room's diffuse light. "We have humans on Shandalar, and they must cut their hair," she says. "I never spent much time around them. I didn't realize it *grew*. That must be very inconvenient for you."

"Do your fins not . . . grow?"

"Very slowly," says Alandra. "They'll be a few feet longer when I'm fully grown, but if they grew like your hair does, I'd be stepping on them, and that would hurt. Doesn't it hurt to cut your hair?"

"No," says Eula. "Hair isn't alive. It's like fingernails. Or scales. Does it hurt when you lose a scale?"

Because she does, a few every morning. Eula has to be careful not to step on them when she gets out of bed, gleaming, jewel-toned razors that they are. Alandra shakes her head.

"Not at all," she says. "So your hair is like my scales, and you don't have anything like my fins?"

"Sounds about right."

"Do you think they might have a book on comparative merfolk and human biology at the Biblioplex?"

It's an innocent enough question, but it makes Eula sit up straighter, a guilty shiver running across her skin. "We could go find out," she says. "I have the rest of the afternoon free."

"Oh, I wouldn't want to waste your time."

"It's not a waste. I like learning things." Eula glances in the mirror one last time as she rises, resisting the urge to get out her bobby pins and start putting her curls exactly where she wants them. "So come on. Let's go learn something."

Alandra follows willingly, and they exit the dorm into a beautiful afternoon. The air is rich with the smell of blooming snarlflowers and the soft, constant crunching of the pests working to prevent them from tearing down the buildings. In the distance, Eula hears cheering from the Mage Tower field— there was no cross-college game on the schedule for today, which means Jamira is probably there, charging through the endlessly confusing rules of the game to bring her team of mixed and undecided students another well-earned victory.

Eula sighs, gesturing toward the field with a quick motion of her head. She doesn't do anything so gauche as look directly toward it, only keeps her pace regular and her arm hooked through Alandra's.

"How does she balance practice and academics *so well* when I'm practically *drowning* in schoolwork?"

She can't quite keep the frustration out of her voice, and Alandra laughs. "Why do you say 'drowning' like it's a bad thing?"

"Because—oh, come on, Al, you know humans need air. Don't be such a law-abiding citizen."

That just makes Alandra laugh harder, bending almost double and hanging on to Eula as a way of keeping herself upright. Orestes launches himself off of her shoulder, darting away to snap butterflies out of the air and swallow them whole. He's a skilled hunter: Eula's seen him take down songbirds on the wing, making her suspect Alandra feeds him more out of habit and kindness than any sort of necessity. Or maybe food is a way to keep the little drake from deciding he could do better on his own. She's still not entirely clear on the relationship between the two, and Alandra's fumbling attempts to explain haven't done much to help.

Clusters of students are everywhere, speaking in small groups, walking to classes, sitting on benches and at picnic tables. She hears snippets of a dozen different academic arguments, some more serious than others. A cluster of merfolk in Prismari colors wave to Alandra, who waves back, while a small group of Silverquill third-years offer Eula a collective approving nod. She stands a little straighter, pleased to have been noticed without censure, and keeps walking.

They're fitting in better as time passes. It's been more than a week since the last blatant display of hostility, when a Witherbloom student "accidentally" spilled a jar of rotting fish entrails on Alandra's bag and she had to go back to the dorms for a replacement before the smell drove them all away. They've made inroads with their chosen colleges, finding their footing on shifting ground.

Jamira has seemed anxious about something, watching the skies and staying behind at the end of their group history class, but Kequia will figure it out, whatever it is. They've never discussed it, but the roommates have silently agreed to take care of one another, as much as they can. Segante takes care of himself, and he doesn't seem to mind.

The dome of the Biblioplex doesn't appear so much as it resolves out of the rest of the campus, like a mist is clearing and allowing them to see what's been there all along. There has to be some sort of subtle magic involved, keeping the massive building and the construction equipment surrounding it from dominating the area. The Biblioplex is still and will always be the center and heart of the university, it's just not so crushingly visible that no one can focus on anything else. It will be breathtaking once the repairs from the Invasion are finished. It's breathtaking *now*, in a shattered, sprawling sort of way.

Activity picks up the closer they get to the Biblioplex, but the great library is massive enough that it never feels crowded. People use the entrances that put them closest to what they're looking for, heading up wide marble stairways and down narrow paths cut into the earth. Each entrance, once reached, is a tall arch that mirrors the shape of the strange stone formations that Professor Kasmina says dot the plane. Eula can see the resemblance to the arch she spotted when they first arrived.

Inside, the air is cool and dry, rich with the smell of ink, paper, and book bindings—cloth and leather and whatever other materials have been used to preserve this impossible collection of riches. Bookshelves line the walls from floor to unreasonably high ceiling, which is vaulted in a way that creates near-perfect acoustics, muffling voices unless they're raised, and then amplifying them throughout the surrounding area. Library attendants and students move from place to place, books in hand, while constructs similar to the campus guides push carts of materials needing to be reshelved. Even after several dozen visits, it remains the most beautiful thing Eula has ever seen.

Although not entirely unscathed. Entire sections of the catalog are missing or misfiled, meaning that finding what you're looking for can become more of an adventure than it's supposed to be. And some of the older, more powerful books have opinions about who gets to read them, opinions they express by growling, or biting, or just trying to flee deeper into the stacks when they don't think a student is ready for the material they contain. Eula could do without opinionated folios trying to bite her fingers because she wants to know more about the history of the school.

Presumably it gets better after you join a college. Deans can give passes to areas of the stacks that would otherwise be off-limits, and the books seem to know their scent. She's seen them settle down and turn docile when someone shows them a slip of paper that says everything's allowed.

She'll have one of those slips of paper one day. They all will, and then they'll be able to come and go without feeling the need to move as a group.

Alandra sets a hand on her shoulder. "I'm going to go see if the librarians have found the book on storm sculpture that I was looking for last week. I'll send Orestes to find you when I'm done," she says.

"All right," says Eula. "I'm going to head deeper and see if I can find the merfolk biology texts." Part of why she likes coming to the Biblioplex with Alandra is that the storm sculptor's studies are so dissimilar to her own, there's never any expectation that they'll stay together. Kequia views trips to the Biblioplex as shared study dates, and Jamira is similar, while Segante is secretive enough to make Eula feel like she's imposing. Alandra, though, is perfect: a companion for the walk and then an absence once they arrive.

Eula starts down the nearest aisle, only to make a sharp left and proceed deeper into the ancient, impossible building.

Geometry doesn't seem to mean much inside the Biblioplex. Neither does architecture: some of the halls she passes through are tall enough to have their own weather patterns, windstorms and clouds caught high overhead with no sign of a ceiling. The interior damage has long since been repaired, books reshelved and corridors restored. It's probably obvious what's been patched if you were here before the Invasion, but to her eyes everything is equally old and equally impressive.

She continues onward until she reaches the edge of a small lagoon, complete with dock. There, she unties a small coracle boat and climbs inside, leaning over to tap the surface of the water with one finger. A ripple fans out, becoming a series of concentric circles that are still echoing outward from that initial contact when the boat starts to move.

This isn't the only body of water inside the Biblioplex; there's at least one river, and a series of decorative ponds, all of them crossable through various means, all of them odd things to keep in a building full of books. But as the librarians don't seem to be alarmed by the water—or by the fish that Eula swears she's seen swimming around in some of the ponds—it's not her place to question.

The Biblioplex is a magical library at a magical university, filled with books of magic that can't help distorting the reality around them in a variety of ways, some subtle, some less so.

Eula has heard stories about students getting lost in here every term, and she has to wonder whether their fatal mistake was asking too many questions about how the building could possibly function. The Biblioplex isn't alive, but anything with this many books and this much magic inside its walls must have opinions of its own, and she doesn't think she'd like having people walking around in her guts wondering how she can possibly exist.

The air cools as the boat carries her across the water to the other side, where she ties her coracle to the small dock and rises to walk even deeper into the near-endless stacks. There are still researchers around, library aides pulling books and frazzled upperclassmen trying to find the books they need to finish out their term papers, but their numbers have dropped dramatically. She heads for the shelf she's been frequenting over the last several weeks, ever since she realized mage-scholars are effectively unsupervised during most of their hours in the library. Still, her heart beats too fast as she takes down a book on the principles of ink-casting written by one of the first Silverquill mages. It's a simple technique, almost laughably so, and yet they have nothing like ink-casting in New Capenna. It's entirely new knowledge.

It's currency.

The book has been an educational read. She's learned a lot already, and it's been helping her pay the true cost of her tuition. She was allowed to leave her city, her home and her family, all because of the things she could offer them in return. She needs to pay. Her father's last letter was clear about *that*. He's had questions from the Family about why he let her go, and while she's been sending back notes from her classes, that isn't enough to count as true repayment. It's time for him to start proving to his masters why letting a budding young shield mage leave the plane was the right decision.

She opens the book to the appropriate spot and places it on the nearest study table before she removes a folded sheet of paper from her pocket, unfolds it, and lays it flat across the pages. No one comes to see what she's doing. No one's even in this section of the stacks. Still, her heart continues to hammer as she pulls a sewing needle from the cuff of her blouse and pricks her finger. A bead of blood wells up, bright and ripe as a redberry, and she begins to whisper the incantation for a basic transcription spell.

The blood rises from her finger, darkening to become as black as proper ink, then splashes down across the paper, becoming a perfect copy of the text beneath it. It dries as it goes, so that when the single drop is expended, her newly duplicated document is ready to fold and return to her pocket.

She glances guiltily around as she does. She's not breaking any rules—people copy books in the Biblioplex all the time, and the things that are considered truly secret are magically resistant to being duplicated, protected by spells she's not strong enough to understand as yet but that seem to be a combination of ink-casting and shield magic that she should eventually be able to untangle. Students have to be able to take notes, and sometimes taking notes means copying out entire pages. So she's not doing anything *wrong*.

Even so, she's not sure the rules about copying materials were intended to apply to copying them for someone else. And there's nothing in the rules as written about sending spells off-plane. She turns the page, pulls out another sheet of paper, and prepares to cast the spell again. Something rustles atop the bookshelf. She looks quickly up, searching for a sign that she's being watched, and finds nothing but books and rolled-up scrolls of parchment. She returns her attention to the book. Once she's duplicated the entire thing, she'll hand it off to Bricen, who's happy to take mail to meet the carriages as they pass through Arcavios.

Most students have to pay to send mail across the planes. For Eula and the others, their scholarships include the ability to send mail home, and they've all been taking advantage of it. She's not the only one who's been considering the ethics of copying library materials to send back to her home plane: she taught Segante the duplication spell last week, in exchange for a few extra coins. It's easier with him if she lets him pay her. He feels less indebted and thus friendlier when money changes hands.

Her father should be able to use this book to buy himself an audience with Mr. Spara, head of the Brokers, who's always looking for ways to streamline the immense amount of paperwork generated by a functional criminal empire. It may be enough to buy her father further into Mr. Spara's good graces, and thus soften the blow of Eula choosing another Family as her future.

She doesn't think this book is going to be enough to buy her freedom, but there are others, and she'll find them all if that's what she has to do.

Her relationship with her father has always been a fraught one. His delight at her first fragile shields quickly faded when he discovered that a surprising magical gift was not enough, in isolation, to bring him fully into the Family fold; after that, she was just another mouth to feed, an expensive one given the costs of her schooling and the social expectations of a girl in her position. He presented her to Falco Spara when she was eleven, and she sometimes wonders if her bone-deep desire to join the Obscura isn't partially fueled by her memory of that encounter, the way the powerful aven had looked at her, like she was a frightened animal for the consumption.

Mr. Spara has been expecting her since that meeting. Not enough to have provided her with tutors or encouraged her to complete her education, but enough that she's always known she'll belong to him, unless she finds her own way out. The Obscura are an escape worth running toward, and her father will never understand, and she's running anyway. It all begins with bribing Mr. Spara so thoroughly that he doesn't think he needs to fight to keep her. That he believes she's already his to have.

That rustle from above catches her attention again just before Orestes's screech of challenge splits the air and the little drake dives into sight, talons extended. He slams into the top of the shelf, where he's met by an unfamiliar screech, and as Eula watches, he harries a small brown owl from its hiding place, pursuing it out of sight, still shrieking. A few feathers drift down, verifying that she saw what she thought she saw.

Hastily, Eula shoves the book back under several others and the second sheet of paper into her pocket, hurrying away from the section and toward where she guesses she might find books on merfolk biology.

She's settled in a study nook when Orestes comes flapping back and settles next to her stack of books, whistling a cheery greeting. She rubs the top of his head with a fingertip. "Hey, buddy. Where's Alandra?"

He whistles again, and she hears footsteps approaching. Eula turns to smile at her roommate, who's clutching a biology text of her own. She sits in the first open chair, leaning over to peer at Eula's notes.

"Anything good?" she asks.

"Depends. Do you know what 'euryhaline' means?"

"Nope," says Alandra, and Eula laughs, and this is a normal day at college, this is normal life, they're just here to learn. Everything is normal.

Everything is fine.

ELEVEN

PARTNERS IN CRIME

There are plenty of books on merfolk biology in the Biblioplex, enough that Eula and Alandra both leave with spinning heads and inky fingers, having learned more than they ever wanted to know about the similarities and differences between their species. There was nothing specific to Shandalar merfolk, but there was enough about other types to give them a starting point.

"You okay?" Eula asks as they walk back into the dorm.

"I think I know what I'm going to do for my term paper in bio," says Alandra. "Maybe I can get extra credit if I send a list of questions to my father and ask him to explain how we compare to other merfolk across the Multiverse."

"I'm sure he'll love that," says Eula dryly.

Alandra laughs. "Sure, but he'll tell me if I ask nicely. Can you come bubble my notes for me?"

"In a little bit. I want to talk to Segante."

Alandra blinks. "About what?"

"Nothing important. Just leave them on your desk, and I'll bubble them up when I get back."

They're approaching the foyer. Alandra hesitates but finally nods and heads for their room.

"See you when you're done," she says, and ducks inside, leaving Eula to approach Segante's door alone.

She knocks and waits. He never answers quickly; sometimes she half assumes he's deactivating some elaborate booby trap before greeting visitors, other times she thinks he's just reminding them that his time matters so much more than theirs that he doesn't have to hurry on their behalf. Either way, she studies her nails as she waits, projecting an air of nonchalance. It won't make any difference, but it might make her feel a little better, and sometimes that's what matters.

When the door finally opens, she's managed to find a hangnail and is wishing she had a file with her. The creak catches her by surprise, and she looks sharply upward to find Segante watching her.

"Blue," he says. "Did you need something?"

"A moment of your time would be nice."

He steps into the foyer, pulling the door tight behind himself. "You shall have it."

"Great, very generous, thanks." She can't quite keep the harried edge out of her voice. "Have you seen anything suspicious recently?"

"You'll have to be more specific. We're on an unfamiliar plane, surrounded by strangers, and culturally completely out of our depths. Someone has vandalized our home. Someone else has thrown rocks, and one of them bounced off my window this morning. Everything is suspicious."

"Wait—someone threw a rock at your window?"

Segante waves her concern away. "It didn't break the glass. We all know that some on this campus would prefer we not be here. Can we focus on your question?"

"Fair enough, I guess. Have you seen owls? Owls during the day, following you?"

"Only in history class." He blinks. "How do you mean?"

"I was just at the Biblioplex with Alandra. Orestes attacked an owl that was perched in the stacks, watching me."

"Were you researching something you shouldn't have been? Looking up naughty secrets that didn't belong to you?"

"No," says Eula, perhaps a bit too firmly. Her ears burn red as she continues, "Just a book on ink-casting. I'm on the Silverquill study track, so the topic is completely within the expected for my studies. I wasn't breaking any rules."

"Then perhaps it was in the wrong place. Was it an owl or an owlin?"

Eula rolls her eyes. "I can tell the difference between a bird and a bird-person. It was an owl," she says.

"Then perhaps you speak to Professor Kasmina about it. It may have been one of hers."

"Why would she be watching me study?" Unless she knows Eula's been copying books to send back to her family and wants to gather evidence against her. But copying books is allowed, according to the student handbook, and the owls were present before she began her duplications. It was just the shock of seeing the owl inside the Biblioplex that made it stand out.

"I don't know," says Segante. "That's why you should speak with her, since presumably if she's been monitoring your library activities, she knows why she's doing it."

"Will you come with me?"

"I'm busy." He looks over his shoulder at the closed door to his room, then back to Eula. "If you don't want to go alone, find someone else who's willing to go with you."

"Alandra just got back," protests Eula. "She's going to want some time in her pool."

"We have two other dormmates, Blue, even if you seem to forget they exist half the time."

"You're not any friendlier than I am!"

"Yes, but I never pretended to be." Segante rolls his eyes and slips back into his room, leaving Eula alone.

Slowly, she turns to face Kequia and Jamira's door. It's true she doesn't hang out with them as often as she could. Outside of class and meals, she can't think of the last time she sought their company. Feeling vaguely guilty, she walks over and knocks, unsure how long she'll need to wait before she can decide they're not going to answer. It's just been . . . easier to spend time with Alandra, her roommate, and Segante, who she isn't sure is a friend but whom she has a relationship of sorts with, based on shared secrets and laundry days.

She's still trying to decide what she should do when the door opens and Kequia appears, the gold beads in her hair replaced by garnets in a dozen shades of red, orange, and honeyed amber. She looks briefly startled, then grins, teeth bright and lovely against dark skin. "Eula!" she says. "This is a nice surprise."

"Hi," says Eula awkwardly. "I need to visit Professor Kasmina, and I was wondering if you might be willing to come with me?"

Kequia looks even more surprised by the invitation, which

just makes Eula feel worse. "That would be great," she says. "I have some questions for her about the role of the Founder Dragons anyway, and I've been meaning to get over there. Let me get my coat."

The heat coming from the open door is intense enough that Eula can't imagine needing a coat, but she nods and waits patiently as Kequia ducks back inside. She emerges a moment later, shrugging into an overcoat of blue linen, still beaming.

"Let's go!" she says, stepping up next to Eula, and side by side, they leave the foyer for the hall, and the hall for the outdoors.

Time has been kind to the afternoon, rendering it crisp and cool, the air bright with diffuse sunlight and with the cheery chatter of passing students. Kequia adds her voice to theirs as she walks, rambling happily on about her classes and everything she's been learning about controlling her psychometry. Eula makes the appropriate listening noises, trying to follow the ins and outs of a school of magic that's entirely alien to her own. Not just Kequia's clear intent to pledge to Lorehold, but the entire methodology behind psychometry as an art. They're both wizards in their own way, but that doesn't mean they have anything in common.

It's a sobering thought, and one that carries her most of the way to the Building of General Historical Studies. It's never one of the busier spots on campus, and right now, it seems virtually deserted, the door unlocked and ajar but no sound drifting from the open windows, no sign that anyone might ever have walked here intentionally. Eula's breath catches, and she glances toward the clock tower, verifying that they're still within Kasmina's office hours.

They are, and so the pair of them continue inside. The building, as always, is quiet and cool; Eula can't remember ever seeing another student in the halls, although there are so many classrooms that she's sure some of them must be in use. Then again, empty classrooms are just one of the subtle reminders of why Strixhaven was desperate enough for students to begin looking off-plane. Expensive as Eula and her dormmates must be for the university, they're warm bodies, and a living reminder that Strixhaven remains secure, safe enough to protect the next generation of mages, whatever world they happen to be from. They are the hope of the future, and that makes them worth coddling, at least a little bit.

Kequia starts walking faster once they're out of the direct sunlight, while Eula slows to consider her steps, letting the other girl pull ahead. Kequia stops, a quizzical expression on her face before she raises one hand, fingers curled into a fist.

"What—" begins Eula.

Kequia shushes her, then motions for her to come forward, slowly, almost creeping toward the door to Professor Kasmina's classroom.

As they get closer, Eula hears voices. One, indistinct accent and all, belongs to Professor Kasmina. The other is unfamiliar, female, mellow and cultured, with the ghost of an accent that sounds almost like Kequia's own, Dominarian and distant and out of place here on Arcavios.

"—being unreasonable, Mina. You know this isn't the way."

"Who are you to tell me what the way is or isn't? You've already given up on any hope of recovery. We don't know this is forever. We don't know this is a permanent change."

"The omenpaths are stable. Dean Adrix says the math resolves the way he'd expect if they're going to endure."

"It doesn't have to stay that way."

"Mina, *enough*. The carriage routes run day and night through the Omenpaths, and Ravnica has all but made an industry of them."

"Ravnica makes an industry of everything. They're as bad as Kamigawa or Capenna like that."

Eula frowns, pressing closer to the wall as she listens.

"Cities are growing in Thunder Junction. Avishkar is hosting races across the planes. People, Mina. Real people have moved through the omenpaths to start new lives for themselves, in new places, and you'd destroy that, stranding them in unfamiliar places, for what? A theory, a prophecy, a dream?"

"I think you should go, Liliana. It's obvious we're not going to see things eye to eye today."

"Or ever," snaps the unfamiliar voice. The door of Professor Kasmina's classroom opens, and a tall, severe-looking woman in a high-collared, low-necked black gown emerges. Her hair is black, her skin is pale, and as she makes her exit, she turns to look directly at Eula and Kequia, a half-amused smile tugging at her lips.

"The professor will see you now," she says, and sweeps off down the hall, moving deeper into the building.

"Maybe we should just go," says Kequia, her voice very low.

"No," says Eula. "You said you wanted to ask about the Founder Dragons, and that woman says Professor Kasmina is here." She straightens and starts for the classroom, passing the frozen Kequia before she looks back and asks, "Well? Are you coming?"

Kequia makes an unhappy noise and hurries to catch up with her, the two of them standing side by side as Eula pushes the still half-cracked door fully open, revealing the classroom beyond. As always when Professor Kasmina doesn't need it to be something else, it currently shows a forested grove, the trees ripe with owls, the ground lush with grass. Of the professor herself, there is no sign.

"Professor Kasmina?" calls Eula carefully, stepping through the open door. "It's Eula and Kequia. We wanted to speak with you?"

One of the owls makes a disinterested sound. There is otherwise no answer from the moonlit forest.

"You said if we had any questions, we could come ask them between classes? Well, Kequia had some questions about the Founder Dragons, and I had some questions about your owls. She's not here, but I know Alandra has some questions about how the Founders relate to her drakes."

"Drakes and dragons are entirely different species; they may spring from a common ancestor and they may not, but to imply that they're the same is to imply that owlin and owls are the same thing, which would get you pecked to death in any reasonable flocking center," says Professor Kasmina, stepping out of the trees. Two owls accompany her, a large tawny owl on one shoulder and a heart-faced barn owl on the end of her staff. She looks weary, honey-blond hair snarled and eyes bright with exhaustion.

"Professor?" says Kequia. "Are you feeling all right?"

"Yes, yes, I'm fine," says Professor Kasmina, waving Kequia's concern away. "I had a late night, and since I didn't have any students after our morning class, I've been allowing myself the luxury of recovery. I'll be fine."

"Where were you?" blurts Eula.

"A new omenpath has been found to the south, and based on the description a Witherbloom student gave of the moths they caught near the opening, I was hoping it might lead to a place I currently don't know how to find my way back to."

"Oh." Eula is quiet for a moment, considering this. All of them know Professor Kasmina is a former Planeswalker. What must it have been like for her, to go from being a visitor in this world to being trapped here in an instant? Sure, the omenpaths have opened the Multiverse in a way it was never open before, but even as Eula couldn't come straight to Arcavios from Capenna, some planes may still be inaccessible, their omenpaths either unfound or unformed. If Professor Kasmina is following up on rumors about moths, she must be truly desperate to get somewhere specific.

It's horrible to think about being stranded with no means of going home, and Professor Kasmina's weariness makes a sudden terrible sense. Eula frowns sympathetically, looking at her instructor. As for Kasmina herself, she focuses on Eula, and after a moment, she asks, "Well?"

"Well?" echoes Eula.

"Well, you said you had questions. Did you come to ask them or just to start building anticipation for the moment in the future where you're *going* to ask them?"

"Oh." Eula shakes her head, recentering herself. She's not sure how to begin asking about owls, but Kequia comes to the rescue, stepping forward.

"The Founder Dragons," she says without preamble. "You told us they were born out of the Snarls formed when the original two planes collided. Does that mean they weren't created from the essence of the Ur-Dragon? If they're the first and only dragons on this plane, why aren't they considered Elder Dragons? If they were born from pure magic, are they dragons at all, or are they sort of elemental constructs that manifested as dragons for some reason?"

"Well, first, I wouldn't recommend wording it that way if you ever have the opportunity to speak to one of them directly," says Professor Kasmina, with a hint of amusement. "They're the first dragons born to this plane, they look like dragons, they act like dragons in every meaningful way, and all you'd do by making them question their nature is confuse and possibly annoy them. Do you want to confuse and annoy an ancient flying reptile with control over powerful magic and tacit ownership of one-fifth of the plane?"

"No," says Kequia quickly. "Not at all. I was just . . . wondering."

"Alandra's asked similar questions," says Eula. "She and her father can speak to drakes, like Orestes, and tell them what to do. She's wondered whether she might be able to talk to the Founders."

"The Founders speak the common tongue," says Kasmina. "No magic is needed to simply communicate with them. Does Alandra want to control the Founders? That might actually be interesting to watch, as long as you give me sufficient warning to have myself and my owls well away from here before you try."

"No," says Eula. "She just wondered whether it would be possible." This feels like the perfect opportunity to ask about the professor's owls, but she's not sure how to begin.

Professor Kasmina doesn't notice the unasked question but keeps going, following the conversation she thinks they're having: "Drakes and dragons are not the same species. As far as I'm aware, there are no drakes like Alandra's companion on Arcavios; something similar might exist closer to the sea, but the drakes this far inland are a very different variety, and I haven't made a full exploration of the plane."

Kequia frowns and speaks before Eula can say anything, asking, "Professor Kasmina, if you're not *from* Arcavios, and you haven't made a full exploration of the plane, why are you the one teaching our history course? Wouldn't it have been better to get somebody with more experience to take care of things?"

"Experience is the key word there. I've been here for quite some time, teaching introductory courses for Quandrix and for incoming students, but I didn't fully join the faculty until after the Invasion, when I woke up and discovered I was looking at a longer stay than I had originally intended. Because of this, I'm a paradoxical combination of established faculty and junior member, meaning I could be spared when we realized we'd need this class if we were going to integrate students from other planes. My ability to view the plane from the outside was seen as valuable: after all, it's hard for me to push an agenda when my agendas aren't related to the school, or to the lands around it. I don't want to plot against the Archaics or become the new Dean of Theory. So while I may need to read up in order to answer your questions sometimes, I'm considered more objective than anyone else."

"Huh," says Eula. "And the owls?"

"Common where I come from, and used by most mages

as a form of security system. My owls are quite interesting in their own right. I have species from several different planes in my parliament."

"Parliament?" asks Eula blankly.

"The collective term for a group of owls."

"We call a group of owls a 'wisdom' on Dominaria," says Kequia.

"Then I suppose you know I'm not from Dominaria," says Professor Kasmina.

"We knew that already," says Eula. "I was in the Biblioplex today, and I thought I saw one of your owls watching me."

"You probably did," agrees the professor. "They go where they like when I don't actually need them, and they know I have a special interest in your group, so they're likely to be hanging around. Honestly, I'm surprised this was the first time you spotted one of them. Did they bother you?"

Eula thinks uncomfortably of the way the owl screeched when Orestes drove it off. "No," she says. "And it wasn't the first time, either, just the most noticeable. So they're not reporting back to you all the time?"

"I have no interest in your collegiate assignations and politics," says Professor Kasmina. "I promise, my owls aren't spying on you."

Eula isn't sure she believes her, but she's not sure how to argue, so she shrugs and says, "Thank you for the explanation."

"Are we going to have an opportunity to meet the Founders in this class?" asks Kequia.

"No," says Professor Kasmina. "The deans of the colleges, yes, absolutely, and they'll all have their chance to make their little recruitment pitches and try to convince you that you should choose them above all the others. Not that recruitment pitches really matter that much, since none of you are suited for more than one or two colleges. Jamira, for example, would do terribly in Witherbloom, and I doubt she'd be able to pass the prerequisites, but she'll be able to sign up for them next term if she really feels like wasting her time. The five of you were selected for your potential and your predispositions, to try and keep things fair."

"You mean we're each supposed to be the cross-planar mascot of a different college, and you don't want to screw that up," says Eula mildly.

"Exactly," agrees Professor Kasmina. "So far, all of you have been falling neatly into the study paths I had projected for you. Admittedly, Eula and her roommate appear to have changed places, but it's endurable. Segante was always going to be a wild card, but even he's following the correct path."

Eula lifts an eyebrow. "Come again?"

"Fiora isn't as repressive and dangerous as he makes it out to be, but this may be the least pressure he's been under in his lifetime. It's only natural that he'd allow himself to relax a bit." Kasmina pauses. "Or did you mean yourself?"

"Yes," says Eula frostily.

"I had expected you to react to freedom from New Capenna's strict societal rules and the control of your parents by exploding into chaotic motion and sliding toward Prismari, while Miss Alandra was raised in a political family, if one slightly more prone to open bloodshed than the majority, and would have fit well within the halls of Silverquill."

"If you'll forgive me for contradicting you, Alandra has said she doesn't enjoy saying mean things to people, or trying to think of what the meanest things she could possibly say might be, and those seem to be half of the purpose of Silverquill," says Kequia. "I can't imagine she'd want to be graded on it."

"And I quite like my strict social rules. If I know the way everything is meant to be, I can work around it without getting into trouble," says Eula. "The obvious troublemaker gets caught. The subtle one doesn't."

"Which is why you'll be an excellent fit for Silverquill. People always change the plan. Segante may have more trouble in Witherbloom if he doesn't learn to stop answering offense with aggression," says Professor Kasmina. "Now, was that all, you two? Or did you want to ask more questions of the 'could get us eaten by irritated dragons' variety?"

"That was all," says Eula, touching her pocket lightly with the tips of her fingers. The professor didn't say anything about her illicit copying of library materials, and right now, that's what matters more than anything else.

"Then you may go. I need to feed my owls."

"Of course, Professor." Before today, Eula wasn't sure the owls were actually alive, not just magical constructs woven for the professor's amusement. She still smiles and nods respectfully as she starts backing toward the door, gesturing for Kequia to follow.

They exit to the hall, the stranger almost forgotten. They have their answers, or some of them, anyway, and it's time to continue onward into the waiting future.

INTO THE STORM

Alandra waits in her coral cove until she hears the bells ring the hour, marking the start of the next round of classes, before she peers cautiously into Eula's half of the room. She enjoys her roommate's company, but the human girl can be so focused on being a pleasant companion that it's uncomfortable, and she doesn't think she can take one more discomfort in this terribly dry, oppressive place.

Her skin itches. Her fins itch. Her *everything* itches, and she's not sure how much longer she can stand it. Everything is so *dry*. This landlocked world is not her own, and after most of a semester with only her room to provide her with something that feels like safety, she's ready to scream. Nothing she's heard of Witherbloom since arriving has made her feel like she would be happy there, but they control the only proper body of water she knows of at the school. It's not fair. She doesn't know what she'd do about that, though, if she were offered the chance: moving other people's coastlines isn't considered diplomatic, and she's here to be a credit to her family and her plane, not get into undertows of trouble.

As to Alandra and her dormmates, their curriculums are almost entirely different, although there is some overlap—enough that it remains convenient for them to take their meals together, breakfast every day before their class with Professor Kasmina, and dinner most nights, save on the ones where Segante's botany course has him gathering pollen from late-blooming snarlflowers or where Jamira is joining the rest of her astronomy class in drawing star charts from the living sky. Still, they have sufficient unity to function as a group when they need to, which is surprisingly frequently.

Alandra should have expected that, she supposes, should have considered that going to an entirely new *world* for her education would mean leaving herself as isolated as an island. She's studying Arcavios, but what she's learning is what Professor Kasmina thinks she needs to know: ancient history and the origins of empire, not modern slang and how people her age talk to one another. The bullies from Lorehold were more blatant than most, but she pays more attention to her surroundings than Eula thinks she does; she's seen the sour looks from other students on the quad, the way some people turn their backs and start talking very, very quickly when they see the trans-planar enrollees coming.

It doesn't hurt her the way it seems to hurt Eula and Segante. She'd think humans were just sensitive to that sort of thing, but Kequia doesn't seem to mind. No matter how sourly people look at her, she continues barreling from class to class, student handbook under her arm and a tsunami of questions nested in her mouth, ready to be spit rapid-fire at anyone who seems inclined to listen. Kequia is her own sort of storm, but not one Alandra can summon or control. She's not sure anyone can control Kequia, but she'd sure like to watch the attempt.

Besides, she has Orestes, and she has her dormmates. She doesn't need more than that. She can be as happy with a small pod as she would be with a larger one. She can.

She just wishes it weren't so *dry*.

Alandra rolls thoughtfully in the water, stretching languidly, then bobs up to the surface. Orestes chirps at her. She shows him her teeth, a quick flash of serrated edges and deadly points.

"Hello, Orestes," she says to the drake curled in his feathered nest. "I hope you didn't get into too much trouble in the Biblioplex."

He chirps again, uncurling from the nest and sliding into the water. He tugs one of her fins with his teeth, and she rolls after him. For a few minutes they play, as innocent as otters, a girl and her drake spinning through the water like a single shared current, unstoppable and wild.

Finally, Alandra stills, turning toward the transparent wall dividing their shared room. Eula doesn't have a class this hour; she's probably off with one of the others if not with a group of classmates Alandra doesn't know. Alandra almost envies her, how easily she keeps trying. They're all isolated in this new place, but Eula keeps pushing for social acceptance like it's something she can actually achieve.

They'll find it next year if they're all still here, Alandra's sure of that. Once they have a college affiliation to their names, they'll be able to fit into a crowd of like-minded individuals, people who have enough in common with them to form a community. She already knows where she's going, assuming they'll have her. Prismari speaks in storms, in the crackle of lightning and the sweetly bitter scent of rain. She'll be at home there, or as much as she can be anywhere but Shandalar.

If she wants to go home to Shandalar, she has to succeed here. She has to show her father that she's strong enough to be his heir, wild enough to sculpt the storms, and clever enough to charm the drakes over to her side. Orestes has never required any charming. Her father bartered his egg for her as a hatchday gift, and when he broke the shell, her face was the first he saw. He knows she's not his mother, is clever enough to know the difference between a merfolk girl and a brooding drake, but that initial impression has left him with an ingrained need to please and care for her. Alandra swims to the wall, and Orestes swims with her, his wings tucked tight against his sides so that he looks more like an eel or a sea serpent than a sky-born drake.

They both break out into the dry, and Alandra shudders, suddenly dryer than she had ever been before coming to this place. The spells maintaining her side of the room also keep the water locked inside their barrier, preventing her from damaging anything by accident. The same spell protects her homework from unintentional dampness, and she appreciates that more than she can say.

Orestes lands on her shoulder, wrapping his tail around her neck, and Alandra reaches up to almost idly scratch the back of his neck, fingers seeking out the small, flexible scales at the base of his skull.

"No class today," she says. "Think the Witherbloom students would let me borrow their swamp?"

Arcavios has an ocean: she knew that before she came here, as did her father, who made her promise not to go out into the open sea until she's been on the plane long enough to understand its possibilities and dangers. That means making friends with the merfolk she's seen around campus, none of whom have been inclined to talk to her when she's tried. She needs a bigger pool than her bedroom, needs to stretch her fins and *move*, but there are more options than a single ocean. Witherbloom has their swamp, which is vast and wet and appealing as the college that controls it will never be. She carries the seeds of neither growth nor death in her hands, and she wouldn't want them if they could be offered to her. But she could ask them if they'd mind a visit . . .

A hard knot of worry begins forming under her breastbone, drawing tight until it chokes her breath off, keeping her lungs from expanding properly. Alandra presses a hand against her chest as hard as she can, catching herself on the edge of her desk with her other hand. Orestes chirps in sudden alarm, then begins shoving his head against the line of her jaw, forcing her to acknowledge him. Alandra turns to look at him, feeling her field of vision begin to narrow to a thin and terrible point.

It feels silly, having a panic attack about the thought of asking the Witherbloom students if she can go swimming in their swamp, but she's been the way she is for her whole life, and she's lucid enough to recognize that the actual source of her panic is the semester as a whole: there's been too much change, too much difference, too many things that set her nerves ajangle. Her father says her anxiety was common for their species in the deep past. Back then, it was the ones with the sense to seek the shallows and flee from shadows who would survive long enough to see adulthood. She's more attuned to those fears than most are, anymore, but her ancestors came by their terror honestly.

Somehow, that doesn't make her feel much better.

Orestes nudges her jaw again, chirping a soothing string of notes. Alandra forces herself to focus on him, and he keeps chirping, creeling and crooning for her attention. In a few years, he'll be able to speak in her mind with words, the way the older drakes do. For now, he does what he can to focus her.

Bit by bit, the knot in her chest lets go, until she starts breathing again. Alandra gathers him in a close embrace, hugging him to her chest like a lifeline.

"I'm sorry, Orestes," she says, glad Eula wasn't here to see that. Her dormmates will see her have an attack eventually, she knows, but she'd prefer it happen when they've had more time to get to know her and won't react badly. She doesn't want their pity. She doesn't want their fear, either.

What she wants is a body of water large enough to cover her, one that's open to the air, not confined like her sleeping pool. She's not used to being boxed in like this, and with her legs weak in the aftermath of panic, she wants to swim freely until she feels like herself again.

But not in Witherbloom. Her mind shies away from thoughts of Sedgemoor.

"Kequia's handbook said there were lakes on the Quandrix and Prismari campuses. I haven't heard anything else about them, but I bet they're still there," she muses aloud to Orestes before shimmying out of her tunic and sliding back through the wall into the water. She kicks off once, swimming into the coral cave that is her bedchamber and dressing room. Once there, she feels around until she finds a clean tunic hanging from the wall, snatches it, and twists into it, allowing the water to ease the process. When she emerges again, she's clothed and ready to face the campus.

Orestes, who has waited patiently for her return, launches himself and reclaims her shoulder, crouching there and wrapping his tail around her neck as she leaves the room.

The public space she shares with her dormmates is empty, all four of them off on their own errands. Alandra exhales, relieved to be alone, however temporarily. Orestes on her shoulder, she heads for the bathroom and then onward to the door.

Outside, the pests are hard at work devouring the ever-growing snarlflowers, chewing them endlessly back. Students loiter on benches and grassy knolls nearby, and none of them give her a second look.

Alandra hesitates. "Quandrix or Prismari?" she asks Orestes. "The book said the Quandrix lake was a miracle of mathematical perfection, and the water is so clear it's like looking into open air. I like clear water. But then, it also said the Prismari lake was a blend of all different temperatures, from hot to cold, and that swimming there would be like streaking through a patchwork of sensations. I think Prismari is going to be my college. I'd like to know their lake."

Orestes chirps. Alandra nods as if she understands him.

"Prismari it is," she says agreeably, and starts walking.

Their dorm is relatively centrally located. She can walk from there to any of the colleges in a little over half an hour, and so she turns toward the Prismari campus, watching the students around her as she goes. Eula was so flustered by Segante wanting her not to go anywhere alone that she forgot to make the same request of Alandra, and Alandra hasn't bothered to remind her—and she's never really alone anyway, not with Orestes.

Most of the students she passes don't pay her any mind: the student body at Strixhaven is varied and chaotic enough that one little mermaid doesn't really stand out very much. Orestes is more of a curiosity here than she is, and most people have manners enough not to stare at other people's pets. He stays on her shoulder, and Alandra walks.

A cluster of students in Pathwarden uniforms stands to one side of the walkway. Alandra waves to them as she passes, earning several sharp looks in exchange. She's not sure why, and as none of them are beckoning her over to them, she supposes she's not going to find out just now. One of them she recognizes, an elf with long pink hair whose expression is as surprised as it is sharp. Veil. To her, Alandra nods and keeps on walking.

She's gone about another twenty yards when Orestes's claws tighten on her shoulder and she hears the sound of running feet behind her. Anxiety tries to spark in her chest again, bright and burning as the ember Professor Kasmina says should slumber there. She pushes it down with all her might, slowing as she turns.

There is Veil, running up behind her, cheeks flushed and hair in disarray. She slows as she sees Alandra turn, and by the time she catches up to her, she is perfectly composed.

"Alandra," she says by way of greeting. "How have you found your first semester?"

"I didn't have to go looking for it," says Alandra. "It came day by day, linearly."

Veil laughs.

Alandra blinks. It wasn't meant to be a joke, and she's not entirely sure Veil has taken it as one: something in her eyes is too calculating, like she's decided laughter would be the easiest way to get Alandra's attention in a positive way. Her father would say that anyone who has to drop a baited hook if they want to catch your eye is probably fishing for an advantage, and she suspects he'd be right, but he isn't here. He's home on Shandalar. She's here without him, and she needs to make friends where she can find them.

So she softens and smiles at Veil's laughter, letting the Pathwarden think she's been charmed. "I haven't seen you since we got here."

"I mean, you're a first-year student, and I'm a third," says Veil. "It makes sense that we wouldn't have classes together. Where are you heading?"

"I want to go swimming."

"Ah. So you're heading for Seichebasin. Do you have a campus sponsor?"

"A what? And I'm going where?"

"The lake on the Prismari campus. I'm just guessing, but the only other lake large enough to swim in that you could walk to is Fractal, over on the Quandrix campus, and you're going the wrong way for that."

"Oh! Yes, that's where I'm going. And what do you mean, a campus sponsor?"

"Seichebasin got its name because it's prone to nasty weather patterns that only happen on and around the water.

I'm guessing you can breathe underwater, but it's still a temperamental place. Since you're not Prismari, you'll need someone to go with you who can promise to keep you safe. Drownings are considered bad for school morale." Veil laughs, like she's never heard anything so silly in her life.

Alandra frowns, fins drooping. "Oh. I don't have one of those. I can ask some of the people in my classes tomorrow, I guess, but I don't know any of them well enough to know where their dorm rooms are. I can't go ask."

"You know me."

Alandra blinks. Somehow, it has never occurred to her that the Pathwardens would have college affiliations. "Really?" she asks.

"I'm not doing anything," says Veil with an easy shrug. "I could walk you to the lake and stay with you while you swim. Are you considering Prismari, then?"

"I am," says Alandra, suddenly shy.

"Then it's my duty as a mage-scholar to show you the best parts of our campus." Veil offers her arm. After a momentary hesitation, Alandra takes it, and they walk on toward the distant clouds of the Prismari campus and the promise of the lake.

Orestes hisses at Veil as they walk, huddling against Alandra's neck. Veil shoots him an inscrutable look and doesn't slow or stop.

Alandra flushes. "I'm sorry. He's not normally—I'm sorry."

"It's all right. He probably knows I don't like him."

"What? Why?"

"Because off-plane people are one thing, but off-plane animals are something else. He could be an ecological disaster.

Maybe he'll eat all the songbirds or maybe his droppings will kill the plants. We have no way of knowing. He's considered medical equipment by the school, but we're putting rules in to prevent pets and to require tighter restrictions for bond animals of all types." Catching Alandra's stricken look, she winces. "It's nothing personal. I don't blame you for needing him. We just want to make sure he doesn't damage our plane without meaning to."

Alandra blinks at her repeatedly. "Orestes would never do anything like that."

"I believe he'd never do it on purpose. And I believe you'll do your best to stop him." Veil smiles. "It'll be all right, Alandra. Let's not worry about this now."

Alandra wants to argue, but not as much as she wants to go swimming, and so she only nods and walks quietly onward to campus as Veil, taking her silence for agreement, babbles happily about the lake they're going to visit, and how wonderful it is to be swimming through a patch of arctic cold and suddenly break into warm tropical waters, carried along by waves that can turn violent in an instant, rain falling from above so that the entire world is water. It *does* sound wonderful, and even Orestes relaxes, letting Alandra carry him toward their destination.

It's all worth it, for the water.

TWELVE

MASKS AND MEANINGS

Weeks slip by, unremarkable save in the way everything about them is strange and new. The five of them go to classes, go to meals, and try to keep up with their homework despite the distractions of the campus. Jamira's all-college Mage Tower team is at the top of the cooperative league, and she can be found at the stadium most nights of the week, joyfully charging down the field with mayhem in mind, often with the other team's mascot clutched firmly under one powerful arm. Kequia can be found in the stands more often than not, cheering and waving a felt pennant on a stick to show her support.

Eula doesn't quite get the point of Mage Tower. When she's not studying, she haunts the Rose Stage on Silverquill campus, watching the performers and applauding the victors of the honor duels that break out there with remarkable frequency. But then, this is what they're supposed to be doing, isn't it? Coming together only to drift apart, setting inexorably off on their own academic paths, their current company only a way station on the journey to the people they're going to become.

She'll miss her dormmates next year when they're all split up and learning to be proper members of their new colleges. But right now the day is beautiful. Eula steps daintily out of her shoes and onto the grass, enjoying the sensation of the blades between her toes. She turns to pick up her shoes before she goes any farther, shooting a smile at Alandra in the process. They're not being split up yet. They still have another term together before that day arrives.

"I can't believe we've almost survived our first semester," she says. Alandra shrugs in response.

Alandra is also walking barefoot on the grass. While she can be coaxed into slipper-type constructs for safety's sake during classes where flying shards might make it dangerous to go barefoot, her anatomy means she's mostly exempt from needing to cover her feet. Webbed toes and low-set fins on the backs of her legs make shoes awkward at best.

"Are you going home for the break?" Some sort of Arcavios holiday is approaching, meaning there's going to be a whole week with no scheduled classes, during which they can stay on campus or return to their home planes as they see fit. Professor Kasmina has warned them all not to become too accustomed to free passage; while their scholarships include their first year's transit, the carriage network is coming under increasing demand as omenpaths are more accurately mapped and as the people in charge begin to understand the difference between permanent and transitory pathways. No one wants to be in the middle of an omenpath when it winks out of existence, and so each path verified as stable and reasonably permanent spawns another cascade of trips, people rushing out to see the Multiverse and seek their fortunes before things change again.

In practical terms, this means that while going home is an option, it can't be a lengthy visit, because there's a chance the carriage won't be available when they want to come back. More important, though, most local students are taking advantage of the break, heading off to see family or attend harvest festivals in their home towns and villages. One of the boys in Eula's Intro to Debate class has been trying to debate anyone who'll listen for weeks, arguing that this is the perfect time of year to visit the beaches near his home, despite their large population of flesh-eating eels. His latest argument has been that the eels manage to devour only two people per spawning season, meaning if they *all* flood the beach, it's unlikely any of *them* will be eaten.

No one's been paying much attention to his eel-centric ranting, and Eula certainly isn't going to leave campus. New Capenna is a risk on multiple axes at the same time: not only might she have trouble getting a carriage back, but it's also possible her father will say that what she's been able to send doesn't make up for needing to get by without her income. Being trapped by an overbooked carriage would be only slightly less awful than being forbidden to come back to school at all.

No, here at Strixhaven, she'll have a week to get ahead on her studies. Having the dining hall and the Biblioplex effectively to herself won't hurt, either. She's got a list of books she wants to copy, and she knows she'll have a list of several dozen more by the time she finishes chasing down the footnotes and bibliographies from the books she's already got. She could study here forever and not reach the limits of what there is to learn—not just about her own field of study, but about so many other things, concepts she's never even dreamed of. If they want Eula to leave campus, they'll have to drag her by her ankles.

She's not as sure about Alandra. The shy storm sculptor has been getting more and more reserved as the days pass, contributing less during their shared classes and jumping more quickly into her watery hideaway when she comes home afterward. The water seems to help, but anyone can tell she's on edge. Orestes is on edge as well, picking up on her moods and discomfort. He's snapped at Eula a few times, and while the little drake always looks ashamed afterward, she doesn't want to share her room with a dangerous animal if he continues down this path.

"I wrote Father and asked if I could come home to Shandalar over the break," says Alandra. She tilts her head back, watching the sky as they walk. "He said this wasn't a good tide for a visit. If I want to come home at the end of the semester, we can discuss it, but he doesn't see the point when I'd just have to leave again straightaway."

The break between semesters is longer—a full month—and the dining halls shut down for what Eula's been told is a "truly epic" deep cleaning. She can't imagine many students will be staying on campus then.

"Discuss?" she asks. "Does that mean he's not planning to let you come home until you graduate?"

"Maybe." Alandra kicks a rock, sending it rolling across the grass. If that hurts her bare toes, she doesn't show it at all. "The Invasion broke some things deep below the surface, natural barriers against the abyss. There are horrors in the sea, and they've been contained for as long as history remembers, and now some of them are loose, and they're hungry. Father doesn't want me there while he's trying to contain them."

Eula stops walking. Alandra continues for a few more steps before she stops and turns to look quizzically at her roommate.

"What?" she asks.

"I thought your father let you go to Strixhaven so you could learn the magic the people on the land refused to teach *him*," says Eula. "You said you won. That violence flows out and peace flows in. You never said you were being exiled because monsters from the deeps might want to *eat* you."

"Actually, I said peace flows out and violence flows in, and war is a constant in the sea," says Alandra. "We all have many reasons for being here. I'd rather go home, if the option is open, but I'll stay if I need to."

"If your father says you can't go back to Shandalar between terms, you can come home with me," says Eula. "We don't have a convenient flooded room for you, but I bet I can get Alton—my older brother—to scrounge up a bathtub you can sleep in, and you can try my mother's sausage rolls."

Alandra brightens. "Truly?"

"Truly," says Eula. "What else are friends for, if not a rusty bathtub shoved into the corner of a crowded bedroom?"

Alandra laughs in what looks like relief, wrapping her arms around herself as they resume walking. A cluster of students has formed around one of the campus bulletin boards, and they angle in that direction without saying anything, curious about what could have attracted so much attention.

When they get there, the board is the usual mixture of

fliers and club announcements, save for a new sheet of purple paper tucked down into one corner. It's been blazoned with silver stars in the corners, and the ink is white, perfectly scribed—Silverquill work if Eula's ever seen it. The College of Eloquence puts so much weight on their ink-based tricks that it's understandable that some of them would become impeccable calligraphers, but the majority of important announcements pass through Silverquill hands to be made presentable before they're hung, which also guarantees that they've been fact-checked and found appropriate.

Not that Silverquill doesn't have their share of pranksters and jerks who might try to pull something over on the rest of the university. They just wouldn't be foolish enough to post it looking like it came from their college. Whatever this is about, it's trustworthy.

And it's advertising a masquerade ball celebrating the approaching holiday break, open to all students, regardless of college affiliation—or lack thereof—to be held in the woods just off campus. Eula can see the sense of avoiding affiliated locations, but she feels a jolt of dismay at the thought that none of the campus protections will be able to kick in if something goes badly. But then, what could possibly go badly at a masquerade ball?

She elbows Alandra lightly and asks, "They have masquerades where you're from?"

Anyone who's paid attention to their little cluster of five knows full well that they're the cross-planar transfer students: even if they'd wanted to hide it, it's written in their faces, their accents, their choice of idioms. Still, they try not to mention their home planes by name when they're around other students. None of them suggested doing things that way. They just did it, aware in some unspoken way that it might keep them safer than they'd be otherwise.

Alandra worries her lip between her teeth and, after a very long pause, nods. "We have masked celebrations at highest tide and harvest. Before the Invasion, the highest tide celebration would be hosted by the human settlement closest to the shore, so the merfolk could attend. Then we would host the harvest gathering, and it was smaller, because most of the humans didn't want to dance in water to their shoulders."

"Huh," says Eula. "Well, my clothes don't tend to stand up to water so well as yours stand up to air, so I guess that's not altogether surprising, but we ought to tell the others about this. Could be a nice way to spend an evening before we break for the holidays, and I think Kequia and Segante are both going home for the week, so it'll be a chance for us to all spend a little time together before we get out of each other's pockets for a while."

"I'm not in your pocket," says Alandra.

"Figure of speech," says Eula, and begins checking her pockets to see if they contain something she can write with.

A Silverquill upperclassman she recognizes from her poetry class, even if she can't quite remember his name, sees her searching and smirks, drifting closer. "Allow me," he says, moving his fingers in an intricate pattern.

One of the Inklings the Silverquill students keep as pets and companions appears, drawing its substance out of the shadow cast by the edge of his shoe. It reaches one spindly hand toward its creator, and he passes it a slip of paper. The Inkling slaps the paper, then hands it to Eula, looking as pleased as an animated wisp of ink can before bursting and dripping back down to the ground, splattering the pavement without getting a drop on the clothing of anyone nearby.

Eula blinks. The upperclassman winks at her.

"I'll see you at the party," he says, and spares a quick smile for Alandra before he vanishes back into the crowd.

Eula looks down at the paper in her hand. It's a perfect replica of the poster, the only difference being that it's black ink on white paper, not white ink on purple. Still, it has the information they need, and she turns to smile sunnily at Alandra.

"All right," she says. "Let's go talk to the others about a ball."

THIRTEEN

WARDROBE MALFUNCTIONAL

They spot three owls during the walk back to their dorm, all watching from high places with enormous, unblinking eyes. Eula glares at them but doesn't make a fuss. She's grown accustomed to the surveillance, and as she hasn't seen any owls in the Biblioplex since she spoke to Professor Kasmina, she's not as concerned as she might be about being spied on. She's been very careful to stay within the lines of the rules as written, but that doesn't mean she wants anyone to realize how wide-ranging the materials she's supposedly been copying for personal study have actually been.

Segante is not a hard sell on the concept of the masquerade ball. He already has a mask, a delicate domino that frames his face in filigree and calls attention to the length of his lashes and the deep blackened brown of his eyes, like pieces of scorched oak left behind after a fire. Eula finds herself looking away, almost reflexively, not quite able to make herself hold his gaze for more than a few seconds.

"The flier doesn't say anything about costumes, but all our nicest things might as well be costumes when you compare them to the fashions the locals wear," she says, all but babbling. "I've been saving a lovely dress I was supposed to wear to the graduation I didn't have . . ."

"So we'll call this our graduation, from the horrors following Invasion," says Segante. "I have a late botany course tonight, gathering night-blooming herbs at the edge of the swamp. I can speak to Dina then. And as it's a night class, the Silverquill boy she continues to insist she doesn't have an understanding with is quite likely to appear. Between the two of them, I can find out whether there's anything we need to know about this 'masquerade' to avoid embarrassing ourselves and our families."

"Isn't Dina seeing Killian?" asks Eula. When Segante nods, she smiles. "He's the TA for my debate class, and while he's not the nicest person I've met at this school, he's definitely not the sort of person who'd give bad information to first-year students for fun. I approve of the people you're planning to ask."

"And as we all know, your approval matters in all things," he says solemnly, before laughing to show that he's making a joke. Eula quirks a smile and turns to walk to Jamira and Kequia's room. The door is closed, but then, the door is always closed; if they're not home, it's closed for security, and if they are, it's closed to keep the heat contained. Kequia is content in the slightly above-average temperature created by Jamira's side of the room, but leaving the door ajar too long lets the heat escape and warm the foyer, where it lingers longer than it should be able to, making it uncomfortable for Alandra. In the interest of everyone being able to socialize, the door stays shut.

Eula knocks, first lightly and then with more vigor, until she hears heavy footfalls, and she steps back as Jamira opens the door. For her part, Jamira appears nonplussed by the sudden appearance of her dormmate and blinks large bovine eyes in bewilderment before glancing over her shoulder and saying, "I didn't think I heard the bell for dinner to be served . . ."

"You didn't," Eula assures her. "Is Kequia here? I wanted to talk to both of you."

"She is," says Jamira. "You may enter."

"Thank you," says Eula, and steps through the door as Jamira holds it for her, into the warm, dry-smelling room.

She's been here infrequently enough that it's still novel, and she looks around automatically, catching the details. The design on Kequia's half of the room has been modified even as it has for Eula and Segante, lines and decorative flourishes twisted until they form a softer, more organic sort of line, not as sweeping as Capenna or as complex as Fiora, but distinctive all the same. Eula has to assume that's what architecture in Dominaria looks like, or at least the part of the plane Kequia comes from. The ceiling here is higher, almost domed, presumably because of Jamira's residency, and the surface of it has been divided into panels etched with geometric designs, which extend to cover both halves of the room.

Apart from the burning desert that is Jamira's half of the room, it's fairly standard, clean and neatly kept, with nothing on the floor. It's a stark contrast to Kequia's desk, which is covered in leaning towers of books and papers that impress and frighten Eula in near-equal measure. Jamira's desk is more controlled, her papers weighed down with interestingly shaped scraps of metal and bits of stone.

Kequia is at her desk, while Jamira has retreated to the heated half of the room, perching on her structure of magma-blasted stone and munching a large apple with a shiny black skin. The interior flesh is golden, making it stand out against the landscape, and flecks of juice stain the fur around Jamira's mouth, bright and gleaming.

"To what do we owe the pleasure?" asks Kequia, setting aside her pen and turning to give Eula her full attention.

Eula blinks. "What do you mean?"

"You never visit our room," says Jamira. "It's too warm for you. You want us to come out to the foyer or the cafeteria or the Biblioplex."

"To be fair, it's not hard to convince me to go to the Biblioplex," says Kequia.

"Or me," says Eula.

"Fair enough, but the question remains," says Jamira. "Why are you here?"

Eula shrugs, looking faintly abashed. "I'm sorry if you felt like I didn't like you as much because I don't come to your room," she says.

"I understand the heat can be a problem," says Jamira. "I take no personal offense."

"I might be offended, but I keep fans around my desk, and when I get too warm, I just touch them and ask them to remember a breeze for me," says Kequia.

Eula blinks. "That's a new application of psychometry."

"Isn't it fun?" Kequia beams. "All my history and archeology classes have been stressing how important it is to remember the origins of an item, not treat it like it sprang into existence for the sake of becoming your artifact. A cracked vessel will still remember holding water, and if you ask the right way, the ghost of that water may be enough to satisfy you. I sit in the ghosts of breezes past, and I never overheat."

"And if that made sense to you, I would love for you to explain it to me, because when she starts going on about turning our dorm room haunted for the sake of cooling herself down, my eyes cross and I stop listening," says Jamira, taking another bite of her apple.

"It sounds—a little—like the theory behind basic shielding," says Eula. "I can try to explain, if you really want me to. But I'm here right now because there's going to be a masquerade ball the night after tomorrow, in the woods off campus. It's not an official school event, but they've been posting fliers around the school, so I'm guessing the administration knows and won't be upset. Alandra and I are definitely going, and so is Segante; I wanted to see if the two of you would come as well."

"What's a masquerade ball?" asks Jamira.

"A costume party?" says Eula. "You put on a fancy dress or a nice suit, and a mask so people can pretend not to know who you are—although it's very rude in New Capenna to wear a mask so good that your host can't tell who you are, and could offend the wrong people if you're not careful—and then you go out and you dance and chatter and drink really overly sweetened punch until midnight or morning, whichever comes first."

Punch, and Halo, if the party is exclusive enough. Eula had her first taste of Halo when her father dragged her to a masquerade ball hosted by his employers. The Brokers were never as free with their stockpiles of Halo as the Cabaretti were, but they could usually be depended upon to produce a few bottles of the glowing, sunset-colored stuff, which had filled her glass halfway with a stolen slice of the cosmos, stars and all. It had tasted like every good thing there ever was on her tongue, like bright, sunny skies and stolen kisses and, oddly enough, raspberries.

There won't be Halo at this masquerade ball. Near as she can tell, there's no Halo anywhere but New Capenna, and she's not even sure it's there anymore, after everything that happened during the Invasion. It doesn't matter. She still wants to go, and punch is enough to make a magical evening, if she doesn't set her expectations too high.

"And it's not against the rules for people to know who you are?" asks Jamira. She waves to the length of herself with the hand that holds her half-eaten apple, indicating her horns, her sturdy legs, and her well-furred muzzle.

"Not at all," Eula assures her. "You put together a costume that works for you, or just a pretty dress and a mask, like I said before, and you dance and you smile and you don't try too hard not to be seen. The idea is to give yourself a little freedom to be the kind of person you aren't necessarily going to be all the time, but to still be enough of yourself to take responsibility for your actions the next day."

"Sometimes the costumes can be quite elaborate," says Kequia thoughtfully. "We have costume parties and masquerades on Dominaria, and some people get very serious about making themselves look like someone different for the night. But beyond that, my experience has been very similar to Eula's. It sounds like a lot of fun. We should go."

"All of us," says Eula, firmly. "It looks better if we attend as a group."

"Better, and not like we prefer the company of our class to anyone else?" asks Jamira.

"As long as we arrive together and then split up, we get the security of numbers, but it still looks like we're making an effort to socialize with the rest of the student body," says Eula. "People know we're from off-plane. That makes us interesting. Haven't you run into anyone who just wanted to talk to you like you were a perfect term paper waiting to happen?"

"Yes," says Kequia.

"Most people," says Jamira.

"So we take advantage of it for a night," says Eula. "We all go, so no one looks unfriendly or like they think they're too good for our classmates, and we have a nice time, and we make a good impression on the people who might be able to help us with our classes next year."

"Sometimes I think you're as calculating as Segante," says Kequia. "What's the main difference between Capenna and Fiora?"

"We don't have mind-control flowers, and we like brass knuckles more than we like razors," says Eula. "You can make a few more mistakes in New Capenna before you run out of chances."

"And when you do?"

"The roses get fertilized, the fish get fed, and your family gets reminded that good manners are worth their weight in gold." She shrugs. "So I'll see you both at the party?"

"You'll see us before then," says Jamira.

"Figure of speech. The flier says the party starts at sunsdown, and we want to be fashionably late, so we'll meet in the foyer when the suns start setting and walk over as a group.

We should arrive about half an hour after they officially begin."

"And this is the way one goes to a party?" asks Jamira dubiously.

"It is," says Eula, and beams at the both of them as she turns to exit the room. "Thanks, both of you. See you at dinner!"

And she's out of the heat, off to tell Alandra the good news. They're all going to attend the masquerade, the five of them presenting a united front to the rest of the school before the holiday break arrives.

Eula's just glad they have a couple of days to figure out what they're going to wear. She spends the entirety of dinner mentally reviewing her wardrobe, looking for something with the right amount of "wow" for the entrance she wants to make. She barely tastes her food, doesn't even notice when Alandra slips some of her monochrome salad onto Eula's plate, and would probably get lost on the way back to the dorm if she couldn't follow the others. But she can, and so she makes it to the safety of her room, where she brushes her teeth and goes to bed still thinking about her dress.

The next morning is rough due to a lack of sleep, which causes Kequia to shoot Eula sympathetic looks and suggest that she spend some extra time in the shower while everyone else goes to get breakfast. They come back with toast and hot, strong tea for her. She accepts both gratefully and shakes off thoughts of masquerade in order to attend her classes and pay attention to what she's supposed to be thinking about: history and tools of debate, mathematics, and physical education.

They're not playing Mage Tower in class this week, and that's a good thing. She would probably hurt herself if she tried.

But she pays enough attention to survive the day and make it back to the dorm, where she begins putting her daydreams into action, pulling clothing from the closet one piece at a time and looking at each critically before she throws it onto the floor. Alandra emerges from her coral cove, stepping over piles of discarded skirts and dresses as she moves to stand beside the slumped, defeated Eula.

"Are you going to wear everything you own to the masquerade ball?" she asks. "That seems like it'll be hard to move in."

"No, I just can't find anything *right*," says Eula. It's frustrating, knowing what she wants to do for the night and not being able to put it together from what she has. Back in New Capenna, she'd always been able to borrow what she didn't have, making up for the failings in her own wardrobe by supplementing it with other people's. That's not an option here. Kequia is too small, Jamira is too large, Alandra is too fond of wearing kelp, and Segante would be insulted if she implied any of his clothing was suitable for her to wear. For the first time since the start of classes, she almost regrets not working harder to socialize with the other students.

Oh, she's been friendly—friendliness is one of the best tools she has, the sandpaper that lets her smooth down the rough edges of cultural disagreement and simple ignorance— but she hasn't been making *friends,* not in the sense of going for coffee or trips to the Biblioplex with them. Her studies and illicit spell copies have been all-consuming, and the dorm has been sufficient to meet her social needs, a neatly packaged and segmented social circle she can move within until it's time to expand into her final home with her college. The Silverquill students she's met through classes and at the Rose Stage have been nice enough, but she's an outsider to them and will be until she finishes the year and declares herself to the silver and black, dipping her hands in ink and setting her tongue to the task of flensing the world. None of them is going to loan her anything to wear.

"Clothes can be wrong?"

Eula gives Alandra a helpless look. "Not for you. You always look exactly like you want to."

"That's because I grow my clothes every day." Alandra meets Eula's blank expression with a smile and a giggle she hides behind her hand. "Oh, I wish you could see your face. I know you've suspected I was making my clothes out of seaweed, but it's not quite that. Father wasn't sure what would be required of me here, and it was important I not go among the land folks and embarrass us by looking like I didn't understand what was required of me by polite society. So he sent me with seeds. Come, look."

She crosses to the closet, crouches, and pulls one of her bags out from where she's had them stashed at the back. Eula hasn't really looked at them since they moved in. Alandra has been good about letting her use the hangers, and anything else has been somewhat incidental.

Alandra lays the bag flat on the floor and opens it, revealing not clothing but a massive pile of shining spherical pearls. Eula blinks.

"Am I the only one who didn't think to bring a banker's fortune in gems when I left my home plane?"

"What?" asks Alandra. "Oh, this isn't a fortune. It's not like pearls are *worth* anything unless you're attuned to them.

They're just spell seeds. Father had them made for me so I'd always fit in well enough to do what needed doing."

"How do you mean?"

"Here." Alandra selects a large, pinkish pearl and presses it into Eula's palm. "Close your fingers tight as tight, and think about what you want to wear to the ball. If you could have everything be exactly perfect, I mean."

Eula blinks but closes her hand around the pearl, which is cool against her skin. Alandra looks at her with bright, hopeful eyes. Eula sighs and closes her own eyes, focusing on the vague idea she had of a masquerade outfit, the thing she was unable to assemble from her existing wardrobe. Seconds tick by, and she feels Alandra's fingers peeling her hand open.

"That should be long enough," says Alandra. She takes the pearl and runs to leap back into her half of the room, swimming out of view behind the coral. She returns to the dry half of the room a moment later, looking pleased. "We can pick it tomorrow, when I pick mine."

"Pick . . . it?"

"I planted it, so we'll know then."

"Don't you need—?"

"I brought three bags of them. I can afford to give a few away."

"Ah," says Eula. "Thank you for your help." She starts gathering her clothes off the floor and returning them to the closet, while Alandra perches on the edge of her bed.

"Do you have an idea about what I ought to wear?" she asks.

"Not green," says Eula. "Everyone sees you in green all the time. Pink, maybe? I'd say white, because it could be really striking with your skin, but I'm planning to wear white, and we don't want to look like we're copying each other."

"I can't wear green because people see me in green all the time, but you wear white all the time," says Alandra, sounding confused. "How does that make sense?"

"I'm intending to try to enroll in Silverquill, and white is one of their colors," says Eula, matter-of-factly. "I could have gone with black, but I don't want to disappear in the crowd. Not this time."

"I can plant something in pink," says Alandra. "Pink and red, maybe? Red's a Prismari color."

"You're definitely leaning Prismari, then?"

Alandra nods. "I want to be a great storm sculptor. Prismari can help me do that."

"I think you're right," agrees Eula, with a quick, warm smile. "And no one's been nasty to you?"

"Not during my classes." Alandra looks like she's going to say more but is interrupted by a knock on the door.

Eula turns and walks over, opening the door to reveal Jamira standing there, looking frustrated. Learning to understand the minotaur's expressions has been a slow process but a rewarding one—it's always best to be able to read the emotional weather of the people around you. Right now, Jamira isn't quite annoyed, but she *is* feeling thwarted, enough so that she's here, peering into the cool, salt-scented room like it's a gateway to some esoteric punishment.

"Everything all right?" asks Eula.

"I'm willing to attend this ball for the sake of social positioning and to make Kequia happy, but I have no idea what one is meant to wear to one of these things, and she's little better," says Jamira sourly. "She suggested I come and speak to you before I break something."

Eula can't help herself. She starts laughing, leaning on the doorframe. Slowly, Jamira's expression melts from frustration into confusion and, finally, into mild alarm.

"What?" she asks. "What have I said that could be construed as so funny that you can't speak? Alandra!"

"Sorry," says Alandra. "We just finished a whole 'Oh no, what am I going to wear?' thing in here, and I think Eula's a little overwhelmed. Are parties always this much trouble? Are we going to have to attend a lot of these while we're here, do you think?"

"If we allow Eula to guide our activities, it seems likely," says Jamira. "Eula. Calm yourself. Please. The problem at hand remains at hand, and I have no idea what I'm meant to wear."

"It's hard when you have to represent your whole plane, isn't it?" asks Eula sympathetically. "Let's go take a look at what you have." She leaves the room and follows Jamira across the foyer to the room where Kequia is waiting, and she just hopes it won't be this difficult every time. She's not sure she can handle an entire academic career of this.

FOURTEEN

MISTS AND MOONLIGHT

Alandra's pearls take the rest of the day and evening to reach maturity, time during which Eula watches Jamira craft Kequia a dress of copper beaten flexible as fabric, with delicate rivets in place of stitches. Kequia helps with the assembly, using psychometry to coax each piece into the exact position where it will show to best advantage, with the least chance of slipping or being knocked askew. The end result is like a delicate suit of ceremonial armor, and when Kequia moves, she gleams like liquid light. Even her hair has been braided and beaded with copper ornaments, creating the suggestion of a crown.

Jamira, in contrast, wears a sort of corset extending down into an ankle-length skirt, open at the front to reveal leather trousers that match the corset itself. Her skirt is patterned in swirls of fractal blue that gleam green under the right light, creating a dizzying pattern of lines and potentials. From the smug look on Kequia's face, she handled the actual needlework, while Jamira supplied the fabric.

They look lovely, both of them, as does Alandra, who emerges from her coral cove in a structural gown of blush pink and rose red, one color fading into the other as it moves around her body, accented with matching conch shells smaller than Eula's palm. The hem is a bloody froth, like foam atop a towering wave, and the single strap is a cascade of red and white pearls, all of it standing out gloriously against Alandra's skin. Orestes takes up her open shoulder, his lithe body creating a sort of asymmetrical symmetry.

Eula claps her hands at the sight of Alandra. "You look amazing," she says. Then she dims. "But I . . ."

"Just need to wait a second," says Alandra, and she leans back into the water. She reaches into the coral structure, producing a length of ice-white fabric attached to a long strand of green kelp, which she snaps off before pulling the dress—and it *is* a dress—through the wall and into the room, where she presents it to Eula.

For a moment, Eula can only stare. This is precisely what she imagined and could never have realized with the materials she had: a column of satin covered in strands of clear beads that move whenever it does, catching the light, shattering it into rainbows, and flinging it back where it came from. The curving architecture of New Capenna is echoed in the beading on the bodice and the cut of the skirt, and the lines of beads form the shapes of feathers when viewed from any sort of distance. It's perfect.

"I'll be right back," she says, clutching the dress as she flees the room, first for the foyer and then onward to the bathroom.

The dress fits Eula like it was grown for her, which it was. She zips herself into it, taking a breath to stare at her reflection.

She needs to do her hair and makeup and get her mask, which feels unaccountably plain in comparison to this dress, but she'll be ready for the ball when it's time to go.

Overwhelmed and giddy, she walks more slowly back to the foyer. Segante has emerged from his room, dressed in a pair of sleek black trousers and another of his heavy velvet doublets, this one a green so deep it looks black until the light hits it. The stitching is done in gold, and he looks at her with amused approval as she appears.

"Charmaid at the ball, is it?" he asks.

"Make all the fun you want, I'm going to dance until dawn," she replies, half flippantly.

Segante responds with a smile and a shallow bow. "Signora," he says. "You will be an honor to your plane tonight. Ignore my jibes. I simply worry I may vanish into the crowd."

"You're wearing the darkest colors you could find to an outdoor ball in the forest," she says. "It's like you *want* to skulk about and disappear."

"I, too, want to be an honor to my plane."

Eula laughs. "Then all you're missing is a flower," she says. "Does Fiora believe in boutonnieres?"

Segante nods. "Yes, but it's considered in terrible taste for a young man to select his own."

"Is that a request?"

"Only if that was an offer."

Eula laughs and turns to pull a flower from the nearest vase, stepping close enough to Segante to thread it through the top buttonhole of his doublet. He watches, and when she looks up, their eyes meet for a moment. Eula's breath catches. It's like she's drowning in the darkness of his eyes, and his face is soft, lips slightly parted, like he can't believe the sight of her.

Then Alandra laughs in the distance, and the moment shatters. Eula steps back, cheeks burning. "That should do," she says.

"Yes," says Segante, sounding half strangled. "Thank you."

"I have to—" She doesn't finish the sentence, only turns and flees back to her room, where Alandra claps her hands at the sight of her wearing the white beaded dress. Eula does a little spin, and Alandra claps harder.

"Perfect, perfect!" she says.

"Is it going to dissolve at midnight or something?" asks Eula, who's read her share of fairy tales, both from the plane of Eldraine and otherwise.

"No," says Alandra. "What would be the point of dresses that come apart at a specific time? Unless you were making them for people you didn't like. Then they could be naked when they didn't intend to be, and that would be funny. It's yours to keep. Can you help with my fins?"

Eula pauses, blinking. "I'm sorry, what?"

Alandra gestures with mild frustration to the long purple fins that crown her head. "I can't style them the way you and Kequia style your hair, but it feels like people will notice if I don't do *something,* so can you help me do something with them?"

"How much flexibility do they have?" Eula asks, moving around behind Alandra.

"A reasonable amount. You can't fold them in half or anything, but you can twist them around each other, and they bend pretty well."

"Hmm." Eula pauses, looking critically at Alandra. Finally, she says, "I have some silver clips that should let me shape them a bit, and they won't clash with your dress. And I was going to use powdered mica on my eyelids—there's enough that I can layer some on the longer fins, which will look nice and give you a little extra sparkle. Not that you need it."

Alandra beams at her. "Thank you."

"What are roommates for?"

The question seems to be the topic of the night, because Kequia is there shortly after, asking for help with her makeup and offering Eula some thin hairpins to hold her own curls in place. By the time Eula's done helping Kequia and Alandra, Jamira and Segante have joined them in the room, making it cramped and oddly warm, despite the chill coming off Alandra's pool, and they're all ready to go.

Kequia has a mask that matches her dress, beaten copper and rivets, while Jamira's mask is hardened leather painted green. Alandra's mask is a piece of carved shell on a stick, and Eula has a plain white domino, which Segante takes one look at before he turns and storms back into his own room, emerging with a silver satin mask, its edges spreading into a delicate spray of moth's wings. He thrusts it at Eula.

"Here, Lady Moon," he says. "It isn't quite a match for your dress, but it's better than that monstrosity you had intended on wearing."

Eula takes the mask and curtseys, offering a half smile. If Segante wants to be nice, she'll let him. He doesn't do it often enough, and it's a nice change of pace.

The bell for sunsdown rings, the campus marking the moment when the suns slip over the edge of the horizon, and they start for the door as a group, ready to face the challenges and delights of the night ahead.

FIFTEEN

A NIGHT IN THE WOODS

Outside, clusters of students are moving toward the wood, dressed as finely as or even more so than the group. The local fashion is layered and structural, with the implication of academic robes worked into even the finest pieces. Eula begins to feel underdressed in her knee-length beaded gown but continues without complaint. She was the one to insist on this outing. She'll be the one to see it to its conclusion.

Soon enough, they're nearing the edge of the central campus, and the trees loom ahead of them, heavy with shadows and rich with the impression of secrets. Eula doesn't have a lot of experience with open woodlands. Some of the wealthier Family members maintain private hunting grounds, but even being part of a social class that might occasionally be invited to a holiday party or company dinner was never enough to earn her father, or herself, access to those lush preserves. Here, though, there's all this green and growth, just free and out in the open where anyone could decide to take it for their own! It feels almost obscene.

She slows, and the others slow with her, allowing the various students trying to be nonchalant to enter the woods before them. Eula studies her nails. They're unpainted, but flecks of the powdered mica she used on her face and Alandra's hair cling to them, adding a hint of sparkle.

"What's wrong?" asks Kequia.

"Nothing," says Eula. "Fashionably late, remember?"

"Is that really a rule?" asks Jamira.

"Trust me," says Eula.

Minutes and students pass them as they stand at the edge of the wood before Eula says, "All right. That should be long enough," and starts walking again.

The group walks with her, all five of them stepping into the trees.

It's like passing through a bubble. There's a momentary sensation of warmth, soft as sunlight, brief as a breeze, and the world explodes into sound. They're standing in the woods, but there's nothing dark about them: light is everywhere, chained globes of glowing brightness hanging in strings from the nearby branches, immensely oversized snarlflowers dripping from the boughs overhead, dancing elementals twisting among partygoers, and gleaming fractals hanging back with slightly more composure. A dance floor has been set up, wooden boards on the ground of the clearing, smooth and polished to a mirror sheen.

Tables of refreshments stud the area, along with smaller tables for people to sit while they get their energy back, and a band has actually taken up one whole corner of the dance floor, not playing yet but with their instruments at the ready. None of that, however, is the remarkable part.

The remarkable part is that Eula recognizes the hanging globes as something they used to do for school dances in New Capenna, and the floral arrangements on the tables look like things she's seen Segante make. Someone has made centerpieces of seashells and twisted loops of iron, and from the way Kequia is looking at the refreshment table, she's sure there's some Dominarian influence as well. Some of the decorations don't look like anything she's seen among her dormmates' possessions or on her own home plane—diamond-shaped rock formations hanging from thin ropes so they appear to be floating, scarecrows with toothy, grinning mouths, dragon-headed boats full of fruit and pastries on the refreshment tables, even a gingerbread castle being scaled by several smaller gingerbread men, the base surrounded by frosting and candy.

She blinks again, then looks more closely at the pattern of the snarlflowers dangling overhead and laughs. "It's an omenpath," she says.

"What?" asks Jamira.

"Not a real one—but that's the theme of the night." Eula smiles to herself. "They've created the idea of an omenpath, and it's like they're sculpting the place where all the planes come together. Whoever managed the decorations deserves some sort of special award from the school."

"That would be me," says a passing djinn. He stops, preening, his smugness too vast to be hidden by his mask, which is shaped like a firebird in flight. "I had help, of course. Pretty much all the Prismari underclassmen chipped in to make sure this theme would work, and we could never have made the clearing without some of the essence-casters from Witherbloom. But I did the conceptual design."

"Fascinating," says Eula. "Can you explain the symbols to me?"

"Of course," says the djinn. He puts a hand on her shoulder, guiding her toward the refreshment table, where he starts indicating objects and naming the planes that inspired them, sometimes with a few facts about the way he thinks those things are used in their home cultures.

There's no Halo in the fountains, so she finds herself disregarding everything he says about the decorations from Capenna and bases her opinion of the rest of his explanations off that shallow understanding. Still, at least he made an effort, and the music is starting, local and lovely.

The djinn looks around, seeming to suddenly realize that he's been focused on one underclassman while the party he helped to design has been getting under way around him. "I—oh, dear," he says. "I need to go check on something. Will you be all right, Miss . . . ?"

"Blue," says Eula. "Eula Blue."

"I'm Anchoa," he says. "And what college do you belong to, Miss Blue?"

"None as yet, but I have my heart and my inkwell set on Silverquill," she says.

"Prismari shall mourn our loss," he replies with joking sincerity, and turns to vanish into the crowd.

Eula is close enough to the table to get herself a cup of punch and turn to survey the crowd, making note of her dormmates' locations. Kequia is near the band, watching them play, while Jamira is off to one side chatting with Bricen, the friendly owlin dressed in a dozen shades of red, the tips of his feathers clearly dipped in dye. Segante has vanished, presumably enjoying the party by lurking in the shadows of the trees, and Alandra—

Alandra is on the dance floor with three elementals, dancing with wild abandon, her dress spinning around her and framing the outline of her body in structural arcs as she moves.

Eula smiles. They all seem content.

The other students are a wide mix of levels of commitment. While most have dressed on par with the five of them—pretty dresses, nice suits, and reasonable masks—some are in much more elaborate costumes. Someone who is either a very wild dryad or wearing an entire shrub as a costume passes by, heading for the snacks, and someone else follows them, wearing a full-body suit that makes them look like the largest Inkling to have ever lived.

Pests creep out of the trees and onto the net of snarlflowers, resuming their endless buffet, and their quiet chewing is so much the sound of campus that Eula relaxes even further, sipping her punch. It's no Halo, but it's tart and sweet and pleasant enough that she's finished the cup and is considering another before she fully realizes it.

A hand plucks the empty cup from her fingers, and she turns, blinking, to find herself facing a human man a little taller than she is, black-haired and dressed in frosted silver-white, a white ceramic mask covering his entire face.

"Killian?" she guesses.

The man shakes his head. "Not tonight, I'm afraid," he says. His voice isn't Killian's, and as she looks closer, she sees neither is his stance. He stands like he expects to be obeyed, like he doesn't know why anyone would argue with him. Killian is confident, but he doesn't stand like he already knows he's the only person in the room who understands what's going on. "You, however, are Miss Blue. Dance with me?"

"You could have heard me introduce myself to Mr. Anchoa," she says. "Knowing my name isn't enough to earn you a dance."

"Take pity, then, that I don't have grander deeds to perform, and dance with me anyway."

Eula smiles. She's performed the necessary pattern of refusals, even if her partner didn't realize there was etiquette at play; no one can judge her for extending her hand and saying, "Very well, then. Lead me out."

He takes her hand and guides her onto the dance floor, where the other dancers are performing some sort of close-step dance, following a pattern she doesn't know. But if her partner can fake his way through proper Capenna dance hall etiquette, she can feign understanding a dance or two. She settles her hand on his shoulder as she sees the women around her doing, letting him guide the way.

"You move well, Miss Blue," he says. "Have you considered Mage Tower?"

"My dormmate plays, and plays quite competently, but I'm not very sporty," she says. "I'd rather study."

"You *are* a studious sort, from what I've been able to observe," he says. "Always looking for something. What are you hoping to discover?"

"Answers, I suppose. Questions, if I need to find those first. You don't always know what's best to be asking before you've gone looking. What are *you* hoping to discover?"

She can't see her dance partner's face, can't read his expression, but she feels his posture stiffen as he considers her question. She's not sure why turning his own query around on him should put his back up like that, but for the moment, she keeps dancing and lets him feel his way through his answer. Masks can make people more forthcoming. They feel like they've hidden some essential part of themselves, and so they don't consider what they might be revealing.

She'd like this man to reveal something, oh yes, she would. He approached her with too much intent for this to be a coincidence, and while he could just have been attracted by her dress—it's a work of art; she'd be drawn to it across a dance floor if she weren't the one wearing it—she suspects there's more to his approach than a love of fashion.

Finally, in a slower, more cautious tone, he says, "You've been spending a great deal of time at the Biblioplex of late. Some people have noticed. There have been questions of what you might be doing—or what you may be looking for."

"I have classes, and classes have homework," she says. "I'm allowed to visit the library in order to keep my grades respectably high. I want to try for Silverquill, and I don't get the feeling your college looks kindly on people who neglect their studies."

"Not as a habit, no." The music continues, and the dance continues with it, the two of them circling farther and farther from the center of the floor. They're almost at the tree line when he gracefully spins her out and says, "People have disappeared from the Biblioplex before."

Eula feigns surprise. She's been wandering the deep stacks for weeks. She knows people don't always make it back from research expeditions. "Have they? During the Invasion, or . . . ?"

"There have been dangerous times on this campus outside of the Invasion, Miss Blue. You would do well to be cautious, and to remember that the company of your friends is safer than solitude."

"I came here with them."

"Then you should be careful to leave with them. Sometimes people who wander the Biblioplex alone don't come back again. Especially when there's no one in this world who'd notice they were missing."

"I don't know what you mean."

"But I think you do, Miss Blue, if you stop and think about it for a moment."

"I don't know anything about people going missing."

"Hope it can stay that way. Be careful. Don't go anywhere alone." The song is ending. The dancers drift to a halt, and he releases her hands. "Don't let strange men lead you too close to the woods."

Eula frowns, reaching for a reply. She's still reaching as he turns and walks away, vanishing into the crowd. Silverquill *are* fond of getting the last word, although most of them are more graceful about it than this. There's a small snapping sound overhead as one of the snarlflower vines breaks, and a pest falls out of the webbing, plummeting toward the floor.

The little monsters must be reasonably sturdy, or Dina and the other Witherbloom students wouldn't sling them around the way that they do. Instinct is faster than reason: Eula reacts before she can think the action through, snatching the falling pest out of the air. Its skin is slick but dry, firm and squishy at the same time, like grasping a particularly ripe banana. It whips around to hiss at her, showing a surprising array of teeth for something that is, at its core, an outsized mutant caterpillar.

"I'm *sorry*," says Eula, "but I thought you might splat when you hit the ground, and I didn't suppose you'd like that very much."

The pest hisses some more but no longer seems to be snarling quite as hard; its mouth droops toward a closed position, and she stops feeling so much like it's about to take a chunk out of her. Instead, it curls loosely around her wrist, forming arguably the ugliest bracelet she's ever seen. Eula smiles as she twists her arm back and forth, studying it.

"Aren't you a charming little fellow? Someone's going to be missing you."

"Not likely," says a voice from the trees beside her. "According to Dina, when they're that small, they don't usually belong to anyone yet."

Eula jumps. "Segante! Don't sneak up on me like that!"

"So sorry," he says, and she can almost hear the smirk in his voice. "Didn't I mention I was from Fiora?"

"You can't use that as your excuse for everything, no matter how clever you think you're being when you do," she chides, squinting into the shadows as she strains to see him. "Lurking isn't very gentlemanly."

"Everyone else allows it, so it must be at least passably clever, and I never claimed to be a gentleman," he says, stepping out of the shadows. In his dark green and black, he blends almost perfectly with the trees. "Did you have a pleasant dance?"

"You didn't offer me one, so I'll thank you not to take that tone," she says. "I'm not a trinket to be passed around. But yes, I had a lovely dance, with a very nice man."

"Ah, but was he nice? I saw your face when he left you here, before you picked up our little friend." Segante leans over and taps the pest with a fingertip before reaching a little farther and resting the same fingertip against her wrist, right above the pounding of her pulse. "They're a lot more clever than most people give them credit for being."

"What *are* they, exactly?"

"You mean beyond the Witherbloom college mascots? They're a sort of magical experiment gone feral. Not wild—they were created tame, and then they got loose. Now they do as they like, until someone tames them again and makes them remember their manners."

Eula looks at the pest on her wrist with renewed interest. "But they're alive."

"So are all the other mascots. So is magic, when you press enough of it into one place that it starts having opinions about the world. Your magic is a part of you. When you make a shield, it's still yours. But if you make that shield self-sustaining and set it free, you're sort of ordering it to be alive, don't you think?"

"My dress is magic," says Eula, plucking at her skirt with the thumb and forefinger of her free hand. "It's not alive."

"It's also not meant to be. Pests, though . . . pests were designed to be a fuel source for essence work. That meant they needed to survive long enough to be used, and also to create more fuel by interacting with the world—eating weeds and the like. So they eat and they grow, and they convert every-thing they eat into more pest, which means more essence. They live, as a sort of a . . . side effect, I guess."

"Like how the Founder Dragons are a side effect of the way the plane was created?"

Segante looks at her with amusement. "Eula Blue, are you asking me whether the Founder Dragons are a sort of supersized pest?"

"I guess I am."

"I wouldn't say it to their faces, but magically speaking, I wouldn't say you're wrong, either."

Eula snorts lightly, then glances back to the dance floor, checking the location of the rest of their friends. Alandra and Jamira are easily spotted. Kequia is less so. A closer look finds her in the crowd still watching the band, her expression rapt as she observes their hands moving across their instruments. Music seems to be a commonality among planes, although Eula doesn't recognize half the instruments and wouldn't be surprised if Kequia doesn't, either. Kequia is so much more interested in the little details, it makes sense that she'd be enthralled.

"Having a nice time?" asks Segante, pulling her attention back to him.

Eula shrugs. "It's a masquerade ball. I've danced with a stranger and had some funny punch. I'm having an average time, I'd say, which is all I was hoping for. How about you?"

"Did you notice how much of the decoration is based on our planes, and the others we know have brushed against this one?" There's a note of irritation in his voice that makes Eula pause and look slowly around, briefly taking in the décor, before returning her focus to his face. His expression matches his tone, lips pursed and skin around his eyes tight.

"Yes. The floral arrangements look like the ones you make . . ."

"Yes. For display among friends and family, signaling

safety. This isn't a safe location. We're not among friends and family. Their presence is an insult at best, a falsehood at worst, and entirely inappropriate."

"Oh." Eula hasn't considered that mimicking attributes of someone else's culture without understanding them could be an insult; she took the presence of Halo fountains filled with punch and sparkling water as a quaint nod to children's parties, not a misrepresentation of something more adult. "I can introduce you to the student who handled most of the decorations. I'm sure he'll be embarrassed when he realizes he made a mistake."

"I don't want to correct it."

"What?"

"It was a mistake, it was a bad assumption, and if any of these people hope to go to Fiora when they're done with school, it's going to get some of them killed, but I don't want to correct anything. He should have done his own research before he decided the floral arrangements I set out in our private quarters were his novelties to emulate."

There's a casual cruelty in that, and it should bother her, but the point that they never invited anyone to come into their space and make half-researched copies of their cultures rings true. Eula frowns, then holds the arm with the pest on it toward him.

"I want more punch, and I don't want this little fellow getting upset and biting somebody between here and the punch bowl," she says. "Can you take it off for me?"

"They should really teach pest handling as an introductory class, if only because the creatures get everywhere, and none of the other mascots bite," says Segante. He strokes the pest's head with two fingers, and it uncurls, dropping off her wrist into his waiting hand. He boosts it into the nearest tree, keeping his hand beneath it in case it slips again as it begins to climb higher, heading for the snarlflower net.

"Do you want some punch?"

"Certainly. I'll be here."

Eula flashes a smile and starts back across the dance floor to the refreshment table. Her dance partner has yet to reappear; while there are other partygoers in white and silver, she would know him if she saw him. Alandra is no longer dancing. That's briefly confusing, until she sees her roommate next to the refreshments, picking through a vegetable platter and putting pieces onto a plate. The young storm sculptor is scowling, which pulls Eula up short.

"Are you all right?" she asks. "Was someone rude to you? Did that nasty Lorehold boy show up again?"

"No, and no, but I learned something I didn't know before this," says Alandra, still sounding frustrated. "I've mostly been staying with all of you, like the five of us aren't *allowed* to go out and be social with other people. Did you know the Phyrexian Invasion started on Dominaria? It's all their fault, Dominaria's, I mean. They did this."

"You mean Kequia's plane? I thought the Phyrexian Invasion started on Phyrexia?"

"Phyrexia started on Dominaria."

Eula, remembering the history of Capenna that had been revealed during the Invasion, the bones of angels and Phyrexians buried so deep beneath her beloved city, frowns. "That doesn't sound like Dominaria *did* anything. It sounds more like they were the first ones to get invaded."

Alandra looks at her, eyes radiating fury from behind her mask. The air around them is starting to feel heavy, the way it does right before a storm. "Maybe not to you it doesn't. I don't know why I thought you'd be willing to listen to me. You're as dry as the rest of them." She turns and stomps away, leaving her plate of appetizers behind.

Eula blinks after her for a moment before turning to scan the crowd again, this time looking for Jamira. She finds the minotaur on the far side of the clearing, no longer talking to Bricen, and heads toward her with determined speed.

Jamira sees her approaching and raises one hand in greeting, the other occupied by a large mug of something. Eula hasn't seen any other mugs, but the vessel is built to Jamira's size, sturdy enough to survive if she tightens her fingers for some reason, and that's an improvement over the flimsier wineglasses. The rhox and orcs who used to show up at Broker parties had a similar gift for locating sturdy dishware, and it's one that's hard not to admire.

"Eula," greets Jamira as she grows near. "I saw you dancing. Are you having a splendid time?"

"I saw you talking to Bricen. Do you think you might try dancing later?"

"Alandra was going to introduce me to an orc from her storm sculpture course who she thought might be well suited to dancing with me, but as it appears Alandra is leaving the party, I shall have to meet this 'Rootha' on another day," says Jamira, somewhat dolefully. "I don't think she's enjoying the party."

"What makes you say that?"

"Apart from the fact that she just threw her mask at a

Lorehold student and now it's starting to rain, I *have* been to parties before. Normally, the people who enjoy them don't leave like that." Jamira sips her drink. "I hope it doesn't rain too much."

Eula glances up. It *is* starting to rain, just a little, the sort of drizzle that turns everything wet and miserable. People in the crowd exclaim unhappily as the first drops hit them, wetting hair and clothing, and a group of students whose costumes make them into fantastic fish, much as Alandra's dress made her a glorious shell, move onto the dance floor. They cut through the dancers already there, both those still dancing and those who have stopped to squint up at the sky.

The new arrivals join hands and begin a complicated, snaking dance that mostly involves ducking under one another's arms as they move in a sinuous pattern around the floor. The air grows heavy again, the way it did when Alandra was expressing her frustrations at the refreshment table, and then, with a snap like a bolt of lightning in the near distance, leaving the taste of ozone on Eula's tongue, the clouds that have gathered overhead begin to thin and drift away.

"Alandra is going to be a very gifted storm sculptor, if it takes that many of her classmates to brush her storms aside," says Jamira, sounding impressed.

"I guess so," says Eula. "I'm glad you're having a nice time. I'm going to go find Kequia."

"Enjoy," says Jamira, and she watches Eula wander away.

Kequia is still watching the band and doesn't seem to have noticed the commotion. She doesn't even seem to have noticed the rain. She smiles politely when Eula asks if she's having a nice time but otherwise keeps her attention on the musicians, clearly enthralled. Eula gives it up as a lost cause, returns to the refreshment table for the punch she promised, and wanders across the floor to the trees where she left Segante lurking.

He's not there. Neither is the little pest when she looks up at the web of flowers, and she has just enough time to start feeling very hard done by before Segante steps out of a different patch of shadow, the pest riding on his shoulder.

"This fellow doesn't know how to hold on," he says, taking the offered cup of punch. "That, or he has an uncommonly strong desire to splat, as you put it, and is trying to fulfill that flattened dream. He almost hit the floor this time."

"Well, that doesn't sound very safe of him," says Eula, barely managing to mask her relief. With Alandra storming out and Kequia and Jamira both lost in their own pursuits, she was starting to feel very alone at this party.

"No, which is why he's been consigned to shoulder duty until he learns to properly hold on," says Segante. "He's small yet, I'm sure he'll get there. I'll leave him in the nest near the dorm door when we're all done celebrating the night."

"Will the other pests accept him?"

"They can be territorial, but that's why I'm letting him ride on my shoulder. The dorm smells like us, he's going to smell like me, I'm hoping that means our local pests will look at him as a normal part of the scenery."

"I'm not sure it works that way," says Eula dubiously. "But I'm not sure it doesn't, either, and I don't know much of anything about pests. How do you know so much about them?"

"You know I've been working my way onto the Witherbloom track, and I talk to Dina whenever something doesn't make sense. I've seen you doing the same with some of the Silverquill upperclassmen." Segante glances up into the branches, like he doesn't want anyone to see the way his eyes soften as he says, "I think I finally see how I can balance growth and destruction, and a lot of that balance comes from essence studies. I might be able to go home when this is all over."

Eula blinks. "Did you think you weren't going to be able to?"

"I know you've gathered by now that the part of Fiora where I grew up isn't a very . . . nice place. Nothing like your bright lights and dazzling parties. The upper classes don't do parades and stage shows and spectacles. They may have them at street level, for the common folk, but those of us in the heights have better things to occupy our time."

"I got that idea, yes," she agrees.

"Well, my father's sister is one of the most unpleasant people in that not very nice place. If there were an award for being not very nice, she'd have won it by now. Or maybe she has won it. She was unpleasant enough to claim a crown, after all."

"Oh."

"Part of why my father agreed to let me leave is that I'm getting old enough for my magic to stabilize, and people were starting to see what I might be capable of. Which means people were starting to make plans that had my involvement as a necessary component, and most of the plans wouldn't end well for me. For them, it depended on how well they played their roles, but for me? No."

"And your father was going to let this happen?" asks Eula, horrified.

Segante looks at her, almost amused. "You've told me

much of your Capenna, and your five Families who control the world. If the Brokers you speak of told *your* father they needed to risk your life in order to have everything they've ever wanted, would he have much choice in the matter? My father searched for every choice he could find, and when he couldn't find any more, he received notice of a wonderful school willing to let me attend classes. A wonderful, faraway school located on an entirely different plane. He has ambitions, even if most of them involve avoiding my aunt's attentions, and no one could question his sending his only heir away for an education. However dangerous it might make me." Segante sighs. "If Witherbloom's teachings are as thorough as they seem to be, I might well return untouchable. I have no desire to chase a crown, but it would be pleasant to feel like I could walk the fields of my childhood without fear, to live in my own city and breathe the air of Fiora. The night air here is too tasteless. Not enough flowers for me."

"Let's dance," says Eula abruptly.

Segante raises an eyebrow. "Pardon?"

"The party can't go on forever, and tomorrow is on the way," she says, grabbing his free hand impulsively in her own. "Let's dance."

"Far be it from me to deny a pretty girl a dance," he says, and allows himself to be pulled, pausing only to set the cup of punch and clumsy pest on a nearby table. Then it's to the dance floor, and the music, and the night that's bright and full of stars.

SIXTEEN

DRY LAND

Despite everything, Segante and Eula are the first ones back to their dorm, walking in giggling and breathless. Leaving a party with a boy is pushing the bounds of acceptable behavior, but Eula's feeling rebellious after hearing how casual some of the people on Segante's home plane were about risking his life, and Segante comes from a different set of cultural norms, one that doesn't seem to care if they're seen walking out unescorted.

That, or he's not interested in girls like that, and the thought that being seen without at least one of their dormmates to play token chaperone might be bad for her reputation never occurred to him. That sort of thing doesn't seem to matter as much here on Arcavios as it did at home, and even at home, how much it matters depends on social status and position far more than Eula cares to admit. Riveteer girls don't need to worry about being seen in public without an escort, and neither do Cabaretti, or at least they didn't have to before the

Invasion. With the Family's recent decline in fortune, their younger members might now find themselves bound by more of the rules of polite society.

She almost wishes she could be there to see it. Just for the mean thrill of watching the untouchable stars of Capenna's sky walking among mere mortals, brought low by the loss of standing and status. Only almost, however. For right now, she's content to enjoy having her room to herself while she removes the pins from her hair and undoes the tiny, pearl-like buttons on her dress, peeling it away a little bit at a time, like she's peeling away a lovely evening in the process.

She's brushing out her hair when a horrifying screech from the foyer catches her attention. She drops the brush and rushes to shove the door open, already calling a shield to hold in front of herself as a defense.

What she finds is Alandra, still in her pink-and-red shell dress, shoving Kequia against the wall, one hand on either shoulder. The screeching is from Orestes, who is flying in circles around the room, wings spread wide and eyes sparking anger. Alandra shoves Kequia again, harder, pinning the other student up against the wall.

"Hey!" shouts Eula. "What are you doing?"

Alandra glances at her. "This is none of your concern, Eula," she says in a low, grating voice. "Go back in our room. This is between Kequia and me."

"I don't know what I did to upset you this much," says Kequia, sounding pained. "Whatever it is, I'm sorry. Can we just talk about it? Please?"

"Oh, like you 'talked about it' before you set Phyrexia loose to destroy the Multiverse? I have nothing to say to you,

Kequia! It's time for you to shut up and stop trying to pretend your plane did nothing wrong!"

Running footsteps from the hall warn of Jamira's approach. Eula, shield still held firmly in front of herself, looks that way and sees the minotaur hurrying toward them, Segante lagging just behind her. He must have heard Alandra's arrival while Eula was brushing out her hair, and used those few extra seconds to go and get Jamira.

Alandra is too focused on pinning Kequia to the wall to hear Jamira's approach, but Kequia sees her. Her eyes go wide, and she fights harder to get away, bucking against Alandra's hands like she thinks she can somehow get the leverage she needs through sheer panic. Alandra shoves her back against the wall a third time. It's clear Kequia is holding back to keep the situation from getting even more violent: if she starts to kick or tries to knee Alandra in the stomach, she'll just escalate things.

The realization causes a pang of unhappiness deep in Eula's gut. Kequia is holding back because she's not sure of her allies in the room. Eula is Alandra's roommate, and while the five of them may move as a unit through the university, they're far less united internally. She never wanted Kequia to feel left out like that. It just sort of . . . happened, a natural consequence of their rooming arrangements. They're all together for meals and classes, but the little moments tend to happen inside their dorm rooms, where it's just her and Alandra, or occasionally in the laundry room with Segante. She didn't mean to shut Kequia out.

"Please, Alandra," says Kequia, sounding oddly desperate. "Let me go. I didn't do *anything* to you."

"You unleashed Phyrexia."

"Phyrexia attacked Capenna a long, long time ago," says Eula, earning a venomous glance from Alandra. "They destroyed the cities that used to be there, the people, the way they used to live. Now it's just New Capenna, and we're doing the best we can. How can it be Kequia's fault if it happened so long ago that my whole city was built on top of it?"

"Dominaria was the birthplace of Phyrexia as we know it," snaps Alandra. "They *started* there. The Planeswalkers and people of Dominaria knew how dangerous Phyrexia was, knew how much damage they could do, and they kept their secrets. They could have gone around and warned all the planes centuries ago that something like the Invasion was going to happen, could have broken their precious rules about secrecy and let us know we needed to be on watch, but no, they didn't want to. They wanted to stay where they were and feel better than us because they knew things we didn't, and people *died*!"

Her last word becomes a despairing wail as Jamira reaches her and grabs her by the back of her dress, hauling her away from Kequia, who sags and puts her hands on her knees. Eula moves to help her, positioning herself so that her shield covers them both, and Kequia shoots her a grateful look that feels entirely unearned. What has she done for Kequia to be grateful for? What, beyond fail to be as good of a friend as she should have been?

Alandra squirms and struggles, trying to break free from Jamira's grasp. Jamira heaves a sigh and lifts Alandra's feet off the floor, still holding the collar of the smaller woman's dress. She gives Alandra a brisk shake and repeats it when Alandra starts struggling again. Only when Alandra is hanging limp and unresisting does she lower her solemnly to her feet.

"If I let go, will you attack Kequia again?" she asks.

"No?" ventures Alandra.

Jamira nods gravely and releases her. Alandra starts to step forward, then sees that Kequia is behind Eula's shield. Her expression cycles fast from disbelief to dismay to disappointment, and she stops where she is, sighing.

"What happened?" asks Eula. "Why are you so angry?"

"Dominaria knew," says Alandra miserably. "They *knew* the Invasion was going to happen, and they didn't *tell* anyone."

"I don't think they did know," says Jamira. "My father was a Planeswalker for years, and he had no idea something like the Invasion was possible. He says the Planeswalkers were trying to stop it before it could happen—they lost several people he considered friends in the attempt to avoid invasion, and when he told me that, all I wanted to do was howl because it could have been him, he could have been lost, and we would never have known what became of him, so far away and under an unfamiliar sun. Dominaria may have known more of Phyrexia than many of the rest of us, but they didn't know the Invasion could happen. The Mending was supposed to stop people from moving between planes without a Planeswalker's spark. Phyrexia should have been contained."

Alandra droops more and more as Jamira speaks, misery appearing to overwhelm her. Eula drops her shield and moves toward her roommate, sliding an arm around the other girl's shoulders. "Alandra? What's really wrong? The Invasion is over. Phyrexia lost."

"So did everyone else," says Alandra, eyes on the floor and voice thick with grief. "No one won."

"Most wars are like that," says Jamira.

"Remember I told you the Invasion broke some barriers in the deep?" asks Alandra, glancing up at Eula, who nods. "The quakes the Invasion caused did more than that. They collapsed tunnels, they created canyons where there had never been canyons before, and they destroyed some of our underwater settlements. I don't even know how much damage they did on dry land."

"That's awful, but I don't understand what—"

"My father can't control the sea when he doesn't know where the next monster is going to come from, and some of the land-dwellers think because we've been weakened, they can come into our waters and take what they want," says Alandra. "He has to set the drakes on their ships, and then they fight back, and sometimes the drakes are harmed. Orestes is only a baby, but his whole family has been lost to the cannons of the land-dwellers. The seas still bleed, although the Invasion's blade has been removed, and we may bleed forever."

"I'm sorry, but that's no cause to attack Kequia," says Jamira.

"I promise, we didn't know," says Kequia. "When Phyrexia came, they came for Dominaria first, every time. Whether we created them or were just the first to defy them successfully enough to become an enemy in their eyes, I don't know. There might be Tolarian scholars who could tell you, historians who spent their whole lives studying Phyrexia and the damage it's done to our world, but I had only ever heard their names in children's stories before the Invasion. I know my grandfather fought them for a thousand years, that he was younger than we are now the first time he faced them. I know they decimated Dominaria twice, and we thought they'd been sealed away forever. No one knew they had retreated to their own world, no one ever even dreamed of New Phyrexia, and once we knew it existed, everything happened so quickly. There were no omenpaths when the Invasion began, and no way for us to get the word to anyone off-plane even if we had wanted to. I . . ."

"I won't feel sorry for you because your world knew this was a risk and never warned mine," says Alandra. "I want to. I want to be the bigger person. But I also want to be a person who's allowed to go home, and I'm not."

"What?" asks Kequia.

"It's not *safe* for me in Shandalar, not while my father fights to hold the seas; I wasn't hatched when he claimed them from the dragon who used to own our shores and cliffs, and I've lived in cultured waters all my life. My father was looking for lakes large enough to house both me and a protective population of drakes when the school contacted him with a better offer, and I'm not *allowed* to go back until he calls for me! I'm an exile from my own home because of the Invasion, because of Phyrexia, because of *Dominaria,* and I'm suffocating here!"

She's yelling by the time she stops to catch her breath, and she stares down at the floor with her thin shoulders slumped and shaking, exhaustion and defeat written in every line of her body.

Eula pulls Alandra a little closer, keeping her from falling. "What do you mean, suffocating?" she asks with bald concern.

"Do you remember when Professor Kasmina was trying to explain mana?" asks Alandra.

Eula nods. "The energy of the planes. Every plane creates its own, which is why magic feels different here than it does at home. What about it?"

"There's a book in the Biblioplex, written by some old Planeswalker, called *Mana-Fest: A Tasting Tour of the Multiverse* that talks about the qualities of mana on different planes. And one of the things he rates is how *much* mana each plane supposedly produces. He describes Shandalar as 'a land of plentiful mana, rich and heavy, stunning the senses and filling the lungs.'"

She stops there, apparently expecting the others to understand what she's trying to say. Eula frowns.

"So . . . Shandalar has more mana than Arcavios? Is your magic failing?"

"No, but there's not enough mana in the air, and I can't *breathe*," says Alandra plaintively. "It's like I'm lying in the sun all the time, even when I'm underwater, like the whole world is pressing down on me and trying to dry me out faster than I can rehydrate. It hurts to be here. The longer it goes on, the more it hurts."

Jamira's home isn't there anymore. Segante can't go home without being in fear for his life. Alandra can't go home because her father won't let her. Eula exchanges a glance with Kequia, suddenly feeling awkward because she *can* leave, she *can* go home again. And she can't bring all her friends back to Capenna with her. There isn't *room*.

Although there might be, if the secrets she's been sending back are big enough for her father to parley them into a better position within the Brokers. Just trying to think of all the moving pieces at the same time makes her head hurt. She's supposed to be getting an education, not orchestrating her own conspiracy.

Not that it seems like any of them have been given the opportunity to go elsewhere. They were chosen for enrollment because they were "embers," but nothing she's read or heard about the nature of Planeswalker ignitions gives her the impression that they had a choice in the matter. They sparked or they didn't, and they had to live with it either way. Sort of like the five of them have had to live with their parents' choice to send them away to school. What happens next is going to be influenced by their actions, but they're all here because someone else wanted them to be.

"Is there anything we can do to help?" she asks.

Alandra makes a miserable hiccupping sound and shakes her head, sagging against Eula.

"Sedgemoor," says Segante abruptly. They turn to look at him, even Alandra, and he shrugs, not flinching away from their collective gaze. "The mana in Sedgemoor is thick and old and, well, swampy. It gathers in the water and in the swamp beasts that fill the place. I've been around the edges with my botany classes. I'm not supposed to go deeper until I officially join the college, which won't happen for a while yet, but . . . do you think going to Sedgemoor might help at least a little?"

Eula blinks and looks to Alandra, waiting for her answer.

The sub-campuses of Strixhaven's colleges are stitched into the body of the university like buttons on a jacket. They're suited to the magic and techniques of the mages who study there, from Silverquill's glorious Grandloft Hall—which reminds her so much of Park Heights that it aches, filled with light and balconies, glorious acoustics and inviting echoes—to

Witherbloom's Sedgemoor, a marshy bayou filled with fireflies and secrets, alive and decaying at the same time, forming something so gloriously contradictory and vital that it takes her breath away.

Maybe it can give Alandra's breath back to her.

Slowly, Alandra nods. "It's worth a try," she says. "I need *something* to knock this dryness out of my lungs, before I drown in it."

"Most of the upperclassmen who would tell us not to go past the border are at the party," says Segante. "We should go now."

Eula wants to offer half a dozen good reasons why they shouldn't go walking into an unfamiliar bayou in the dark of night when they know there won't be anyone there to help them if they get into trouble. She doesn't. Alandra needs this, and they need it as a group if they want to keep Alandra's anger from splitting them apart. The more Eula learns about where they all came from, the more convinced she is that they need to stick together. They would never have known one another without the Invasion, but it changed their lives forever, and now their best way forward is as a group.

So instead of arguing, she nods and says, "Just let me go and change into something more suitable. Alandra, you want to put on something a little sturdier? I don't think your dress is a good choice for the bayou."

Alandra sniffles and nods, allowing Eula to lead her into their room. Eula looks back before she closes the door. Jamira is comforting Kequia, and Segante flashes a quick thumbs-up, one of the few hand gestures their planes have in common. She gives him a nod and shuts the door, turning to Alandra.

The young storm sculptor is already fighting with the fastenings on her dress, tugging at them with an almost violent intensity, like she's afraid the others will leave without her if she takes too long. Or, maybe worse, change their minds. She manages to undo two buttons and pop the third off entirely before she stops and sags, breath coming in small, anxious hitches.

"Alandra?" asks Eula. "Do you need my help?"

A small nod, and no further movement. Orestes, perched on Alandra's shoulder, looks pleadingly at Eula and chirps. She flashes him a smile as she moves to unfasten the rest of Alandra's buttons, turning politely away as soon as she's done.

"There you go," she says. "Go grab something you can get muddy."

Clutching the dress to her chest so it won't fall onto the floor, Alandra nods and dives into the flooded side of the room, Orestes riding with her. She kicks her way into the coral structure at the center of the space, and Eula turns to her closet, pulling out her most tattered pair of trousers and a thick canvas shirt. They'll wash, and if they don't, they're no big loss.

Shoes are a bigger problem. She has only three pairs, and losing even one will be a blow to her limited options. In the end, she settles on the shoes she used to wear when she served with the cleanup crews, and hopes their general sturdiness will stand up to mud and slime.

She's dressed and ready to go by the time Alandra emerges, wearing one of her standard green tunics, head fins tied back by a braided web of seashells that Eula's seen her wear as a belt. She's barefoot, as always, but if any of them won't need to worry about stepping on something unpleasant in the swamp, it's Alandra. Eula flashes her roommate a quick smile.

"All right," she says. "Let's go."

Orestes flies through the hanging wall of water as soon as Eula opens the door, circling Alandra's head twice before he lands on her shoulder, and together, the three of them exit.

The others are waiting in the foyer, Kequia looking far less shaken, Segante still wearing the same clothes. Eula looks at him and raises her eyebrows. He shrugs.

"If I can't handle a little muck and mire, better to find out now, when I can still change the direction of my classes, than next year when I can't," he says.

"Fair enough," she agrees. "Lead the way."

The dorm is echoingly silent as they head for the door. It's not uncommon for them to go days without seeing any other students in the building, something that occasionally bothers Eula but doesn't seem to be a part of any organized shunning or exclusion. Maybe all the unassigned students fall into their own little clusters, bound by proximity if nothing else, and figure themselves out from there. Maybe this is the normal Strixhaven experience.

The night air is still crisp and cool—they weren't inside long enough for anything to have changed. Segante pauses next to a cluster of snarlflowers, plucking the pest he rescued from the party from its perch and letting it wrap around his wrist again. He gives Eula a challenging look when he sees her watching him.

"They're happiest in Sedgemoor," he says. "I just want to make sure he gets home."

She puts her hands up, smiling. "I didn't say a word. You do what makes you comfortable."

"Thank you, I will," he says, and walks on, a little stiff, chin raised high. Eula smiles and follows, Alandra by her side, Kequia and Jamira trailing after. Kequia is still leaving space between herself and Alandra, as if she fears another attack might be forthcoming.

"You like him," says Alandra.

"I like all of you."

"Yes, but you like him like him," says Alandra.

Eula heaves a put-upon sigh. "I already have a younger sister, and I think you're older than me," she says. "The role is filled; you don't need to audition for it."

Alandra giggles, and Eula smiles. They're not even at the swamp yet, and Alandra's feeling relaxed enough to joke around. That's a better result than Eula could have hoped for.

They cut across the school grounds, heading in a direction she normally avoids, away from the light of the central campus and the gleaming magic of the other colleges, toward the welcoming dark of Witherbloom. The air gets warmer as they walk, turning humid and heavy. Eula can feel her hair wilting, but when she glances to Alandra, she sees her roommate walking taller, eyes getting brighter with every step. Maybe Sedgemoor *is* the answer to what ails her.

"Doesn't Conjurot Hall help you?" she asks.

The center point of the Prismari campus is the site of many introductory courses, and she knows Alandra spends a reasonable amount of time there, sunk in her studies and calling clouds into places where clouds have no business being. Alandra, for her part, shrugs.

"Prismari isn't as much about letting magic mature and settle; it doesn't pool the way it does here, not even in the lake, although swimming helps," she says. "Maybe a bit in the Furygale, but that's dangerous, and I haven't been desperate enough to dive into the center of a storm that doesn't love me. Not yet."

Eula shudders at the thought of the hectic, dangerous slice of the Prismari campus, where so much elemental energy has gone awry over the years that it self-replicates and eternally churns, ready to overwhelm and undermine the unwary. She can't quite understand how Prismari students can be so calm about their proximity to that unending storm. But then, Prismari students seem to be unnaturally calm about a lot of things, too sunk in their dreams of great art yet to come to notice when they're walking on the edge of a cliff and about to plummet into the depths.

The walk from their dorm to the Witherbloom campus is a long one, but pleasant enough. The night is clear and bright, and if Kequia keeps Jamira between herself and Alandra, that's an ordinary enough thing, even if it's not always quite so pointed. As for Alandra herself, she holds tightly to Eula's hand, face turned in the direction of the swamp, hope almost palpable in her expression. She's looking for relief. If she can find it in Sedgemoor, she'll accept it.

The five of them pass a discreet brass sign with the Witherbloom insignia on it, and the night transforms. The warmth that's been gathering in the air slams down with the weight of a midsummer midnight, humid and heavy and immediately smothering. Eula coughs. So does Kequia, who staggers for a moment before she catches hold of Jamira's arm to hold herself upright. Segante keeps walking without missing a step, and Alandra—

Alandra takes a deep, deep breath, then laughs and does a little spin as she's walking, scales gleaming in the moist night air. Orestes launches from her shoulder and flies a wide circle above them all, wings spread and fins extended as he creels.

"It's this way," says Segante, gesturing for them to follow him along the walkway to a narrower path paved with water-smoothed river stones pressed down into the earth to form an almost glossy surface. Tall ferns and grasses surround the path, waving without wind, and the omnipresent munching of the pests gets louder with every step they take.

Unfamiliar bushes dripping with ripe red and purple berries grow tantalizingly near, their fruit presented for the taking. Eula keeps her hands to herself. If the fruit were safe, surely the Witherbloom students would have picked it all by now, rather than leaving it as a temptation for wandering strangers.

A frog croaks up ahead, the sound shocking and sonorous. Orestes chirps and dives after it, vanishing into the grass. Eula walks a little faster, pulling up level with Segante. "Is he going to be all right?" she asks, her voice low.

"Unless he's foolish enough to get swallowed by a frog, he'll be fine," says Segante, to another peal of laughter from Alandra, whose spirits have definitely recovered since reaching the swamp.

Jamira looks around with wonder as they walk, finally leaning toward Kequia and saying, "I don't know that I'll ever get used to this much water, just open in the earth, and so much unburnt vegetation. We had nothing like this on Aranzhur. Our tower gardens might have had this much grass in them at the very height of the growing season, and they were guarded such as you can't imagine. This is an embarrassment of riches."

"I think this is more normal for a lot of planes," says Kequia. "My part of Dominaria is fairly arid, but we have wetlands and marshes. Nothing quite this . . . intense, I don't think, although I've heard stories of the great swamp of Urborg, where the ground itself is alive and the trees watch your steps, but I've never been there. I haven't seen as much of my home plane as I think I should have. Maybe when I'm done with school."

Jamira nods, and the group keeps walking.

The path is growing soft under their feet, every step seeming to almost ripple through the stones. Segante motions for them to stop, and they do, even Alandra, who whistles and lifts her arm for Orestes to return to. He lands, damp and muddy but sans frog, still looking pleased with himself.

"Is this enough?" Segante asks, looking at her solemnly. "Is the air thick enough to fill your lungs?"

Alandra lowers her arm, Orestes settling into the crook of her elbow, and appears to seriously consider his question. Finally, voice gone small once more, she asks, "Does it go deeper?"

"It does," he says. "This way."

He continues along the path, leading them deeper into the weeds and ferns. Every step sends a ripple rolling behind him, like he's walking on thick slush rather than solid ground. The others follow more cautiously. The rolling continues, the feeling that the world is getting less solid with every step.

Then, between one step and the next, the path pops like a soap bubble, and they're standing in brackish water up to their calves. Eula shrieks. Kequia squeals. Jamira snorts, stomping one foot in the water. It's barely past her ankles, but she still looks unhappy about the transition.

Alandra, however, laughs and claps her hands before flinging herself forward. She hits the water face-first and is gone in an instant, diving into the muck and vanishing despite the brightness of her scales and fins, her green tunic somehow counterbalancing the brilliance of her skin. Orestes bobs to the surface, sitting like a very strange duck, wings folded against his back. He even goes as far as to crane his neck and preen himself briefly before starting to snap at the water, presumably pursuing some small fish or other tasty target.

"Flooded room good, actual swamp better," says Eula, moving to stand closer to Segante. His elegant trousers are wicking up water, the fabric growing darker by the second. She eyes them. "As the person who does your laundry, I can't say I'm thrilled about this."

"I'll pay you extra," he says, almost jocularly, and she pauses to blink.

"Who are you and what have you done with Segante?"

He laughs at that and is still laughing as Alandra surfaces some twenty or so feet away, beaming and waving one webbed hand at the group.

"Have you been under yet?" she asks, swimming toward Segante. "Oh, it's beautiful down there! The water has so much to *say*. I hope people are listening to it the way they ought to be."

"I'm afraid submersion has never been one of my favorite activities," he says solemnly. "Tell me, do they have karoks on Shandalar?"

"Karoks?" asks Alandra blankly.

"Like logs, but alive, reptilian, and filled with an unreasonable number of teeth."

"Oh! Like kitefins? Although I guess kitefins are fish . . . Can karoks fly?"

"No," says Segante. It's his turn to sound blank as he stares at her across the water. "Karoks don't fly. It's one of their few truly redeeming qualities."

"Karoks," says Eula, turning the word over in her mind and trying to connect it to something familiar. Finally, she blinks and looks at Segante. "Is another word for them 'crocodiles'?"

"Yes," he says.

"Alandra, you should come out of the water right now," says Eula.

"Why?"

"We have crocodiles in New Capenna. They live in the sewers, and they have mouths like spring-loaded traps."

Alandra shrugs. "So, like kitefins."

"They will eat you."

Alandra beams. "They will *try*," she corrects, and goes under again.

This time, several minutes go by without her returning to the surface. Orestes continues to bob contentedly atop the water, which Eula assumes would stop if his mistress were grabbed and eaten by a crocodile, and she returns her attention to the others.

Jamira has hoisted Kequia to sit across her shoulders as she wades deliberately around the area, studying flowers and hanging ferns. A large frog hops out of the brush and into the shallows with a plop. Jamira studies it in turn.

"I knew there was a great deal of water here, but this is excessive," she says.

"I'll take you to Dominaria and you can see the ocean,"

says Kequia. "More water than you can dream of, in all directions, stretching on into forever."

"You jest."

"I don't."

That quiets Jamira for a time, the minotaur turning her vast head to stare at the girl on her shoulders.

Finally, in a soft voice, she says, "My father told me stories of the sea. I never thought to see it with my own eyes."

"I would be proud to show you all the wonders of my world," says Kequia, and both of them are quiet after that, lost in some private, unspoken communication.

Eula wades through the water to stand next to Segante. "Are you sure we're safe here?" she asks.

"No," he says. "I'm actually pretty sure we aren't. You should never assume you're safe in Sedgemoor. Too many things with teeth like to lurk in the bayou. But I think we're collectively bigger and meaner than anything likely to attack us this close to the edge. If we went much deeper, it would be a different story."

"You take us to the nicest places."

"Alandra seems to be enjoying herself."

"She is. Segante . . . thank you." When he turns to look at her, bewildered, Eula smiles. "This was really very kind of you, and it seems to be helping."

"I'd rather not have to deal with assassination attempts right outside my room when I don't have to," he says, dismissing her praise. "If this keeps her away from Kequia's throat, it's worth it."

Eula snorts lightly, then pokes him in the arm. "Just keep telling yourself that. I'm sure you can convince yourself you're as heartless as you pretend to be."

"There's no pretense in me, I swear," he says, and appears to be preparing to say something else when he goes still, staring off into the trees across the water.

Eula stiffens, following his gaze. The night has gone silent, save for the sound of Jamira trudging through the water. Even the pests have stopped their endless chewing, and while the fireflies continue flitting around the weeds, they're not as dense as they were. Orestes lifts his head and chirps, querulous and clearly uneasy. Jamira stops wading and turns to look in the direction Segante and Eula are staring.

About ten feet away, the crown of Alandra's head breaks the surface of the water, rising just high enough to let her see what's in front of her. Then she submerges again, not a word said. The humid air seems to quiet, growing heavier still, this time with anticipation rather than moisture.

Someone shouts in the distance, and a group of white-masked figures come charging out of the trees, dressed in black and gray, with no college affiliations to be seen. Their masks match the one Eula's dance partner was wearing at the party, but that's where the identifying marks end. At least one of them is an owlin, long brown and white feathers trailing from their arms, face as concealed as all the others.

Eula puts a hand on Segante's arm, stumbling in the murky water. "Are these friends of yours?" she asks, keeping her voice low.

"No," he replies, taking a step backward.

There's no guarantee these people mean them any harm. Maybe they're here for the same reason, seeking the thicker mana of Sedgemoor for themselves. Maybe they had no idea anyone else would be here. Maybe they have nothing to do with dire comments about disappearances and taking care.

Maybe. But Eula's nerves are jangling as the strangers approach, faces hidden with no masquerade ball to excuse it. She can't see their eyes. It's hard to credit them with a peaceful reason to approach so aggressively when she can't see their eyes.

Segante takes another step back, raising his hands like he thinks he's going to hold them off through an intimidating gesture alone. Eula holds on to him, trying to take deep, calming breaths as she reaches for the magic of this place, the weight of the mana that is Sedgemoor. They came here because the magic might be heavy enough for Alandra. Maybe it has the weight to lend to her . . .

Her shields have always been woven from the opposition of structure and decay, identifying the weaknesses in an attack and building a barrier against them. Reaching into the swamp for power is like driving her fingers into a pool of rot, natural and revolting and oh so very familiar at the same time. She pulls as hard as she dares, remembering other entropic pools, the smell of the New Capenna sewers, even the brief glimpses she's had of Raffine's tower on the occasions when she's been able to get close enough to the Obscura to see them at their most relaxed.

Mana floods her senses, thick as swamp dirt and black as loam, the smell of rot and rebirth filling her nose. It's hard to find the structure in all this collapse, but she does what she can with what she has, pulling it close and leaning on the decay as she throws a shield between herself and Segante and the approaching figures.

There's a splash behind her as Jamira lowers Kequia to her feet, followed by a tearing, bubbling sound. Eula glances over her shoulder at the pair. Jamira is bent forward, moving her hands like she's trying to hoist something unspeakably heavy off the ground, and the water around her is roiling with furious activity. Then, long whips of earth and stone break the surface, lashing at the air like the tendrils of an octopus, grabbing at nothing. They're glowing from within, lit up red by an electric heat.

Kequia steps behind Jamira, taking cover from the fight all of them can see approaching, but stays close, not fully retreating. Jamira gives her a quick glance, which she answers with a nod. It's unclear what good psychometry will do in an outright battle. Still, it's enough that she's staying, that she's willing to fight with them.

There are at least eight masked figures moving forward, entering the water some fifteen feet away and wading closer. Eula pulls more entropy out of the swamp, weaving it as fast and as hard as she can into the substance of her shield, forcing order out of chaos, ordering her magic to protect them.

Try as she might, she can't expand the shield to cover more than herself and Segante, and so she focuses on reinforcing it, building it thicker, stronger around the edges, like the Inklings she's been studying in the Silverquill foundation texts. She's always used entropy in her shielding: this is just a purer dose of the stuff, and she can hold it as long as she needs to. She wishes she could call Alandra back, but her roommate is somewhere deep under the brackish water, doing whatever it is she's going to do, and isn't there to be reached for.

Orestes is still bobbing serenely between them and the oncoming strangers, which means either they're all overreacting by preparing for an attack or he isn't quite clever enough to recognize danger. But then, danger probably looks different when you have wings. One of the approaching figures pulls a leather sling from one pocket, aiming it at the small drake and whipping it around in a whistling circle before releasing one end and sending a stone hurtling at Orestes.

For his part, he appears to realize the danger right before the stone would have hit him. He launches himself into the air, wings beating frantically, and makes a long, shrill shrieking sound as he rises to a point well above their heads and starts to circle.

"Orestes, here!" calls Eula, hoping the drake will recognize his name when uttered by someone other than his mistress. Orestes looks at her and goes into a dive, arrowing for her shoulder.

He doesn't see the second stone coming. The sling-wielder has had the time to reload, and this time the shot flies straight and true, hitting Orestes in the chest and knocking him off course, sending him sprawling into the swamp.

"*Orestes!*" yells Eula.

Segante is already moving, diving from behind the safety of her shield and racing for the point in the bog where Orestes fell. He reaches the floating drake quickly, scooping him out of the muck and gathering him close to his chest. He pauses to snarl at the attackers, then runs back to Eula, flinching as another stone hits him in the shoulder, much of the impact absorbed by his velvet doublet.

All questions of hostility have now been answered, save for the central and all-important *Why?* This is definitely going to be a fight. Eula digs her heels into the mud beneath her feet, determined not to let it be a fair one.

Jamira gestures sharply, and the tendrils of earth she's called from beneath the water lash and quest around her, looking for things to strike. The attackers continue advancing. Eula shifts position enough to intercept Segante, getting him—and Orestes—back behind cover.

And then the strangers are upon them, hands raised. They have no knives or brass knuckles, nothing she would recognize as the marker of a street fight; they fight with fists and feet, with planks of rotten wood, with slings and slingshots, and, of course, with magic. One of them starts flinging small balls of flame at Jamira's twisting tentacles, which dry and harden every time they're struck, mud becoming baked clay. Jamira snarls, and the electric red at the center of the tendrils glows brighter, the ones that had been frozen shattering their outer shells and beginning to twist and writhe anew, now translucent as glass.

One of the attackers gets too close. Jamira's tendrils grab and hold them in place, refusing to let them retreat, and Kequia steps forward, one hand extended to brush her fingertips against the stranger's mask. What can a psychometrist do in combat? Gather information that might turn the fight in your favor.

Kequia pushes away from the attacker, half shouting, "They want to drive us back to the main campus. They don't want to seriously hurt us."

"Wanting doesn't matter much when you have weapons," snaps Segante, stepping out from behind the shield. "Injuries will happen."

He leans down to touch the water, and the tiny floating weeds speckling the surface begin to pull together, forming an almost straight line from him to the strangers. They clot as they cluster, becoming larger and larger, small buds forming in the middle of the larger formations. It's enchanting, or it would be if it didn't look innately dangerous.

A series of projectiles hit Eula's shield, snapping her focus back to the attackers. She shoves more power into it, reinforcing it against the assault. Two more of them have gone around her to get to Jamira, who grabs her tendrils like whips and lashes them at the approaching figures, knocking them backward into the water.

"Go back where you came from!" shouts one of the masked figures. "We don't need you here!"

"Is this how Witherbloom always says hello to unaligned students?" demands Eula.

"These aren't Witherbloom students," says Segante. "None of them would insult the swamp in this manner."

Another volley of projectiles, followed by two lightning strikes that slam into Eula's shield hard enough to rock her back onto her heels. She feels the shock all the way through her body, hair standing on end in response to the impact.

Kequia grabs another attacker, slapping her palm flat across their mask. Her eyes roll back in her head as a wash of dry air radiates out from her, the perfect antithesis to the humid swamp around them. She steps away from the attacker, who grabs for her, only to find Jamira's hand wrapped around their throat, stopping them from making contact.

"No," she says implacably. "Kequia, what did you see?"

"They want . . . they want to capture us and take us to the omenpath so they can push us through," says Kequia. "They want us off the plane."

"You don't belong here," hisses the attacker with Jamira's hand wrapped around their throat. "This isn't your world."

"Maybe not, but it's our education," snaps Eula.

Another lightning bolt hits her shield, which is cracking under the pressure. She can't hold it much longer against this kind of assault. Segante's weeds are still spreading and pulling together, until he ducks back behind the shield just as the buds swell and burst, releasing some sort of spores into the air.

"If anyone here can make wind, this might be a good time," he says.

The spores drift toward the masked attackers, a cloudy smudge against the night. The first ones to be enveloped stop moving and start to cough.

Eula can't create wind, but she can expand her shield by making it thinner. It's almost a relief to stop focusing on thickness in favor of teasing out the edges, creating something that should filter the spores out of the air, even if it won't stop a sharp stone.

The choking attackers don't seem to be thinking about rocks right now. They're too busy pounding their chests and grasping their throats, trying to breathe.

Eula is waiting for the next sally when a column of water erupts to her right and Alandra bursts back into view, standing atop a watery platform, feet spread and hands raised. The sky above them begins to darken with clouds, stars disappearing as the storm rolls in.

She raises her hands and brings them crashing down again, the gesture like a wave itself, and the sky bursts open. The spores are washed away in the torrential rain, which stops roughly three feet away from where Eula stands, still holding up her shield.

Segante straightens, taking his hand away from the water, and strokes the back of Orestes's neck and wings, cradling the drake close as he stares at Alandra. He takes a step closer to Eula. "Remind me not to draw your roommate's ire," he says, voice low.

"Got it," says Eula.

Jamira still has her two captives, holding them in place with earthen tendrils that are beginning to dry and harden, becoming effective shackles. The two attackers struggle, watching as the remainder of their companions turn and flee until only they remain.

Alandra's column of water gradually collapses back into the body of the swamp, and she wades toward the others, eyes going wide as she sees how limp Orestes is.

"One of these dishonorable curs hit him with a rock," says Segante, offering him to her. "He's stunned but doesn't seem to be seriously injured."

It's hard not to wonder whether that was true before Segante started soothing him. Eula folds her shield back into abstract nothingness as the rain tapers to a stop, and Alandra turns on Jamira's captives with blazing, furious eyes, leaving Orestes with Segante. They struggle harder, seeming to realize for the first time just how much trouble they're in.

Alandra advances toward them, and despite everything, Eula can't help but note how much better her roommate looks after her immersion in Sedgemoor: her scales gleam with a luster Eula hadn't even noticed fading away, and the fins on her head are standing up again, not wilted as they'd become over the last few weeks. It's wonderful to see her looking so well. It's painful to realize how much she'd faded without any of them noticing.

And she's furious, which may be the most important thing of all.

"You *hurt* Orestes," she says, still glaring at their attackers. "He's just a baby. Why would you hurt him?"

"We didn't come here to hurt your pet," says one of the attackers, no longer struggling. Instead, with Alandra so close, they've frozen like mice confronted with an unexpected snake. "We came here to convince you to leave Strixhaven. You don't belong here."

"We don't?"

"This school is for us, not for people from other planes! You'll never understand what it's like here, and you'll never belong!"

Jamira snorts. "We were invited."

"Not by us! What will it take to convince you that you're not wanted here?"

"More than an ambush under cover of night, cowards," says Alandra. "More than an attack on a *baby*."

She snaps her fingers, and two bolts of lightning lash out of the clearing sky, shattering the frozen tendrils that held the attackers in place. The pair waste no time before scrambling to their feet and running off into the darkness of the swamp, their masks glimmering through the dark before they pass out of sight.

Kequia turns to stare at her.

"Why did you do that?" she demands. "We could have learned more about them! We could have found out what they wanted!"

"We know what they wanted," says Alandra. "They wanted us to leave. Well, we're not going anywhere. If we'd unmasked them, we would have been able to recognize them, but it wouldn't have done us any good—unless you wanted to go to the administration and say, 'Gosh, we snuck into Sedgemoor in the middle of the night and some other students tried to chase us away, so we engaged in an unauthorized duel to make them stop.'"

Jamira blinks, brows lifting. "You seem very clear on the rules of dueling."

"It's all most of the Prismari students can talk about some days. Who's dueling whom, who wants to duel whom, who's going to challenge whom to a duel. They really like making things explode in exciting ways, and a duel is sort of like an argument with rules and also more opportunities to set stuff on fire."

"You are also very calm when your companion is injured."

Alandra takes a deep breath, lets it out slowly, and smiles. The expression has edges a smile shouldn't have, unsettling and sharp. "If I'm not calm, I'm going to flood this whole swamp, and that wouldn't be fair to the things that live here. I'll stop being calm once I'm safe in my room. Lightning can't get through the spell that keeps my water contained."

That's good to know, and Eula files it away for later analysis. The wall that keeps the water where it belongs must be a type of modified shield. Maybe she could learn to do something like that, cast shields that stayed static and controlled environments, rather than moving and protecting people.

It's an interesting thought, and she holds it as she offers her arm to Segante and begins wading toward the shore. The others follow—five wet, muddy, bedraggled students stepping back onto solid land. Segante must be repulsed by how much mud she's managed to pick up, since he keeps staring at her until they reach the shore and he lets go, turning his eyes away.

"Do they all hate us that much?" asks Kequia, once they're free of the water and turning their backs on the bayou.

"I don't think they do," says Eula. "I never felt like that before."

A light comes on beyond a stand of wide-leaved trees, casting rays of ghostly gold out across the water, and a mild, aristocratic voice whose accent mirrors Kequia's in a distant, familial way calls, "Hatred is better than indifference. And I am not indifferent to your challenges to curfew. Here, if you would please."

Segante winces, and all of them turn to plod, obedient and weary, toward the light.

SEVENTEEN

ACADEMIC GUIDANCE

The light proves to be attached to a small ground-level balcony, on which stands the tall, aristocratic woman Eula and Kequia saw leaving Professor Kasmina's office not that long ago. Her long black hair is pulled into an elaborate chignon, and the sight of her makes Kequia stop and cock her head hard to the side, frowning.

"Yes?" asks the woman, with a hint of impatience.

"You look familiar," says Kequia. "And you have a Dominarian accent."

"Which would make sense, given that I am Dominarian," says the woman, sparing a smirk for Eula, who clearly recognizes her. "We have that much in common, if not much more. My name is Liliana Vess, and I'm a professor of necromancy here at Witherbloom College. Some of you I've met before. All of you, I know. You're Kasmina's little experiment, her 'embers' brought to hearth. What I want to know is what the lot of you are doing in Sedgemoor this late at night, and why I was just woken by a massive storm coming out of nowhere."

She doesn't look like she just woke up. She doesn't look like the kind of person who ever relaxes enough to sleep, but instead the kind who leans in a corner with her eyes open for a few hours, watching spiders spin their webs across her face.

It's a funny image, but not funny enough to wash away the dread that comes from being interrogated by a professor, especially one wearing a long black robe and gesturing them imperiously forward. She opens a narrow gate in her balcony wall.

"All of you, inside," she says. "I want to speak with you, but not here in the open. The trees have eyes, and sometimes it's better not to be observed."

Eula follows Liliana's gaze to a large branch, where a tawny owl is perched and watching them in silence. Looking back to the professor, she nods.

"Privacy is important," she says, and steps through the gate.

The others follow her, too surprised by her easy obedience to argue.

Liliana waits until they're all on the balcony to gesture them inside, then turns to the owl with narrowed eyes. "You can go," she says. "They've survived the night, no thanks to you, and I'll handle things from here."

The owl takes off in a flurry of feathers, flying soundlessly back toward the central campus. Liliana watches it go and manages not to sigh. "Some people think they're so subtle, and have no idea what the word means," she mutters. "Some people do so enjoy making their shortcomings my problem. And yes, I know you're probably still listening."

She turns and follows the students inside, closing the door firmly behind herself. The five of them are standing in the middle of her front room, clustered together as if they think tracking mud into a professor's quarters won't be such a crime if they do it all in one place. Alandra has reclaimed Orestes from Segante and is cradling the drake against her chest, rubbing the underside of his jaw with her fingertips as he looks adoringly up at her and makes tiny chirping sounds.

Liliana looks them up and down, assessing, before she sniffs and asks, "Don't any of you have some sort of cleaning magic that you can deploy before you ruin my rugs?"

"Sorry, ma'am," says Segante with uncharacteristic meekness. Eula blinks at him, then realizes this is a Witherbloom professor. Even if he hasn't been taking classes from her yet, he probably knows who she is and doesn't want her to speak against him when it comes time for admissions.

"Very well, then," says Liliana. "Just don't touch the furniture, all right?"

"You're a Planeswalker," says Kequia, watching her. "My grandfather told me all about you. Liliana Vess, the necromancer."

"I *was* a Planeswalker," Liliana corrects mildly. "Like so many others, I was deemed naughty after the Invasion and have been sent to time-out to think about my crimes. My spark no longer burns."

"Oh," says Eula, taken aback. "I'm . . . sorry?"

Liliana gives her a half-amused look. "It's a difficult sympathy to express. So many of our kind don't seem to mind the loss of their freedom. Others, well. They feel trapped, unable to complete the duties they were sworn to. Some of them might do next to anything to have their sparks ignite again. You can't trust every former Planeswalker you meet."

There's an edge to her words that, combined with the way she dismissed the owl outside, makes Eula pause and look at her more closely. Liliana continues to look amused, like she's not saying anything of any real importance, only talking through her thoughts on some inconsequential matter.

"Now, then," continues Liliana. "Why are you here? Only the Fioran boy is considering Witherbloom as his future rooting place, and the rest of you have no real business in Sedgemoor, especially not after dark. You could have been seriously injured. The trudges don't ask why you're there, they just eat you, and you'll find your classes much harder if taken while decomposing. Would any of you like some tea?"

She doesn't wait for them to answer, just turns and sweeps out of the room, heading for the small kitchen attached to her quarters. The slice of it Eula can see through the open doorway is clean and cluttered, filled with small jars and dangling bundles of herbs. Precisely what she'd expect to find in the home of a swamp-dwelling former Planeswalker. Although there isn't nearly as much grime as she would have anticipated if she'd been asked to predict this scene.

Kequia turns to the others, whispering fast and urgent: "My grandfather's told me stories about her. She was a great necromancer from our home plane. She destroyed her family, consigned her ancestral homeland to defilement and decay, and made bargains with demons to have power and eternal youth. She's . . . not a very nice person."

"Did he also tell you how I fought alongside the Gatewatch on more than one occasion, or that I only ever raised armies of the dead against people who deserved it?" asks Liliana mildly. Kequia squeaks, turning to see the necromancer standing in the kitchen doorway, still looking more than half amused by the situation. "Not that anyone ever feels like they *deserve* an army of the dead, I suppose, but it's subjective in a lot of ways. I didn't ask you all how you take your tea."

"Black," says Jamira.

"Honey," says Segante.

"Saltwater?" asks Alandra half timidly.

"Honey *and* sugar, and cream," says Eula.

"D-do you have Sewa bark tea?" asks Kequia, cheeks burning bright with mortification.

Liliana lifts an eyebrow. "What do you take me for? Of course I have Sewa bark tea. Morning or night harvest?"

"Morning," says Kequia, and watches as Liliana walks away again.

"Do you always insult powerful necromancers who *control our grades* as soon as they leave the room?" asks Segante mildly.

"I didn't think she could *hear* me," protests Kequia.

"Well, she could, and now we're having tea with her, so let's all put on our best company manners and not give her a good reason to raise an army of the dead against *us,* all right?" asks Eula, watching Liliana move around the kitchen out of the corner of her eye. The woman may be a formidable necromancer and a professor at Strixhaven University, but she makes tea the same way anyone else does, no magical shortcuts or demonic interventions.

That part's almost disappointing.

Eula turns back to Alandra. "How's Orestes?"

"All better," says Alandra. "I hope we don't see those people again. I don't think I can be that nice a second time."

"You called a lightning storm against them in the middle of a swamp," says Jamira. "That wasn't very nice."

"I let them go before I flooded them back to their dorms," says Alandra. "That was *extremely* nice of me."

It's difficult to argue with that, and so for a moment, Eula just looks around, taking in all the details she can. The décor is a mixture of Arcavios standard and little things that remind her of Kequia's room, knickknacks and trinkets that don't look like they're from around here. The out-of-place items are mixed in among the rest, bits and pieces that don't look like they came from any plane Eula recognizes. Some of them could be from Capenna, or Shandalar. Others are completely unfamiliar, draped in an intangible strangeness she could never have explained to someone who wasn't there.

It's not surprising that Professor Vess used to be a Planeswalker. It would be almost more surprising if Professor Kasmina were the only one at the school. The Biblioplex alone should have been attracting Planeswalkers to Strixhaven for as long as it's existed, and they all had to be somewhere when the Invasion happened, which means they all had to be stranded somewhere, right?

"Here we are," says Professor Vess, emerging from the kitchen with a tea tray covered in individual cups. She holds it out toward them, and what follows is almost a master class in nonverbal communication, as she doesn't say a word, only glances from person to cup and back again, and they each unerringly pick up the correct drink.

Eula's tea has so much cream in it that it's almost white, and enough sweetness to make her back teeth tingle. She sips slowly, savoring it, and looks up to find Liliana watching as intently as a cat watches a mouse.

"When I was first starting to walk the planes, it was the little things I had to learn to watch out for, the little things that always gave us away," says Liliana. "Now that the omenpaths are open, I wonder how many of those little things will be sanded into dust and brushed aside. How long before everything's the same everywhere you go, and no one drinks New Capenna hummingbird tea any longer?"

"Ma'am?" asks Segante.

Liliana shakes her head. "Ignore me—the meanderings of another age. The time of Planeswalker dominance and cultural isolation is over, and how things will be done is how things will be done. Now that everyone has a cup of tea, meaning each of you has accepted my hospitality and will be expected to repay it in proper kind, why were you all in Sedgemoor?"

"It was my fault," says Alandra, eyes on the floor.

Liliana frowns at her. "I find that difficult to believe, considering what I know of your behavior on campus. You're not a troublemaker. And how would you even know to seek the swamp?"

"The mana here in Arcavios is so much thinner than it is at home in Shandalar," says Alandra, glancing up at Liliana. "I felt like I was suffocating. And then tonight, at the party—"

"Ah, yes, the Masked Ball. Are they still holding that in Hawkswood? It was always a fun night when I was a student, although half the time the upperclassmen would spike the punch—is that why you decided to go wading in the moonlight? Too much punch?"

"No," says Alandra. "At the party, someone came to dance

with me, and he told me about how Phyrexia originally came from Dominaria. How it was Dominaria's fault that all of this happened."

"That's a bit unkind," says Liliana. "My home plane is responsible for a lot of things, but the first people we hurt were always ourselves. We didn't create Phyrexia on purpose—we didn't create Phyrexia at all, we just had a megalomaniacal bastard decide he should become the god of the machine hells, and the first thing he tried to destroy with them was us. I grew up in the wake of the devastation they wreaked on my home plane, and I was on Dominaria when the multiversal Invasion began. Believe me when I say that our world suffered as much as any other."

"How did you get back here?" asks Jamira.

"I said I was there when the Invasion *began*. They had sufficient defenders. I returned here to do what I could for my colleagues and students. I was . . . not enough. None of us were enough." She looks away, and her eyes are the silent screaming that Eula knows so much better than she ever wanted to. She's seen that look in her mirror and on the faces of her parents and her peers. They're all still at war and may be until they die. "But the Phyrexians fell, and it was over. I tried to reach across the Blind Eternities to return to Dominaria, to check on my friends, and no echo answered me. I had been extinguished, and I hadn't even noticed the loss. I, who notices the death of flies, didn't feel the death of my own soul. Perhaps there hadn't been enough of it left for me to notice the loss. I was . . . distraught? I suppose is the best word. Displeased, at the least. I didn't dare tell anyone what had happened to me. Few enough knew about the Planeswalkers, and those who did thought poorly of us, blamed us for the Invasion. So I went to Kasmina, as the only other Planeswalker I knew of at the school. I found her . . . but that's getting off the point. Dominaria didn't do this. Phyrexia did. If Dominaria nurtured Phyrexia at times, it was an accident, a crime committed by terrible people, and blaming the entire plane is unfair."

"I . . . didn't know all that," says Alandra. "The man I danced with . . . he told me it was all Dominaria's fault, and it made so much sense, and I was so tired. The Invasion is the reason my father sent me here, where he thought I'd be safer. No one warned either of us how thin the mana is on Arcavios."

"And with you being from Shandalar, it was like taking someone who grew up at sea level into the mountains for an extended period," says Liliana. "Why didn't you speak to your advisor?"

"Professor Kasmina hasn't said anything about the mana being thin," says Alandra. "I don't even think she's noticed. She watches us with her owls, and they couldn't tell her I was having problems. I didn't think she'd care. It's been getting harder and harder to breathe, and then I thought I had someone to blame, so I . . . I said some pretty awful things to Kequia."

Jamira snorts lightly, turning her face away.

"It's all right, Alandra," says Kequia. "I didn't realize how much you were suffering. None of us did. I should have known something was wrong."

"Be that as it may, discomfort is not a valid reason to bully other students," says Liliana. "As punishment, you're going to stop dancing around the question and tell me why you were in Sedgemoor."

"I was trying, and you interrupted me," protests Alandra.

Liliana eyes her. "Surely that's not right."

Eula opens her mouth, thinks better of it, and sips her tea instead of saying anything. If Liliana—Professor Vess—wants to toy with them as punishment for trespassing, well, there are worse and more painful punishments they could be enduring right now.

Alandra makes a small, frustrated noise, and Kequia steps in, voice perfectly modulated, no sign of tension in her tone.

"Alandra and I had an unpleasant exchange about the nature of Dominaria's involvement in the Invasion, leading to her confession that she was suffering from the lack of Shandalar's natural mana reserves. Segante suggested the mana pooling in Sedgemoor might be sufficient to make her feel better."

Liliana looks to Segante for confirmation. He shrugs. "It's wet, she's wet, I thought it would be a good match."

"You mean you read the essence of her magic and the essence of Sedgemoor's magic and saw a reasonable alignment," says Liliana mildly.

"That, too."

She sighs. "You shouldn't have come alone, in the dark, and you certainly shouldn't have come with a group of students who aren't familiar with the area. Someone could have been seriously hurt. Do you have any idea how much paperwork is involved with student injuries in the bayou?"

"Alandra could have been seriously hurt if we'd continued depriving her of the mana she needs for her health," says Segante. "And allowing hostility to linger when we had a quick, easy resolution seemed unwise."

"That's not how they do things on Fiora," observes Liliana.

"No. I've found the best way to navigate this plane is to ask myself, 'What would I do at home?' and then do exactly the opposite," says Segante.

Liliana snorts. "So you brought her here at night, without an escort, on an untried theory, to be *kind*?"

"I didn't say I was good at it."

"I heard a ruckus—that's what attracted my attention to your little field trip to begin with," says Liliana. "Do you want to tell me what that was all about?"

"No," says Jamira.

Liliana blinks at her, then laughs. "Honesty. I suppose that works. *Will* you tell me what that was all about?"

"There was a crocodile, like the ones we get in the sewers at home," says Eula. "Big, scaly, too many teeth. It startled me, and I panicked, which freaked everyone else out a little."

"And I was feeling so much better after some time in the water that I called up a storm when Eula started yelling," says Alandra. "I didn't even mean to, it just happened."

"Hmm," says Liliana. "I know you're lying to me, but I suppose a few lies are a small price to pay for a night without fatalities. Finish your tea and get back to your dorms. Even with the Oriq and the mage hunters largely destroyed—it's all right to look confused; they were before your time, and you'd best hope they stay that way—we have curfews for a reason."

"Yes, ma'am," says Kequia.

They drink their tea in anxious silence, and Liliana collects their cups when she's done, then walks them to the front door, rather than the balcony door they arrived through.

"Be sure you don't have any more unsanctioned karok fights in my bayou," she says, mild as anything. "I'll be watching you."

"Thank you, ma'am," says Eula, and the five of them flee into the night, Orestes chirping at Liliana as she closes the door.

Segante waits until they're halfway down the pathway back to the main trail to their dorm before he punches Eula lightly in the arm and asks, "What was that about? A crocodile attack? You know as well as the rest of us that that's not what happened."

"Yes, and I could tell that no one wanted to tell her we'd been attacked by a group of students. I did what needed to be done," says Eula primly. "When you're dealing with authority figures, polite lies are better than rude truths. 'We think part of the student body wants us to leave, and we can't identify them, and now it's your problem' is a *very* rude truth."

"It would have been inappropriate to tell her what really happened," says Jamira.

Segante shakes his head. "I thought you people were supposed to be the honest ones," he says.

Eula dimples at him. "Whatever gave you that idea, sir?" she asks, and laughs at the look on his face, an odd mixture of frustration, pride, and almost speculation that she doesn't fully understand.

No one attacks them on the way back to their dorm, and although Jamira catches a glimpse of something in the trees, it's too far away and obfuscated by branches for them to tell whether it's another owl watching them or just some sort of odd swamp creature coincidentally passing by.

There are no other students. The midnight campus might as well be deserted, filled as it is with silence and darkened windows. As soon as they leave the Witherbloom campus for the main university, the temperature drops, and the air turns dry again. Eula and Kequia both shiver, while Jamira, Segante, and Alandra don't really seem to notice.

Segante shrugs out of his doublet and drapes it around Eula's shoulders, taking a moment to be sure it's secure before he steps away. Eula shoots his back a startled look that turns slowly thoughtful as she pulls the thick fabric around herself and follows her friends back into their dorm.

WITHER AND BLOOM

Segante wakes alone in his bed well before the morning bell and stretches languidly, breathing in the sweet, familiar perfume of the dreamwaste flowers arranged on surfaces throughout the room. The pollen is soothing; if not for the near-intoxicant effect the flowers can have on people from other planes, he would suggest a garland for Alandra. The merfolk's nerves might be calmed by the natural ease of the flowers, the way they blunt some of the edges off the world.

Or she might succumb to them as too many have before, finding herself more interested in dreaming pretty dreams than she is in continuing to live her own life—a life that will already be more limited than he cares to consider, if she needs regular visits back to Shandalar to keep her body and magic healthy. He wants to be able to return to Fiora when his time at school is finished, if only for the sake of his father, but he would chafe if it were to be somehow *required*. Adulthood should be about freedom. Before the omenpaths, he would never have seen an entire plane as confinement. But the Multiverse is open now, and he's not going to be locked away again.

A childhood spent trapped inside a single house and the surrounding grounds was more than enough confinement for a lifetime. His mother had been content to live and die as a hothouse flower, but he wants more. He wants all the Multiverse at his fingertips. A strong young man with a backing in the magical arts can write his own ticket, and that's what he intends to do.

Slipping into his robe, he cracks the door open wide enough to be sure that he's alone, then exits to head for the bathrooms. Next year will be its own challenge, but for this year, waking early has been enough to reliably let him shower alone. Perhaps the colleges include dorms with en suite bathrooms. One more thing to discuss with his advisor, whoever that proves to be.

The thought is enough to remind him to hurry. His first class today is on the importance of proper mana resonance in flower arranging, a relatively niche subject that attracts students from all five colleges. People on Arcavios—both those native to the plane and his dormmates, who are otherwise fairly sensible people—seem to dismiss flower arrangement as a casual art more often than not, something playful and transitory. The bouquets at last night's masquerade ball were an illustration of *that*.

Put the wrong flowers together, issue a cutting insult. Even a deadly one, depending on the flowers in question. Combine flowers grown under the wrong magical influences, create a weapon with no trigger to pull or ammunition to remove. People should pay more attention to flowers.

He showers quickly, dresses just as fast, and leaves the dorm before the breakfast bell can ring to wake the others, heading back toward Sedgemoor.

The amphitheater where they'll be working today is brick and wrought iron, open to the elements. Their professor likes it that way. Yedora is the groundskeeper for Strixhaven as a whole when not teaching for Witherbloom. It's an honor to be in one of her classes, and the fact that Segante was able to enroll at all is just one more piece of proof that people don't take flowers seriously enough.

He's not the first one there—that would attract attention—but he's early enough that he can watch most of the other students trickling in, a mixture of years and colleges that turns the long desks set up for them into a patchwork of colors. Yedora watches from the front of the amphitheater, the tall treefolk instructor leaning against the wall with patient unconcern. Like Dina, she's as much plant as she is mammal; unlike Dina, her skin is bark brown, not green, and her hair is made up of twisting, gnarled roots, like her hands. There's a quiet strength in her presence, a serenity that radiates out from her position to quell any student rivalries or conflicts that might have otherwise erupted.

The last student arrives just as the bell rings to begin the class, and Dina moves among the desks, distributing the bundled flowers they'll be working with today.

"These were grown in Sedgemoor and in my personal greenhouses," says Yedora, her voice carrying effortlessly through the space. "They have the potency necessary for today's assignment but have been cultivated to do no harm. Using at least four different flowers, selected for harmony in appearance, scent, meaning, and magical potential, I want you to make me an arrangement suitable for placing in the office of a dean. Which dean will depend on how well I appreciate your efforts."

This is a solo exercise, which means he doesn't have to play nicely with the other students. Oh, some of them are harmless enough, and the few who've seemed inclined to join the group that opposes his presence on campus are nowhere near as subtle as they believe themselves to be: he's been surviving the ins and outs of a noble household on Fiora since he was old enough to be trusted with solid foods, and a few guileless college students aren't going to get the better of him. He's honestly not sure some of them fully understand the mischief they've tried to get up to over the course of the semester. The swampvine thorns someone embedded in the strap of his book bag could have caused a nasty allergic reaction if he hadn't evaded and removed them, and the starflower sap someone else smeared on several of his vases could have seriously damaged his vision.

Still, he's managed to deflect or defuse all their pranks, even the ones that were almost subtle enough to get through his defenses, and is thus taken by surprise when, only moments after Yedora steps out of the amphitheater to consult with one of her TAs, something hard and spiky impacts the back of his head. He yelps, dropping the flower he was considering for his arrangement, and reaches around to feel the place where it hit.

His fingers come away sticky with sap and reddish with blood. He stares at them for a moment before turning a hard look on the other students.

"Who threw that?" he asks.

The offending object is on the ground by his feet: a seedpod, oblong and hard, covered in little grasping hooks that would help it grab the fur of a passing animal in the wild and travel to a new spot where it could germinate. *Tangletrap pod,* supplies his botanical training, followed by a list of the attributes such a thing could bring to a proper flower arrangement.

No one answers him. No one even meets his eyes. He glares at them all the same, picking up the pod with exaggerated care. It scratched his head without embedding itself, but those hooks are sharp, and it could easily latch onto his fingers if he doesn't pay attention.

Blood matting his hair, he turns back to his station, setting the pod next to his practice vase. There are a few whispers from behind him, quickly hushed, as the room gets back to work.

Casual cruelty is nothing new. If anything, it's refreshing: this place is too soft for him most days, too inclined to pad the corners and pretend that people aren't essentially selfish beasts at their hearts. Of his dormmates, only Eula is willing to snap and snarl at him, and even she spends too much time hiding her teeth behind a veneer of polite manners and senseless social rules that no one else on this plane can understand. Throwing things while the teacher's back is turned may be juvenile, but at least it's honest in its hostility.

The best response that can be offered to that sort of cruelty is to remain as unruffled as possible. He's already failed to be truly untouchable by reacting at all. Now he just has to hope his pride can recover.

Professor Yedora comes back into the amphitheater. The atmosphere seems to shift as the rest of the students tense, waiting to see if he'll betray them. Segante keeps working.

He's been many things in his life, and he intends to be many more before he's finished living, but he's not an informant. He handles his troubles in his own time and in his own way.

A thin trickle of blood works its way down his neck and below his collar, and he squirms slightly as he works. Maybe that motion is what catches Dina's attention, or maybe that's just what gives her the excuse to approach him, coming up quietly on his left as he's working.

"You're bleeding," she says, voice low. "I'm not going to ask what happened, but I am going to ask you to come with me before you get blood on the flowers and turn this into a larger incident."

"What are you going to do about it?" he asks, not looking at her.

"Clean out the wound, give you a dressing, and make sure you're not going to pass out."

"It would take more than a little blow to the head to fell a son of my house," he says smugly.

"So prove it."

Segante sighs. "You're not going to let this go, are you?"

"Nope," says Dina, with excessive and borderline-offensive cheer. "And if you think you can out-stubborn Killian, you need to spend more time with my boyfriend. No one will tamper with your station while the professor is watching. Come along."

Defeated—but amused at the same time—Segante puts down his flowers and allows her to lead him out of the amphitheater and around the side to a small bench. She settles him there, producing a medical kit from inside her robes, and begins dabbing at the back of his head with a dampened piece of cotton.

Voices drift through the curved wall, and Segante stiffens, realizing they're in a natural acoustic bubble. From here, he's able to hear anything said on this side of the amphitheater. He shoots Dina a startled look, and she smiles, nodding. This was intentional.

From beyond the wall, a male voice says, "She'll find the note. She'll come."

Another answers: "Alone?"

"Have you watched her? Snotty little thing, she'd never ask for help. Her plane must be even worse than Segante's, with the way she carries on."

A female voice answers, low and tight: "Quiet, both of you! This doesn't work if we're clumsy about it. She'll take the bait, and we'll take the girl. It's a simple plan, as long as you don't screw it up."

Dina is stitching the back of his head now, but he barely notices, focused as he is on listening. These people—these students, whoever they are—are planning to hurt someone. To hurt *Eula*, no matter how careful they are about avoiding her name. And he's not going to let that happen.

Some forms of intrigue simply cannot be allowed.

EIGHTEEN

HARRIER'S WOOD

Alandra's color is still improved come the morning, and she has more energy than she's had in weeks. Eula feels bad all over again that she hadn't noticed how much her roommate had faded; watching Alandra bounce around the room, diving into the wet to retrieve something she forgot and then returning to the dry to make a note on one of her papers, is like being back in their first days at the school.

"I'm sorry," she says finally, turning away from the mirror where she's been putting the final adjustments on her hair. "I should have noticed you were so miserable, and I didn't. I'm a bad roommate."

"You're a fabulous roommate," says Alandra. "I've never had a roommate before, but I can't imagine having a better one. I wouldn't have liked it if you'd gone asking a bunch of questions about why I wasn't feeling great, not when I didn't know exactly why. Can I still come home with you for the break between terms?"

"Of course," says Eula. "We can read up on mana and how it works between planes, and find the best way for you to stay healthy in New Capenna. I can't wait to show you my city!"

"D'you think Kequia is going to be mad at me today?"

"Maybe. I would be, if you'd attacked me without provocation. But honestly, it sounds like whoever told you all that stuff about the Invasion was *trying* to provoke you. Like they wanted you to get upset, so we'd be fighting amongst ourselves."

"I guess so . . ." says Alandra. "But if that was what they wanted, were they part of the group that attacked us? And how did they know they should follow us to Sedgemoor?"

"I don't know," says Eula, giving the dorm-room door a measuring look. "But that's a really good question."

It had been Segante to suggest they go to the Witherbloom campus, and he liked to talk about how differently they did things on Fiora, how it was every man for himself on his home plane. Maybe he'd seen an opportunity to betray them all without getting blamed.

And if he had, *can* she blame him? They're all products of their planes, every one of them, and the places where they clash are just as important as the places where they fit together.

"It's almost time for breakfast," she says, and heads for the door.

The foyer is currently empty, but there's a sheet of paper tacked to her door. She pauses and takes it down, unfolding it to find her name written inside, along with a short message.

Miss Blue—

   It is of the direst importance that you meet with us in the Harrier's Wood this afternoon, following third bell. While last night's altercation ended with no serious injuries, things could have gone very, very poorly, and we wish to discuss the matter with you more openly, as polite people and fellow students of the arts.

Please come to the wood, and come alone. You have our solemn word that you will not be harmed.

The note is unsigned, which isn't much of a surprise, given that it reads like a thinly veiled threat. "Come alone" and "we're not going to hurt you" aren't usually the sort of things people say when they have your best interests at heart.

But still, she's curious. Those aren't friendly words, but they're also the sort of thing the Families say right before they make someone an offer, and offers can change your life. Her life's been changed so many times recently—what's one time more? Thoughtful, she folds the note and slips it into her pocket, tucking it away for later.

Jamira and Kequia approach from the bathroom down the hall, both freshly showered and wearing robes cinched tight around their waists. The height difference between them never ceases to be striking—it's not that Kequia is particularly short, it's just that Jamira is so toweringly *tall.*

She waves and mentally pushes the note even farther down in her pocket. Kequia might be able to use her psychometry to learn more about whoever wrote it, but whoever it was must have known the general strengths of all five students before they crept into the foyer and left a message for Eula; they'll have taken precautions. So instead of offering it over, she smiles and asks, "How'd you sleep last night?"

"Horizontally," says Jamira gravely, and laughs at the expression on Eula's face. "Quite well, thank you, once I washed the mud out of my fur."

"That trick with the tendrils was neat," says Eula. "Did you learn that here? Or— I can't even imagine what class that would come from. Never mind me."

"It's something I learned at home," says Jamira. "I am a blacksmith, and it's best if I can bend soil and metal both to meet my needs. The differences are subtle but concrete. My father makes chains of iron and flame; I make grasping arms of whatever I can find. I've been able to apply some concepts from my theory classes to keep them flexible longer by encouraging the moisture in the soil to move according to its own needs, rather than solidifying into clay. Once I'm formally a part of Quandrix, I'll be able to take their material sciences classes, and what I learn there will make me a better blacksmith."

"Wow," says Eula.

"How's Alandra?" asks Kequia.

"She seems better," says Eula. "I think visiting the swamp helped her a lot. Next time I write home, I'm going to ask my father if he can get me an invitation to take her to visit Raffine's tower. The energy there is strong and heavy, and enough like Sedgemoor that it might be good for her."

"Raffine?" asks Jamira.

"The sphinx who rules the Obscura—one of the Families on my home plane."

"Is Alandra going home with you for the term break?" asks Kequia.

Eula nods.

"Nice. Jamira is coming home with me."

Jamira nods. "It will be pleasant to visit another plane, and we should take the opportunity while we can. Kequia tells me there are minotaur on Dominaria; perhaps we'll find we have things in common beyond our species. Perhaps it will be a place where my family and I can one day settle."

"That would be nice," says Eula. "You two coming to breakfast today?"

"I need to finish a paper," says Kequia. "I'll just eat a sausage roll on my way to history."

"I have already eaten," says Jamira. "I want to get a head start on researching an equation for my theory class. Apologies."

"It's no big deal," says Eula. "As long as you reassure Alandra that you're not mad at her, it'll be fine."

"Oh, I'm not mad," says Kequia, looking alarmed at the very concept. "I understand why she was upset, and I'm not going to blame her for having bad facts. That can happen to anyone. That could happen to *me*."

That idea seems to alarm her even more, and Jamira snorts, amused.

"Yes, you could have a wrong answer one day," she says. "It happens to the best of us." She slips into their room then, leaving Eula and Kequia alone.

"You're really not upset?" she asks.

"Really," says Kequia. "My mother says grudges are like acid. If you hold them too long, you burn yourself as badly as your enemies."

"All right; if you're sure." Eula shrugs, then crosses to her own room, opening the door and poking her head inside. Alandra is in the dry part of the room, gathering her books. "Kequia's here if you wanted to say sorry. She's not coming to breakfast today."

"Oh!" says Alandra, and whistles for Orestes before hurrying to the door and past Eula to the foyer. "Thanks, Eula."

"It was nothing," demurs Eula, and slips into the now-empty room, pulling the note out of her pocket again to study it more closely. The handwriting isn't familiar; the ink looks like the standard-issue stuff they sell in the student store. If she tells the others about the message, they'll probably insist on coming with her. She was told to come alone.

If she asked her father what to do, what would he say? Listening to the mysterious letter-writer and going alone could be dangerous, but it could also be an opportunity. People are more likely to spill their secrets when they think they're in a position of power, and going alone to a place she doesn't know will certainly create that impression. She's supposed to be learning everything she can. This is something to learn. This is knowledge, and knowledge is power, and power is what's going to get her family in tighter with the Brokers. She takes a deep breath, and she knows what she's going to do. There was never really any question.

The day passes in a daze. She and Alandra eat breakfast outside, their toes digging into the grass under the table and the chatter of nearby students washing over them like a gentle tide. Segante joins them briefly, then runs off after a group of students from another of his classes, his mouth full of questions Eula doesn't understand and his eyes bright with the joy of chasing answers.

Professor Kasmina seems distracted during their history class, which focuses half on the Blood Age—every plane has had its wars, it seems, even those born out of chaos with a full complement of dragons to guide it into the future—and half on her questions about what each of them intends to do during the holiday break. All five of them are staying on campus, for one reason or another, although Eula suspects those reasons are more alike than any of them is quite admitting. Professor Kasmina relaxes slightly when Kequia confirms that she's not going back to Dominaria after all, the last of them to say so.

"Excellent," says Kasmina. "You can all use the time to get ahead on your studies. Most hopefuls to the colleges will have been bending their interests in the appropriate direction for years before they reach campus. You have a lot of catching up to do if you want to seem appealing to the colleges of your choice."

"I thought they had to take us if we declared for them," says Eula.

"They have to let you *try*," says Kasmina. "It wouldn't do anyone any good if we forced the colleges to take unsuited students. Most people are constitutionally suited to at least two of the available colleges, and while they may come to us with preferences, they can be swayed. More than one would-be Lorehold historian has found themselves doing cultural dance within Prismari, or resurrecting ancient poetic forms alongside the rest of Silverquill. Your paths are not yet set. So study and work while you can, to find that clear road into your futures."

Segante scowls at her. "You make this sound like some sort of game, with the colleges we didn't want as consolation prizes."

"There are no consolation prizes here, only better fits, and you'll all end up where you fit most cleanly," says Kasmina. "It won't be easy. It will be *right*."

"Will you be remaining on campus, Professor?" asks Jamira.

Kasmina nods. "I will, and I can be of unique assistance to you, my aspiring Quandrix. But I'll be available to any of you who might have questions during the break. About half the staff will remain present. That would have meant more before the Invasion, when we weren't running with a skeleton crew, but still, you won't be alone here."

Kequia puts up her hand. "Professor, what can you tell us about this holiday?" she asks.

"Ah, Sea's Rise," says Kasmina. "The time when the Snarls are at their most powerful, and when their connections are the loosest. The observance of this holiday dates all the way back to the Blood Age, when—"

They learn more than they ever wanted to know about the observance of Sea's Rise, but Kasmina seems to forget about making dire predictions about everyone's future academic careers. At the bell, they rise and scatter, off to their individual classes.

Eula attends her classes, dutifully taking notes and turning in her papers, but her heart isn't in it. She's leaving Intro to Debate when she walks straight into a wall of black-and-white satin. She rocks back on her heels, blinking, and the wall becomes the front of Killian's jacket, worn by the TA himself, who's standing to block the door. He has his arms folded and a half-supercilious, half-concerned look on his face.

"Blue," he says curtly. "Where were you today?"

"My seat?" she ventures.

He lifts an eyebrow, and she flinches, unable to stand up under his attention.

"I'm sorry," she says. "I was just distracted."

"Distraction in a debate can be deadly," he says, and never has that statement been truer than in Silverquill, where words are weapons, honed sharp as steel and swung like swords.

"I know," she says. "I'm sorry. It won't happen again."

"What has you so preoccupied that you couldn't defend

yourself against a simple logical fallacy?" he asks. "If you'd been debating alone, that's where you would have lost. I've been watching you all term. You're better than that."

"I need to find a place, and I haven't had any luck so far."

"Did you try asking the campus guides?"

"I'm not sure it's *on* campus." Eula shakes her head, frustrated. "I checked the map before I left my dorm, and there wasn't anything with the right name. So I don't know where I'm going."

"Did you try asking me?"

Eula pauses. "What?"

Killian shrugs, his expression bored and faintly smug, as always. "Did you try asking me? If you're not finding the information you need through some other means, asking an upperclassman is always a good idea."

"I didn't want to bother—"

"Also, Dina asked me to keep an eye on you when it became obvious you were aiming for a Silverquill study track. She said you had a keen wit, which I've seen, but she worried you'd never been in a real-world situation without backup. I try not to make my girlfriend mad when it's just as easy to do what she asks. So maybe you should try telling me what you're looking for and see what happens."

Eula pauses, strangely uncomfortable at the obvious offer of help. Everyone has their own agenda. That's as true at Strixhaven as it is in New Capenna. But people here wear those agendas more openly on their sleeves, and right now she can't see any agenda in Killian beyond wanting to keep Dina happy, and maybe keep Eula out of trouble.

She takes a breath and says, "I'm supposed to meet someone in the Harrier's Wood. Do you know where that is?"

Killian pauses for a moment before he frowns and shakes his head. "No. I know all the off-campus spots—Dina likes trees, and most of our dates involve going for walks in green places—but that's not a name I've heard before. Be careful, okay? If someone's trying to get you to go someplace where no one can find you, that's not normally a *great* sign."

"I can take care of myself," she promises gravely, swallowing the urge to laugh at the ludicrousness of the entire situation.

"See that you do," he says, and turns back to his desk, tacitly allowing her to pass.

Eula heads briskly away from the classroom, trying to make up for lost time. Her next class isn't affiliated with any specific college: Principles of Magical Shielding is a prerequisite for many advanced courses taught throughout the university, and she's seen people raise shields using techniques she could never have imagined on her own, shields of wood and shields of water, shields of swirling, prismatic light. They make her own shields of hardened air and concentration feel oddly uncreative, like she could be trying harder. It's probably her favorite class, and not only because it plays so directly into her strengths. It reminds her how flexible and glorious magic is, and how lucky she is to live in a world where magic is real— it's not all invasions from the sky. Sometimes it's a shield growing around your hand, thin and delicate and weightless, and still the heaviest thing that's ever existed.

Sometimes magic is everything.

So she hurries across the campus, trying to make it to her next class before the bell tolls and marks her down as tardy. She's almost there when she spots a familiar figure heading the same way, moving with more patience and deliberation than she thinks she's ever felt in her life. She brightens and hurries toward him, waiting until she's close before she calls, "Bricen! Wait up!"

The owlin upperclassman stops where he is and smiles as he turns in her direction, facial feathers puffed out in friendly acknowledgment. Eula realizes with a blink that she's started recognizing owlin body language as easily as she does cephalid or rhox. She's adapting.

Is that a good thing or a bad thing? That's a question for another time, and she trots to a stop in front of him and flashes him a bright smile of her own.

"I was hoping I'd run into you. I have a question about campus."

Bricen's eyes brighten. Apparently, being asked local history questions is just about the most fun thing he can imagine. "All right, hit me."

"I'm trying to find a place, and the campus guides can't help me. But you're Lorehold, so I thought maybe if something had changed names or whatnot, you'd know about it."

Bricen nods. "Good thinking. We tend to keep track of that sort of thing. What are you looking for?"

"The Harrier's Wood."

Bricen's smile fades. "Why are you looking for that? That's not a good place for you."

"I'm supposed to meet someone there. Please. Is it on campus? Or just off?"

"I don't know if I should say." His feathers are pressed flat now, slicked down against his head and body. He looks like he's trying to make himself small. It's not going to work, but it's a nice trick.

"I'm not going to get myself into trouble, Bricen."

"But you could. You and the rest of your class tend to stick together, I've seen you, and it's the only reason I don't spend more time worrying about you. You don't understand this plane yet the way someone who was born here does, and you don't always know what's dangerous."

"I'm a Strixhaven student like any other! I can make my own decisions about what's safe for me and what isn't. Or I can ask my advisor."

"But you didn't. You asked me."

Eula shrugs. She doesn't want to go into her complicated feelings about secrecy right now, or why she feels like it's important to listen to the letter-writer and go to the wood alone. Or why she might not hurry to inform her advisor of everything she's doing outside of class.

Bricen sighs. "Do you remember where I picked you up on the day that you arrived? Where you were all having that little picnic?"

"I do," says Eula. "I wondered at the time why the transport arrangements left us alone on a strange new plane for so long. Was it some sort of team-building exercise? Make sure we'd start to bond with one another before anyone else could get a foot in? If that was the goal, I wish you'd been able to arrange dropping Jamira off in the same place."

"Bonding was the idea," Bricen admits. "As for Jamira, she was busy seeing her family off to their next destination, or she would have been there. And it worked. You're a very functional unit, the five of you."

"Until next year, when we all go to separate colleges and have to make new friends," says Eula.

"Yes, until then," says Bricen. "But regardless, the wood near where you stopped to wait for me, that's the Harrier's Wood. Named after both the bird and the tendency of mage hunters to harry students through the trees."

"Mage hunters?" asks Eula, alarmed.

"They're not a concern any longer, or at least not at the moment," says Bricen. "They were driven back before the Invasion, and while they might be regrouping somewhere off campus, they've shown no sign of coming back anytime soon."

"That isn't an answer."

"It's all the answer you're getting from me right now."

"Right. Okay. So that little patch of green is the Harrier's Wood? Why didn't you want to tell me that?" There's something fascinating about what people decide needs to be kept secret as opposed to what they'll say openly. Arcavios likes to pretend it's an open and honest place, but Eula knows the truth. It's as powered by secrets as New Capenna, and sometimes the only way to live with them is to let them lie. Mage hunters aren't a concern right now, and she needs to go to the Harrier's Wood; she'll let this secret pass her by, for the moment.

"It's dangerous."

"If there aren't any mage hunters there, how is it dangerous? And why did you leave us there for so long if it wasn't safe?"

Bricen looks uncomfortable. "We should get to class. I hope you're not thinking about going out there alone."

"Of course not," Eula lies. She starts walking again, faster now; the bell for the start of Principles of Magical Shielding is only a matter of seconds away. "You know me. I'm a city girl. I don't go wandering around in the bushes when I have a choice in the matter."

NINETEEN

SNEAKING AROUND

They make it to class a beat before the bell, cutting it narrowly enough that Dean Veyran looks at them and shakes her head—a towering condemnation from the normally reserved Prismari professor. Eula sinks into her seat, trying to avoid notice, and focuses on the lesson.

It's enthralling—the principles of magic always are—and by the time the bell rings for the end of class, she's put everything else out of her head. She's actually surprised when Dean Veyran waves her hands and collapses the delicate elemental shield she's been constructing all period, letting it dissolve into lines of mist that waft around her in a silvery haze.

"Thank you all for your attendance and attention," she says formally. "I hope I have granted you the knowledge to better survive the remainder of the term."

The students murmur thanks as they rise. Eula does the same, stopping when someone grabs her wrist. She turns to find Bricen standing behind her and looking at her anxiously.

"Promise me you won't go alone," he says with sudden urgency.

Eula pulls against his grasp, and he lets her go, looking only a little bit reluctant. "I can't do that," she says. "But I promise I'll be careful."

Bricen sighs but doesn't grab her again. "I guess that's all I can really ask for," he says glumly.

Eula nods and heads for the door. The rest of her day is dedicated to study periods and a class on Biblioplex access that has felt frankly remedial for weeks now. The Biblioplex is large, but it's not *that* confusing, and she certainly doesn't need to spend another hour learning how to call the boats. She's been calling them just fine since midterm and isn't going to forget everything she knows before their final exam.

Instead of going to her useless class, she turns away from the classrooms and starts to walk. No one stops her as she approaches the main gates and continues onward, exiting to the pastoral landscape outside the university.

She's not the only person skipping class on this beautiful day. There are people on blankets near the walls, sprawled out or picnicking or just enjoying the sun. One group appears to be playing a less violent variation of Mage Tower, slinging a flat disc through the air and chasing after it, whooping and clapping one another on the back after a particularly clever catch. Eula ignores them all and keeps walking.

The spot where they arrived on Arcavios and had their interrogation with the Pathwardens was about three miles from campus. That's a long walk in the wilderness for a city girl; even a full term at Strixhaven hasn't acclimatized her to the way the ground can be so uneven when it's not paved and planned, and while the field looks smooth and open, the ground is filled with hidden holes and jutting rocks, slowing her considerably until she reaches the road.

Once she's on the smooth-packed earth, she speeds up and makes most of the trip at what she considers a halfway reasonable pace, coming into sight of the picnic point while the suns are still riding high in the sky. Eula pauses, taking a deep breath, and starts up the shallow hill between her and her destination.

When she reaches the top she stops, looking into the woods beyond. The Harrier's Wood, where she's been told to go. The trees are well spaced and seem healthy; there's nothing eerie or unusual about them, and the branches that reach for the sky above are well clothed in lush green leaves and small, hard fruits that look entirely inedible. She turns to look back at the campus, which perches in the distance like a strange half-tamed beast, familiar and still not entirely trusted.

A bird flashes by overhead, feathers bright blue against the paler blue sky, and Eula follows the arc of its flight to the trees.

"Well, there's a sign from the house if I've ever seen one," she says. The house always wins, but there can be quite a lot of fun on the route to losing. She shakes off her brief hesitation and continues onward, into the shadows of the trees.

A narrow path has been pressed into the leaves and loam, feet following the same route enough times to wear it into the earth. Eula follows it, preferring the ease of the desire path to the difficulty of picking her way through the roots that break the ground.

It's different in the shadows of the trees. The air is cool and still, smelling strongly of leaf-rot and clean soil. Sedgemoor was warm and vibrant, pulsing with the life of death and the death of life. This place is patient, growing at its own pace, not hurried by anything. Tiny chirps and rustles sound all around her, the birds and small creatures of the wood reacting to her presence. And Eula keeps walking.

She isn't truly alone very often these days. They try to stay together to avoid possible harassment from the students who would prefer they leave the school entirely. When she's not in class, she's in her room with Alandra, or studying at the Biblioplex, or eating at the dining hall. As she walks, it occurs to her that she can't remember the last time she was alone on purpose for any length of time—not even before leaving New Capenna. Since the Invasion, everything has been moving very quickly, and in arcs designed to benefit everyone around her. Her family, the Families, the cleanup crews, and now the school. It's been so long since she could just *think*.

So she does, pressing deeper into the Harrier's Wood. The man she danced with at the party mentioned disappearances from the Biblioplex—but why? There haven't been any disappearances this term, or else they've been kept so quiet that she hasn't heard anything about them, despite spending an unreasonable percentage of her waking hours in the stacks. She's made her fair share of copies, either writing things out carefully by hand or using the transcription spells she's committed to heart, or asking the assistance of the Inklings who stay in the vast library full-time. They can be cajoled to copy almost anything, and when they don't want to, there's usually a Silverquill second-year around who can be convinced to make them do it.

Her carefully selected file of secrets too good to portion out without a specific reason has been growing since the start of term, and some of the spells and historical records she has should be enough to help her father *and* buy her freedom. There's information enough for everyone, and she knows Raffine will be enthralled by some of the things she's copied out.

She can't even feel bad about stealing Strixhaven's secrets. For one thing, no one asked her to promise she wouldn't. If you're going to call people from across the planes and offer them access to your wild candy store of mystic knowledge, you should say something about what you don't want them to do before you leave them to their own devices, or you should expect them to do exactly what she's done. Not just her, either—she's seen Alandra with quill in hand, copying spells in a messy, borderline illegible script, and Segante lurking in the deep stacks, doing foundation-knows-what. They're all the same, all here to benefit themselves, their planes, and their families, and she'd be in the wrong *not* to take proper advantage.

She's broken no rules, done nothing wrong, only guaranteed her ability to return and finish her education. Coming home empty-handed could so easily end with a command that she *stay* home. But if she comes home with something valuable enough to lift them out of the lower city without her, if she buys her way free . . .

Everything is transactional. She thinks that's why she gets along so well with Segante. He understands it. Alandra and Kequia still think the world knows how to be generous, and Jamira is difficult to read, but she and Segante understand that reality is a transaction, and whether you're the belle of the ball or holding a server's tray when the party starts is determined by how well you balance the books before they call the score.

Birds twitter nearby, and Eula keeps walking, following

the path around thick-trunked trees and dense, woody shrubs until it deposits her at the mouth of a clearing. Unlike the clearing where the masquerade was held, this one is plainly artificial: someone has cut back the trees, leaving a ring of stumps. The ground is marked with shallow pocks where the rest of the stumps have been pulled, the holes filled in as much as the forest has allowed. Sunlight slants through the latticed branches overhead, dappling on the leaf-litter.

Roughly a dozen students are gathered there, wearing the colors and sigils of all five colleges, talking quietly among themselves.

Eula stops dead at the end of the trail. A leaf crunches underfoot, and the students turn to look at her, giving her no chance to run or hide. She doesn't know any of them well, but she recognizes some among their number, people she's seen in the dining hall or passed on the quad. One girl wearing Quandrix colors is in her Principles of Magical Shielding class, always sitting at the back of the room, never making eye contact with the instructor or the other students. Another she recognizes as the Lorehold student who was so rude to Alandra on their very first day.

Maybe seeing him makes her bold, or maybe she's just feeling reckless, but either way, she folds her arms and says, "One of you said you wanted to talk to me, and that I wouldn't be hurt. Well, I'm here like you asked. Now talk."

"Miss Blue," says a goblin in Witherbloom colors, stepping forward with a polite, well-rehearsed smile on his face. She recognizes him as Abtin, the Pathwarden from their arrival day, made briefly anonymous by his lack of uniform. "It's a pleasure to see you—"

"I came to talk, not hear you spit pleasantries at me like they're going to be repossessed if you don't use them all right now." Eula tilts her head, watching him closely, and sees the way the corner of his eye twitches, discomfort radiating off of him. She makes him nervous. That doesn't make a lot of sense. He's at least a year ahead of her, and all she really knows how to do is shield—great for getting her out of this situation alive if this is some sort of nasty trap, not so helpful for letting her walk away the winner in any conflict.

"I'm sorry," says the rude boy in Lorehold red and white, taking a step forward of his own. "It *is* nice to finally meet you properly, without your swarm of bodyguards. I'm Larin, and I appreciate you coming to speak with us."

Eula eyes him but doesn't say anything. She's said enough. Now it's his turn.

Indeed, only a few seconds pass before Larin says, "We've been meaning to approach you for some time, but now, with everyone going home for the holiday break, it seemed urgent we meet. This is the Arcavios Preservation Society, and we have a favor to ask of you."

"Oh?" Eula doesn't mention the fact that none of the transplanar students will be going anywhere over the holidays. If these people don't already know that, they can learn it when the campus closes down and the five of them stay precisely where they are.

"Yes." He pauses, looking at her with a grave, deep-set sincerity, like he has never in his life prepared to make a more important request. "Don't come back."

"Excuse me?" Whatever she'd been expecting him to say— and she'd had a mental list of possibilities going, ranging from

"Bring us some of that Halo we heard you talking about" to "Carry this rock with you to your home plane so we can form a sympathetic link for a class project"—it wasn't *that*. Even if these were some of the same people who'd attacked them in Sedgemoor, that kind of blunt approach showed a tiresome lack of subtlety and an utter unwillingness to negotiate. "We're enrolled through the end of the year."

"Yes, but surely you can see that you don't belong here." Larin sounds entirely serious. "This is dangerous foolishness, and if there was going to be some sort of pilot exchange program, it should have waited to launch until we'd had the time to complete ecological studies on the impact of the omenpaths on our home plane. We'd barely even started looking at the possible impacts when this program was announced."

"And if they were going to launch despite our objections, they should absolutely have restricted themselves to students who came from planes directly connected to our own," says an elf from Witherbloom. "There are stable omenpaths from Arcavios to at least four other planes, and we don't know yet about the temporary ones, or how to predict new omenpaths forming."

"I've been working on that math," says a djinn in Quandrix colors. "We need a few more unstable omenpaths to get the equations right, but once we do, we'll be able to predict the formation and dissolution of omenpaths. Or I hope so, anyway. Because right now, we're undefended. An omenpath could form anywhere, anytime, and there's nothing we can do to stop it."

"Is four an unusual number?" asks Eula.

"We don't *know*," says the djinn, frustration evident.

"There's so much we don't know, and here we have people rushing to set up carriage services and cross-planar mail delivery and imports!"

"And you," adds Larin grimly. "We don't know what you being here is going to do to the plane—or what the plane is going to do to you. Haven't any of you noticed that things here don't work exactly the way they do when you're at home?"

Eula thinks of Alandra, slowly suffocating in the ambient magic of Arcavios, so thin compared to the bounty of her faraway home. "No," she lies. "We've all been fine."

That seems to take some of the wind out of Larin's sails. His lips firm into a hard line, and he looks at her sternly. "That just means you haven't been paying attention. There *must* be complications. Students from the Pinzari Isles are cold all the time because they're not used to the climate this far inland. And students from Chimneycomb find the air as thick as treacle and almost as difficult to breathe, at least until they finish adjusting to the local environment. You came from other *worlds*, other places, where everything works differently. If you haven't noticed any issues, you just need to look harder."

The accusation of not paying attention stings enough that Eula lifts an eyebrow and gives him a withering look. "Or maybe people are people wherever they are, and any plane that can support people is going to have some things in common. The Planeswalkers have been going back and forth forever, and they haven't caused any problems like you're hinting at."

Too late, she realizes that saying Planeswalkers haven't caused any problems is probably not the best way to get her point across. If there's one thing the Planeswalkers have definitely done, it's cause problems.

"The Planeswalkers passed through the Blind Eternities when they traveled from plane to plane," says the Quandrix student, garnering nods and murmurs of agreement from the other students in green and blue. "Nothing else could survive in the Blind Eternities. The ability to make that transition without being vaporized is what made them Planeswalkers. So if they had biting insects in their hair or seeds stuck to their boots, those would just burn away during the crossing. There's nothing like that to protect us from the omenpaths."

"So just because someone *could* track something invasive through the omenpaths, you want us to drop out of school?"

"No, because someone already has," says Larin. "More than one someone, and more than one kind of invasive thing."

"Explain."

"We've found odd flowers growing around the edges of Sedgemoor," says the elf. "Nothing from this plane. But I was near your dorm the other week and saw the boy from Fiora making a flower arrangement with some of them. He looked approving, like they were normal flowers, the sort of thing he was used to using."

"Those are dreamwaste flowers from Fiora," says Eula. "He got permission to bring them with him as a cultural artifact. We declared them to the Pathwardens when we arrived."

"Be that as it may, there have also been odd moths around the cafeteria lights," says another student. "Wings too big, eyes too bright. They're not from around here."

"Some sort of fungus is eating the snarlflowers, and we don't know what it will do to the pests if they catch it," says yet another student.

"So you see, the omenpaths are dangerous, and you need

to go home so there's less reason for them to be used," says Larin. "It's a small sacrifice for the safety of our plane—and your own."

"But the omenpaths will still exist," argues Eula. "Sending us home doesn't do anything to solve the problem."

"But you could," says Larin.

Eula blinks. "What?"

"You could solve the problem," he says, and gestures toward the Quandrix student who mentioned studying the omenpaths. "Via, explain."

Via smiles and nods, stepping forward with the brisk efficiency of a teacher's pet getting ready to deliver the correct answer. "We don't have the models to let us predict the formation of new omenpaths yet, but we have the mathematical underpinnings of the tunnels themselves. They all follow a very similar aetheric fractal tunneling matrix. I've been leading a team in building . . . I guess you'd call them explosive charges."

"Bombs?" asks Eula.

"I suppose you could describe them as bombs," says Via. "You set them up and set them off, and they destabilize the quantum tunnel when they explode. They can theoretically collapse an omenpath. We just need someone to plant the charges."

"And you're not sure whoever does it will get out before the collapse crushes everything inside, so you're asking the transfer student none of you cares about to take the risk," concludes Eula grimly. She finally unfolds her arms. "There's no way. When I *do* leave this campus, I'm going home, not blowing myself up in a quantum tunnel because you're worried about flowers and bugs. You're cowards for even asking. I hope you understand that."

"But this is for the good of *all* the planes," protests Via. "Your home won't fare any better than ours does if you just leave these open paths between it and the rest of the Multiverse!"

"The Multiverse is opening the omenpaths on its own; it can deal with closing them on its own," says Eula. "It surely doesn't need me to do it. Thank you for your proposal, but I'm afraid I must be going." It takes every ounce of etiquette she understands to remain unflinchingly still, watching the group of students shift uncomfortably from foot to foot.

"People have been vanishing from the Biblioplex," says a man in Silverquill black and white. Eula's head snaps around, her eyes narrowing as she focuses on him. She knows that voice.

And after this, she'll know his face, too. He won't be able to run away from her again.

"You keep *telling* me about people disappearing, and I don't know anything about that," she says.

"I didn't think you did," he replies. "But it's been happening for as long as anyone can remember, and you spend a lot of time at the Biblioplex. If you disappear, people will just assume you're the latest abductee, and they won't look for you any harder than they have the others."

That's alarming. Eula takes a step backward.

The man she danced with looks genuinely regretful. Larin looks almost pleased, like he's been hoping she would refuse to help them.

"You promised I wouldn't be harmed," she says, voice trending toward frantic.

Via sighs. "We did," she agrees. "But we had hoped you would be open to seeing reason and taking the necessary steps to preserve the sanctity of Arcavios. This is just the place you go to school. This is our *home*. If becoming Pathwardens isn't enough to let us protect it, then we'll be Preservationists, and we'll do what we must."

Eula doesn't wait to see what they're going to do or demand next. She turns on her heel and bolts into the trees, avoiding the desire path and its clear ground in favor of making a disappearance into the underbrush. She runs as hard as she can, suddenly grateful for the physical education requirement she's been grappling with since the start of the term. She's always been reasonably fit, capable of running along city streets and shoving herself through shortcuts as the need arose. Now she feels like she could run forever, especially when she has a good reason.

The people she hears thundering along her trail are definitely a good reason, or the beginnings of one. She doesn't know if they'll actually harm her, but the continued references to disappearances in the Biblioplex make her think they will. She has no one at the university who would lead the charge to find her if she vanished. Oh, she knows her dormmates would notice, and Alandra would probably *try* to search for her, but she's far away from the dorm, and no one knows she's here.

Bricen might be able to tell people where to start looking, if she doesn't come back. Or Killian. But she can't count on the kindness of people she barely knows, and she can't count on Professor Kasmina paying enough attention to her students to notice her disappearance. A few reports that she was last seen in the Biblioplex, and she'll vanish into someone else's mystery.

She supposes the people following her might wait until Alandra's in class, then break into their dorm and remove Eula's belongings, leaving a note behind to make it look like she left of her own free will. That would almost be better than claiming she'd just disappeared.

Kequia's psychometry would tell her the truth as soon as she inevitably touched the note. But there's no telling how long that might take, and Eula will still be injured, imprisoned, or even dead in a ditch somewhere, rotting into the earth of a plane that has never felt so unlike her own. She puts her head down and keeps running, not allowing herself to look back. Looking back means either stopping or running without looking where she's going. One way loses ground, the other sees her slamming into a tree. Better to run and count on her ears to see her safely to the end.

Something hits a nearby trunk, embedding deep in the wood. Eula dares a glance and sees what looks like a short arrow made from some sort of natural quill or feather spine protruding from the bark. She finds another burst of speed and races into the wood, mumbling under her breath and knotting her fingers together in an intricate pattern as she runs, until the thin black lines of an ink shield blossom in her hands, and she slings it over her shoulder, protecting her back from sneak attacks.

She keeps running, and the woods drop away, and she realizes with a lurching hitch that they're not giving up. They're going to keep following for as long as it takes, and they know these woods better than she does, by far. It's momentarily terrifying, before she digs deep for another burst of speed and forces herself to keep going. She survived Phyrexia. She's not going down here, chased through the trees like some sort of prey animal. She *won't*.

So she runs, and she pours her magic into the shield at her back as she keeps her eyes on the wood ahead of her—the last thing she wants to do is knock herself out by running headlong into a tree because she's too panicked to watch where she's going. But she can't be looking everywhere at once. She doesn't see the pursuers moving up behind her, doesn't even realize they're there until something grabs hold of her shield and yanks hard enough to send her toppling over backward, landing like a turtle flipped onto its shell.

The Quandrix girl from her Principles of Magical Shielding class is standing behind her. There's nothing that looks quiet or shy about her now. There's a vicious scratch down one cheek, probably from running into a tree branch, and her eyes are hard, cold, and unforgiving. She's not touching Eula's shield with her hands. Instead, she has a web of blue and green strands spread between her fingers and has somehow managed to loop them around the shield on Eula's back. It feels like an impossible interaction of magic, and yet it's happening, threads wrapped around the jagged edges of Eula's shield until she's held fast, trapped on her back on the cold forest floor.

More of her pursuers loom above her, and there's no getting out of this. For a moment, she wishes her magic were more offensive in nature, that she had Alandra's lightning or Segante's deadly blossoms or even Kequia's psychometry. She dismisses the desire. She is a daughter of the streets of New Capenna, and she will not cower, even if she's caught and captive. She's better than that.

She is.

She has to be.

A caul of power settles over her face, a shield of a sort, impermeable to everything, even air, and she can't breathe, she can't *breathe,* and her vision goes black, speckled with tiny pinpoint sparks of brightness, rising and popping like the bubbles in a glass of Halo, and then even those are gone, and all is darkness, silent as the grave.

TWENTY

ETERNITY

Eula wakes up in a world made entirely of light.

There was a Crescendo party several years before the Invasion where she'd finally been judged old enough to stay awake and watch the old year slain on the horizon in a cascade of fireworks and scintillating sparks, giving the new year a path to follow into the newborn now. Some clever Cabaretti engineer had figured out how to make the falling sparks look like the bubbles in a glass of Halo, glittering and iridescent. This is like that. She blinks, and the bubbles don't go away.

Her hands are tied behind her, and her feet are bound at the ankles, leaving her sprawled and all but helpless on the jagged ground. Whatever's beneath her feels like rock, none of the soft edges of leaf-litter or loam, but relatively level for all of that. She can't see more than a few feet in any direction, all the details of the world softened and blurred by the falling cascade of bubbles. She even *smells* Halo, that ineffable brightness, like biting into a sugared lemon and a raspberry at the same time. But she can breathe. This isn't Halo, and as that thought forms, the subtle wrongness of the scent follows. There's an undertone of char and superheated metal to the sweetness, burnt sugar coating the citrus brilliance in a brittle shell.

Her skin tingles, like she's lying in an exfoliating bath, like the bubbles she can see bursting all around her are more physical than she initially assumed. She squirms, trying to sit up, and the tingling gets stronger, becoming a light abrasion.

Eula stills, pondering her situation. She's in an omenpath: that much is terribly clear. They caught her, they bound her, and they threw her into an omenpath while she was unconscious.

She catches her breath, feeling the tingling bite of the bubbles against the back of her throat. Via said her team was *building* explosives, not that they were already finished. Are there bombs in here with her? Are they using her to somehow feed the charges? They were clearly able to come far enough into the omenpath to strand her; there's no reason they couldn't set the explosives themselves unless they need a living person to somehow make the reaction work. Martyrs, not murderers.

It's the exact sort of self-serving distinction drawn by people who want to think of themselves as the good guys. She tries to roll, tries to look around, and when both attempts fail, she tells herself the bombs aren't ready yet: she's a sacrifice to their ideals, but she's not going to take anyone with her. The feeling of abrasion is getting stronger, beginning to burn, and she knows it doesn't matter whether there's a bomb in here, because she's not going to survive for long. Whatever the omenpaths are made of, they're meant to be traveled through, not lingered in, and the Halo gleam of the air is going to consume her.

She closes her eyes and focuses on continuing to breathe, which is getting more and more difficult as the burn advances. She just needs to keep breathing. A mail carriage will come along eventually, or Bricen will come looking for her, and she'll be fine. She'll be *fine*. Silently, she promises to pay twice as much attention during gym class if she can survive this. If she can just make it back to her dorm, with the door closed and locked between her and the rest of Arcavios.

It's all right if Alandra is there. She likes her roommate and isn't worried about Alandra deciding to make her disappear in the name of some weird new form of planar purity. But no one else. No one—

Her eyes snap open and her entire body tenses as she hears a foot crunch in the gravel near her. Whoever it is, they're coming from behind: she can't see anything of their approach. But they're coming closer. They're getting closer, and she's trapped.

Half desperate, half instinctive, she reaches for a shield and finds the mana of this space slips through her mental fingers like a thin mist, unwilling to be caught or contained. She grabs again, and the second time, she feels the magic catch, just for a moment, like a spark landing in a heap of kindling. She grabs a third time just as the stranger reaches for her, and the hands that would have grasped her arm and rolled her over onto her back bounce off the suddenly sealed shield instead.

There's no point in pretending to be unconscious anymore. Eula glares at the glittering emptiness ahead of her, demanding, "Who are you, and what do you want?"

Segante's answering chuckle is dry and brittle and utterly recognizable. Hope surges through her.

"I'm your dormmate, and I thought I might drag you out of here before you passed the point of recovery," he says.

"How did you—?"

"Find you? That part was reasonably easy. You weren't as subtle about looking for your meeting point as you thought you were, and I followed without your knowledge. Once I realized what was happening, it was a small thing to hide myself until your assailants finished trussing you up and tossed you into the omenpath to die. I'm sorry to have interfered with your fun game of 'get chased through the forests and maybe get my throat slit like a ceremonial stag.' It seemed rather a waste of a good shield mage." Segante's voice is mild and soft. He pauses to exhale, almost like a sigh, before he continues.

"Let me guess; they told you to come alone," he says. "You're clever enough, if sometimes a bit conceited, so they must have promised not to harm you before you decided it was a good idea to leave campus. They lied. You didn't."

"Sorry I trusted them," she says bitterly.

"As you should be. Can you release this shield so I can untie you?"

"The air burns."

"I don't think we're supposed to stay inside the omenpaths for this long. Come on, Eula. Just drop the shield."

Eula worries her lip between her teeth for a long moment before she lowers her hard-won shielding. The feeling that the air is trying to eat her immediately surges back, stinging all the more after her brief respite.

Then Segante's hands are there, undoing the knots at her

wrists and ankles with quick, efficient gestures. When he's done, he guides her into a seated posture, and she sees his face for the first time.

He looks terrified, the skin around his eyes bruised and drawn, his lips thinned into a hard line. She starts to comment and stops as he crushes her against him, holding her close. Eula takes a deep breath of tingling air. Her lungs feel like they're being squeezed, like every breath is an effort too immense to be shouldered on her own. She lets herself go limp against him, resting her cheek on his shoulder and coughing so hard that she shakes.

Segante shifts one hand to her back, rubbing in tight, concentric circles, like he's going to ease the air back into her. It seems to help, and before long, the tightness in Eula's chest begins to loosen and let go. She shoots him a grateful look, and he acknowledges it with a quick nod as he pulls first his hand and then his arms away.

His sudden absence is a cold wound in the world, and she almost reaches for him again, barely catching herself before she does. He straightens, reaching for her hands to tug her gently with him.

"This omenpath closes in an hour, and we don't want to be inside it when it does," he says. "Come with me."

Eula squeaks and doesn't resist. Bad enough that they left her inside an omenpath, but to leave her inside one that's on the verge of closing? "I could have been—"

"Lost," he says firmly. "Nothing more than that. If I allow myself to consider their actual intentions, I would have to hunt them down, and this little adventure would end in my expulsion. My father would be most displeased if I returned home before finishing my studies."

"Which you would have to do if you committed a bunch of murder on my behalf."

"Precisely. Do try to keep up, Blue."

Despite his commanding tone, he's gentle as he leads her out of the omenpath and into the cool air of the evening. One sun has fully set; the other is well on its way. The sky is the bruised beauty of twilight, and the air—

The air stings her skin. Eula stops, looking down at her hands and arms. They're bright red, redder than she could easily see inside the omenpath. "The bubbles really *were* eating my skin," she says with frustrated wonder.

"It's no worse than a bad sunburn. I can fix it once we have a moment."

"What do you mean?"

"I mean, we're not alone here." Segante gestures down the road to where several small carts wait. "I think your friends are still at large."

Eula's face hardens, and she grabs his hand again, pulling him toward the trees. Segante stumbles after her, looking too confused to resist. When they're almost there, he pulls his hand away and demands, "What are you doing? They could still be *in* there."

"And we can hide better with cover," she says. "If we walk down the road, they'll see us. I thought the goal was *not* committing murder tonight."

He looks at her sharply for a long moment before he yields and lets her tug him into the trees. They stick close to the edge, moving through the wood in the direction of campus. They've made it a reasonable distance before Segante stiffens and pulls her close to his side, making an exaggerated shushing motion at the same time. He turns, pressing his palm flat against the trunk of the nearest tree. The thin branches of its crown dip downward, contracting and growing denser as they twist together, until the two of them are covered by a screen of woven twigs and wide, glossy leaves.

Eula blinks, then nods and tucks her head toward her reddened breastbone, focusing for a moment before a shield begins to form around them, thin as a soap bubble and gleaming with flecks of light like the glitter inside the omenpath.

"What did you hear?" she asks.

"Footsteps in dry leaves," he replies. "Keep your voice down."

"No need," says Eula dismissively. "My shield will keep them from hearing us, and your tree will keep them from seeing us. How long do you think we're going to stand here?"

"As long as we have to," says Segante. He turns his attention to the web of twigs blocking them from the rest of the forest. "Are you sure your shield blocks the sound?"

"I have an older brother and two younger siblings," she says. "I learned how to make shields that could stop sound before I learned how to reliably stop a rock. Do you have any brothers or sisters?"

"Is this the time for small talk, Eula, really?"

"If we're about to die, I'd rather do it making polite conversation."

"Now that their clever 'throw you into an omenpath and hope no one notices' plan has failed, they're not going to kill us." Segante's tone is witheringly dismissive. Eula shoots him a startled glance.

"What do you mean?"

"I mean if they'd been intending to kill you, they wouldn't have taken so much time explaining themselves before they trussed you up and tossed you away," he says. "They're students. Pampered, sheltered students who'd probably never even considered that people our age *could* die before the Invasion came and upset everything they thought they knew about their lives. They aren't killers. Oh, maybe that one boy from Lorehold could kill someone if he really put his mind to it—he's got the look of someone you shouldn't trust around sharp objects—but the rest of them? No. They're academics, not assassins. They left you inside the omenpath, which I truly believe *would* have killed you, and they walked away with plausible deniability. They were never going to *murder* you. They got too involved for that."

Eula gapes at him. "You make that sound so *reasonable*," she finally says.

Segante shrugs. "It is reasonable, when the other option sees you dead on the forest floor. I would be . . . most displeased if you died in such a pointless, wasteful manner."

"I guess that would be wasteful," says Eula. "But be careful saying things like that, or people will start to think you care whether I live or die, and that could damage your reputation."

Segante makes a noncommittal sound and reaches up to tweak one of the leaves—or tries, at least. His fingers don't pass through the shield; they press up against it, a thin barrier between him and the rest of the world. He turns a half-amused look on Eula.

"Very funny," he says. "I need to see if they're close enough to worry about, or whether we can start moving again."

"Be quiet, then," she says, and twists her fingers, redefining the scope of the shield. It expands first, then pulls back into a rough disc, coming to rest against her back. The sound of the forest comes whispering back, leaves rustling in the breeze, birds chirping in the boughs—but there's no sound of pursuit. No running footsteps or crunching branches. Eula shoots Segante a hopeful look.

He nods, grabbing her hand, and brushes the branches aside with a quick gesture, leaving them with a clear shot into the nearby trees. Holding tight to each other, they bolt from shelter into the unknown and run as hard as they can for the forest's far edge.

TWENTY-ONE

ANGLES AND ALLIANCES

Finding their way out of the Harrier's Wood and back to the side that faces campus is easier said than done. Even pausing only periodically to listen for signs of being followed, they're losing the light, leaving them wandering through the increasingly dark woods long after they had hoped to be back on clear ground.

"We're going to miss dinner," mutters Segante.

"I'll buy you coffee and dessert," says Eula.

"What did they want from you, anyway?"

"Didn't you hear?"

There's still enough light to let her see the quick, sharp shake of his head.

"Ah. They wanted me to drop out, go home, and blow up the omenpath on my way there. I guess they didn't know I'm at least two omenpaths away from home, or maybe they were planning to have someone else blow up the link between here and Fiora. Maybe you. Anyway, I turned them down and they didn't have the bombs yet, so they just threw me in there and left me."

"Why would they—"

"They say things can come through the omenpaths. Bugs and plants and other things that aren't good for the plane."

"Ah," he says, more thoughtfully. "When I was a child, I used to help Father's cook in the garden. She had all manner of herbs and simples that she grew herself. And then, one of my aunt's rivals became aware of our location and threw a dozen little clay balls over the garden wall. They broke when they hit the ground, and when we swept up the mess, bits remained. What we didn't know at the time was that the balls had been packed with seeds, and those seeds were poisonous plants that mimicked many of Cook's herbs. She tasted everything before it could be served to us, and her death was . . . quite unpleasant. We moved at once, of course, but the damage had been done, and we had lost a very skilled cook. All because of some plants that weren't where they were meant to be."

"That doesn't mean the omenpaths are going to kill us all, which they seemed to think they will." Eula shakes her head. "There are professors—former Planeswalkers—and that Firemind guy who's going to fix the situation with the bandits on Fiora, and they're all comfortable with the omenpaths. I don't think a bunch of students should get to make a decision that big. Especially not if it means blowing ourselves up in the process."

"I am definitely opposed to blowing myself up, being blown up, or having you blown up," says Segante. "No explosions, please."

They pause, listening to the dark woods around them.

There are no sounds beyond the faint rustle of nocturnal wildlife beginning to emerge from their burrows and take to the night. Eula takes a shaky breath and starts moving again, Segante beside her.

"I'll try not to get exploded," she says.

"See that you do," he says imperiously. "Or I'll tell Alandra to have her father arrest you."

"He's a warlord, not a king," she says.

"Arrest you!"

Eula snickers at that, unable to quite help herself. "All right, all right. Why Alandra's father? Why not your aunt?"

Segante sobers. "I would never wish a Fioran prison on you, or on anyone else I wanted to see alive again," he says. "I haven't the money or influence to get you out, and imprisonment there would break you, regardless of how small your original offense had been. They would break you and be proud of themselves for having done it. So clever, to shatter the spirit and strength of a girl who'd done nothing wrong. So powerful, to destroy an enemy before the battle can begin."

"Oh," says Eula, more softly. They walk on, and the light starts to brighten as the trees thin around them. "I wish one of us had magic that could lead us out of this wood. I know I'm the one who wanted to use it for cover, but there are limits."

"Shields aren't the best wayfarers, I suppose?"

"No. I could use a shield to *create* a trail—if I made one of the little bubbles I use to pass messages to Alandra, I could break branches with it while I was moving—but once I'm trying to backtrack, it's too late to create anything."

"Alas, much the same for me. I can heal injuries and encourage plants to grow, and I can do a certain degree of damage to living tissue, but none of those sets a thread for me to follow out of the wood if I didn't do it in the first place. I'm as stranded here as you are."

"At least we're not stranded alone?"

"There is comfort in company," Segante agrees, and they keep walking.

The light continues getting brighter until Eula can see the outline of his face. His hair is dark enough that it's just one more patch of shadows among the trees, and she wonders if her hair is the opposite, if it's a beacon he could follow through the wood. She would never have managed to get away if not for his intervention. She doesn't have the disposition, or the camouflage, to have pulled it off. It would be easy to resent that, and the girl she was before the Invasion probably would have. Now . . .

She's learned to let herself rely on other people when she has to, and to understand that she can't save anyone unless she's willing to allow herself to occasionally be saved. It's a difficult adjustment to make. She still thinks it's a good thing that she's been making it.

The edge of the wood is so abrupt that it's almost a shock. One second, they're walking through trees without end, and the next second, those same trees are falling away, leaving them to face the wide expanse of field between them and the distant shape of campus. The lights are still on; they haven't missed curfew yet.

But that means their pursuers haven't missed curfew, either. They could easily be lurking out there in the tall grass, concealed by shadows, ready to attack and still get back to their dorms before it's too late. Eula glances at Segante, alarmed. He looks grimly back.

"You spent more time with them than I did. Do you think they're going to jump us out in the open?"

"I think they're cowards," says Eula. "Tricking someone to come alone into an ambush? Why, I never. The facebreakers back home might offer you a parley, but they'd never *lie* about it like that. Hired muscle that lies to a victim will lie to an employer."

"The more I learn about your city, the more fascinating I find it," says Segante. "All right. We walk fast, we walk together, and you don't look back, no matter what. Can you make one of those shields around us that keeps any unpleasantness in the air from getting in?"

"I can make them airtight, but I'll have to drop them so we can breathe."

"How long will we have with the air you catch inside?"

"Ten minutes, maybe?"

Segante nods. "That will do."

They hold their positions while Eula casts her shields, drawing them into large spheres around their heads. She looks at Segante and nods, and he mouths, "Don't look back," before he takes her hand and starts walking, pulling her quickly across the field.

She thinks she sees motion out of the corner of her eye several times, and she tenses, trying to keep her attention fixed forward. They're almost at the end of their ten minutes when something flashes by—one of the flat discs she's seen thrown back and forth on the green. She gasps, whirling to look behind her.

There is no motion behind them. Everything is still and dark, and Segante tightens his grip on her hand, tugging her along. The air inside her bubble is getting thin and strange-tasting.

Time to let the shields go. She does, and takes a deep breath of fresh air like a draught of Halo, sweet and welcome.

"I thought I asked you not to look back," he says.

"I don't understand why," says Eula, letting him pull her as she continues to scan the dark fields behind them. The grass seems taller than it should have been, topped in too many places by blossoms nodding in the wind. She glances at Segante again. "What did you do?"

"I made sure we'd be safe," he says. "That was all."

She feels like he did more than that, but she doesn't want to argue. "Shield's down," she says. "Are we still being followed? Is this where we run?"

"I don't think so at this point, and it might be a good idea, if we want to get back to campus before curfew," he says.

Eula nods, and they run for the distant shape of campus, hand in hand and side by side. Nothing comes out of the fields to assault them, and almost before they know it, they're approaching their dorm, wreathed as always by blooming snarlflowers and munching pests, their hearts beating hard and their lungs aching but with no one in visible pursuit.

Segante waits until they're inside the dorm to let go of Eula's hand. He heads for their foyer, which is empty, although someone's left a pile of books on the central table. Kequia, probably. Segante continues toward his room, and Eula follows him, too keyed up and jangled to want to be alone. He pauses at the door, one hand on the knob, and gives her a hard look. "Did you want to come in?" he asks.

"If I could?"

"I don't have guest bouquets out," he says, as if that should mean something to her.

Eula shrugs. "I don't know what those are, so I won't mention the lack if you won't."

Segante opens the door and gestures for her to follow him. "We observe a lot of pleasantries and social rules on Fiora, so people will know whether they're protected by the laws of hospitality or not," he says. "You can't kill someone after you break bread with them, for example, but that doesn't include drinks or canapés. You can absolutely invite someone around for a light snack and an assassination."

Eula blinks.

Segante isn't done. "One of the ways you can signal the status of a household is with the flowers you put out in public areas. All my current bouquets say, 'The master of the house is home, no others reside here, trespass at your peril.' You would be within your rights to take that as a threat, and none of the laws of hospitality would be broken if I killed you."

Eula blinks again, then turns to look at the flowers arrayed on the shelf nearest the door. "I don't see any of that," she says. "It's just flowers to me."

"Are there not seemingly innocuous things that could be viewed as dire insults on your home plane?"

"Oh, sure. If you go into the home of someone of a higher social status and don't remove your shoes and hat, you're insulting them, saying they're not important enough to relax around—unless they called you there for work, and then you'd be insulting them if you *did* take those things off, because that implies their time isn't valuable enough to respect. It would be *intensely* rude of me to invite you in and not immediately offer you a drink, or for me to eat in your presence without offering you something first."

"Ah. Well, by inviting you in without welcoming bouquets, I have done all those things. On Fiora, this would be a dire insult."

"I guess it's a good thing we're not on Fiora, then."

His bed is easily twice the size of hers, and he has space for a table and two chairs in addition to his desk. Eula crosses to the table and sits, admiring the flowers displayed there. Insulting or not, they're pretty, even if the pollen does make her head spin a little.

"What did you do back there in the field?"

"I encouraged the local flora to release pollen into the air. It was a mildly toxic mixture. It shouldn't have killed anyone, if that's what you're worried about; they'll wake up in the morning with headaches and blurred vision, but nothing worse. Unless there are wolves. Oh, I hope there are wolves."

Eula laughs. "That's not nice!"

"Neither was luring you into the trees without backup. As they started it, I am allowed to finish it."

"With wolves?"

"With wolves." Segante moves to adjust the flowers in the nearest vase, visibly uncomfortable. "Where I come from, no one helps anyone else for free. Coming to your defense tonight would have been construed as my trying to get you into my debt so I could force you to do something equally beneficial for me. Outside of family members and sworn alliances, there are no casual 'favors.' Your home seems to be the closest to my own of everyone's here, and even that is so different as to be constantly disorienting when you choose to discuss it."

"Oh."

"The way this group does things . . . you handling my

laundry makes sense, because I give you money for the favor. But Kequia helps Alandra copy her homework more nights than not."

"Alandra's handwriting is atrocious," agrees Eula fondly. "It's the webbing between her fingers. She has trouble holding a pen. I've tried to teach her some basic ink-casting, but she doesn't seem to have any talent for it."

"I've never seen Kequia ask for repayment."

"Alandra brings Kequia pastries from the cafeteria on the days when she sleeps in too late to make it to breakfast, but not because Kequia asks. Because it's the nice thing to do."

"And Jamira—I've seen her help so many people carry things across the campus, even when doing so took her in the wrong direction."

"It's nice to help sometimes."

"It doesn't make sense. This isn't the way things work between people who aren't family, or even between people who *are* family. A familial hand is the most likely to hold the knife."

"Maybe that's the thing they're really worried will spread between planes," says Eula. "Better manners, or at least not stabbing each other nearly as much."

"Maybe," says Segante, somewhat sullen. He looks at her across the room, and Eula looks away, not sure what she's supposed to say now. When did everything get so unclear?

TWENTY-TWO

ADMISSIONS

Eula takes a short, sharp breath and rises, wincing as her reddened hands press against the table. "I'm intruding, you're not set up for guests, I should go."

"No," says Segante. His cheeks redden for a moment at the sheer bluntness of the negation, and he rises in turn. "Not yet. We need to repair the damage to your skin."

"It's not that bad," says Eula, looking at her arm. In the cool light of Segante's room, her lie is even more obvious. She doesn't just look sunburnt, she looks like she's been pressing her entire body against the side of a furnace, baking the top layers of her skin away, leaving her raw and on the brink of blistering.

"Brave words," says Segante. He steps toward her. "I may not have put out the proper flowers for a visitor, but you can't truly mean to reject my hospitality so blatantly. It would be a terrible insult. Are all young women from New Capenna so rude?"

"It would be ruder for me to insist on staying when you've already established that you weren't expecting to entertain," counters Eula, her own cheeks flushing. This is a script of sorts, one she's seen play out with her peers but never followed on her own.

She's nineteen years old, well past the point where she's considered an adult in New Capenna, and from what she understands, she's an adult here in Arcavios as well. Each plane must have its own rules of courtship and comportment—just the process of comparing notes with her fellow Silverquill hopefuls has made that perfectly clear—and in some places, it's more common for young people still in the process of their schooling to begin stepping out with their peers. Why, even in New Capenna, people her age have been known to forge and negotiate understandings between one another, although not normally people in her social class. The rules are different for the children of the Families, and for the children of the Caldaia, born with no hope of upward social mobility, but for her, well. She's been carrying the weight of her family's expectations for a long time.

It's been heavier than she ever realized it could be. And now, hearing the start of this familiar script from Segante's lips, the only person outside of New Capenna who might anticipate her lines, she wants to put it down more than anything. So she smiles and waits to see what he'll say next, waits to find out whether the polite refusal is a part of this performance in Fiora as well.

Segante shakes his head, moving toward her.

"Of the two offenses, my allowing a guest to leave injured when I could have addressed the matter is the greater slight," he says. He reaches for a bouquet, then holds it toward her. "I clipped these flowers myself this past morning. They're fresh and carry no harmful toxins or biting insects."

This is a new direction for the script to take. Eula blinks. "What?"

"Essence work is simplest when there's a source to pull from," he says, still holding out the bouquet. "Please, let me help you."

Eula nods, very slowly, and reaches out to take the bouquet. Segante wraps his hand around her wrist as she does, his fingers cool against her burning skin, and ducks his chin down toward his breastbone.

She can feel it as he begins to unwind the essence from the flowers in her hand. It comes apart in two distinct streams, a stinging rush of entropic decay and a fainter, more distant brightness. She can't quite feel the second the way she does the first, and in fact, it's hard not to think that just the day before, she wouldn't have felt it at all. Her time in the omenpath has rubbed more than just her skin raw.

Then the ribbons of essence wrap around her fingers and her hand and all the way along the length of her arm, and there's a cooling sensation, like someone is running an ice cube from her elbow to her wrist. The petals on the bouquet begin to wither and crisp around the edges, drying out and dying. The feeling of coolness expands, spreading down her torso and along her legs.

The ribbons tighten, and the bouquet collapses into dust as the coolness fades, leaving her hand empty. She looks down at it. The redness is gone from her skin, replaced by her normal pallor. A quick twist and her wrist is free of Segante's grasp, allowing her to raise her arm to the level of her face.

The damage there is gone as well. She's restored.

She lowers her hand and lifts her gaze to meet Segante's, her eyes wide. "You healed me," she says.

"It was only polite."

The echoes of the script she knows are still there but tattered, reshaped by their progression. His eyes are so dark, and her fingers are dusty with the crumbled remains of his bouquet. She should look away. It would be the polite thing to do, the proper thing to do.

She doesn't look away. He's so close, the heat from his body a comfortable contrast to the coolness of her skin.

"If we're both being polite," she says.

"Yes?"

"I should . . . thank you."

"No gratitude is needed for proper hospitality." But he doesn't move away when she starts to lean toward him, and she knows this script, she knows what happens next, and she doesn't shy away.

His kiss tastes of honeyed tea, and he offers it with a hunger she couldn't have predicted. She returns it the same way, leaning closer still, until she slides off her chair and he catches her, pulling her close as he continues to kiss her, and kiss her, and kiss her.

The coolness on her skin is replaced by an electric tingle that has nothing to do with magic *or* manners and everything to do with his hands, one splayed flat against her back, the other sliding up the curve of her neck to tangle in her short-cropped hair. She lets herself be molded against him as his hands move against her, and keeps her focus on kissing him, endlessly.

The rug looked soft the first time she saw it, and it *is* soft as she kneels on it, as Segante lowers her onto her back, as he begins unbuttoning the front of her dress, fingers moving with a quick deftness that must serve him well in his flower arranging. For one dizzy moment, Eula can't remember what comes next. Then she catches her breath and reaches up to unfasten the buttons of his doublet, exposing the tightly fitted vest beneath.

She hesitates then, tilting her head slightly back as she studies his eyes, looking for some sign of whether she should stop or continue pressing onward. He's stopped kissing her for the moment, gone still when the doublet came open, and the eyes that meet hers are—not worried, precisely, but filled with a strange, thick waiting, as heavy as melted metal.

Eula swallows, then says, in a soft voice, "I can stop, if you'd prefer."

"We could both stop," says Segante.

"Or . . . ?" Eula offers.

His next kiss is searing, his fingers tracing along the front of her bandeau like he can read the future in the boning there. She takes that as the invitation it seems to be and keeps unbuttoning, her own fingers unfastening his vest until it hangs open, exposing the paler skin of his chest. One nipple is pierced, shockingly silver against a dusting of dark hair.

Segante pulls back slightly, saying, "It seems unbalanced that you should still be so covered."

"It hooks behind my back," she says breathlessly, and laughs as he pulls her up enough to reach behind and unfasten the bandeau, sliding it downward with a quick tug before simply staring at her. There's no urge to cover herself. She gazes up at him, barely breathing, hair a tangle of wild, unkempt curls.

Then he leans down and kisses her again, and some scripts really are the same between planes.

Some things don't change at all.

ACADEMIC EXCELLENCE

While Segante and Eula explore each other in a dorm room filled with flowers and soft rugs, Kequia sits in the cafeteria with a bowl of lentil soup and a plate of thick, unleavened bread, which she dips methodically as she reads her current textbook, moistening each bite before she eats it. The noise of the cafeteria fades into the background, easy to overlook in the face of the grand historical drama of the Blood Age, a time of turmoil and strife for all Arcavios that even her home plane of Dominaria would be hard-pressed to match.

Oh, they'd succeed—digging through various planar histories in the Biblioplex has provided her with proof that the people who used to complain about the world never slowing down to take a breath between crises were correct: things really *did* happen on Dominaria more often than should have been statistically possible. Dominaria was once considered the literal center of the Multiverse, the hub around which the entire impossible wheel of reality spun. That changed some time ago, but the echoes and the scars remain. Dominaria was a plane in constant chaos, and that chaos makes the histories of all the other planes she's been studying seem comprehensible and contained.

Kequia turns a page in her book, dips her bread again. It's hard sometimes, looking at the old histories, not to get an inflated sense of her home plane's importance. Everywhere is important, Dominaria included, and history has been happening across the Multiverse since it came into being, malleable and mutating and magical. Even Lorehold falls into the trap of thinking one plane's history is more important than any other's with surprising frequency—for all that she's been able to read about planes she had never even imagined, places with names like Innistrad and Eldraine and Kaldheim, most of the archeology texts are about Arcavios, digging into the history and heritage of the plane she's on. That makes a certain degree of sense, since there wasn't much point in trying to specialize in another plane's history before the omenpaths— doing so would only frustrate anyone who tried, unless they were fortunate enough to spark.

She pauses then, thinking about what Professor Kasmina has said about Planeswalkers and embers. She doesn't *feel* like anything changed in her after the Invasion: she's as connected to her magic as she's ever been—more, even, now that she's learning how to use it in her own way and not according to what people who think she can grow up to be her grandfather want from her. It doesn't feel like a fire burning in her chest, or like a coal getting ready to burst into something brighter. It's just . . . hers, warm and safe and steady, and ready to let her use it to explore as many planes as she can find. Whatever

Kasmina thinks she is, or was, the former Planeswalker is wrong.

She dips her bread again, eyes still on her book, and almost misses the scuff of feet approaching her table. She tenses, shoulders growing tight as she casually—oh so casually—reaches for the fork she always takes with her meal, even when she has no intention of using it as any kind of eating utensil. Even when she knows she doesn't need it. Can't carry weapons to the cafeteria, but the cafeteria provides them, if you pay attention.

"Miss Akosa," says a disapproving voice, northern Jamuraan accent heavy and clear. "You can't be intending to *eat* with that little piece of metal, can you? How unsanitary."

Kequia looks up and finds herself facing an older man in Tolarian chancellor's robes, the collar pressed and starched, the sleeves loose to the elbow and tight to the wrist, leaving the wearer's hands free for mystic gestures and runic summonings. His mantle is brown leather, with the knotted fringe of a dedicated historian. In case all of that wasn't enough, he has the seal of Tolaria West on his breast, high above his heart. His skin is as dark as her own, and his expression is twice as solemn, but it's the robes and her response to them that steal her breath momentarily away. They're such a familiar slice of home. They shouldn't seem so shocking, and she shouldn't be questioning their presence. But they are, and she is, and the bite of bread and soup in her mouth is suddenly tasteless and dry as paste. She swallows with an effort.

"Silverware isn't unsanitary when you have running water to clean it reliably, sir," says Kequia politely, feeling as if she's eleven years old and defending her grandfather's most recent disappearance to her village schoolmaster. Somehow he had always managed to time his visits to other parts of the plane to correspond with her needing him to come in and talk to her class about some facet of local or planar history. The ghosts of a dozen detentions dance before her eyes as she struggles not to look anything other than politely interested in what this man may have to say.

"I see." He sniffs. "Well, if you're quite done with your meal, your presence is requested."

"Where, sir?"

"The administration building. Your advisor will be meeting us there, along with"—another sniff—"others."

"Should I return to my dorm to find the rest of my class?"

"No, Miss Akosa. We want to speak specifically to you."

That never bodes well. Kequia closes her book, puts her bread regretfully down on the edge of her tray, and rises. "Can you wait a moment while I clear my table?"

"Isn't there staff who can manage it for you?"

"Yes, and school constructs when the staff aren't available, but it's rude to assume I can just go around making messes and they'll handle everything." She picks up her tray, tucking her book up under her arm as she does, where it won't be dropped. "It should only take a moment."

"If you must," he says sourly.

Kequia walks her tray to the return station, where she scrapes her leftovers into a bin for the Witherbloom composters to collect and places her dishes in the appropriate tray. True to her word, it takes only a moment. True to the promise of his attitude, the man in the Tolarian robes is scowling when she returns to her table.

"Ready, sir," she says.

"You had best be," he replies, and starts walking, clearly expecting her to follow.

Curious and confused in roughly equal measure, she does exactly that, letting him lead her out of the cafeteria and into the early evening air. The campus is still well lit enough that she can see the students making their way along the paths, the budding astronomers setting up their telescopes and the would-be athletes throwing balls and discs to one another on the green. The man from Tolaria West looks at all this activity with dispassionate disapproval, and Kequia blinks in her confusion, hurrying to keep up with him.

"Does this campus have no curfew?" he asks.

"Several Witherbloom core subjects work best when taught at dawn or dusk, and not many Witherbloom mages are awake at dawn," she says. "The ones who are sort of scare me."

She's seen them walking, their eyes bright with fanatic fire, their smiles wide as the horizon and filled with the artificial energy of too many cups of coffee, tea, or even stronger stimulants. They're almost entirely upperclassmen, so she hasn't had to interact with them much, and she's grateful for that.

The man from Tolaria makes a noncommittal noise and keeps walking.

Kequia is quiet for a time, hugging her books to her chest and trying to focus on her feet, on not tripping over the little irregularities in the brick of the path. When the silence gets to be too much, she looks up and blurts, "Is there something wrong? With my family? Did my mother . . . is she okay?"

The man blinks, looking bewildered by her question for a long moment before he says, "Your family is entirely fine.

I spoke to them before coming here. Your grandfather sends his regards."

With Teferi, that could mean nearly anything. "Please, what did he say?" she asks.

"Nothing I should be repeating to a child," says the man. "Here we are."

Kequia isn't a *child,* but she doesn't argue. Instead, she considers both his tone and his words, his constant attempts to reduce her agency in this discussion. There are answers in his behavior, if she can dig deep enough to find them. As for swearing in front of a scholar, well, that sounds like her grandfather if nothing else does. Her family knows the chancellor is here.

They're approaching the main administration building. Kequia's seen it before, has been inside a few times, but not at night and lit entirely from within, making its glassine walls shine with nacreous color. It's eerie and almost unsettling, making her stomach turn unhappily. She should be in her dorm right now, working on her papers for tomorrow's classes and occasionally answering Jamira's questions. The Quandrix hopeful has paths of study very different from Kequia's own, and by comparing their work, they've found that they can better understand it. It's like the mismatched parts light up and clarify the similarities.

One thing about the administration building stands out as unusual: there's a whole group of people in Tolarian robes on the steps, murmuring amongst themselves. They look up as Kequia and the man approach, their faces smoothing into neutrality, their postures shifting toward something more formal: arms down, hands folded either in front of them or behind their backs. Some of them nod to her, like she's someone of actual importance and not just a Strixhaven first-year waiting to find out whether she's in trouble.

"Vitha, if you please," says the man who came to fetch Kequia from the cafeteria.

One of the women nods and steps forward, opening the door to the administration building. The woman is apparently human, missing two fingers on her left hand, with scars twining up her arms like the skin has been torn away in odd, tangled strips. She holds the door wide as the rest of them file past her, finally stepping inside and letting it swing shut once everyone else is through. Kequia glances back at her, eyes wide.

She's heard that name before. Vitha Thenwe, shield mage and professor of mathematics. The chance to study under her had been one of the main endorsements of Tolaria West before the Invasion, when Kequia had still been considering colleges. Now here she is, in the living, if slightly tattered, flesh! Given what she's heard about Professor Thenwe's shielding techniques, Eula is going to be *so* jealous.

Kequia allows her steps to slow until she's walking alongside Vitha. "Professor," she says with the utmost politeness. "I didn't expect to see you here."

"No, Scholar Akosa, I don't suppose you did," says Vitha, tone perfectly polite. "After the Invasion, I remained at Tolaria West, to help my plane recover."

Kequia isn't a scholar by Tolarian standards; that title must be earned. If they're giving it to her so freely, they want something. She holds this firmly in mind as she smiles and bows her head to the professor, her posture perfectly composed.

"Was the school badly damaged?" she asks.

Vitha actually stops walking for a moment, taking a deep, strained breath. When she starts to move again, her eyes are shuttered, like she's trying to hold back some terrible wave of memory. "Tolaria has battled Phyrexia before," she says. "We were created for this battle, and we have survived it every time the need arose. We survived this time as well, although not without costs. There are always costs."

Kequia doesn't want to ask what those costs may have been, not with those scars and that endless, empty look in Vitha's eyes. So she swallows her reply and merely follows, letting the group lead her into a small, well-appointed conference room dominated by a large hardwood table. The walls are decorated with banners of the college seals, with a larger banner of the university seal hanging directly across from the door.

Two figures are already seated when they arrive: Professor Kasmina, a large, tawny-feathered owl perched on the back of her chair and watching them all with unblinking, unforgiving eyes, and Professor Vess, sitting well away from her with a steaming cup of tea in one hand and her face set in an expression as unreadable as the owl's.

It's not really a surprise to find the two former Planeswalkers waiting for them, but the sight still causes Kequia's stomach to sink toward her toes. Whatever's going on must be very serious indeed.

She looks to Professor Kasmina with urgent, pleading eyes. "Is my grandfather all right?" she asks.

"Teferi?" asks Professor Kasmina in surprise. "I assume so. He's not immortal anymore, but he's still a human wrecking ball. Blowing out his spark won't have changed that. I don't think anything could have. Didn't they tell you what we were going to discuss this evening?"

"We thought it best to have this conversation without prejudicing the scholar," says the man who first collected her from the cafeteria. "Unlike some institutions, Tolaria believes in the integrity of education."

Kasmina bristles. Professor Vess sips her tea.

"Proceed, then," says Professor Vess. "You requested this meeting. It sounds as if you've already made up your minds about how it's going to go. Let's see how correct you are."

Her tone is lightly interested, like she's suggesting a child carry on playing with matches and dry grass. The delegation from Tolaria react by looking uneasy and mumbling among themselves, moving one by one to take their seats around the table. Kequia remains standing, unsure what she's supposed to be doing, until Professor Vess pats the open seat next to herself. Kequia hurries to sit, wedged between Professor Vess and one of the professors from Tolaria West, with the rest arrayed around the table and looking attentively toward the first man, waiting for him to start their meeting. Professors Kasmina and Vess both look at him with anticipation, like adults who've been told that a child is going to do a particularly clever trick.

"Well?" prompts Professor Vess. "This is your meeting."

"Yes," says the man, shaking off whatever brief fugue had fallen across him. "I am Chancellor Feren, and we are here to discuss your unethical student recruitment practices, in hopes that we can come to some sort of an accord moving forward, to reduce competition over students."

"Is that really in the best interests of the students?" asks Professor Kasmina. "I would think competition could only be good for them, as it forces us to improve our offerings and provide them with a more thorough educational package. Really, we should be seeking an accord that *increases* competition, not eliminates it."

"The academic situation has been changed by the omenpaths," says Chancellor Feren. "They allow cross-planar student recruitment on a scale that has never previously been possible, which makes poaching possible on a scale that we've never had to worry about before."

"Is it really poaching if you haven't offered a student a position before we do, or is it slowness on your part?" asks Professor Vess. "I just want to be sure we're all working from the same basic definitions."

"Why are we speaking with you?" counters Chancellor Feren. "It's my understanding that you're both college faculty—and not the most senior among them, either. Neither of you is a dean."

"No, but as former Planeswalkers we are considered uniquely suited to matters of policy that impact cross-planar relations, and the students you're objecting to are in my care," says Professor Kasmina, her voice cold. "I'm their primary advisor until they reach second year and pledge to a college, and then I'll remain their general advisor after that, making sure they get everything they need and deserve out of their university education."

"If you would prefer, we can leave you here and go to see if Director Taiva will be willing to take this meeting on our behalf," offers Professor Vess. "I would recommend against it, of course, unless you have a decade to wait and enjoy being shut in a room with the high-strung, traumatized director of a rival academic establishment. He's always put Strixhaven first, and I don't see you having an argument that will make him change his mind about doing so in the future."

"That's quite all right," says Chancellor Feren quickly. "I didn't mean to imply that you weren't qualified to take this meeting, just that I had expected something . . . else, given the reputation of this establishment."

"He means he thought he'd be meeting with one of the Founder Dragons," says Kequia. Both professors give her curious looks, and she wilts. "Professor," she adds, not quite sure which of them she's addressing, only that she wants to keep them happy with her, at least until she understands what's happening here.

"Indeed," says Chancellor Feren. "We didn't know you existed until we came to offer Miss Akosa admission and her grandfather informed us she'd gone off to study at Strixhaven. He's a Tolaria man, her grandfather—one of our greatest graduates. He's been doing great things since he was a student with us."

"Notice how it's always 'great' things," says Professor Vess to Kequia mildly. "We forget that 'great' and 'terrible' become interchangeable when looked at from a sufficient distance, like history can sand the edges off atrocities."

"Lady Vess," says Chancellor Feren sharply. "I hardly think you're one to speak of atrocities."

Professor Vess makes a disinterested humming sound and sips her tea.

"Regardless, your presence on the faculty of this school proves our point that you have moved to keep the playing field unbalanced," says Vitha abruptly. "You were born in

Dominaria, the same as we were. You knew about Tolaria, while we were ignorant of you. Shame on you, luring good students away from our world to this one."

"The luring was entirely my doing, I'm afraid," says Professor Kasmina. "I was the one who provided the list of proposed students, and while Liliana did assist in winnowing it down to find our inaugural class, Miss Akosa was not our only prospect from Dominaria. We would have been, as you say, 'luring good students' away no matter what. If blame must be assigned, allow me to have it."

"Why *are* you here?" asks Professor Vess. Kequia is starting to understand what they're doing: by trading questions quickly, they're forcing the delegation from Tolaria to continually switch focus between the two of them, not allowing Chancellor Feren or the others to relax long enough to choose whom they're going to talk to. It's a subtle unbalancing, but it appears to be working, judging by the looks on the delegation's faces.

"We want you to send your stolen students home," says Chancellor Feren. "They were recruited under false pretenses, and they deserve the chance to choose where they pursue their educations, not be lured in with promises of scholarships and fancy colleges."

"What?" squawks Kequia. The delegation turns to look at her. She hunches in her seat, cheeks burning under the weight of their attention, then forces herself to sit up straighter, meeting Chancellor Feren's eyes. "I've done nothing to warrant expulsion, and I'm not going to leave of my own accord," she says sternly. "I'm almost done with this term, and next year I can pledge to Lorehold. I've been waiting for that opportunity since Grandfather handed me a student handbook to study.

I know about Tolaria. I know what you can offer me. I choose Strixhaven."

"You see, sir, Strixhaven is the premiere magical institution in the Multiverse," says Professor Kasmina. "There's nothing that can't be learned here, if you're willing to put in the work."

"We have professors older than this campus," says Chancellor Feren. "I can't believe any other school could surpass what we have to offer."

"Yet somehow, we have," says Professor Vess. "Blame the Founders, or the Snarls, or the web of spells that stabilizes and controls the Mystical Archives. Regardless, we have more to teach than any one mind can ever learn, and more resources than you can dream of."

"We can rebuild our reserves if we have *students*," counters Chancellor Feren. "Unlike your gilded towers of patronage and privilege, we're a working school. We depend on tuition to keep our doors open. If you're not willing to return the students you've already stolen, we must request you restrict your student recruitment to a curated group of planes, ones occupied by cultures that would not be a good fit for the student community we're working to encourage."

Professor Vess sips her tea and raises an eyebrow. "Fascinating that you now claim we could skewer a venerable establishment with a little healthy competition. I was under the impression that your agricultural programs and efforts to provide Dominarians with food security made up the bulk of your income. Given your description, I assume you have some manner of list you'd like to impose upon us?"

Chancellor Feren reaches into his robes and produces a small scroll.

"How droll, you do," says Professor Vess. She leans over to take the scroll, unrolling it enough to read. Then she blinks and shoots a sharp look at the Tolaria designation as she pushes the scroll down the table to Kasmina. "You must be kidding."

"I assure you, I'm not."

"So we're to be allowed the great privilege of students from Fiora, Muraganda, and *Mirrodin*, which we both know no longer exists, while you claim all students from planes known to have stable precollegiate education systems? We'd be converting half of our campus into remedial studies just to keep our students from accidentally killing themselves! To say nothing of the cultural conflicts that would arise if we put students from some of these planes together. Do you know how hard it was to find a balance that allowed us *one* Fioran student without the constant fear that someone was going to be poisoned?"

Kequia grimaces. No one ever mentioned poison as a hazard of dorm living. Then again, no one mentioned sulfur, either, and even with the magical barrier keeping Jamira's room environment out of Kequia's own, both of them smell like sulfur most of the time. Some hazards simply can't be seen.

"Given your resources and stated academic goals, we would think you'd be willing to support us and agree to our requests," says Chancellor Feren. "Academic health arises from varying points of view."

"Am I correct to assume your potential student body also took a beating during the Invasion?" asks Professor Kasmina.

Chancellor Feren nods, his expression grim. "So many students were lost. So many students, so many teachers, and so many brilliant young minds that *would* have been students in a year or two. We lost an entire campus to Phyrexia, and it will be years before it can be restored to its former glory. Dominaria's survivors are dedicating their resources to rebuilding, not to paying for the education of their younger children, who will never be able to inherit their family lands, and who would once have been sent off to us to bring honor and renown to their family names."

"It sounds like your concern is more about families choosing not to send their children to school at all than it is with them choosing to send their children to study with us," says Professor Kasmina. "We've only recruited one student from all of Dominaria so far, and while there are others on my list, there aren't many. We're not going to restrict ourselves to the planes you don't want just so you can feel competitive."

"But—"

"No. I'm sorry, but no. I can get Director Taiva in here if you'd like, but he'll tell you the same thing. Your struggles, tragic as they are, do not belong to us. If you're meant to survive reconstruction, you will, without punishing us for having a different academic structure. We lost . . ." Her expression hardens. ". . . so much, during the Invasion. So many professors, so many students, so much history and knowledge, and we didn't give up. We lost little less than everything, and we're not going to bow to the autocratic demands of a university that isn't even on this plane. If you missed out on Miss Akosa, maybe you should have been faster. A legacy of her caliber should have received offers from all of your campuses years ago. If you need tuition to keep your doors open, it's time for you to recruit better. We did."

"Will you really elect to work against your fellow academic establishments?" asks Chancellor Feren, voice low and cold.

"We would prefer to work *with* you," says Professor Vess. "We need to develop a competitive cross-planar curriculum, one that can prepare our students for the new reality. Who knows better what literature and history from Dominaria should be taught than the preeminent institute of Dominarian learning? There's no need for us to fight over prospective students. We can't possibly admit every hopeful in the Multiverse, and our offerings wouldn't be right for all of them anyway. *Without* giving you any input on our admissions, I can offer to help you come up with a screening process and promise to throw any students who wouldn't thrive here your way."

Kequia frowns. This feels . . . wrong. It's true that the omenpaths are bringing the planes into contact with each other more than ever before, but when planes cross, it leads to glorious adventures and exciting feats of magical skill, not administration and student enrollment.

But maybe administration is the foundation they need to build a solid and peaceful collaboration among the planes. The representatives from Tolaria are all talking at once now, sentences spilling over one another like eager puppies as they argue for the standards they want to see shared between campuses.

None of which changes the feeling that she shouldn't *be* here, that this is a conversation meant to happen behind closed doors, without its subject in the room.

Kequia puts up her hand.

"Yes, Miss Akosa?" asks Professor Kasmina.

"I have homework; can I go back to my dorm?" she asks. "Since I won't be leaving the school until I get my degree, I mean."

Professor Kasmina looks at Chancellor Feren and smiles as she replies, "Of course, dear. Hurry along. I'll be by later tonight to check on you."

Kequia rises, feeling rather like a game piece that's just been kindly dismissed by the game master before she could be sacrificed in some complicated gambit meant to benefit the other side. She hugs her books close as she hustles for the door and doesn't look back until she's out of the building entirely. The sky has grown even darker while she was in that room, and only the campus light posts are there to guide her back to the dorms.

She's halfway there when the bell rings to signal primary curfew: after this point, everything is closed, and students are expected to be in their housing if not actively participating in a class. The dining halls will be wiping down the tables and portioning out the leftovers to go—well, to go wherever it is that leftovers go. To the pests, most likely. The little things are everywhere, and their endless hunger is amusing, as is the way most of the campus seems to tune them out. They belong to the Witherbloom mages, as much as they can be said to belong to anything or anyone, but they're tolerated on all five college campuses as well as the central university grounds.

Kequia hugs her books and keeps walking, more grateful than ever that the offer from Strixhaven arrived when it did. She used to dream of Tolaria, and maybe it's still a place worth dreaming about: maybe what she saw today just seemed petty and small because they're scared and temporarily safe enough to focus on things that don't actually matter. Maybe focusing on small things is a way of handling the big things going wrong.

It doesn't make her feel any better about being dragged into the middle of a fight that had nothing to do with her, but it's something to hold on to as she approaches her dorm, grateful to see that the exterior lights are on, guiding her safely home.

When she gets there, Segante's door is closed, as always, and so is the door to her room. Peeking inside, she finds Jamira passed out cold on her rocky bed, muzzle pointed toward the ceiling and faint snores drifting through the shield. No company there.

Kequia eases the door gently closed. She should be going to bed, she knows, but she wasn't tired before she was pulled into an administrative meeting, and now she's so spun up she feels like she could climb the Biblioplex in order to sprawl on the roof and count the stars.

Segante has never been open to her attempts to socialize, but Eula and Alandra often are. Kequia crosses to their door and knocks lightly. Then she steps back to wait.

A few seconds tick by. She takes another step back, starting to feel increasingly foolish. Why would anyone be hanging around in their dorm rooms waiting for her to need company? Sure, the curfew bell just rang, but there are plenty of nighttime activities on campus for people who want to go looking for them. She's quite sure they've found something to do, something far more interesting than—

The door swings open, and there's Alandra, Orestes on her shoulder, a polite smile on her face that turns genuine when she sees Kequia.

"Kequia!" she says gleefully. "What's going on? Eula's not here, if you're looking for her. I don't know where she is. That's a little strange—I normally know where she is, because it makes things easier when I need to be someplace that she isn't."

"It's easier to avoid someone if you know what and where you're avoiding, yes," agrees Kequia. "I wasn't looking specifically for Eula; I just wanted some company."

"I'm company," says Alandra happily.

"You can be. Got any ideas about where we can go to burn off a little energy? It feels like my skin is full of ants, and I'd like to shake them loose."

She should probably find Alandra's sharp-toothed grin alarming, but after a term spent sharing the same housing, it's comfortingly familiar, as are the small, inquisitive chirping noises Orestes starts making, spreading his wings and standing up on Alandra's shoulder.

"Go see her if you're so eager, you silly lizard," says Alandra, nudging Orestes with her chin.

The drake leaps into the air and glides over to land on Kequia's shoulder, wrapping his tail loosely around her neck for balance. "Hello to you, too," she says, before she notices Alandra plucking the books out of her hands. "Hey! I was reading those!"

"Not right now you're not," says Alandra, putting the books on the foyer table. "Don't worry, no one's going to take them. Jamira checks your homework against her own while you're asleep, not when you might come back and catch her, and Segante isn't focusing on the same magical problems you are."

Kequia blinks. Alandra shrugs.

"What?" she asks. "I pay attention. Or did you think I was so busy trying not to suffocate on this plane's cruddy mana to notice what's going on around me?"

"Are you drunk?" blurts Kequia.

"No, but I did go to Sedgemoor for an hour this afternoon,

while the Witherbloom novices were gathering flowers." Alandra beams. "I caught a few frogs for them, and they were totally willing to let me hang around soaking in the atmosphere. I'm not drunk. I'm just feeling full and happy."

"All right," says Kequia. "Where are we going?"

"That would spoil the surprise," says Alandra, and grabs her hand. "Let's go!"

TWENTY-THREE

SNARL

Eula and Segante lie side by side on their backs, her head resting on his shoulder, his hand splayed across her stomach in a manner less possessive than wondering, like he's trying to convince himself she's really there. A second bouquet has joined them on the floor, knocked off the table during their enthusiastic rolling, and its crushed flowers perfume the room even more strongly than their sweat. Their silence is easy, comfortable, the silence of the satiated and content.

Finally, Eula rolls away from him and rises, sliding her bandeau back on as she goes. "I've abused your hospitality long enough," she says. "I should go."

"You've abused nothing," says Segante, sitting up and watching her intently. "I extended my hospitality, and by taking it, you avoided a possible insult between our houses. Everything is balanced as it should be, and there is no danger here."

"I should still go see whether Alandra needs me; I could

use a little normalcy tonight, and helping her figure out how to get her notes put away without water damage is always good for a half hour of healthy frustration." Eula flashes him a quick smile. "Thank you again for the save, and for a very pleasant evening. I guess if they want to drive us all out of school, it impacted you, too, but it still felt like a very big hero moment for you."

"All I've ever dreamed of," he says dryly—but there's a note of sincerity there that takes the sting out of his words. "I assume you'd like to discuss this with the others before we take it to Professor Kasmina?"

"Authority figures are a good last resort," says Eula. "As long as we don't involve her, we're not doing anything wrong by trying to figure things out on our own. Once she knows the situation, she gets to have input on how we handle it. I want the others to agree that it's the right time."

"Fighting with other students could see us expelled," cautions Segante.

"Yeah, but I'm not foolish enough to go off alone with them again: this was their one real chance to take us out. And for right now, this is the very definition of 'they started it.' I just think we need a better idea of what we want to see happen—and how big this group is—before we involve the professors."

"Fair enough." He hesitates. "And as to what happened between us . . ."

"That was very enjoyable, and I wouldn't object to another dance, but I won't expect anything from you. You needn't worry about that."

Segante nods, making no effort to conceal his relief. "I enjoyed myself as well."

Eula smiles as she opens the door and slips out into the foyer. Kequia's books are on the table. She makes quick note of it as she crosses to her own door, opening it and poking her head in.

She withdraws a moment later, her expression perplexed. Segante, vest and doublet refastened, has emerged into the foyer. He's leaning against the wall near his dorm room. As she steps back out, he lifts his head and frowns.

"What's wrong?"

"Alandra's not here," says Eula. "She doesn't have any night classes in the middle of the week."

"You aren't responsible for her."

"I know. I'm just . . . she's usually home around now, and I don't like that she's not right after those people lured me off alone." She looks to Kequia and Jamira's door, then crosses to it and knocks briskly. "The timing is just worrisome."

"So you're going to make it everyone's problem?"

"That's the New Capenna way," she says with forced cheer. "No problem is too small to make somebody else deal with it, or too big to break up and share around."

"But not with authority figures."

"Not if we can help it."

"Your home city is weird."

"So is the treacherous flower shop you grew up in." She knocks again. "Everything's a matter of perspective."

The door opens and there's Jamira, wiping the sleep out of her large bovine eyes, the hair atop her head ruffled and sticking up at the back. It adds an oddly vulnerable cast to the massive minotaur, making her look smaller, somehow, with the loss of her imposing outline.

"Eula?" she asks, bewildered. "What do you need?"

"Do you know where Alandra is?"

"I normally track my roommate, not yours," says Jamira. "She was heading to the swamp this afternoon, but that was well before dinner. I had Mage Tower practice at the same time; I finished my workout, ate a quick meal, and came back here to sleep until my back stopped aching. I haven't seen her. Or Kequia, for that matter."

"Maybe they're together," says Eula. She's about to say more when there's a clattering noise from Segante's room. She whips around, as does Jamira, and sees him lunging for the door and through it, vanishing into the room.

"What are you doing, you overgrown chicken?" he demands.

Eula and Jamira approach his door cautiously and are almost there when Segante emerges, holding Orestes in one hand. The drake isn't struggling to get free. There are scrapes and scratches on the scales of his throat and sides, and one of his wings has been cut, not enough to penetrate the membrane, but enough that he's bleeding, a thin, ichorous trickle washing his wing in red.

"Something's wrong," says Segante.

"Orestes!" Eula focuses on the drake, starting to reach for him as she moves toward the pair. "What are you doing here? Where's Alandra?"

"My room is the only one with a window that actually works," says Segante. "He pried it open from the outside. Jamira, could you . . . ?"

"I can fix the lock once we know where Alandra is," Jamira says.

Segante nods. "A reasonable order of actions. If the drake has come home without his mistress, something must be keeping her from us."

"Logical," says Jamira.

Eula gathers Orestes into her arms. He tilts his head back so he can look up at her, eyes half lidded and weary.

"I wish Kequia were here," she says. "She could use her psychometry to get a better idea of where you've been."

There's no mud on the little drake, and his scales smell faintly of ozone, like he's been flying through a large storm.

"He didn't just come from Sedgemoor," says Segante.

"No, or the Cultivarium," says Jamira. "He'd be covered in pollen if he'd been there."

Eula nods and gives Orestes another careful once-over. He doesn't show any signs of having been in the woods recently; Alandra probably isn't lost in the Harrier's Wood. "Jamira, I know you mostly focus on your geomancy, but have you learned *any* sort of useful tracking magic in your intro classes?"

"I can run a line of probability from Orestes to Alandra, if that's what you're asking," says Jamira. "It won't be perfect: all it can do is tell us where the drake is most likely to have left her, and whether she's likely to still be there. If she's moved since they separated, or if she's in someplace that's not usual for her, it won't work. I'm not a tracker."

"No, but every little bit will help. Orestes is injured. She wouldn't let him fly away hurt if she had any choice in the matter. Please, Jamira."

Jamira nods ponderously and presses her hands together in front of herself, palms flat. She follows by pulling them apart, moving her fingers like she's trying to work a particularly complicated cat's cradle. Separating her palms appears to take effort, more than the motion justifies, as she grits her teeth and pulls harder. The air begins to sparkle and fizz, like it's been filled with tiny bubbles. Orestes sneezes, and the bubbles all pop at the same time, a thin string of mingled blue and green light forming in their place.

The cat's cradle around Jamira's fingers becomes visible as the string manifests, a tangled web of light and angles that extends from her hands and out of the dorm entirely. "Follow it," she says, sounding strained but satisfied. "If she's where probability says she should be, it will lead us to her."

"And if she's not?" asks Eula.

"It won't."

That makes a certain sort of blunt sense. The three of them start walking, Orestes moving up to perch on Eula's shoulder, his tiny claws digging into her skin to keep him from slipping. He's definitely exhausted; the little creature is breathing too fast, and when he presses against Eula's ear, she can hear his heartbeat still struggling to come down from what must have been a deeply alarming tempo.

The curfew bells have rung: the campus is silent, save for the rustle of the trees and the distant hooting of some of the owlin students, who respect curfew in their own way but still give in to their nocturnal urges from time to time. Strixhaven never really sleeps. It just goes through various stages of activity and quiescence.

Following the gleaming line of light through the dark makes Eula grateful for the campus web of walkways, which are smooth and clean and mostly devoid of tripping hazards. This could be so much worse of a walk. And despite that little advantage, she finds herself remaining as close to Segante as she can manage, each of them lending proximity to the other as a sort of quiet support.

Alandra is a grown woman, and it would be worth leaving her alone if not for Orestes, who droops more and more on Eula's shoulder until he slides off and lands in her arms, cradled and supported while he goes as limp as a cat, content to be carried along.

"How much farther?" asks Eula.

"I don't know," says Jamira.

"Pass him to me, I can patch him up a bit," says Segante, and Eula does, pouring the unresisting drake into Segante's hands. They keep walking. They're committed enough at this point that doing anything else would feel like giving up. Orestes came home injured, without Alandra. That means she needs them, whether she knows it or not.

The thread leads them toward the Prismari campus, which glows in the night with an eerie combination of flickering red and glacial blue light. It's like the whole thing is made from plasma on the verge of exploding, unstable and beautiful and dangerous all at the same time. But they're following the thread, and so they head into the glow, letting it envelop them in glittering, scintillating brightness.

Curfew is taken somewhat less seriously on the college campuses than it is on the main university grounds; Prismari students move through the light in ones and twos, focused on their own unknowable errands. None of them looks at the little group for more than a scattering of seconds, glancing at them, taking their measure, and dismissing them as unimportant. Eula bristles. She'll show these people unimportant.

Orestes chirps, landing heavily on her shoulder. She glances over at him, and he mantles his wings in greeting, looping his tail around her neck as a stabilizing anchor. She turns fully to Segante, who is smiling, a little wistfully, as he watches the drake get settled.

"Good work," she says, and he preens in the shifting light, looking pleased with himself. She smiles and lets him have the moment. Orestes is looking so much better; the man who helped him feel that way deserves the praise.

Most of the students are heading toward a long promenade that appears to wind its way through some sort of sculpture garden. Eula, who hasn't spent much time on the Prismari campus, frowns to herself as she tries to remember what they call that area. Finally, the answer comes to her: "That's the Opus Walk," she says to Jamira, gesturing. "There must be some sort of performance going on tonight. That's not where the thread is taking us?"

Jamira shakes her head. "No. It seems Alandra is not likely to be attending a student production."

The thread continues twisting off into the distance, and they follow, moving deeper into the Prismari campus, until the Opus Walk has fallen away behind them and the only sound is the increasingly loud howling of the distant wind. The air is still where they are, but it sounds as if a storm rages just up ahead.

A storm, contained on the Prismari campus . . . "We're approaching the Furygale," says Eula. "Alandra wouldn't go there. I'm sure she wouldn't. She's said before that she wasn't desperate enough to dive into a storm that doesn't love her."

"Maybe the storm has learned to love her," says Segante. "Or maybe her desperation has changed."

"It's not safe."

The Furygale is where the Prismari dump their abandoned experiments and half-finished spells, a teeming tempest of unpredictable wild magic. It's a graveyard of the lost and unlamented, workings that will never be finished and concepts that have turned feral. Prismari students go there to duel when they don't want to be caught by their professors, and Prismari professors pretend they mysteriously forgot about the place on the day they graduated, unless they have good reason to slip across the line between the endless storm and the rest of the campus.

And the thread is leading them directly there. Eula calls a shield as they walk toward the howl of the storm, holding it in front of herself as a precaution, and Segante slows, putting her between him and the storm. Eula shoots him a half-amused look and keeps walking, following Jamira as she plods deliberately toward the sound of the wind.

The first warning sign is small, easily overlooked. The signs that follow it are not. They get progressively larger, and their warnings get progressively more graphic, going from DANGER PAST THIS POINT to DO YOU LIKE THE NUMBER OF LIMBS YOU CURRENTLY HAVE? BOTH MORE AND LESS ARE POSSIBLE IF YOU CONTINUE to THE ENERGIES IN THIS AREA WILL KILL YOU, AND IT WILL HURT THE ENTIRE TIME. By the time the roaring wind has started to ruffle their hair, the signs are becoming more and more alarming, and Eula is starting to question the wisdom of looking for her roommate.

The thread extends into what looks like a deserted quad, the ground covered by a pattern of colored bricks that has been obscured by the sheer amount of damage to the stone.

Half a fountain sits at the very edge of what can be clearly seen, water still flowing through it to spray out the top, where it shatters into prismatic light. Jamira continues on, following the thread. Eula hesitates, then yelps as Orestes nips her ear.

"The drake wants us to continue," observes Segante.

"I got that," says Eula, somewhat dourly. She sighs and starts walking again, hurrying to catch up with Jamira.

"This is where Alandra is logically most likely to be," says Jamira.

"The thread's still going," says Eula.

"Yes, but Alandra is clever enough not to have gone deeper without good reason. As I can't imagine a good reason, she's nearby."

Segante shakes his head. "Sometimes Prismari students come here looking for inspiration, or answers to what might help them with a project. Is it possible Alandra just needed some inspiration?"

Eula starts to answer, then stops as someone deeper inside the storm screams. The sound is high and furious, shrill as a seabird, and sets all the hair on her arms standing on end. Orestes lifts his head and chirps, then launches himself into the air and flies toward the sound, moving with swift and focused purpose.

"This way," says Jamira needlessly, and breaks into a run.

The others run after her, plunging into the storm.

The edges of the wailing, crackling vortex are warm and almost pleasant, like a tropical breeze washing across their skin. The hair on Eula's arms doesn't lie back down, and the hair on the back of her neck is starting to stand up in sympathy with it, leaving her feeling itchy and out of sorts, like something has gone terribly wrong. The wailing remains at the same volume, loud enough to be distracting but distant enough that none of them feels the need to raise their voices.

"At least the signs of dire peril have stopped," says Jamira.

"Yeah, because we're *in* the dire peril at this point," says Segante.

Eula looks around. There is one more sign, presumably erected by a student with a good sense of humor. TOO LATE NOW—TURN BACK WHILE YOU'RE STILL YOU.

"Okay, so the Prismari are dangerous and need to clean up their toys," she says. "Orestes went that way. Alandra must be nearby."

"Or else she's a ficus tree," says Segante, following her.

Jamira frowns. "Transmutation magic is more the purview of Quandrix. Prismari students are more likely to vaporize you or perhaps turn all the water in your body into steam than they are to turn you into a tree. I suppose someone could do a cross-disciplinary project . . ."

"Yes, fitting things into tidy little baskets is definitely something the Prismari are interested in, and not an occasional accidental side effect of blowing stuff up to express their big, big feelings," says Eula dryly. She keeps moving, trying to catch a glimpse of Orestes in the distance.

It's hard to see, what with the occasional random gouts of flame and bursts of icy light leaving their afterimages and complicating the night. The path isn't exactly clear from here, either; someone has cordoned off portions of it, making forward progress equally likely to be sideways progress, or gently curving progress. Still, they press onward.

"How does anyone in this college survive going to class

long enough to graduate?" asks Segante, sounding faintly horrified.

"The Furygale is not used to hold classes and is officially off-limits to all but the most advanced students," says Jamira. "I have been here once, when I was invited to observe a work of towering geomancy that would have been a tour de force, had it been successful. As it stands, it exploded twice, and I had to intervene to prevent it going up a third time in a much more unpleasant and dramatic way than any of us would prefer. At the time, I stated my intention not to return here unless absolutely necessary."

"Well, Alandra's missing, and that's pretty necessary," says Eula.

"Is she missing, or do you just not know where she is?" asks Jamira.

Another scream splits through the ongoing storm, as long and tortured as the first, and the sky overhead answers with a crack of lightning and a slow, menacing roll of thunder. Eula runs toward the sound, treating the obstacles in her path—rocks, strange crystal spikes, half of a bench whose other half has been reduced to twisting elemental spires—the way she would the city walls at home, going over them rather than around, using their height to propel her forward. They don't slow her down, and soon enough, she's whipping around a half-eroded corner to face Alandra and Kequia.

The two are back-to-back, Orestes flying tight circles above them. They're both bleeding from multiple small, clean cuts on their arms and necks. And surrounding them . . .

Surrounding them in a rough circle are students with blank white masks hiding their faces, dressed in a mixture of college colors, as diverse as the group that cornered Eula in the woods. Eula stops running and simply stares at them for half a moment, giving Jamira and Segante a chance to run up behind her.

"Are those . . . ?" asks Segante.

"Looks like it," says Eula. She pulls more power into her shield, making it as solid as she can, and starts advancing.

The students aren't just standing there. They're throwing every form of magical energy they can conjure at Alandra and Kequia, lashes of light and pure, ink-black shadow, whips of earth and woven vegetation. One of them tries to call down lightning, a streak of blazing electricity from the sky, and is thwarted when Alandra thrusts one webbed hand into the air and grabs it, holding the crackling bolt as if it were no more dangerous than a piece of ribbon. She coos to it, and the lightning almost seems to nuzzle her hand before she releases it, sending it at the student who called it to begin with. The student screams. Alandra adjusts her position, planting her feet a bit more firmly, and shrieks a third time.

The sound is just as piercing as it was before, cutting through the air. Now that they're at the epicenter, the reason for the shrieking is more evident: when Alandra shrieks, the storm overhead doubles in size and strength, the clouds growing heavy with rain even as they continue to roil with electrical charges. Alandra is summoning a tempest, and they're all going to be swept away.

Segante makes a complicated gesture. The scrubby plants growing around the area stand up straighter, growing visibly healthier, their leaves turning glossy and green as they stretch upward. The vines some of the attacking students called twitch and root themselves, then begin to follow the same pattern of growth, getting taller by the moment.

Eula looks down at her shield, which is so solid it feels less like a magical construct than like something that simply *is*, magic notwithstanding, and turns to offer it to Jamira. "Here," she says. "It should stay manifest for about a minute after I let go."

Jamira doesn't argue, just takes the shield in one hand as she grabs the line of probability in the other and snaps it like a whip. It responds by growing shorter and thicker, becoming a five-foot braid of scintillating blue-and-green mathematical light. Then she bellows, the sound lower and deeper than Alandra's screams, and charges toward the attacking students.

Eula calls another shield, this one light and thin, and uses it to block a lash of ink from the attackers. She stumbles back. Segante is there to catch her, bracing her upright while she drops the shield and calls two more, locking them around her forearms. He yells something, but the storm takes the sound before she can hear it.

Jamira, meanwhile, is still charging toward Kequia and Alandra. She uses her borrowed shield to smack one of the attackers aside, then bellows again as she wraps her whip around the leg of another, jerking them off-balance and sending them crashing to the ground. Alandra almost casually grabs a bolt of lightning out of the air and flings it at a third attacker, forcing him to fall back into some of Segante's plants.

The plants surge upward, easily doubling in size as they entangle the student foolish enough to step on them. They wrap tight and begin putting out little puffs of pollen, necrotic yellow and unpleasant to behold. The student they've ensnarled struggles before going limp, eyes fluttering closed.

Jamira stops when she reaches her dormmates. Kequia squeaks in surprise, then whips around and locks her arms as far around Jamira's waist as they can go, pressing her cheek to the taller woman's chest. Jamira bows her head briefly, nuzzling Kequia's hair before releasing her and turning to parry another attacker, her light whip deflecting a trident made of ice.

Eula and Segante continue fighting their way through the fray and have almost reached Alandra when there's a sudden gout of dazzling elemental energy from deeper in the storm. It lashes upward and explodes into starbursts of light, little silver flecks drifting down toward the ground. When they touch skin, they leave patches of frostbitten cold behind. For a moment, all fighting is put on hold in favor of dancing out of the way of the drifting specks. Eula raises her arms over her head, pouring more power into her shields until they expand to provide an umbrella she and Segante can huddle under.

Jamira holds the shield Eula handed her over herself, Kequia, and Alandra, while Orestes wraps himself around Alandra's neck and buries his face under her fins. The attackers have no such easy shelter. Those who have fallen scramble to their feet, all trying to hide their exposed skin by pulling down sleeves and tucking hands into pockets. The sparks are thinning, and as they become scanter and scanter, some of the attacking students begin to brace themselves like they're planning on another swing.

Before they can, Alandra throws back her head and wails, high and ululating. The storm above them doubles, lightning lashing down, and the elemental energy responds, sending up another terrifying blast of light and danger. That seems to be the last straw for the attackers, who regroup and run. They don't seem to be moving deeper into the storm, which has been cut out along the edge of the Furygale itself and is still shallow where they're all standing.

The thought is both terrifying and sobering, and Eula shudders. How bad must it be deeper inside the Furygale, where those terrible bursts of elemental energy are manifesting? How deep is it even possible to go?

"We need to leave, *now*," says Segante, grabbing her arm and trying to pull it down, breaking the umbrella formed by her shields. Eula blinks at him, then allows herself to be pulled along.

Jamira is doing the same with Kequia, leaving Alandra to hurry after the pair. None of them stops or slows until they reach the warning signs at the border and stumble out into the safe, staticky air of the campus night.

Once they're clear of the Furygale, although still close enough to hear the energies crackling and erupting within, Alandra wobbles before sitting down abruptly in the grass. Orestes croons and rubs his head against her chin, lending comfort.

Jamira also wobbles, seeming suddenly off-balance. She drops Eula's shield and releases her lash at the same time, raising her hands to cup her side, where the leather of her vest has darkened dramatically. Eula stiffens.

"Jamira!" exclaims Kequia. She hurries to reach for the staggering minotaur, hissing between her teeth as her fingers touch the leather. "That's a deep cut. We need to get you to a healer, now."

"Can't," says Jamira. "We're out past curfew, dueling in

the Furygale without a Prismari supervisor . . . we'll all be in serious trouble if we get caught outside of our dorms."

Something flickers by overhead. Eula looks up in time to see a barn owl landing in a nearby tree, the heart-shaped disc of its face a pale smudge against the night.

She still doesn't want to involve the authorities. But Jamira is bleeding, and now the hostile students are targeting more than just her. This has to end.

"Go get Professor Kasmina," she orders the owl, which spreads its wings and takes off, vanishing quickly and silently into the dark.

"I think you'll find that was a mistake," says a voice behind her. She turns, shoulder bumping Segante's, and gapes at the sight of Professor Vess stepping out of a pool of inky shadow. The necromancer looks at the group of students as dispassionately as if she'd just found them playing a card game in the cafeteria. Her gaze lingers on Jamira for only a few extra seconds.

Then she sniffs and turns, beginning to walk away from them. She goes only a few steps before she stops and looks back, eyebrows raised. "Well?" she asks. "Are you going to bring her, or are we leaving her here? I didn't think you lot were that cold-blooded—no insult intended, Miss Alandra, I know you're ectothermic. It's a colloquialism."

"I've heard the phrase," says Alandra. She's bleeding, too, from tiny cuts on her face and arms, as well as from a long slash down one leg. She looks flatly at Professor Vess. "The humans where I come from use it as an excuse for raiding us, since we clearly can't have feelings if we're cold-blooded monsters."

"My apologies, then, for the insensitivity, but the question remains: Are you going to bring your injured friend, or are we leaving her behind?"

"We're *not* leaving her," snaps Kequia.

"Very well," says Professor Vess, and watches as the other four help Jamira back to her feet.

Now with a faculty escort, the group staggers away from the Furygale, and the eternal, semi-captive storm rages on.

TWENTY-FOUR

TRIALS AND TRUSTS

Professor Vess leads them all the way out of the Prismari campus and then through the main campus to where it connects with Witherbloom, moving with a tight efficiency that makes the long walk almost bearable. Jamira leans on Kequia and Segante for about half the distance until it occurs to Eula that a shield is a solidified piece of protective magic, and the shape of a shield is a surprisingly malleable thing. With that idea in mind, she calls another heavy, solid shield, this one shaped into a long, narrow cylinder with a hook at the top, sized for Jamira to lean on.

Eula hands over the walking stick, and Kequia steps aside, letting Jamira test it against her weight. When it holds the minotaur without breaking, Jamira smiles, and so does Eula, focusing on keeping it intact as they continue their walk onto the Witherbloom campus.

Unsurprisingly at this point, Professor Vess beckons them toward her quarters, waiting until they're safely inside before she says, "All right. I'll need you to explain what just happened, if you don't mind."

"Why did you say addressing the owl was a mistake?" asks Eula. "I thought Professor Kasmina was a friend of yours!"

"She is, as much as someone who thinks the only secrets that matter are her own can have friends," says Professor Vess. "I'm sure you've noticed that her owls are always watching you, even when civility says they shouldn't be. There are things . . . oh. I'm sure you've all found that there are things about your lives that you can't explain to one another, no matter how much effort you put into trying. Aspects of growing up on your respective planes that don't make sense to people who weren't there."

She shuts and locks her door, then turns to open a glass-fronted cabinet and withdraw a small wooden crate filled with glass jars and rolls of linen bandages. She puts it brusquely on the small table at the center of the room, looking to Segante. "Well? You're going to be the healer. You can heal them."

That seems to be her final word on the subject, because she returns her attention to Eula. "Kasmina is a friend as much out of necessity as any actual affection. We were both Planeswalkers, and we weren't enemies; we shared something unique and immense and impossible to explain, and we can still find comfort in that reminder, although there's an element of pain to that shared history now that the Blind Eternities no longer call us home. She would slit my throat without hesitation if she thought it might reignite her spark. She would hold my hand while I bled out, and tell me she was sorry, and promise to carry my body home to Vess Manor to rest among the bones of my ancestors, but she wouldn't put down the knife."

"A friend, then," says Segante.

Jamira looks at the wall, seeming oddly uncomfortable.

"Oh, I like you, but that isn't the way most people would define friendship," says Professor Vess. "Kasmina will hesitate at nothing to accomplish her own goals, whatever those goals may be, and in her eyes, the ends will always justify the means. She does what she does because she truly believes it's for the best."

"So she might not have helped us against the other students if she thought it was for the best that we lose?" asks Eula.

"Something like that," says Professor Vess. "Now, would you little ruffians care to tell me what happened back there?"

Somehow she makes the insult sound like an endearment, and there's no rancor in her expression as she folds her arms and looks at them. Kequia squirms. Alandra starts to answer, then stops, hissing through her teeth, and puts a hand over one of the nastier scratches on her arm. Segante moves toward her with the first aid supplies he received from Professor Vess, beginning to bandage her wounds.

Professor Vess sighs heavily and turns to Eula and Kequia. "The two of you look less damaged than your peers. What happened?"

"I . . . Segante and I got back to our dorm to find Alandra and Kequia absent, and Jamira asleep," says Eula, mentally editing her reply even as she speaks. "We thought they might have gone for a late snack and were going to leave them alone to do whatever they needed to do when Orestes came crashing through Segante's window."

"Orestes is the drake, is it not?"

Eula nods. "He is. He came with Alandra to keep her

company, and because she gets anxious when she's alone. He keeps her calm."

"You don't need to justify the beast to me. I've seen people with stronger attachments to stranger, and I studied at Witherbloom before I became a professor. If you can find me five of our students who don't rely on their pests to survive the day, I'll be very, very impressed by your skills as a scavenger. Orestes is rarely seen without Alandra, I assume?"

"He doesn't like to be separated from his girl," says Eula. "We knew something was wrong when he came back without her, so Jamira cast a probability spell to figure out where Alandra was most likely to be."

"Not infallible, but a vital tool for any budding Quandrix mage-scholar," says Professor Vess. "They can be used to find your peers when they've been swallowed by their own experiments, and to bring them back before it's too late to restore them to a physical form. I was unaware that she had progressed to that level of scholarship already."

Jamira looks away from the wall, frowning. "Why?" she asks.

Professor Vess gives her a level look. "Because you're a first-year student not pledged to a college yet, and it seems unusual for you to have focused your independent studies so efficiently. Also, I've met your father, and I didn't expect him to have nurtured a love for scholarship. My fault, for the assumption."

"I work hard," says Jamira.

Eula hurries to resume the story, wanting to get past the inexplicable awkwardness of the moment. "We followed Jamira's spell to the Prismari campus, and from there to the Furygale, where noises from inside told us we'd found our missing friends. We pressed on and found them in the middle of a fight against a group of unidentified students."

"They're always unidentified when you don't want to get them into trouble, aren't they? You're not going to be condemned for tattling on people who initiated an unsanctioned duel in a dangerous area in the middle of the night," says Professor Vess.

"I didn't know them, and most of them were wearing masks," counters Eula. She pauses, looking at Professor Vess. Professor Vess, who used to be a Planeswalker, who speaks against their advisor, who might have her own ideas about the omenpaths and how they're meant to be used. "I think some of them were part of the group that jumped me earlier this evening."

Professor Vess lifts an eyebrow. "Jumped you?" she inquires.

"Yes." Eula looks at her levelly. "They invited me to an off-campus location to talk, and when I didn't agree to drop out of school, return to Capenna, and blow up the omenpath on my way out of here, they attacked me, tied me up, and threw me into an open omenpath to die. They want the omenpaths destroyed, and they want those of us who came here from other planes to go home and leave them alone."

"The people who attacked us said something a lot like that," says Kequia. Eula and the others look over at her. She shrugs. "They didn't ask us to go to the Furygale. I asked Alandra to take me someplace where I could blow off a little steam after my meeting with the envoy from the Tolarian Academies—"

"I'll explain later," says Professor Vess, before Eula can ask what that's supposed to mean.

"—and she took me to the Furygale, said we could duel

each other until I felt better. But psychometry isn't very useful in combat, and I was trying to find a way to use it to predict her attacks when someone threw a rock at my head. And then they came charging out of the storm." Kequia pauses. "I didn't know any of them, but they knew us. They didn't start targeting Orestes until we refused to fight with them. Alandra said no, over and over, and they got mad."

"Twice in one night doesn't sound like much of a coincidence, and there are no omenpaths on campus," says Professor Vess. "Miss Blue, were they aware of your escape?"

"I don't know," says Eula honestly. "Segante got me out, and we got away through the woods."

"And didn't immediately notify campus authorities, I see." Professor Vess purses her lips briefly before returning her attention to Kequia. "Is there any way these people could have predicted the two of you heading for the Furygale?"

"Only in that I go there often enough for Jamira's spell to predict I would go there if I was trying to clear my head," says Alandra, pulling her arm out of Segante's grasp. It's swaddled in bandages from the shoulder to the wrist; they tug and pull as she flexes her hands, studying them. Satisfied, she turns and offers him the other arm. "I think it was an ambush of opportunity, more than anything planned."

"It would make sense for them to be not just the same group, but some of the same students," says Eula. "They seemed to think I'd be an easier target than I was, and they could have gone looking for another target while they were feeling powerful and successful."

"It's possible," says Professor Vess. "I was aware we had a certain anti-omenpath sentiment brewing among the student body but not that it would have reached a level of size and intensity where attacking their fellow students would seem like a good idea. What did you say about blowing up the omenpath?" Her head swings around, attention suddenly locked on Eula.

"Before they threw me into the omenpath for telling them no, they wanted me to carry an explosive device with me when I was leaving and detonate it inside the omenpath. I'm not sure what they think that's going to do, but it's what they were asking me to do."

"Your world has elevators, does it not?"

"Er, yes?"

"What would happen if you were to drop an explosive device down an open elevator shaft?"

"It would bounce off the elevator operator, and probably break the cable." Eula looks alarmed. "A bunch of people would get hurt. It could even set fire to the building! You don't get elevators outside of Family buildings, so now you've killed people *and* burned down a Family building! I would get in *so* much trouble if I dropped an explosive device down an elevator shaft."

"I didn't mean literally, Miss Blue," says Professor Vess. "Where would the fire go?"

"Oh. Um. Up, probably? And out any open doors."

"But would the elevator shaft survive?"

"As long as I didn't burn down the building in the process, I think so, yeah." Eula shrugs. "The fire would exit through whatever means it could find, and the shaft would remain. Are you saying if someone set off a bomb inside an omenpath, it would just . . . squirt out the openings into whatever planes it was connected to and leave the omenpath itself mostly alone?"

"I'm saying we don't know, not really, but that seems as likely an outcome as the entire omenpath collapsing inward on itself. And as we haven't exactly been setting up *inside* omenpaths to start performing complicated magic, we don't know whether the nature of physical reality within an omenpath would do something to the explosion. Maybe it would be snuffed out, coming to nothing; maybe it would be amplified and lay waste to those innocent connected planes. We have no *way* of knowing without substantial research, which hasn't been a priority up until this point."

"Is it going to be a priority now?"

Professor Vess sighs. "If we have would-be student reactionaries threatening explosives, I suppose it has to be, if only so we know what's going to happen when they put their plans into action."

"The people who attacked us were wearing emblems from all five of the colleges," says Segante. "Is there nowhere we can consider ourselves safe from the threat of attack?"

"I was under the impression you were from the upper echelons of Fiora," says Professor Vess. "You've never considered yourself safe anywhere."

Segante nods his understanding and turns his attention back to Alandra, quickly checking her remaining wounds, the first aid kit open in his hands. The injured storm sculptor is drooping, the fins on her head as flat and lank as they were before her first trip to Sedgemoor. Orestes is clinging to her shoulder, clearly concerned as he nuzzles her cheek and croons.

"She'll be all right, little beast," says Professor Vess. "Your precious keeper has been hurt, but not so direly that you need to worry about her. Come here and let me patch the tears in your wing."

"You?" asks Kequia, clearly wary.

"Yes, me," says Professor Vess. "I was a healer before I was anything else, and I learned the ways the body moves and mends itself in the course of learning to understand my magic. If that same magic is better suited to raising and reanimating the dead, well, that doesn't make it any less potent. It seems I'm to be a professor in residence for a time—at least until they find a stable omenpath to my home region of Dominaria, or until I feel like putting myself to the trouble of travel. I may as well practice some old skills, lest they turn fallow on me."

Orestes chirps and leaps into the air at Alandra's nod of assent, gliding over to land on Professor Vess's outstretched arm. She smiles, ever so slightly, and runs her fingertips lightly down his spine, barely grazing his scales.

"Why must the path lead to your home?" asks Jamira. "I would be content with any means of returning to my plane of origin."

"Because her"—a quick jerk of the chin toward Kequia—"reaction to my name isn't an uncommon one. I had a very long time to do a lot of very questionable things. Not all of them were as bad as some people would make them out to be, but some of them were even worse. I made deals with demons, I raised armies, I killed people, even if I didn't always do it with my own two hands, and I desecrated more graves than there are hairs on my lovely head. Every monster in your storybooks has their own version of the truth, and my truth is this: I became what I became for what seemed to be the best of reasons, and I remained what I was out of selfishness and necessity. My choices were often enough my own that I deserve the guilt for my crimes, and often enough someone else's that I deserve a chance at redemption. At . . . a quiet life beside a swamp that welcomes my presence, knows and appreciates me, where I can teach the next generation of mage scholars to avoid my mistakes."

"What mistakes would you admit to?" asks Eula.

Professor Vess's smile is quick, sharp, and more than faintly amused. "Murder and resurrection can *seem* like the answer to someone who refuses to stop interrupting you, but it's almost always worse in the long run. You can't just kill people for getting on your nerves."

"You *can*, you just *shouldn't*," says Segante.

She turns to give him a politely disbelieving look. "This is another thing we should be considering in our recruitment going forward," she says. "We've ruined you. If you truly believe that, you can't go back to Fiora. Your own people would eat you alive."

"You're making assumptions, the way outsiders always do when they're faced with our customs," he says stiffly. "It would be impolite and impulsive to kill someone just for getting on my nerves. I would politely correct them and make it clear that there would be consequences going forward. Then, if they persisted, I could kill them with no stain on my reputation and, more important, no damage to my household's hospitality. We don't kill on first offense. No one would survive to adulthood if we did."

Eula blinks. Fiora really does sound more and more like New Capenna when he says things like that. She insulted and interrupted plenty of people when she was a child too young to understand that what she was doing was wrong. That's what children *do*. But adults who kill kids aren't viewed positively, not even by the facebreakers or the disposal experts. Fiora must have similar rules, or Segante's right: no one would live long enough to learn the rules, much less keep passing them along to the next person.

Professor Vess has been cradling Orestes close as they spoke. Now she takes her hands away, and the drake spreads his wings as wide as they can go, bowing low as he stretches them out. He chirps, sounding pleased, and Professor Vess smiles at him.

"There you are," she says. "Now, be a good boy and try to keep your mistress from diving back into the Furygale before she's officially a member of Prismari College. I think her father will be most put out, with both of us, if something happens to her."

"You know my father?" asks Alandra.

"I've encountered all your families at one point or another, except for yours, Miss Blue. I'm not particularly eager to see how any of them would react if they heard you'd been injured on my watch," says Professor Vess. "Thank you all for being so frank about what happened tonight. These are things I needed to know, and things that may not yet be finished haunting you. I will speak with the deans and the other professors about how we can answer to this attack on our students and how best to keep you safe. For now, don't go anywhere alone, any of you, and if you could make sure that someone who *isn't* with you knows where you are, that would be for the best. I'm afraid I have to ask you all not to go looking for the students who attacked you."

Jamira begins to object, as does Alandra. Professor Vess puts one hand up, palm facing outward, and they quiet.

"I'm not asking you not to defend yourselves if they come after you again, or to hide out of fear of further encounters. Only that you not try to force another confrontation." Professor Vess is solemn as she looks at them. "I know you're brave. I know you're capable. But you only need to make it through another week and it'll be Sea's Rise, and you'll have much of the university to yourselves. You can regroup and decide what your next steps will be, from a position of relative strength. I think you need that. And as a professor with some measure of authority over you, I'm afraid I must insist."

One by one, they nod, some more reluctantly than others; Jamira looks like she'd rather gore Professor Vess with her horns than agree to this demand, while Segante looks oddly relieved, like he was afraid the others were going to rush out and start assaulting people at random in their quest for revenge.

"Very good," says Professor Vess. "Now, if no one's actively bleeding, come along. I'll walk you back to your dorm. No arguments! You need to get some rest. You have classes early tomorrow morning."

Once again, none of them objects, and as she heads for the door, they fall into step behind her, letting her lead them out of the room, back into the territory of owls.

TWENTY-FIVE

ALLIANCES

Professor Vess was right: it's late, and they have History of Arcavios with Professor Kasmina in the morning. Eula isn't entirely comfortable with the idea of going back into that classroom, with its impossible forest and silently staring parliament of owls. She's less and less certain that she trusts Professor Kasmina, and if she doesn't trust her advisor, who *can* she trust?

They wouldn't be here without Professor Kasmina—*she* wouldn't be here without Professor Kasmina. She'd be back in New Capenna, trapped in the inevitability of a life she never wanted to live, growing roots among the work crews, becoming more and more destined for a future of sweeping streets and patching brick. There's nothing wrong with any of those things—if she ever thought there was, she got over it fast when her beloved older brother chose that life for himself and thrived there—but it's not what she wants, not what she needs. Kasmina *saved* her.

Kasmina saved them all. They *owe* her, for giving them the chance to live up to their full potential. Without her, they'd all be sitting on their home planes, twiddling their thumbs and waiting for the future to catch up to them. Here, though . . . here, they have a genuine chance to become the best versions of themselves.

Segante looks like he wants to say something as they reach the foyer and Eula turns to follow Alandra to their shared room. She doesn't stop moving. There will be time for confessions and questions later, time to decide what their earlier intimacy means for them going forward; right now she's exhausted, and morning will arrive sooner than anyone thinks.

Kequia and Jamira head into their own room, and after a long moment of hesitation, Segante does the same, vanishing into his solitary space.

Eula doesn't stop to undress before she collapses into the bed, arms flat at her sides and face pressing hard into the pillow, the world wisping away in a moment, replaced first by blackness and then by a cascade of colors scintillating across an infinite sky, bright as a Prismari art project, complex as a Quandrix equation. Some of them are familiar, greens and blues and purples and reds. Others are colors she has no names for, shifting shades that make perfect sense here, in what she can only assume is a dream, but which could never exist in reality as she knows it. Everything is rimmed in Halo-bubble brightness, like she's viewing it through the prismatic lens of the omenpath.

She stares at the sky, open-mouthed and rapt. She's had detailed dreams before, but never anything like this, never anything that felt so real she could reach out and touch it, hold it in her hands and keep it close forever. She feels warm and weightless, like she could run forever across the unseen, oddly untextured ground beneath her bare feet.

There's a sound behind her, and she turns to see Professor Kasmina walking under the cascading sky, her hands cupped around something at chest level and her head bowed, as if with grief or exhaustion. She doesn't seem to have noticed Eula yet, and so Eula holds her position, motionless. There's nowhere to hide. May as well soak in what details she can before she's inevitably caught and has to come up with some explanation for what she's doing here.

As if there's ever a real explanation in a dream. Dreams are where you go when you don't want things to be explained. She steals one last look at that glorious, scintillating sky—a sky like that deserves a name, something special, not just "the sky"; it's like looking into eternity, or like looking into eternity layered on top of itself, rendered plural and perfect and even more unending than it was in the beginning—and then follows Kasmina, walking carefully in case the formless ground seeks shape between her steps and sends her sprawling.

Indeed, the ground starts to find a shape under her feet. Each step makes it more solid, like walking the path into Sedgemoor in reverse, until she's walking across one of the main antechambers in the Biblioplex, a vaulted ceiling spinning itself above her. The customary stained glass is missing, replaced by clear panes that do nothing to filter or fade the beauty of that impossible sky, and she's grateful for that, even as she knows she'll never be able to look at the Biblioplex ceiling the same way again.

Kasmina turns down a narrow hallway lined with books,

and Eula stops where she is, trying to figure out what the dream is trying to tell her. Dreams are either the mind's way of processing things too complex to be worked out in the waking world or they're the result of some sort of interference from a more powerful mind-mage or oracle. Well, she's not a mind mage at all, and if some oneiromancer wants to start messing with her, she needs to pay attention or they're going to run rampant through her mind and memories. Not something she wants to encourage.

So she turns slowly, looking at the room around her. She's *been* here, when she was awake. The Biblioplex is vast and sprawling, but it doesn't tend to rearrange itself without good reason. This antechamber is accessed from one of the southern entrances, connected by a book-lined hallway to the foyer looking out on the distant spires of the Prismari campus. When she's awake, it often smells of char and ozone, the wind carrying the reminders of distant, glorious devastation into the building. The Biblioplex has protections against fire and lightning, of course, but that doesn't stop it happening outside.

She's *been* here. This is the entrance Alandra uses most often, and she's met her roommate here a few times. And indeed, as if summoned by the thought, here comes Alandra now, wearing the green tunic she had on the day they met, fins loose and streaming out behind her as she runs. Her bare feet make little slapping sounds against the marble floor, and Eula marvels momentarily at the dream's dedication to detail.

Then she notices the books in Alandra's arms, clutched like she's afraid someone will try to steal them from her. The titles are incomprehensible scrawls, distorted by the lens of the dream, but Eula knows them all the same: she checked them out early in her time on campus, using them to take careful notes on the strengths and weaknesses of the school. They weren't entirely accurate, unable to account for the changes brought about by the Invasion, but they were enough to let her send a fairly thorough write-up home. She doesn't know why Alandra has them.

But she saw her with them, didn't she? When they were both awake, she saw Alandra with those same texts, spreading them out across her desk like some sort of strange treasure map, taking notes of her own. Those notes had never come to anything—unless, as with Eula's own careful notation, they had been tucked into an envelope and sent off-plane as an offering to the past, paying for the future.

Alandra runs out of sight, and Eula turns to watch her go. When she turns back, the antechamber is different, the scent in the air still ozone-sharp but also cool petrichor, stone drying after recent rain, bright and clear and constantly changing. She knows that if she followed the narrow hall to the exit, she would find herself looking out at the Quandrix campus, and so it's not entirely a surprise when Jamira walks slowly into view. She isn't carrying any books, but there's a boy beside her, human, tall, moving in a way that Eula almost recognizes. It's strange how he can seem so familiar and be a complete stranger at the same time, like someone she saw once in a crowd or—and she smiles with the irony of it all—in a dream.

Then he waves his hands, punctuating a point she didn't hear him make, and she knows who he is, pictures him wearing a white mask and knows him for the boy she danced with in the wood, the one who warned her away from the Biblioplex. But she remembers this moment. It's in a dream, but it doesn't *feel* like a dream. It feels like something she witnessed and dismissed as unimportant, something that's only coming back together now.

She turns away, suddenly feeling like an intruder, and the room shifts again, subtle but real. Eula winces. She knows that whatever she sees when she looks back again will be something she doesn't *want* to see, something that changes what she thinks she already knows, and yet she can't stop herself from moving. The dream has its own demands, and it wants her to understand what she doesn't know she doesn't know. So she turns again, and this time the air is dry dust and aging paper, and it's Kequia she sees crossing the antechamber.

She doesn't have a companion, no books in her arms, but there are ink stains on her fingers and a guilty look on her face, like she's been doing something she shouldn't be doing. She heads quickly down one of the halls that branches off the room, and she doesn't stop, and she doesn't look back.

The antechamber doesn't change before Segante comes walking through, shoulders straight and chin high, looking like he hasn't a care in the world. But he's carrying a scroll, one of the long parchment texts that are meant to remain in the research shelves, never leaving the Biblioplex. As Eula watches, he tucks it away into his velvet tabard and walks onward as if he's done nothing wrong.

She's seen that scroll, hasn't she? On the bedside table in his room, when he allowed her inside? When he trusted her?

"There are spells that sound the alarm when a book is removed from the Biblioplex without going through the proper channels. They're for the protection of students as much as for the protection of the texts. But there are ways around them, if you're cunning, or clever, or from a plane where being both is the best way to survive to reach adulthood." Kasmina's voice comes from right behind Eula, who whirls with a gasp caught like a stone in her throat.

Her advisor is standing there, looking calm as anything, although the marks of grief are still etched deep around her eyes. She looks exhausted, like she hasn't slept in months, and the front of her tunic is charred, as if she'd been holding a candle close to her breast only to have it blow out in the wind. She carries no candle now. Her hands are empty, fingers smeared with wax.

"I'm not an oneiromancer, if that's what you're worried about; I haven't been spying on your dreams," she says, watching Eula's expression. "But when I was at my strongest, I could open scrying portals between planes, and what is a dream but a personal plane? You come from outside this world. The dreams of Capenna cling to you still, and always will. I can show you what you need to know, what you've already seen without putting the pieces into the proper order."

"And how do you know I've seen those things if you haven't been spying on me?" It's easy to be angry inside a dream, easy to raise her voice and demand answers. Eula glares at the woman in front of her, trying to radiate anger.

"I haven't been spying on your *dreams*," says Kasmina. "I'm your advisor. It's my job to keep an eye on what you're doing on campus when you're awake. My eyes are everywhere."

She waves her wax-tipped hand, and a full parliament of owls glides out of the shadows among the shelves, landing on every surface that can support them. Their wings are silent as ever, muted by their feathers. Some of them begin to preen, digging at their feathers with talons and beaks. Others simply settle, eyes on Eula, eerie in their silent regard.

"I know everything you and your little classmates get up to," says Kasmina. "I know what you think you've been hiding. I know Liliana is trying to turn you against me, and I know that she won't succeed. I won't allow her to."

Eula stares at her for a moment, then grabs hold of the flesh of her own upper arm with two fingers and twists, viciously.

There's no pain. This dream won't end that easily.

Kasmina sighs. "You really want to believe her over me? I brought you here. I made this world a haven for you. I saved you from what your own world would have forced you to become, and while I won't demand loyalty for something you never asked me to do, I'll request a little consideration. Maybe you shouldn't be so quick to judge me on another's word."

Eula takes a step backward, the floor cool beneath her feet, and shakes her head.

"No," she says. "I'm not a toy, and I'm not a pawn to be used in whatever game you think you're playing here. I'm not going to trust you."

"A pity. You seemed so morally flexible in the beginning— or did you think I brought you here for your looks? All my embers have the potential to be powerful, but you five, you had the potential to be *great,* if you would just stop holding yourselves to other people's standards. Two scions of the most politically minded planes I've ever had the displeasure of visiting, a Planeswalker's child, a Planeswalker's grandchild, and the daughter of a man who ran the seas red with blood before he settled into his own ascendancy. You should have been *easy.* You shouldn't be listening to the moralistic bleating of a villain who treats the loss of her spark like it doesn't matter, who thinks she can transform into a hero after everything she's done. You should be listening to *me*."

Eula scowls. "I don't think so, ma'am. I think I should be doing exactly what I've been doing so far. It's been working pretty well."

"Stealing secrets and sending them home to buy yourself a berth with a stronger crime family?"

Eula manages not to flinch. The accuracy of the accusation is more than she expected, but then again, nothing has matched her expectations since the day her admission papers arrived, has it?

Kasmina sighs. "Time's growing short, but it's not running out, not yet." The Biblioplex is dissolving around them, becoming streaks of pastel color that melt toward the darkening ground. Eula looks up, heart in her throat as she *hopes*—

And there it is, that wash of impossible colors whirling and sliding one around the other, that glorious eternity that she knows, on some level, should have been *hers*, should have been the song embedded in her heart, should have sung her to sleep each night and warmed her awake each morning. But it isn't and will never be, and this may be the only time she sees it.

Held rapt, Eula watches the swirl of the Blind Eternities above her until morning comes, and she awakes.

TWENTY-SIX

CONSEQUENCES

Alandra sits at her desk, carefully copying her homework over onto a clean sheet of paper, one not wrinkled by water stains, and frowns. "What do you mean?" she asks.

Eula, eyes still on the mirror she's using to carefully pin and set her hair, sighs. "I just think we should be listening to Professor Vess. Maybe Professor Kasmina isn't who she says she is. Maybe we need to be . . . careful."

"Because you had a bad dream?"

"It wasn't a 'bad dream,'" says Eula, frustrated. That makes it sound so basic, so small, and it wasn't either of those things, not really. It was . . . huge, and confusing, and infinite in a way that she doesn't have the words for and never will. She woke feeling like something had been given to her and something had been stolen from her at the same time, and they weren't the same things. "It was . . ."

"A nightmare?"

"No. I don't think it was a dream at all. I think it was . . . a conversation."

Alandra glances around at that, frowning. "You're not making any sense."

Eula takes a deep breath and turns away from the mirror. This will go easier if they can see each other, assuming there's any way this goes well at all, which she honestly doubts. "I'll let it go if you'll answer a question for me."

"All right."

"How long have you been copying books to send home to your father? And how have you been doing it?" Alandra doesn't have any talent for ink-casting; she can't have been making her copies using the same tricks Eula does.

Alandra stares at Eula, her cheeks paling as her fins turn a darker purple and rise slightly away from her neck and shoulders, bristling. "What did you say?"

"There's no rules against it, I know, I looked, but you've been hiding it all the same, just like I have. How are you making your copies?"

"Sand patterns," says Alandra slowly. "I sculpt tiny storms and use them to fuse the sand into patterns of words and letters. It works for copying glyphs, too. They're fragile, but my father knows how to reconstruct them if they break. I pack them in shells grown from my pearls and send them home with the mail."

"How long?"

"Since we first got here. How did you know?"

"I saw it last night, in the dream that wasn't entirely a dream." Eula looks to the door, her expression going blank. That wasn't all she saw, and while Alandra's "crime" is the same as her own, not forbidden even if it's not necessarily something the administration would approve of, the others are more questionable.

Jamira, who, according to the dream, is working with the Preservationists and may not have been ambushed at all. Segante, who isn't just copying materials to send home but outright stealing them. And Kequia, although Eula still doesn't understand the significance of her inky fingers.

Alandra looks uncomfortable, like she can't decide how she's supposed to react to this information, like she doesn't know what it means.

Eula starts for the door. "I think Professor Kasmina wanted me to see that if I can't trust her, I can't trust anyone, because we all have our own agendas, and no one is above suspicion. But I've been doing the same thing you have. They never told us not to. If they didn't want us to keep our families informed about what we were doing, they should have told us not to."

"That sounds sort of like an excuse," says Alandra miserably. "Have we been doing something wrong?"

"I don't know," says Eula. "But I'm going to find out."

She steps out into the foyer, leaving Alandra staring after her.

The door to Jamira and Kequia's room is closed. Eula hesitates, then turns toward Segante's door. It's also closed, but she feels more welcome there, and less like confirmation will turn into an accusation. It's possible she just saw the signs of what Alandra was doing and put them together in her sleep. Verifying that her roommate has also been sending information home doesn't *prove* her dream was a conversation with their advisor.

Verifying that Segante has been stealing books, on the other hand, or that Jamira has been working with the people who attacked them . . . either of those things will change everything.

Segante is the more dangerous of the two, for all that he's physically smaller than Jamira; not only does she have a healthy respect for his magic, she knows he comes from a plane that taught him not to hesitate to strike an ally who's turned against him. Her lessons were similar enough that she has no illusions about how quickly he would turn on her if he thought she was a threat. That's almost soothing, in a way. She and Jamira come from such different backgrounds that the minotaur could be planning to trample her to death while Eula still thought everything was fine between them.

As she has this whole time. Jamira is the reason she hopes the dream was just a dream, despite the thin proof she's already received from Alandra. Alandra and Kequia both could have been hurt when they were cornered in Sedgemoor, or in the Furygale. Eula could have *died* in that omenpath. She's not sure she can forgive Jamira for that if she's been working with their enemies here on campus.

Eula walks to Segante's door, raises her hand, and hesitates before knocking.

The door swings open a moment later, and Segante blinks at her, hair mussed, vest misbuttoned and sitting askew on his narrow torso. "Eula," he says with evident surprise. "Did you need something?"

"I need to talk to you." She takes in his unkempt appearance and asks, "Can I come in?"

Segante nods, clearly recognizing the question as a safety

line. He steps back, pulling the door wider. "Enter as a friend," he says.

Eula steps inside. It's early enough that Segante hasn't thrown out the previous night's flowers yet; they're drooping and wilted, limp in their vases. The rug is still rumpled, scattered with dried petals. He sees her looking at the flowers and reaches out to run his fingers over the top of the nearest bouquet, which perks up and blooms again as it responds to his magic.

"Eula, what's wrong?" he asks.

"I had—last night, I saw—" Trying to explain the dream that may not have been a dream to Alandra just frustrated them both, and so she stops herself, squares her shoulders, and watches as he rebuttons his vest, covering his undershirt.

Eula sighs. "How long have you been stealing books from the Biblioplex?"

His fingers slow, then still, remaining lightly pressed against the buttons. "That's a large accusation, Miss Blue," he says, and his voice has cooled to something closer to what it was in the first days they knew each other, before she understood his flowers and he paid her for his laundry, before their time together after the wood. "Are you sure you should be throwing large accusations at a man in the morning? I haven't set out the guarantees of hospitality yet."

"There are dreamwastes in the bouquet you just refreshed, and I can see you've removed the stamens to stop the pollen," says Eula. "That's as much a sign of peace as any I've encountered."

"But not a formal one."

"Maybe not, but I think the administration will be annoyed

if you kill me, so." Eula looks him squarely in the eyes. "How long have you been stealing books?"

"How do you—ah." He exhales, swearing under his breath as he turns away. Eula doesn't know the words, but she recognizes the intent. "From the beginning. My father wanted to be informed as to what I was learning here."

"Copying is easier."

"He wanted to study the materials the books were made from. Every time I send a volume home, he sends me a new installment on my allowance. There are so many. A dragon's hoard of knowledge. They'll never miss a few."

Privately, Eula thinks the "dragon's hoard" comparison may be more accurate than he realizes. Not one dragon—five. The Founders won't be happy if they find out about this. Neither will the librarians.

"You could get expelled," she says hotly.

"I've learned enough to survive."

"Have you?"

Segante looks at her gravely. "I must have. I don't have the choice you think I do, Eula. This isn't something I decided to do because I wanted to, or even to please my father. He orders, I obey. That's how you survive in Fiora, as a dutiful child. Or are you going to stand there and tell me you have no idea what's expected in the name of family loyalty?"

"I can't," says Eula. "But I wish you'd be more careful. Professor Kasmina knows."

His eyes harden. "How? Did you tell her?"

"No. She told me."

He frowns. "What?"

"Last night, I had a dream that wasn't a dream, more like a

vision, induced by a scrying portal. Professor Kasmina wanted me to see that none of us is blameless; we've all been serving our own ends, whatever that might mean, and even if she is what Professor Vess says, she's not our enemy—or not our only enemy. Some of the things she showed me were things I might have figured out on my own, put together from memories I could recognize. Others were . . . more complicated." She's not ready to mention her suspicions about Jamira, which are more than suspicions now.

Segante pauses. "She can read your *mind*?"

"No, I really do think this was a creative application of a scrying portal. She opened it between my mind and hers, rather than between herself and another location. She said she could scry between planes, and someone else's dream is sort of like another plane of existence. My magic doesn't work remotely like that." Eula shakes her head. "She knew we'd been talking to Professor Vess. She wanted me to see that we all had our own reasons for being here, and that her having reasons for *bringing* us here shouldn't mean we stop trusting her."

"Oh? What have *you* been doing wrong, princess?"

"I've been hand-copying books and sending their contents to my father so he can negotiate a stronger position with the Family he works for." Eula shrugs. "He asked me to—well, told me to, really—but I did it because I wanted to."

"Why?"

"I don't want to work for his Family." She's never said it so bluntly before, the words out in the open where they can betray her. "I want to work for a different Family, one I think will take better care of me, and where I can be a lot more valuable in the long run."

"It's all about power and position where you come from."

A very small nod. "Yes. I didn't always understand that, but after the Invasion, yes. I'll do whatever I have to do in order to secure myself a position that can protect me. I'm never falling to the bottom of the world again."

"Then you understand why I did it."

"I do. Not the specifics, any more than you understand the specifics of our Families, but close enough that it makes no real difference. But Segante . . . stealing books can get you expelled."

"And? If it sees me expelled to a better position than I had before, is it such a tragedy?" He looks down his nose at her. "Are you planning to report me?"

"I wouldn't," she says, and her voice is little more than a sigh. He looks at her sternly for a few seconds more, then nods to himself, apparently content with her reply.

"Very well, then."

"But Professor Kasmina might, if she thinks she has to."

His shoulders stiffen at that, and he begins to turn away.

"She wanted me to see that she's not unique because she's not completely trustworthy, and she showed me how all of us have been acting for our own interests. You stealing books, Alandra and I copying them . . ." Her voice trails off, unsure how to continue.

Segante doesn't miss the pause. He glances sharply back at her. "And?"

"And I'm not sure what Kequia has been doing that we should question." Eula shrugs. "I just saw her with inky fingers, hurrying somewhere. It could mean almost anything. Jamira, I . . . I wanted to talk to you first, because if it wasn't true that you were stealing books, what I saw about her probably wouldn't be true, either. And now I guess it is, and we're going to have to deal with that."

"What did you see?"

Eula sighs. Once she says it, everything will change, and there won't be any taking it back. The end begins with this.

"She's been working with the students who attacked us, the Preservationists who want to see the omenpaths destroyed," she says. "I don't know why—she's as much a stranger here as we are. But I saw her walking with the one who approached me at the party, and I don't think Professor Kasmina would have shown me that if it didn't mean something."

Segante's face hardens. "It means she's going to explain herself," he says, voice hard, and strides toward the door.

Eula momentarily considers grabbing him but dismisses the idea. She wants to know as much as he does. Instead, she follows him out of the room and across the foyer to Jamira and Kequia's door, where he knocks briskly before stepping back to wait.

Kequia opens it a few seconds later, her hair still tucked up in her sleeping bonnet, safely contained. She'll oil and pin it into her customary elaborate braid before they leave for breakfast, but she rarely bothers before that. "Yes?" she asks, half yawning.

"Where's Jamira?" asks Segante.

"She had practice this morning. Mage Tower. She's going to meet us at the dining hall in an hour." Another half-smothered yawn as Kequia begins to turn away.

Segante reaches for the door before she can pull it closed, his face a mask of bland civility that sends a chill along Eula's spine. "My pardon, Kequia, but we must speak with her at once. It's important. Did she happen to mention where her practice would be taking place today?"

"This time of week, they're normally at the stadium," says Kequia, seeming to wake up a bit as she blinks at him, some of the clouds clearing from her eyes. "You can catch them before they start the first game if you go now."

"Eula, you'll want your shoes," says Segante, releasing the door and turning his back on Kequia. "I'll walk slowly."

He starts down the hall, and after a beat to process what just happened, Eula whirls and runs back to her room, leaving Kequia to slowly close her door, utterly perplexed.

A few seconds later, Eula is chasing Segante toward the front door, hopping as she pulls her shoes on. He barely spares her a second glance, he's so focused on his goal. The air around him is like a static shock, spiky and startling without crossing the line into causing actual pain. She's never seen him this angry.

"Segante?" she asks as they step outside. "What are you going to do?"

"I'm going to ask her a question," he says. "And if she gives the wrong answer, I'm going to fight her. She may win—her magic isn't stronger than mine, but it's less subtle, and that can turn the fight in her favor. Those stone whips of hers would be a hard thing for me to beat. But it doesn't matter."

"You don't *have* to fight her."

"She endangered you. She endangered *me*. My honor and safety both demand satisfaction, and she'll provide it, either by proving this accusation untrue or by meeting me on the dueling grounds."

"I'm very tired of duels," says Eula.

Segante glances at her, and for a moment, he looks almost amused. "Then I suppose we'll hope she can refute the crimes she'll be accused of."

It's early enough that the campus is quiet, the green all but deserted, the pathways sparsely used. The dining halls will be packed, she knows; freshly woken students want calories and caffeine, in that order. It's a little jarring to think about how naturally she's fallen into that rhythm, how quickly she's been able to trade a slice of toast and a cup of black coffee gulped down hot and bitter in the kitchen for proper meals eaten slowly while debating the previous night's homework with her friends.

Jamira endangered all that by working with the people who want to see her driven off campus, who think she has no right to be here. The only real question between her and true, burning anger is "why?" Why did Jamira do this; what possible reason could she have had? Until she knows for sure, she can't allow her temper to run away with her.

Segante seems to have no such compunctions. The air around him is practically sizzling by the time the stadium comes into view up ahead, doors open and students in athletic gear jogging in and out. There's no sign of Jamira among the crowd. Segante starts forward, and Eula puts a hand on his arm, stopping him.

"What?" he demands, shooting her a sharp look.

"They're still doing warm-ups," she says. "If we wait, she should come out, and we can try to get her alone. Unless you want to do this in front of witnesses who might be a part of the group that's been targeting us?"

Segante startles, like he never considered that Jamira

might be spending time with the people she might have been working with. The Mage Tower team would be a perfect opportunity for her to talk with them across college and year-group lines and without fear of her dormmates overhearing; even Kequia, who spends more time with Jamira than the rest of them do, doesn't usually attend practices. Jamira can be reasonably assured of privacy here.

Only reasonably. Segante and Eula find an open bench and settle in to wait, eyes on the stadium door. They don't speak. Maybe for the first time in her life, Eula doesn't feel like she has anything to say. That static continues to crackle in the air around Segante, not quite like the electric buzz that sometimes hums around Alandra, fuzzy and sharp and strange. It's almost like being back inside the omenpath. After the third time it stings her, Eula can't take it anymore.

"Why is your magic biting me?" she asks, voice low.

"Is it?" asks Segante. He frowns, and a moment later, the static stops. "My apologies."

"But what—"

"We've discussed our strengths and weaknesses," he says. "I'm advancing my study of the essence arts. There are always tiny living things in the air around us, pollen and insects and the like. When I'm on the brink of losing my temper, I can start pulling the essence out of them to prepare myself for battle."

"Oh." So the tingle was the death of countless tiny creatures? That isn't a very pleasant thought. Eula pushes back the urge to inch away. "Have you always done that?"

"Wiped out a few of my mother's gardens when I was little, when she used to take me to gather flowers with her."

The corner of Segante's mouth twitches upward, the shadow of a smile.

"You've never mentioned your mother before."

"Haven't I? She was my best friend in childhood. She was kind and stern and said that knowing who you were mattered more than anything else. If you didn't know who you were, how could you know what you were willing to die for? She was the first person I told when I figured out who *I* was, and she offered me her father's name to replace the one I wasn't using anymore. She would be so proud of me for making it this far, for leaving Fiora, for living as myself and knowing what I'm willing to die for."

"Would be?"

"She died." The words are simple, mildly said, and so calm that they silence the world for a moment.

Eula swallows. "The Invasion?" she asks delicately.

"No. One of my aunt's men came in through the window of her quarters. They were looking for me. They didn't realize I'd changed rooms when I changed my name. She caught them, and she stopped them, but not before they poisoned her. I was too far away to help. Even if I'd been closer, I wasn't as good at delicate healing as I am now. I could have tried to pull the poison from her veins and pulled her veins from her body in the process. It was better that she die quickly and without knowing I had failed her."

"It's not your fault, Segante."

"Isn't it?" He turns to look at her. "The killer was coming for *me*, my father's heir, and found my mother instead. I was too far away to intervene. How is this not my fault?"

"You didn't send the killer to your mother's room?" Eula

shakes her head. "You didn't do it. When a Family gives an order, the people who follow it aren't entirely to blame, and the people it rolls over aren't to blame at all."

Segante sighs. "I hope I can believe you eventually."

Eula stiffens. "Look," she says, raising her hand to point.

He follows the gesture and rises, starting briskly toward Jamira, who has just emerged from the stadium. The towering minotaur is wearing gray-brown athletic gear, sweatshirt and shorts, and she looks utterly perplexed to see Segante striding toward her.

Her perplexity grows as Eula joins him, hurrying to be the first to reach Jamira. "Hey," she says, all bright, artificial cheer, so brittle that it might shatter under any pressure. "You slipped out early, Jamira. We wanted to talk to you."

Jamira's eyebrows raise. "Talk to me?" she asks. "About what?"

Eula is reaching for a believable lie when Segante renders it moot, half snarling, "About the way you've been selling us out to your friends."

Jamira goes still, bovine nostrils flaring as she exhales. "What do you mean?"

"He means we know you've been working with the people who attacked us," says Eula, and any chance that she was wrong, that she was acting based on a dream that meant nothing, dissolves, because Jamira's ears flick back and half flatten against her head while the thin line of coarse hair that runs down the back of her neck like the outline of a mane bristles, virtually standing on end.

Eula's heart sinks. The dream was truth. Jamira did what they're accusing her of.

For a moment, Jamira seems to waffle between panicked helplessness and a sort of self-righteous anger before landing on the side that offers her a sliver of comfort. Her mane bristles further, her head swinging to focus on Eula.

"So clever," says Jamira. "Do you know *why* I would be willing to do something like this, something that could hurt me, too? That could hurt Kequia, who never deserved anything like this? Do you think I don't feel terrible about it? But I did it anyway, and I won't say sorry."

"We don't know," says Eula. "Why?"

"My father loved us so much," says Jamira. "He loved our mother more than anything, and he welcomed my sister and I as a blacksmith welcomes the fire. All he wanted was to be with his family, to have and to hold us, and then his damned Planeswalker spark woke up and pulled him away from us. Do you have any idea what that was like, the first time? When we saw our father wreathed in ash and fire for an instant before he was gone? We thought his magic had consumed him. We thought he was gone forever. My mother wore a widow's weeds and grieved him in the town, my sister and I walked in his shadow, deemed a dead man's daughters, and we had buried him in all but body by the time he returned. He named himself 'Planeswalker' and promised to never leave us again. He would travel and bring us trinkets from other worlds, swearing he would protect us forever, no matter what came. Scarce two years gone, he was gone with them, vanished into the night. He didn't come home for fourteen years, and then it was to find us grown almost into women and his wife gone to the ground. My entire childhood was spent in fear for his life, and for what? A spark he never asked for or wanted? When he told us it had been extinguished, I laughed. Rumi cried. She was the one who'd always hoped to ignite like Father did one day, to travel with him. I used to lie awake at night dreading the day it happened."

"So when Kasmina said you were one of her embers, that must have been very frightening," says Eula, keeping her voice level and as devoid of horror as she can.

Jamira snorts. "It was the worst thing I could have imagined. The planes were never meant to mingle. The omenpaths were an error, and removing them only sets things right. Any trust I've broken, any crime I've committed, I did it for my father, and for the fathers of everyone else, so that they can stay safely home and not be lost between the worlds. I did it for my sister. And yes, I did it for Professor Kasmina, for the Planeswalkers who deserve to be restored so they can leave the rest of us alone. And I would do it again, joyfully."

Eula stares at her, momentarily speechless. Jamira and Kequia have both spoken so easily of the Planeswalkers in their family. She's always seen it as an advantage if anything, an easement into the way their lives are now. All the shocks of Arcavios must have been less shocking when the existence of worlds beyond their own was less of a surprise.

"Kequia and Alandra could have been direly hurt," says Segante, cutting off her wandering thoughts. "Eula could have been *killed*."

"They wouldn't have killed her, even if she hadn't been able to get away," protests Jamira. "They were only going to tie her up and throw her into the omenpath. The next carriage would have picked her up and taken her out one side or the other."

Eula gasps and turns her face away. Segante catches her eye, giving a small shake of his head. If Jamira doesn't know, they're not going to tell her until the moment is right. This is an arrow they have in their quiver that she doesn't yet have in hers. "What happens to someone abandoned inside an omenpath?" asks Segante, his tone treacherously gentle. "None of our classes have mentioned stopping in the middle and allowing yourself to be subjected to that ongoing energy."

Eula's breath catches in her throat as she realizes why the impossible colors in her dream had seemed so confusingly familiar. She saw them in the omenpath. Not all of them, not the glorious sweeping sky of her dream, but flickers around the edges, like the embers of some vast, harshly banked flame.

"She could have been killed," continues Segante, unaffected by Eula's silent epiphany. "How dare you. You said she was your *friend*."

"She *is* my friend," protests Jamira. "You're all my friends. Nothing actually happened. There's no reason to be angry when nothing *happened*."

Eula and Segante stare at her, united in their horror. "You think a betrayal only matters when it succeeds?" asks Eula, after several seconds of silence. "You think the outcome is the only important part?"

"The iron doesn't care what shape it was after it's been beaten, or how many mistakes the blacksmith may have made along the way," says Jamira patiently. "Have you expressed your anger enough that I can return to my workout?"

Segante sputters for a moment, then looks to Eula, silently asking her to handle this. She nods once and steps forward.

"I think you should talk to Professor Kasmina about

transferring dorms," she says. "Most people don't like to be set up, and what you did could have gotten someone seriously hurt. It *did* hurt me, even if you don't want to believe it did."

"But—" says Jamira.

"You've said before that you don't *need* the desert environment to stay healthy, only to stay comfortable," says Eula. "Kequia will understand, especially when we tell her you were partially responsible for the attacks in Sedgemoor and the Furygale. I know it's probably too early to move you into Quandrix housing, but there are other places for unaligned students, and this is for everyone's safety."

Jamira blinks, looking briefly much smaller and more uncertain than she normally does. Eula looks unflinchingly back, refusing to let herself be intimidated. It would be so easy to back down now. That's why she can't.

Finally, Jamira snorts and says, "I need to get back to practice."

"We'll see you in class, or when you come to move your things," says Segante, and turns away. Eula follows, not allowing herself to glance back, and side by side, they walk away.

The trip back to the dorm is silent, neither of them quite finding the will to speak, neither of them sure that they have anything to say. It's not until the door comes into sight that Eula makes a small, unhappy sound, sniffling at the same time.

Segante puts a hand on her arm, and side by side, they walk into their dorm.

As soon as they're inside, they hear the yelling coming from their foyer. They exchange a glance and break into a run, Eula faster by a few long steps. They reach the foyer to find

Alandra, arms empty of Orestes, and Kequia, both dressed, both distressed.

"Where is he?" demands Alandra, whirling toward the sound of footsteps. The air is thick and humid, filled with the seeds of a gathering storm. There were no clouds outside. Whatever's coming, it's centered here. "I went back to my side of the room to get him, and he was gone. He never goes anywhere by himself. You must have taken him with you. Where is he?"

"Alandra, I've never taken Orestes anywhere without you," says Eula, trying to keep her tone level. "I'll help you look for him."

"All right," says Alandra, some of the humidity falling out of the air as she reins her anger in as much as she can. Kequia looks at the others, her anxiety not fading.

"Alandra knocked on my door, said she couldn't find Orestes," she says. "He isn't in my room."

"Did you see the drake this morning, before you came to see me?" asks Segante, looking to Eula.

She shakes her head. "I thought he was still sleeping. He does that sometimes, when Alandra's in the room. He doesn't go anywhere without her. He knows his job."

Which was keeping Alandra's anxiety from over-whelming her—something that he isn't doing now. Even with the gathering storm reined in, Alandra's scales are paler than they normally are, and she's breathing too fast. Eula has never seen her actually have a panic attack. She doesn't know what would happen if Alandra was pushed too far, but she's reasonably sure it would involve more lightning than she's comfortable with.

Stepping over to Alandra's side, she slides her arm around her roommate's shoulders. "Come on," she says. "Let's go search our room again. I'm sure he's just asleep under a pile of clothes or something, and we'll find him in no time."

She's not actually sure of that, but she *is* sure that saying so won't help, while keeping Alandra busy might. So they step into the room and begin searching, methodically at first, then with more and more urgency as the tiny drake doesn't appear. He's not in the water, and he's not in the closet, and he isn't under Eula's bed, where she's occasionally found him curled like a cat.

They're on the verge of giving up when a shout from the foyer catches their attention. Eula rises from where she was looking under the bed, but she's slower than Alandra, who is already out of the room. Eula follows quickly, and they find Segante standing outside his half-open door.

"Someone's been in my room," he says, voice grim. "Between when we left and when we came back."

"How do you know?" asks Eula.

He holds out his hand, showing a few crushed clamshells. Eula blinks.

"These were mixed with the decorative stones in my bouquets," he says. "There are still bits of clam stuck to them. The smell is going to be horrible in a few hours. I'm going to have to dump and sterilize all the vases or it'll become unlivable."

"And that smell would have been irresistible to a hungry drake," says Eula. "Is he in your room?"

"The window was open. Whether he pried it open himself or someone broke in, I can't tell," says Segante. "If he *was* in there, he's long gone."

Alandra makes a despairing sound, something akin to a seabird's cry. It would seem over the top and exaggerated if not for the obvious anguish in her face, or the way her knees start to buckle. She almost hits the ground before Kequia rushes to hold her up, keeping her from falling.

Eula frowns, moving to support Alandra's other side. "Did you smell clams this morning?"

"No," says Segante. "But they were in the water, and still fresh enough not to become obviously pungent to a human nose. I think they were put there last night, to attract Orestes to the only room in this block that has an openable window."

"You think this was a trap?"

"If it was, I can try to unravel it," says Kequia. She reaches out one hand to Segante, beseeching. "Give me the shells. I'll read what I can from them."

Segante nods and walks over to drop the clamshells into her hand, careful not to touch her skin. Eula watches, chest tight with worry, and keeps as much of her attention on Alandra as she can.

Alandra is still swaying, still pale, still seemingly on the verge of losing consciousness, but she holds fast to Kequia's arm, her eyes still open. As for Kequia, she closes her hand around the shells for a moment, swaying in place. The smell of old, dry parchment washes through the air, and Kequia closes her eyes.

"Cold," she says. "Cold and wet. Water. The ocean, very far from here. Someone's raking the beach with a tool I don't recognize. The clams don't know what it is, either. They only know it by the absence it leaves behind."

"Can we move beyond the inner lives of clams?" drawls

Segante. "I'd like to find Orestes before my room begins to smell like low tide."

"The clams are in a bag, and the bag is on a Skycoach, and they're delivered here, to—" She gasps, catches herself, and shudders. "Veil. From the Pathwardens."

"Veil?" asks Alandra, her voice sounding small and miserable.

"Yes," says Kequia. "She takes the clams and carries them to the Mage Tower stadium, where she meets with . . ." She stops mid-sentence and opens her eyes. "I can't see anything else," she says. "That's where it ends."

Eula's stomach clenches. "Kequia, we need to know. Did you see Jamira? Did she put the clams in Segante's room?"

"I know you don't spend much time with us, but Jamira is my friend," says Kequia. "She's kind to me, and she pays attention to me. She doesn't treat me like I'm stuck-up or strange because I like to study history and finish my homework on time."

"I thought we didn't, either," says Eula.

"You try not to," says Jamira from the entryway, her voice heavy with weariness. "You can tell them, Kequia. They already know."

Kequia sighs. "Jamira put the clams in Segante's room when he wasn't there."

"I left the door open, and once the smell got out, the drake followed," says Jamira. "Alandra, were you aware he could open the door of your room?"

Alandra blinks and says nothing.

"He stands on his hind legs like a caracal and pushes down on the handle with his forelegs, then drops back before his weight stops it from opening. The door will naturally swing a few inches open, and he can slip out. You must not have noticed him making his exit."

"I was getting ready for class," says Alandra, sounding shaken.

"You were already gone when we left," objects Eula.

"I was gone from my room. You didn't check the showers." Jamira looks at her challengingly. "I waited. I am very patient."

"Jammy . . ." Kequia steps toward her, expression unsure and hands half lifted. "I don't understand what you're saying."

Jamira glances at her, shoulders slumping, then returns her attention to the others, clearly gathering her courage. "I waited until he had gone into Segante's room, then went outside and around the building. The window was easy to pry open, and I dangled the meat from those same clams for the drake's attention. He came quickly. He was easy to restrain."

Alandra makes a pained sound, lunging for Jamira. Eula is too slow to stop her but not too slow to throw up a shield between them, her roommate slamming into the thin black-and-white barrier and shooting Eula a stunned, horrified look before she starts slamming her hands against it, trying to break through. Eula feels every blow like a vibration through her bones but doesn't drop the shield.

"Alandra, please," she says through gritted teeth. "We need to find out what she did."

"I delivered him to Professor Kasmina. She informed me that you knew what I'd been doing and would be confronting me soon—which, indeed, you did. She will bring this to an ending that is well past due."

Eula drops the shield then, and Alandra stumbles,

off-balance. Kequia has no such issues; she just lunges, grabbing Jamira's hand in both of hers.

Her pupils expand, swallowing the dark irises of her eyes. "She grabbed him gently," she says. "She treated him like something fragile and precious. He bit her, twice, but she didn't let go, only swaddled him in a burlap cloth and took him to the history building. She handed him to Professor Kasmina and left for the stadium, where she met with you."

"How do you—?" asks Alandra.

"Psychometry isn't just for inanimate things," says Kequia. "Most people think it's a useless specialization, but that's just because most psychometrists never learn how to use it properly. Once you know what you're doing, you can unlock the world."

"Kequia—" begins Jamira, but Kequia is already pulling her hands away and turning toward Eula and Segante.

"I don't know exactly where Professor Kasmina is taking him, but she left campus right away, and we should go after her," she says. "I don't feel like we have a lot of time."

Looking at Jamira, who watches Kequia like her heart is broken, Eula can't help but agree.

"Are we all going?" she asks.

"We are," says Segante. "We're here for an education, not to be used as pawns."

"All right," says Eula. "Kequia, do you know what direction Professor Kasmina went?"

Kequia nods.

"Good. I'll be right back." She starts for the hall.

"Eula?" asks Alandra. "Where are you going?"

"New Capenna teaches you a lot of things when you grow

up there, but right now the one that matters is that when somebody else has a head start, you need a fast car and a good driver or you're already out of the race," says Eula. "Get ready to go. I'll only be a little bit."

And out she goes.

TWENTY-SEVEN

GOING FULL CIRCLE

One nice thing about living on a university campus: people's movements tend to be predictable and familiar. Eula leaves the dorm and cuts across the grass, first walking fast, then running, and finally sprinting to get to the shallow amphitheater where undecided students and Lorehold upperclassmen mingle for a general archeology course. Kequia would normally be there by now, and she's seen Bricen heading in that direction often enough to be certain she can find him there. So she runs.

More students are out and about now than there were earlier. Very few spare her a second glance. Someone's always late to class, someone's always trying to catch up to their schedule, someone's always running. If her run has an edge of panic around it, well, no one's looking closely enough to see.

When the amphitheater comes into view, she slows so as to better scan the faces around her. Bricen isn't outside. She steps into the amphitheater proper, where a Lorehold professor she doesn't recognize is in the middle of a lecture, and there he is, down with the rest of the TAs.

There are too many stairs between her and him. Getting there will take more time than she has to spare. Eula doesn't pause, only throws down a shield and steps onto it, standing solidly in the center as it slides frictionlessly down the steps. It's like riding a sled during one of the rare midwinter snowfalls back home, and her shield is a surprisingly stable surface, like it doesn't want to buck her off. The professor stops speaking and stares. Several of the TAs do the same. Bricen lifts the feathers atop his head in distress, then closes his eyes, keeping himself from seeing what must seem like her inevitable crash.

Instead, she reaches the amphitheater floor and dismisses the shield, turning the lingering momentum into a quick forward jog that stops when she gets to Bricen and puts a hand on his arm.

"Do you have access to the cart?" she asks. "It's an emergency."

"Huh?" He uncovers his eyes, feathers smoothing down against his head. "Eula, I'm in the middle of a class—"

"I wouldn't ask if it weren't important," says Eula. She seizes his hand. *Please.*

Bricen freezes, looking uncertainly from her to the professor, who is watching this scene play out with an expression on her face somewhere between confusion and amusement.

"Go," she says. "I'm sure you'll tell me all about it later, when you're explaining why you shouldn't be penalized for disrupting my class."

She waves her hands in a shooing gesture, and Eula takes a step backward, Bricen's hand still clutched in her own, trying to tug him with her. Their respective heights make this difficult, but he follows anyway, choosing to be led. She's more relieved by that than she realized she was going to be. She didn't want to make a fool of herself in front of a whole class of Lorehold students.

Bricen lets her pull him all the way up the stairs, which seem twice as long now that she has to take them one by one, climbing as fast as her legs will carry her. It's not until they're outside the amphitheater and no longer in danger of disrupting the class that he digs his heels in and pulls his hand away from hers, crossing his arms and prodding her in the shoulder with a wing.

"Will you tell me what's going on?" he demands.

"Do you have the cart?"

"It's not mine, it belongs to the college," he says.

"Can you *get* the cart?"

Bricen frowns. "I can get the cart, but I'll need a good reason," he says. "Why am I getting the cart?"

The urge to say "It will take too long to explain" is strong, but not quite strong enough to overwhelm the small voice telling her not to antagonize her allies. "Orestes has been stolen," she says. "Jamira thinks she knows where the person who took him went, but they have a head start over us, so we need the cart to catch up and get him back. He's so small. He can't be away from Alandra for long."

Bricen's feathers rise in what looks like agitation. "Someone *stole* an emotional support companion?" he demands. "Who would do such a thing?"

"That's what we're trying to figure out," says Eula. She knows who did it, but she's starting to think she never knew Professor Kasmina at all. "Will you get the cart?"

"I'll be at your dorm in fifteen minutes," says Bricen, and turns, taking to the air in a frantic flapping of wings.

Eula watches him go for a second, absorbing her own success, then turns and runs back toward the dorm, where she can only hope the others will be waiting.

They are, all four of them standing outside. There's an uncharacteristic distance between Jamira and Kequia, who stands with her back to the minotaur, studiously not looking at her. The air around Jamira's hands is already glowing blue-green, a thread tangled around her fingers as she casts the probabilities on where Kasmina would have taken Orestes. The spell found the drake's mistress once before. Hopefully it can find him now, when the stakes are different but even more dire.

Eula waves as she runs up to them, sliding to a stop in the still-damp grass. "Bricen is bringing the cart," she says. "I told him we needed his help to get Orestes back."

"But not from who?" asks Segante.

"No," she says uncomfortably. "He's not one of us, not like that, and he might not be willing to come if he knew we were going up against a professor." She shoots a sharp look at the thread twisted around Jamira's hands. "I wasn't sure all of us would be willing to come."

"Professor Kasmina made me certain promises, encouraged me to pursue certain associations, but never said anything about hurting Alandra's companion, or forcing me to act against people who've been kind to me," says Jamira. "Kequia explained . . ."

"I told her that if Professor Kasmina had the power to remove an ember, she'd have already done it," says Kequia. "She's just been using Jamira."

"I still believe the planes should be separated, independent and free of even Planeswalkers," says Jamira. "But we're here, and I value what you are to me." She glances to Kequia last, frowning slightly. "I value you more than anything else outside my family."

"I don't think we can trust her," says Segante. "Someone who betrays you once will betray you again. But that doesn't mean we can afford to refuse her help."

"I think we should," says Kequia. "I don't want to be near her."

Alandra says nothing, only hugs her middle and rocks on her heels, looking like she's on the verge of an anxiety attack. The sky overhead is pulsing with clouds that roll in and dissipate in uneven waves. Eula moves to put a hand on her roommate's shoulder, trying to reassure her. Orestes doesn't only stabilize Alandra's mood; he makes it possible for her to control her magic by making it possible for her to control herself. Without him, she's likely to pull a tempest down on their heads.

"Alandra, are you all right?" she asks, voice low.

"No," says Alandra. "What if he gets hurt? He's not supposed to get hurt. He's supposed to be here, with me, so we can keep each other safe."

Eula doesn't have an answer to that, and so she stays where she is, trying to soothe Alandra through proximity alone. The silence is almost as oppressive as the electricity in the air. Finally, hand still on Alandra's shoulder, she says to the group, "Professor Kasmina knows everything we've all been doing. She knows I've been copying books and sending them home to my family."

Alandra shoots her a quick, guilty look. "Me, too," she admits.

"I've done no such thing," says Segante. "Copying is a scribe's work, and well below me. I've been sending the originals back to my father. They'll help him to solidify his position. They might make it safe for me to go home."

"I haven't been doing anything like that," says Kequia. "You were *stealing*?"

"You know how to manipulate the angles almost as well as I do," says Segante. "You aren't the only one of us to retain your innocence."

Kequia bites her lip and looks away. "Does it matter what I did?"

"Professor Kasmina knows about it," says Eula. "Whatever it was, she's been taking note, and she knows what you did. She showed me the edge of it last night. Isn't it better if you tell us on your own?"

Kequia doesn't turn back to face her but keeps looking away as she says, "I guess. My mother always says it's better to admit when you've done something wrong than it is to keep pretending that you haven't. I . . . I didn't do anything to hurt anyone here." The words *not like Jamira* hang unspoken in the air.

"So what did you do?" asks Alandra.

"My psychometry is good for knowing when people tend to come and go," says Kequia. "I used it to check the schedules of my professors, and I . . . made changes to their grades, to make sure I'd be at the top of all my classes."

"But you're so smart," protests Jamira. "Why would you need to do that?"

"My family expects a certain level of performance from me, and allowing me to come here instead of attending

Tolaria West on my home plane was difficult for them," says Kequia. "I haven't needed to change anything major, but it was important my grades match their expectations."

"So we stole, and you cheated, and Jamira betrayed us all," says Eula. "Aren't we a fabulous inaugural class of transfer students? I wouldn't blame Strixhaven for deciding we were a failed experiment and never doing this again."

They all look at one another, quiet and uncomfortable, and are still silent when the cart comes rolling down the pathway, Bricen at the reins and elk harnessed at the front. He's not driving as fast as he could be, but probably faster than he should be on campus. As he pulls the elk to a halt, he looks at the lot of them, frowning.

"Am I interrupting something?" he asks.

"No," says Eula, and hurries to swing herself up into the back of the cart. The others follow, with Jamira settling on the driver's bench next to him. "Jamira, finish your casting," says Eula.

Jamira nods and releases the tangled threads that fill her hands. They pool around her hooves for a moment before one of them extends outward on its own, drawing a hard line into the distance. "That way," she says. "It's the most probable direction for Orestes to have been taken."

"Please, drive," says Alandra.

Bricen nods and flicks the reins, sending the elk back into motion. They trot down the path toward the edge of campus, gathering speed as they go. Jamira's thread is bright and easy to follow, as steady as a guideline on a map. Eula shifts closer to Segante in the back of the cart, studying his frown.

"What's wrong?" she asks, her voice low.

"This all seems to be happening at once," he says. "It's not how I would have deployed a grand betrayal."

"So s—the person who's doing this doesn't have your experience. Isn't that a good thing?"

"Maybe." Segante's frown deepens into a scowl. "Why this? Why now? Why not wait to the end of the week, when the campus would be all but deserted and we wouldn't have been able to go to anyone for help?"

"Maybe it wasn't an option."

"Why not?"

"Maybe . . ." Eula pauses, her thoughts filling with that impossible rainbow sky, those colors she's never going to see again. "Maybe Sea's Rise is important somehow. It marks the highest tide of the year, doesn't it? High tides usually have something to do with the motion of the moon, or moons. So if this person wanted to do a large working with the plane's energy, wouldn't a time when everything's already heightened and being pulled out of its normal shape be better than most of the alternatives?"

"There's a lot of 'maybe' in that sentence."

"Professor Kasmina said the Snarls were at their strongest and their most undone during Sea's Rise. There are probably rituals that can only happen while that's the case," says Kequia.

Eula nods. "We know about the Preservationists now. That changes how we're going to behave, and how we're going to react to things. So say the original timeline gave our opponent more time to get all the pieces into place, only the anti-omenpath group acted too soon and tipped us off. Things get a little accelerated when someone doesn't stick to the plan."

"Speaking from experience?"

"Sort of." Eula shrugs. "I never planned whatever this is, but I ran with a pretty ambitious crew at my last school. We all wanted to impress our teachers, and through impressing them to impress the Families. Sometimes we'd have plans that should have worked, and then someone would slip up and we'd have to start moving really, really quickly in order to accomplish what we were trying to do before it all came down around our ears."

Alandra shifts closer to her, not speaking. The forming storm is chasing them as Bricen drives, the sky turning dark and pale by turns. There's nothing natural about that pattern, that lurking deep-sea pulse of power and pain. The air is sharp with static. True electric static this time, not the growth and decay of Segante's magic. Eula puts an arm around Alandra's shoulders, letting the blue girl burrow against her side, and the cart plunges on.

Jamira's spell isn't losing strength or clarity, even with Jamira's attention mostly fixed on Kequia, who rides with her eyes fixed on the horizon, not looking at anything or anyone else. Jamira starts to reach for her, catches herself, and pulls back, clearly thinking better of the gesture. Instead, she looks down at her hands, watching the brilliant immaterial thread spilling out between her fingers.

"You going to tell me what this is all about, or you going to make me guess while you mutter back there?" calls Bricen, twisting his head around at a seemingly impossible angle to help his voice carry.

Eula jerks upright in her seat, turning guiltily to focus on him. "What do you mean?"

"I mean, no one's going to snatch your roommate's pet and run away with it just to play a prank," he says.

"Orestes isn't a pet," protests Alandra.

"Apologies—companion," says Bricen. "He's a very good companion from what I've seen, but he's not a student, and that means he should get a certain protection from pranks and troublemaking unless you do something to start it. Which you didn't, so far as I've heard or can see. So I'll ask again: What is this all about?"

Eula shifts in the back of the cart, moving closer to Bricen. "Have you heard anything about people being uncomfortable with us being at the school?"

Bricen shifts in his seat, and it's clear that *he's* uncomfortable now; he wasn't expecting the question to be asked so bluntly, if it was asked at all. "I've heard—I mean, some of the students in the lower years have been a little narrow-minded about the transfer program. But it doesn't make sense! We have the room for you, and we needed the students. If people want to complain about you taking up resources that could have been used for locals, well . . . some people don't pay attention to how many enrollments we need for most classes to actually happen. Numbers matter."

"But we don't pay to be here," says Alandra. "The school takes care of everything."

"All right, that *is* a little odd, but I trust the bursar knows what's going on," says Bricen. "We have the Pathwardens. That's enough to make sure you didn't bring anything dangerous with you, and your presence opens new courses of study for the rest of us."

Eula blinks. "You don't object to us being here because it means you can do more homework?"

Bricen shrugs. "Yeah, pretty much. I've heard a few people

grumble, but they usually shut up when they see me, I think because they know I like you guys. You're all interesting in different ways, and since the omenpaths opened, being in Lorehold doesn't just mean being ready to study the history of Arcavios. I love my world, and it has plenty of mysteries we haven't unsnarled yet, but the Biblioplex is full of books that never made any sense because they're unfinished histories of places we've never been able to go before. Well, we can go there now. When I graduate, I'm going to finish all those books. If I'm going to go out and ask other planes to welcome me, I'd better be welcoming to people from other planes who come here."

Eula pauses, considering the wisdom of that approach, but before she can say anything, Alandra's storm comes alive.

Lightning arcs slam into the ground ahead of them again and again. Every time it strikes, it illuminates something that had been unseen, an elegant elemental tangle of curves and twists etched in glittering silver-bright lightning shards that snap and fizz, somehow suspended in midair. The lightning isn't creating the structure, just revealing it.

The lightning finally stops, but the structure it revealed remains, elegant and chaotic and artless all at the same time. Alandra leans forward, eyes going wide.

"It's a Snarl!" she says, voice loud enough to carry. "There's supposed to be one under the school somewhere, but we're not allowed to go down there, so I've never seen one before!"

"It is," confirms Bricen, his own voice much lower. "It's always here, but you can't always see it unless someone's feeding magic into it."

"Or assaulting it with a large, crudely conjured storm," murmurs Segante, giving Alandra a hard look.

She shrugs it off, more interested in the Snarl ahead of them—the Snarl they're still moving toward. "Why would she take Orestes to a Snarl?" she muses.

"I don't know, but whatever her reasons, I don't think I trust them," says Eula. She's read about the Snarls just as much as any of them have: great tangles of wild magic formed when Arcavios was born, scars of the union between the two protoplanes that birthed it. If not for the Snarls, she's not sure anyone would have figured out how Arcavios differed from any other plane.

In the Snarls, the old magics of Apex and Zenith still clash, prehistoric power preserved through the ages, frozen and unchanging. She can't believe it hasn't curdled, at least a little. Power isn't meant to be held static like that. It's meant to run wild and free, feeding the plane and being fed in return. Everyone she's spoken to about the Snarls has said to steer clear of them until she's further along in her studies, until she's stronger; where planes braid and blend, magic does as it will, and not always as the mage who casts it bids.

Every Snarl is different. Surviving one won't prepare her to survive any of the others. And she doesn't know how this Snarl in particular will distort the world.

And now Kasmina has taken Orestes into the Snarl, and Eula can't conceive of any good reason for her having done that. Eula leans forward, eyes on the Snarl as she addresses Bricen.

"Is this one of those things where if we drive the cart into the Snarl, it vaporizes us on the spot?" she asks.

"I don't think so," says Bricen. "The elk won't like it, but they're elk. They don't like anything. The cart's not magic, so there's nothing about it for the Snarl to distort. We should be fine if we have to go in there." He hesitates, then asks, somewhat uncertainly, "*Do* we have to go in there?"

"I think we do. I say we go."

Jamira's thread still leads them straight and clear toward the Snarl, and so they drive onward, toward the gleaming structure of captive lightning, toward a confrontation that none of them has been hoping to have.

Toward Orestes.

TWENTY-EIGHT

INSIDE THE SNARL

They reach the Snarl and keep going, driving into the tangle of translucent electric strands, which crackle and break across their skin like whips of static light. Space itself distorts as they move deeper, but not in the kaleidoscopic colors of an omenpath; this is less like a slice of impossible light from the walls of creation and more like a series of thinly sliced shadows, each so thin that it becomes light and darkness at the same time, a pressed butterfly's wing of pure contradiction unfolding all around them. When the thread finally ends, they are in what looks like a vast cavern with walls woven from strands of butterfly-shadow and stolen light. It's bright enough to see. That's the only small blessing Eula can find.

It feels like the Caldaia, where true sun never reached but a thousand electrical wires and captive cantrips saturated the air with light all the same, making it impossible not to see the surrounding world. It feels like the Mezzio, bright playground of her childhood. It feels like everything and nothing at once, and it makes Eula want to claw her own skin off to resolve the contradiction. She raises one hand, fingers bent to scratch, and stops as Segante leans forward and grabs her wrist as nimbly and easily as anything, holding her in place.

She shoots him a shocked look. He shrugs.

"No," he says. "I've grown reasonably fond of your skin where and as it is, and I think we'd both care for it less if you took it off."

"Is that so?" Eula twists her wrist out of his grasp. She can't keep up the imperious expression for long; it breaks down and dissolves into a smile, one that he willingly returns.

It feels strange, to be smiling in this cathedral of light and shadow, with a former Planeswalker somewhere ahead of them and Orestes's life potentially on the line, but it's what they have, and she's not going to give it up just because they might all be about to get into serious trouble. When you're about to get into serious trouble is exactly when you *ought* to smile.

As if he's following her thoughts, Segante leans back and says, "You might have trouble taking us to see New Capenna without your skin. I still don't quite understand—is that the name of your city, or the plane?"

"The plane is Capenna; the city is *New* Capenna, because the city is where everyone went to rebuild after Phyrexia invaded our plane the *first* time."

"Oh," says Kequia. "Yes, that makes more sense. I always thought it was strange that your plane and your city had the same name. Like calling Arcavios 'Strixhaven' or calling Dominaria 'Tolaria.'"

"Or calling Fiora 'Paliano,'" says Segante.

Jamira says nothing, only hunches her shoulders, and Eula

winces. It can be so easy to forget that Jamira's plane was lost in the Invasion. There are no cities there to carry on the name, and even the name of the plane itself will one day be forgotten. It's a terrible thing, to lose a home.

It doesn't forgive what Jamira's done, but it makes her fear and desperation a little easier to understand. Eula lost her home when Park Heights fell, and there was a time when she would have done anything in her power to get it back. She still wants the heights of the city, still wants the sun and the freedom, but it's less pressing now. She knows there's more.

She thinks no one told Jamira that. Or maybe their losses, while similar in shape, are so different in scale that there's no comparing them.

The cart rolls deeper into the Snarl, and Eula feels something that has a shape similar enough to one of her shields to be familiar snap into place a bare second before a dome appears around them, gleaming blue with pearlescent streaks of white, perfectly rounded and slicing into the ground with such precision that she knows, on a theoretical but visceral level, that it forms a sphere, locking them inside.

That kind of shield is finicky to cast and dangerous to maintain too long. Keeping it porous enough to let air in and out without weakening it to the point of collapsing is difficult enough to verge on impossible, and this is a shield-sphere large enough to contain six people, a cart, and two elk . . . and perhaps, somewhere, Kasmina. They may be in over their heads.

Bricen pulls the elk to a halt, their hooves clattering against the hard, stony ground, and twists to look at the five underclassmen. "You never finished telling me what was going on here," he says, voice stern. "This isn't just a search for a lost pet. What have you dragged me into?"

"Professor Kasmina asked me to help her abduct Orestes," says Jamira, her voice dull. "She has him. She told me that by helping her abduct him, she would be able to forward her goal of removing us from campus. She wants to close the omenpaths. And she promised she could save me from my spark. That she could make it so it never ignites."

"She was the one who proposed the cross-planar student recruitment," says Bricen, sounding baffled. "It was her pet project. Why would she want to close the omenpaths? She's been helping draw up lists of other potential students to recruit over the next several years. This doesn't make any sense."

"And why would she promise to extinguish your spark when she brought us all here *because* we had the potential to ignite?" asks Segante. "If that was something she could offer, why not offer it to all of us?"

"It doesn't make sense if you believe my goal requires omenpaths, or that I could truly extinguish something so precious as a spark—or that this is my first class," says Kasmina's voice, echoing out of the shadows surrounding them. It seems to come from everywhere and nowhere at once, reverberating against the walls of her shield. "My first students were Will and Rowan Kenrith, of Eldraine. They came willingly and well aware of their potential, and they proved to me that Strixhaven can be the shaping of a new generation of Planeswalkers. This is where we sculpt the future. Omenpaths are an aberration, a temporary scar on the body of the Blind Eternities. They will heal. They will fade. And if we love the Eternities as they have always loved us, we will help that healing along. We should be sealing the omenpaths, not exploiting them."

"What are you *talking* about?" demands Kequia. "We're not Planeswalkers! We're students!"

"The first does not preclude the second, child," says Kasmina. "Your deaths, however, might. It's a tragedy to lose a Planeswalker-in-waiting. Losing all five of you will break my heart."

"What are you talking about?" demands Jamira.

"I cannot extinguish you, but I can take what should always have been mine," says Kasmina. "I tried to focus the anger of your fellow students to awaken your potential—fires catch in pain, and I arranged to have you hurt. Not enough, it seems. The scruples of my fellow professors and my inability to move against you directly kept you safe. Here and now, with Sea's Rise upon us and the Snarl awake, I can unmake your futures to remake my own. The Blind Eternities have never known you. They grieve for me. The Multiverse itself will forgive me for what you are about to lose."

Jamira gasps, realization flooding her face, then shifts positions to put herself between Kequia and the voice, like her body will be enough to shield her friend from Kasmina's magic.

Bricen narrows his eyes. "I'm pretty sure professors aren't supposed to harvest students for their magic," he says. "I think it's against school rules."

Kequia nods so fiercely that Eula wants to laugh. She stands, balancing on the back of the cart, and glares into the distance. She can't quite feel the full shape of the shield, but she knows the principles behind it well enough to guess where the walls will be. "We're not spare parts," she snaps into the darkness. "We're not going to sit back and let you hurt us."

"Do you have a choice?"

Eula leans forward, toward Jamira, whose hands are still full of threads extending outward into the dark, and drops her voice as she whispers, "Can you lead us to her?"

Jamira nods, holding up the tangle of her spell with placid resignation. Eula claps her on the shoulder, then jumps down from the carriage.

Alandra—eager, anxious Alandra—follows suit, staying close to Eula. Without Orestes, her store of bravery is small; without the open sky, her access to storms is limited. Still, she stands, ready to fight if fighting is required of her.

Eula lifts her chin and looks into the dark. "Come out and talk to us like a reasonable person," she says. "Have some *manners.*"

Kasmina's laughter answers her, bright and sharp and wild, stripped of hope and sense in the same sound. "Manners? Oh, child of Capenna, you'd speak to me of *manners*? We were playing games of etiquette and spite on Antausia when your people were still bowing at the feet of angels. You know *nothing* of manners. You only know the petty rules you've decided can stand in for true propriety. I no more need come out and talk to you like a 'reasonable person' than I need to abandon the Blind Eternities to the consequences of the actions of a few."

Segante jumps down from the carriage, snarling into the dark. "You have no right to judge us for the worlds that made us, or to judge those worlds," he says. "You were a Planeswalker. You could have come to us with anything you thought we needed to know and taught us in our homes. You had the Multiverse, while we were locked in our rooms like children, and now we can go where we will, and you're still as free as you've ever been. You've lost nothing. We've gained everything."

Eula reaches behind herself, momentarily fumbling before she finds Segante's hand and holds on tight. He squeezes her fingers, and she pulls what strength she can from the gesture.

Kequia is climbing down from the cart, Bricen and Jamira alongside her, and the six of them are unified in glowering into the dimness, waiting for Kasmina to show herself. The Snarl remains illuminated and wild, not moving when faced directly, but flickering when seen from the corner of an eye, endlessly changing, endlessly static.

And then Orestes chirps, off in the dark. It's a small, plaintive sound; it could almost be overlooked in the layered echo of their voices.

Alandra's eyes go wide, and electricity crackles in the air around her. She steps sharply forward, the crack of lightning accompanying the motion. A jagged bolt shoots from the top of the Snarl to the bottom, but before it can touch the ground, it's grabbed and absorbed by the Snarl itself, fading into nothing more than memory with a crackle and the faint smell of ozone. Alandra shrieks, the wail of a maddened seabird, and more bolts streak down, all meeting the same fate as the first while, deeper in the Snarl, Kasmina starts laughing.

"Alandra!" Eula grabs her by the shoulders, looking into her wide, blank eyes, and gives her a sharp shake. "Snap out of it! This isn't helping us!"

Kequia steps away from the cart, moving toward the shield wall that surrounds them. She has one hand lifted, like a curious child about to touch a soap bubble and see if it will burst. Segante watches her go but doesn't say anything.

Then Kequia lays her palm flat against the barrier, jerks, and collapses. Jamira is there before she can hit the ground, catching the smaller girl in both sturdy arms, sweeping her from her feet into a close, worried embrace. She studies Kequia's face much as Eula studies Alandra's, but while Eula looks with the eyes of a deeply concerned friend, Jamira looks with something more.

Segante smiles as he looks away from the pair, focusing instead on Eula and Alandra. Eula is still holding her roommate by the shoulders, fingers digging in until the scales beneath them start to pale from lack of blood.

"You have to stop slinging storms, Alandra," says Eula, her voice dropping. "You're just feeding them to the Snarl. I don't know what that means, but I don't think it's good for us. You have to stop."

Alandra blinks, finally focusing on Eula. "She has Orestes," she says, her voice small and petulant.

"I know she does, and we're going to get him back," says Eula. "You have my word."

"This is very dull," says Kasmina from the shadows. "You came here to fight me for the drake's return, didn't you? Then fight me. I've set up this lovely arena for us. It's six against one. Don't you think that means it's time for us to answer once and for all whether a Planeswalker without a spark is still something to be concerned about?"

"Come where we can see you and we'll discuss it," says Segante.

"I think not," says Kasmina.

"What happens if we lose?" asks Eula.

"I split open the chambers of your heart and remove your

embers," says Kasmina. "Five of them combined should be enough to relight my own."

It doesn't sound like she means their literal hearts, but something more ephemeral, something that's meant to be stored in the depths of the soul. Eula takes a half step back.

"No, thank you," she says primly. "Just give Orestes back and we'll go."

"No," says Kasmina. "The only way out of here is through me."

"Then I'll have to show you what we learn in Lorehold," says Bricen, tearing his attention away from Kequia, who still lies motionless in Jamira's arms.

"What's that, little historian?"

"When you're trying to navigate a dig site you don't already know by heart, the first thing you need to do is *light. It. Up.*" He spreads his wings and moves his hands through the air like he's gathering and molding a ball of clay, something weighty and ancient that only he can shape.

When he brings them together, there's a flash of light as bright as day, and he throws a small, temporary sun into the air in front of him, where it hangs, shedding light throughout the cavernous center of the Snarl. They see Kasmina against the Snarl's far wall, Orestes prisoned in her arms and a full parliament of owls in attendance behind her, perching on the body of the Snarl itself.

Then the same force that drank Alandra's lightning begins to pull at Bricen's sun, rapidly draining it into the tangled weave of the Snarl until the dark returns completely.

But the damage is done. Orestes saw his person in that moment, his duty and his close companion. Drakes aren't as clever as dragons, but they're smarter than most people give them credit for; he saw Alandra and he understood what the rigidity of her fins meant. In an instant, his teeth are embedded in Kasmina's arm, and she yells, releasing him involuntarily. He never hits the ground. His wings are spread before he can even start to fall, launching him toward Alandra.

The owls follow, their claws extended, but the drake is faster than they are, streaking toward his person without a sign of hesitation. The edge of his wing brushes Eula's cheek as he slams into Alandra's chest, sending her stumbling backward.

Owls fly without a sound, and Eula has no way to know when they'll attack. But she knows Kasmina, and she knows the tactics she's come to expect from her, even before she realized they were enemies; she grabs the swirling, staticky mana of the Snarl and throws her shield up around Alandra almost without thinking, catching merfolk and drake together in a dome of streaky black and white.

Three owls collide with the shield a bare second later. It's almost comical the way they hit, wings outspread and feathers flying everywhere, and Eula does, in fact, crack a smile.

Jamira turns back toward the others; Kequia's eyes finally open. The young Dominarian sits up in the minotaur's arms, and she pushes a handful of braids out of her eyes before she says, "I saw what she was planning when I touched her shield. We have to get out of here."

"What?" asks Eula.

"What?" asks Bricen.

Kequia looks at the others, her eyes wide and grave. "She didn't bring us to Strixhaven because she thought we'd make good students. She brought us here because she was planning to traumatize us enough to ignite our sparks, then use their fire to relight her own."

"We got that part," says Segante. He glances venomously back to where they last saw Kasmina. "She wanted her *embers*," he says, like there's no greater insult he can conceive of. "She brought us here solely because we might have been Planeswalkers before the universe changed. I'm no one's potentiality but my own. Even my father, who has no other heir, has been forced to admit that I don't do well with molds or assumptions."

"She brought us here because out of everyone on her list, she thought we were the most likely to ignite if she pushed us far enough."

Jamira looks horrified as she sets Kequia to her feet. "I would never become a Planeswalker," she says. "Not for all the power in all the planes."

"I don't think you get a choice. I think if you go through enough trauma, you become a Planeswalker, and it just *happens*."

"Which is what she's been trying to do to us all year," says Eula. "Setting us up to be attacked by the Preservationists, isolating Jamira when she's already reeling from losing her entire home plane . . ."

"Setting the scholars from Tolaria on me," says Kequia.

Eula frowns. "I don't know what that means, but sure," she agrees. "She wanted us to ignite, and when that didn't happen, she decided to use Sea's Rise to take our magic for herself. Let's get back to getting out of here." She releases the shield around Alandra, who moves to stand beside her.

"Why didn't the Snarl swallow your shield?" asks Bricen. "Why isn't it swallowing *Kasmina's* shield? If we want to get out of here, we need to know how to get through, and I'm really not sure how we're supposed to do that."

"I have an idea," says Eula, looking at the dome around them. "Bricen, how much trouble do you get in if you leave the cart?"

"More than I want to deal with, but most of it will go away when I tell them I was trying to get away from a professor who wanted to kill a group of underclassmen who were technically in my care. Once the professors start attempting murder, you can get away with a little property destruction."

"Great." Eula looks to Jamira then. "Can you give me one of those mathematical lattices you use for spell construction?"

Jamira frowns. "*Give* you?"

"Yes. Make a lattice and hand it to me. The Snarl didn't swallow your tracking spell; I think it won't swallow the lattice, either."

Jamira keeps frowning as she presses her hands together, then pulls them slowly apart, a complicated web of twists and knots forming between them. It looks like a massive lace doily stitched in green and blue, and she holds it out toward Eula, who plucks it from her hands with ease.

"Hold on," says Eula, and narrows her eyes, mentally pressing a shield into the space defined by the doily. It stretches as her shield expands, becoming a delicate overlay atop her disc of black-and-white iridescence. Shoulders locked in a hard angle that betrays how much effort this is taking, she glances at Kequia. "Touch the shield, but try not to look too deeply. I want you to push facts *into* the shield, not pull them out of it."

Kequia looks confused for a moment before her eyes widen in understanding. She nods, reaching over and tapping Eula's shield with one finger. A delicate ripple of red spreads outward from that point of contact, adding a ribbon of brilliance to the combination.

Eula flashes her a tight, strained smile, then begins walking toward Kasmina's dome, her own held out in front of her. When the two barriers touch, there is a chiming sound, loud and lingering, and it continues as Eula keeps walking forward, extending the shield behind herself as she goes.

The dome spreads to let Eula's shield through, seemingly unable to resist the pressure, and Eula keeps walking until she's formed a short corridor. She looks back then, allowing the shield in her hands to flow into the shield walls behind her, and calls, "Well? Are you coming?"

The others hurry to join her. Once they're all through, she releases the shield and drops to her hands and knees on the ground, panting. Segante helps her back to her feet, and she leans against him, letting him hold her up.

"*Very* impressive, little shield mage," says Kasmina's voice, still echoing from the darkness. "You could have been amazing, if you'd been allowed to ignite in the natural way of things. Mana synthesis of that level is normally the purview of much more sophisticated mages—or Planeswalkers. You would have been magnificent. You still might be."

Eula glares into the darkness. "I'll be sure to raise a glass to you when I get home, fine, *upstanding* citizen that you are."

Her companions look briefly confused. Only Segante, who has come to understand some of how things work in New Capenna, barks a short, dry laugh.

They turn to exit the Snarl.

Kasmina is there waiting, a serene expression on her face

and a parliament of owls behind her. She smiles, raising her hands in a seemingly careless gesture, and none of them can move, none of them can breathe as the floor rushes up to greet them.

Eula can see the cart still as their former teacher's spell takes hold, and she doesn't remember it being so large, or so far away.

And then there is darkness.

TWENTY-NINE

EMBERS

Eula is the first to wake, hands and ankles tied, body stretched out along the floor of the Snarl, which still lights up around her in iridescent swirls and eddies. It's like being inside the body of a vast terrestrial jellyfish. She tries to sit up, getting nowhere.

"Oh, good. You're awake." Footsteps approach as Eula squirms until Kasmina looms over her. "Transmutation hits some people like that. It's as if your bodies don't care for being shaped by someone else's will. Strange. On Antausia, transmutation is a game for children. Can you survive a game of tag without becoming something amphibious or scaled?"

"Why are you *doing* this to us?" Eula demands, still struggling against the ropes that hold her.

"I already told you that, or you already figured it out; either way, the question is beneath you," says Kasmina. "This Snarl was formed when Apex and Zenith collided, two planes becoming one in a single moment of terrible trauma. Neither of them lived to realize their full potential."

"What does that have to do with us?"

"You demonstrated what it has to do with you when you synthesized your group's various magics into one," says Kasmina. "You can shape a spear of your combined powers. You can make them into something new. Sea's Rise is coming. The tides will be high, and the moon will be as close as it ever comes. I can take the weapon you make for me and use it to slice the Snarl away, unbinding the planes from each other. Apex and Zenith will be free. They will separate and go their unique, individual ways."

"The school . . ." Eula stares at her, horrified. "The school is built on top of another Snarl."

"Yes, and when it rips open, the campus will be lost. Some students may survive—the upperclassmen, especially, have already been through an Invasion, and they know the way to run for safer ground. Professor Vess is a rat in human form. She'll live no matter how many sinking ships she sets sail upon. But the school will fall. The Founder Dragons will probably die when the Snarls are sundered—they pull their power from the union of the two planes, and I doubt they can endure without it. If they do, I'll be most impressed. I'll also be very far away from here."

"How?"

"Sparks ignite in times of trauma and great power, little ember. The little traumas I can craft for you individually haven't been nearly enough to do the job, and so I'm going to use you to create such a trauma that the very sky burns. The power it releases will burn through you like a wildfire, scorching everything it touches. You may not all ignite, but at least one of you should, when you consider everyone you've come to know and care for on this plane is lost forever—and they might have lived, had you just been a little less preoccupied with your own lives. Had you just been fast enough to stop me."

Kasmina smirks, and Eula writhes, and Segante's voice rises from the other side of her, calm, measured, and utterly furious.

"If we ignite, we still won't help you," he says. "We'll save each other, and we'll leave you to rot."

"Oh, no," Kasmina says, switching her attention to him. "An ancient dragon gave me the idea, before all this began. A candle can light itself from another's wick. If you ignite, the shock of your spark realizing what it was always meant to be should be enough to reignite my own. I'll burn with you."

Segante lifts his head and stares at her like he can't believe she's saying something so unreasonable. Then he turns, looking toward Eula, who has closed her eyes again.

Her eyes are closed, but the air around her hums with a current all its own—not electric, not static, but low and thrumming. There is a deep, resonant note to it that he recognizes from his own magic, the power of swamps and still, dark places pulled to shroud and cradle her. She's building a shield around herself, although he can't say to what end, beyond that Eula is most confident when she's protected.

He looks around at the others. Jamira, Kequia, and Bricen all appear to still be unconscious, their skin gleaming with a faint bluish nacre and wet with some kind of unfamiliar mucus left over from Kasmina's transmutation spell. Kequia is in front of him, where he can't see her face. And Eula is working so hard to pull her shield together that he can't look at her for very long or he'll betray her.

One of them is missing. One of them . . .

"Where is Alandra?" he demands.

Kasmina scowls. "That little lizard of hers grabbed her while she was still a frog and flew away with her. She'll have reverted to herself by now, but I don't know where. No matter. Four potential sparks should be enough to do what must be done, and she won't get through my shields without her little Capennan friend to help her."

Segante squints into the darkness and sees the curve of her rounded dome bent around them once again. Alandra can call all the tempests she likes; she won't get through that wall.

"Now what?" he demands. "You just rant at us until we Planeswalk away out of sheer irritation?"

"No," she says. "Now I cleave the world to save the Multiverse." The desperation in her voice is unmistakable. She's doing this because she doesn't see any other way to make things right. Horrible as this moment is, she enacts it with the very best intentions.

Kasmina reaches out with both hands, eyes glowing blue-white as she gestures toward the five of them, and Segante jerks as he feels something hook into the body of his magic, digging deep into something that ought to be untouchable and safe from such intrusions. She begins to pull, and the air fills with the rich, organically fetid smell of things rotting in the mire, plants collapsing in on themselves, compost and time. She turns away from him, repeating the gesture over Kequia, and the smell of air rushing across sunbaked prairie joins the miasma.

From Jamira she pulls water sizzling on steel, the smoky burn of green wood on a clean fire, and from Eula she hooks sunlight on brick walkways, the bright taste of copper going to patina, and something sweet and sharp and citrusy, heavy as blood and light as bubbles all at the same time. Finally, she turns to Bricen and extracts more sunlight, this falling on ancient canyon walls, the taste of dust and charcoal in the air, the excavation of the past and future. Funneling their stolen power together, Kasmina whips a ball of brilliant, prismatic light at the wall of the Snarl.

It changes shapes as it flies, smooth sides becoming jagged, until it appears to be a ball made of countless razor-sharp blades. It smashes into the Snarl, which absorbs it as it's absorbed so many other magical displays, its tangles flashing in a prismatic display of colored lines, then, one by one, the tangles go ashen gray and begin to crumble.

The ground beneath them groans, trembling. Kasmina laughs.

"The Snarl will break down, and the planes will separate!" she declares. "Arcavios was an aberration, and it will be reborn as the places it should always have been. New places, clean, good places, that can grow free and wild and into their own realms! And it wouldn't have been possible without the four of you! Rejoice and embrace your own ascension, as the campus crumbles and you rise! Rise and—"

Something slams into the back of her head, and she stops mid-sentence, lifting one hand to touch the point of impact. Her fingers come away bloody. She makes a confused sound, then wobbles, the light from the Snarl wall in front of her growing brighter, prismatic and burning. It's too much to look directly into. Kasmina gestures with her bloodied hand, trying to pull the light back, and it lashes out, wrapping around her wrist and forearm. She screams then, high and agonized, as the snarled lines of her own spell begin dragging her forward, toward the dying wall of the Snarl.

Eula finally moves. The shield she's been spinning close to her skin expands, snapping the bonds on her wrists and ankles, and she rolls to her knees, kneeling as she moves to untie first Segante and then Kequia.

"Alandra, you need to come out now," she shouts.

Segante scrambles to his feet, looking around for threats even as the Snarl wraps more tendrils around Kasmina, pulling her endlessly forward.

"We need to hurry," snaps Eula. "Alandra! Come *on!*"

"I couldn't use magic, the Snarl just eats it," says Alandra, stepping into the light. Orestes is on her shoulders, his tail wrapped around her neck.

"Did you throw a *rock* at our evil professor?" asks Segante.

"I needed to do *something!*" says Alandra, hurrying to untie Bricen.

It seems odd to be talking about the situation while Kasmina is still screaming, but the tendrils have formed a cage around her, pulling her deeper and deeper into the Snarl, and there's no breaking her free. They need to get out, whether or not they can save her.

Something sparks deep inside the Snarl, like flint striking against stone, and the brilliance from Kasmina's spell grows even brighter, all-encompassing.

Eula moves quickly to untie Jamira. As soon as she's free, Jamira moves to help Kequia sit up, and there's a tenderness in the minotaur's hands that's impossible to miss, although Eula somehow missed it growing there. She'd feel bad about that, except that she feels like it's something she's not meant to see.

"We're going to need a new advisor," says Kequia.

Bricen makes a strange, strangled sound, almost drowned out by Kasmina's wails, then stops as he glances upward at the Snarl. Half of it is still turning gray, crumbling from the top down. The other half is filled with bright flashes of brilliant light, and they're somehow even more terrifying, like their hunger may be unconstrained and unstoppable. The ground gives another shake.

"Uh, everybody?" he says.

"What?" asks Eula.

"How do we stop a Snarl from breaking apart?"

"I have no idea," says Eula, scrambling to her feet and staring upward. "I think . . ." She glances desperately at Kequia.

"I have an idea," says Kequia. She pulls away from Jamira, pausing to kiss the other girl on the temple, then runs for the nearest twisting tendril of the Snarl itself. Gritting her teeth, she closes her hands around it and is immediately blown backward six feet.

Jamira catches her before she can slam into the ground. Kequia gives her a dazed smile and closes her eyes.

"Kequia? Kequia, stay awake," says Jamira.

Kequia groans. "Kasmina's magic is snapping the strands inside the Snarl," she says. "It's consuming her spell, but it needs clearer magic to retie the broken pieces. It needs fuel."

"Fuel, we can do," says Alandra. She brings her hand

down in a hard slashing gesture, and lightning begins to lash from the ceiling, striking the walls again and again. Rather than hastening the collapse, the lightning restores the Snarl where it hits, illuminating healthy tangle in place of ashen gray or dazzling light. Bricen yells approval and begins tossing tiny suns into the air, feeding them into the structure, which devours them with greedy speed. Segante calls small, prehistoric-looking plants from the rock-hard soil, and they wither as quickly as they grow, swallowed by the Snarl.

Eula begins crafting small spheres of shield and throwing them at the ground, but they only bounce and roll away. She tries throwing them upward, but they fall, uneaten. She stops, frowning at her hands until Kequia puts a hand against her shoulder.

"The magic of shields is connective, like the Snarl. It can't use them. But it can use everything else we're giving it."

The Snarl is growing brighter with every volley of swallowed spells. Kasmina isn't screaming anymore. She's been pulled fully into the explosive brilliance of her own working, and her silence is so loud it hurts. The ground is still shaking beneath them, however. Eula looks down, sickening echoes of the fall of Park Heights ringing in her head. Then she turns, bolting for the cart, and climbs up into the back.

"Here!" she calls. "Everyone get over here!"

The others come as quickly as they can, Jamira with Kequia riding on her shoulder, Alandra with Orestes curled against her chest. Only when they're all on the cart does Eula reach for them, taking Segante's hand with her left and Alandra's with her right. She closes her eyes, and Alandra calls the heavy ozone crackle of a closing storm around them, while Segante summons the hot closeness of a greenhouse under heavy sun. Eula accepts the magic each of them has to offer her, and once again, the shield she forms has eddies of red, green, and blue mixed into the black-and-white foundation she provides.

The ground shakes harder. Bricen hoots distress and puts his hand on Eula's shoulder, more red and white appearing in the swirling shield, which expands from a disc in front of her to a sphere that contains all six of them. Jamira puts her hand on Eula's other shoulder, and the green and blue intensify as the shield-bubble expands to encompass the entire cart.

Then Kequia takes Eula's wrist, just above Alandra's hand, and the red expands as well, all five colors appearing in almost equal measure. The shield-sphere grows to contain the elk as well as the cart, enclosing them all in a field of safety.

And the ground beneath them splits open, and they fall.

It's not a very far drop, maybe ten, maybe fifteen feet, before they wedge in the crevasse that has formed beneath them and go no farther. If they hadn't been contained within the shield, they would have dropped all the way to the bottom of the newly formed abyss, and some of them would certainly have been lost. The elk shriek, bouncing against the bottom of the shield.

Alandra looks wildly around, Orestes chirping and creeling on her shoulder, nudging her cheek with his head.

"It's all right," says Eula. "I have Jamira and Kequia and Bricen helping me to maintain your parts of the shield. You can let go." The strain is starting to show in her voice, compressing the syllables into something sharp and bitten-off, but her chin is up and her eyes are open; she isn't finished yet.

Alandra drops Eula's hand and slams her palms flat against

the base of the shield, magic flooding outward, accompanied by the sharp ozone smell of a gathering storm. A few seconds pass, and then a gust of wind blows from beneath them, hard enough to dislodge the shield sphere from its place. The elk bleat in terror as the sphere is rocked loose and blown out of the crevasse, rolling away, sending them all tumbling end over end.

As soon as the wind escapes the crevasse, it dies, absorbed by the Snarl. And they roll on, out of the Snarl's boundaries. The ground isn't shaking anymore. Eula exhales, weary, and lets the shield dissolve.

"Are we dead?" asks Kequia.

"I don't think so," says Jamira. "Are you still angry with me?"

Kequia frowns at her for a moment, then thaws and throws her arms around Jamira's neck. The minotaur stands, hauling Kequia into the air as she does, so that the smaller girl's feet wind up dangling well above the ground. Jamira puts her arms around Kequia's waist, smiling, and kisses her.

Eula's cheeks flush red as she looks away, and she finds herself looking at Segante, who quirks an eyebrow.

"They may have the right idea," he says.

Eula bristles. "I am a good Capennan girl, and there will be none of that until we've stepped out properly at least twice."

"Ah, then you'd be amenable to another walk in the woods?"

Eula sputters and is still sputtering when Alandra looks around and asks the question they've been too busy indulging their relief to ask before this:

"Where did Professor Kasmina go?"

SEA'S RISE

Professor Kasmina is well and truly gone. Whether she was swallowed wholly by the Snarl or caused herself so much trauma that she succeeded in reigniting her spark is irrelevant for now: what matters is that they're here, they survived, and none of them got into *too* much trouble for first commandeering and then destroying a school cart.

Although they've been firmly informed that if they ever do something like that again, expulsion will be on the table.

With Professor Kasmina gone, they needed a new advisor as quickly as possible, and none of them was particularly surprised to find Professor Vess elected to the position. She's been gruff but fair, and only somewhat critical of Professor Kasmina's curriculum—which is to say, she's not insisting they all take the class over again next term, although she's made it clear that she wishes she could do exactly that.

"Sea's Rise is tomorrow," she says, facing their small class. The classroom is less fantastic without an illusionist at the helm but no less imposing. Professor Vess can make any room imposing just by standing in it and looking disapproving. "Most of your classmates have departed. If you need anything during the next week, please bother someone else whenever possible, as I'll be observing the festival in my own manner and do not wish to be disturbed."

"Professor Vess?" Eula puts up her hand and waits to be acknowledged before she continues, asking, "Has the Snarl been fully restored?"

"That's part of what I'll be doing during the festival," says Professor Vess. "The Snarl has almost fully recovered, but I'll be feeding it mana to help that process. Tanazir and Galazeth have agreed to come and aid me with the restoration."

"Aren't those two of the Founder Dragons?" asks Alandra eagerly.

"Yes, and if you are all *very* well behaved while semi-supervised on campus, I will ask if either of them has time to listen to your inane ramblings." She pauses for a moment, looking at the group with slightly less sternness in her expression. "I trust you're all well? No lasting effects from your . . . experience?"

"We're fine, Professor," says Kequia. "Better than fine. We're learning."

"I have finally verified the nature of the punishment for your various transgressions," says Professor Vess. "It was difficult. Some thought you should face censure or be restricted in your movements. Others felt you had been led astray and deserved a second chance. The final answer is somewhere in the middle. At the start of next term, while you will be allowed to pledge to your individual colleges, you will be unable to relocate to their dorms. It seems you need more time to learn how to be responsible citizens of a Multiverse, rather than a single plane. This will also allow you to serve as residential advisors to our next incoming class of cross-planar students."

"You're continuing the program?" asks Eula sharply.

"We are," says Professor Vess. "This is a school, Miss Blue, and we need students. Moreover, there are many students like yourselves scattered throughout the Multiverse, promising mages who need a proper education. We can help each other. Knowledge will unite us."

"Something has to," says Segante, and the others murmur agreement as Professor Vess moves to begin their last lecture before the holiday.

Eula glances at him and grins, receiving a small, restrained smile in answer. The holiday will see them all here, and the summer will see them all in New Capenna, for a season of cultural exchange, friendship, and not being traumatized by authority figures. Well. Not beyond the normal, anyway. Eula's quite sure they'll wind up at any number of ridiculously overblown parties as the Families jockey for a look at the newcomers. Cross-planar visitors are nothing new anymore, but scholars full of secrets and the potential to work great magics are something else altogether. Segante has even promised to rent them an apartment where they can all stay together and tailor the environment to their individual needs. She can't wait to see what her friends will make of her plane, or what her plane will make of *them*.

Outside the classroom window, a great tawny owl watches the class, then turns and flies away, vanishing into the clear blue double-sunned sky of Arcavios. And life at Strixhaven, as all across the Multiverse, marches on.

ABOUT THE AUTHOR

Campbell, Hugo, and Nebula Award–winning author SEANAN MCGUIRE lives and works in Washington State, where she shares her somewhat idiosyncratic home with her collection of books, creepy dolls, and enormous cats. When not writing or playing too much *Magic: The Gathering*—which is fairly rare— she enjoys travel and can regularly be found any place where there are cornfields, haunted houses, or frogs. Her first book was *Rosemary and Rue,* the beginning of the October Daye series—with more than a hundred books following since. Seanan McGuire doesn't sleep much.

For more fantastic fiction, author events,
exclusive excerpts, competitions, limited editions and more

VISIT OUR WEBSITE
titanbooks.com

LIKE US ON FACEBOOK
facebook.com/titanbooks

FOLLOW US ON TWITTER AND INSTAGRAM
@TitanBooks

EMAIL US
readerfeedback@titanemail.com